CANADIAN BESTSELLER!

"An intriguing novel . . . richer and stranger than a mere thriller" *Guardian*

"A chilling study in male obsession" *Macleans*

"A classic tale of suspense . . . one of the finest you'll read in its genre . . . a lyrical page turner and a rare creation" *Ottawa Citizen*

"A gripping murder mystery . . . thoroughly engrossing . . . Appignanesi's piercing probe into the psychology of the deranged fanatic is in itself worth the price of the book" *National Post*

"At once a murder mystery, a psychological study of obsessive jealousy, and a meditation on gender relations and political ideals, this book aims high and hits its targets with deadly accuracy. This is a novel of real depth, and, I suspect, lasting impact" *Montreal Review of Books*

"Appignanesi's fifth novel explores love and jealousy, image and reality, and confirms her reputation as a compelling writer" *The Times*

By the same author

Fiction

MEMORY AND DESIRE

DREAMS OF INNOCENCE

A GOOD WOMAN

THE THINGS WE DO FOR LOVE

Non-Fiction

LOSING THE DEAD

FREUD'S WOMEN (with John Forrester)

SIMONE DE BEAUVOIR

CABARET: THE FIRST HUNDRED YEARS

FEMININITY AND THE CREATIVE IMAGINATION:
A STUDY OF JAMES, PROUST AND MUSIL

THE RUSHDIE FILE (edited with Sara Maitland)

DISMANTLING TRUTH:
REALITY IN THE POST-MODERN WORLD
(edited with Hilary Lawson)

POSTMODERNISM (editor)

IDEAS FROM FRANCE (editor)

SCIENCE AND BEYOND (edited with Steven Rose)

THE DEAD
OF WINTER

Lisa Appignanesi

McArthur & Company
Toronto

THE DEAD OF WINTER

Published in Canada by McArthur & Company
322 King Street West
Suite 402
Toronto, Ontario
M5V 1J2

Set in 11/13pt Sabon by Falcon Oast Graphic Art

Canadian Cataloguing in Publication Data

Appignanesi, Lisa
The dead of winter

Novel.
ISBN 1-55278-069-4 (bound)   ISBN 1-55278-122-4 (pbk)

I.   Title.

PS8551.P656D43 2000   C813'.54   C98-932704-3
PR9199.3.A66D43 2000

Reproduced, printed and bound in Great Britain by
Cox & Wyman Ltd, Reading, Berkshire.

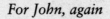

For John, again

Prince Escerny: 'Can you imagine a greater happiness for a woman than to have a man wholly in her power?'
Lulu (jingling her spurs): 'Oh, yes!'

Frank Wedekind, *Earth Spirit*

'Desire does not so much transcend its object as ignore it completely in favour of a fantastic recreation of it.'

Angela Carter, *Nothing Sacred*

PROLOGUE

Ste-Anne-de-Beaulieu is a good place for death.

Unrepentant snow covers the ground for seven months out of twelve. There is no spring. In the sapping heat of summer, the old people congregate on their creaking wooden porches. They rock. They watch thick honey strips grow black with flies buzzing towards the sweetness of a sticky end.

Autumn brings the hunters. They inch along the narrow streets of the town and proudly display the bounty they have transported from the remoter reaches of the Laurentian range. Heavy-jowled moose and tender-faced deer decorate the four-wheel drives. Unblinking animal eyes point heavenwards with all the solemnity appropriate to funeral processions.

The town itself stayed black with the swish of priestly robes far longer than Montréal, its cosmopolitan neighbour some hundred kilometres to the south. The nuns, too, refused the permitted shorter lengths. Change is not Ste-Anne's principal business.

On the main street, the one recent building of note is a funeral parlour as sumptuous and glistening as the images which once played across the screen of the cinema it has replaced.

The body was found in winter. Christmas Day, 1989, to be exact. It was hanging from a rafter in the old barn behind the house on the hill. Amidst the cobwebs and frozen earth and little heaps of powdery snow which had blown through cracks, there was still some hay left over from a past life when it had served a purpose. The light clung to the scattered bale as it had once clung to that vivid face.

It was only as I gazed at that body, so slight and vulnerable within the folds of a brashly fake fur, that it came to me that I, too, had returned to Ste-Anne with a longing called death.

PART ONE

1

That night the bells of Ste-Anne's tolled out midnight mass with jubilant abandon.

In my half-sleep, the sounds grew into giant birds travelling through the December darkness. Propelled from the arches of the silvery belltower, they rode the currents above the red-tile and slate and metal roofs of the town, skirted the trees in the valley and landed here in the house on the hill to cover me with their wings. I let them lull me. I wanted sleep. I was eager for the morning.

When a shriller ring set up a cacophony from my bedside, I thought it was the bells again. It took me a while to reach for the phone and by the time I did, only silence followed by a click and a signal answered my 'Allo'.

Madeleine. I knew it must be her. Who else would dare to ring so late? I almost punched out her grandmother's number to return the call, but a mixture of tact and timidity prevented me. I could be wrong. In any case, it would do Madeleine no harm to think there were moments when I was unavailable.

The red numbers on the clock radio beamed out 1.18. I shook away the irritation that comes with broken sleep. After all, I didn't have to leap out of bed before dawn this morning. There were no appointments awaiting me – no ancient Mme Groulx demanding yet another in the interminable changes to her will; no prospective divorcés, rigid in mutual hatred, haggling over the property clauses spelled out in the outdated promises of a marriage contract.

On Christmas Day and for a week thereafter, the offices of Pierre Rousseau, *Notaire*, are soundly closed, the answering machine deaf to calls. The week is necessary, I have learned. Like hangovers, the rashes of irritation family Christmases induce have to be allowed to settle before action is embarked on. And I am fond of my clients. I have known many of them for years. Sometimes I prefer to keep them distant from those expensive, binding clauses and intractable codes which make up the official part of my work. The law is blind to the upheavals of individual emotion.

When I first took over the practice, I had no idea I would feel this way. It was with a grudging, sullen reluctance that I had let the mayor ambush me at the funeral reception which he honoured my father by holding in his own suitably gilded salon.

His plump, ringed hand resting on his girth, M. Desforges gave me his preening smile, turned his small shrewd eyes up at me and said, 'Enough travelling, now, eh? Time to come home. When will you begin?'

He was both determined and already convinced that I would step into my father's well-polished shoes: there would be a third generation of Rousseaus to serve as notaries to Ste-Anne. Perhaps Desforges thought I would order his affairs, his slippery land and building deals, his municipal contracts, as smoothly and silently as my father had done.

Weeks passed, but eventually I decided. Desforges had tickled my sense of justice by mentioning the Mirabel Airport scandal. Several families in the vicinity of Ste-Anne had had their land expropriated by the federal government at the time the gargantuan airport was planned and now, thirteen years later, when only 5,000 of the 97,000 prime agricultural acres had been used, reappropriation claims were going ahead.

To tell the truth I was also at a low ebb, a piece of brittle flotsam flung back onto the shores of my native Québec. I had no desire to carry on with the journalism that had taken me to France, to North Africa and then to the Ottawa bureau of *Le Devoir*. My convictions had abandoned me. Maybe too much time abroad had undermined my sense of Québecois patriotism.

I couldn't summon more than verbal outrage at the injustices a constitution repatriated from Britain to a federal home in Ottawa would engender for my French-speaking province. And I had an uncomfortable sense that the once desired language laws, which enforced the use of the French language and a French education, were building walls of parochial intolerance between and around us.

In that state of personal uncertainty, the dry precisions of the civil code for which I had once been trained took on all the charm of a siren call.

I moved into my father's office, a red-brick building with its afterthought of plaster columns, at a stone's throw from the rather better columns of the town hall. I moved into the inherited house as well. I even took over the car. With all the panache of a sleepwalker, I slipped into the routine of a small-town notary – which my youthful ideals had taught me to loathe as a corrupt bastion of traditional power.

It took me a few years to wake up. When I did, I realized the job was nothing like I had imagined it. Maybe I just wasn't corrupt enough or interested enough in money. In any event, it occurred to me then that in fact my practice was half-way between a priest's and a psychotherapist's. I was the keeper and recorder of the town's secrets. Confidences can be dangerous. And lonely. Luckily, these days I am adept at solitude.

In the warmth of the duvet, thoughts of Madeleine steal over me again. I need to see her. I have to explain. Yes, I must explain. The temptation to slip over there now is overwhelming. I switch on the bedside light. The sudden brightness dazzles. Through lowered lids, I fumble for my clothes and make for the front door. As I leave the shelter of the porch, a gust of freezing wind attacks and scatters my purpose.

This is folly. Can there really be any point to this

trudge through cold darkness? I will see Madeleine as planned later today at her grandmother, Mme Tremblay's house, for what she calls Christmas dinner though it begins in mid-afternoon. It is odd that I call her Mme Tremblay, just as I did as a boy; odder still, since she is my nearest neighbour again, a mere garden and small wood away on the southern slope of the hill – which is not too far in the vastness of this countryside. We meet regularly for Sunday tea.

Mme Tremblay, despite the passage of years, keeps to the habits of her Scottish childhood, though she speaks French to me, a French which is clear and correct and as insistently not Québecois as her checked woollen skirts and muted cardigans, her iron-grey hair and rigidly upright school-teacher's back, her taciturn dislike of gossip.

The only thing Madeleine took from her was that French. It served her well in Paris.

Madeleine in Paris.

The next thing I know I am back in bed and mellow images of those early days in Paris lull me to sleep as surely as an oft-repeated childhood fairy-tale.

When the cold grey dawn creeps reluctantly through my window, the images have grown darker, fraught with the drama of our lives. I banish them and dash for the shower. I do not want to think of these things. Not today, when I shall meet Madeleine in an ordinary way – if anything can ever be said to be altogether ordinary in my meetings with Madeleine.

The fluorescent lights in the bathroom cast an irritating glare. I remind myself that this is something else I must change in the house I still think of as my father's, though I also know that the longer the list grows, the less I do. I close my eyes and let the water stream over me, hot and strong.

When I last saw Madeleine some two weeks ago in Montréal, she wasn't her teasing, quicksilver self. She was wearing an old pair of jeans, a dark sweater which swallowed her shape. Her hair was tousled, her eyes red-rimmed from lack of sleep. The week before, she had opened in a new play at the Théâtre du Nouveau Monde, her first theatrical appearance in Montréal for some time, and the critics had savaged her performance – the French press even more so than the English. All the trademark venom of a city which wishes itself big and knows itself small was deposited at the feet of a star who had made the cardinal mistake of coming home.

The date of the opening was unfortunate. On the 6th, just two days before, a lone deranged assassin had gunned down fourteen women students at the Ecole Polytechnique, the engineering faculty of the Université de Montréal. The event had a grim horror to it. Like some concentration camp guard from another time and place, the killer had ordered men and women into segregated lines. Then, with his Sturm Ruger semi-automatic he had picked off only the women. 'You're all a bunch of feminists,' he shouted. 'I loathe feminists.'

It was the last day of term. At first, in the

18

cafeteria, then in the classroom, the students had thought the baseball-capped youth was a prankster. He had a smile on his face. But the blood which flowed was appallingly real. His own too. The carnage over – fourteen dead, thirteen others wounded – he had killed himself.

In his pocket, the police had found a three-page letter proclaiming the political nature of his act. Feminists, he stated, had ruined his life, had robbed him of opportunity. Attached to the letter was a hit-list of television personalities, senior government and trade union figures, an array of successful women.

A stunned province mourned its dead. This was the kind of event we could imagine in New York, in California, in Texas – but not in Montréal, where it still isn't altogether unusual for people to leave their doors unlocked.

Thousands streamed to a silent vigil at the university, transforming the mountain road into a ribbon of light. Ten thousand queued to pay their respects the next day to eight of the dead, whose white, flower-strewn coffins were laid out in the university hall of honour. The funeral mass at the vast Notre Dame Basilica overflowed into the forecourt and found its echo in smaller memorial gatherings throughout the province and further afield.

Madeleine had attended both communal rites. She was still in a state of shock when we met, as if the killer's hatred and gunfire had leapt over the mountain and been targeted directly at her. Her hand trembled as I lit her cigarette. She could concentrate on nothing but the unleashed horror of the event. My attempts at reason held out little comfort.

We sat in a small Portuguese restaurant off the Main: whitewashed walls made whiter by the slash of brightly turquoise slats, pictures of fishing boats in distant harbours. A cold, crystalline light poured through high windows which in summer drew back to create a *terrasse*. Madeleine didn't like the light. She wanted to burrow into some obscure corner. Her dark glasses went on and off and on again as we talked.

She told me she had tried to cancel the play's opening; to stage a reading in honour of the dead women instead or close the theatre for a few days in an act of mourning. It was no time for plays, let alone a portrayal of the grand, pistol-loving daughter of General Gabler, that Hedda who provokes a man to a botched death.

But the management had forced her to go on, had permitted only a brief tribute to the assassinated women before the curtain rose.

Madeleine's hand repeatedly brushes her cheek as if an invisible fly were trying to land on it.

'I don't understand it. I don't understand why you hate us. Tell me, Pierre.' She lashes out suddenly, finding a ready target in me for her vehemence: 'Why do you want to hurt us, kill us? Why?'

'Please, Madeleine. This Marc Lépine was an isolated case. He was demented.'

'So many of you seem to be demented. Men hating women. Violent men, killers, serial killers everywhere. Even here.'

'There are far more serial killers in novels and in movies than in life, Madeleine. Most violence against women happens in the home. You've been reading too much, watching too many films.'

She glares at me. 'What about Bill *l'éventreur*, our very own ripper? And before that, the strangler, Bill *l'étrangleur*?'

It comes to me with uncomfortable force that Madeleine is obsessed by serial killers because she is a serial lover. I banish the thought and say the first thing that leaps into my mind. 'Next you'll be telling me all serial killers are called Bill.'

My humour falls as flat as a concrete pancake. Madeleine scowls at me.

'OK then. Just explain the hatred to me. Tell me why. And don't tell me you don't know what I'm talking about. Don't tell me you haven't heard them. Even this week, on the phone-in programmes, there's been a slew of them. Men venting their spleen, as if all their failures were women's fault. As if the victims of Lépine were to be blamed for their own deaths.'

'I don't know, Madeleine. But I don't think it's a generic hatred. It's not men against women. It's just the losers – men whose wives have left them, men who've lost or can't find jobs while women seem to be successful, men who might carry the childhood wounds of broken or brutal homes. It's not the whole sex.'

My attempt at reasonableness does little to dent her emotion. She puts her glasses on again. Her voice is suddenly low. There is a tremor in it.

'Yesterday, as I was leaving the theatre, I accidentally brushed against a man. A stranger. And he turned on me, just like that.' She snaps her fingers and the voice which comes out of her is a snarl. '"Who do you think you are, eh? Eh? Bloody bitch! Marilyn Monroe? The Queen of Sheba? *Maudite pute!*" And he spat at me. Spat.'

'Horrible.' I am quiet. I don't know what to say. I want to hold her, but I know she won't let me.

'I apologize for my sex, Madeleine. But remember, Lépine was a single instance. There's nothing to be afraid of.'

She prods the salad leaves on her plate, moves them round. Not a single one has found its way to her mouth.

'Nothing to be afraid of? You can say that today? This week? After all that's happened. All that savagery.' The face she lifts to me is now that of a waif, forlorn, abandoned. 'And there's something else.' Her voice crumbles into a whisper. 'Eyes. Staring at me. Hot. Peculiar. I can feel them sometimes in the audience. In the street. Tailing me.' She shivers. 'As if they possessed me. Were entitled to all of me. Stalker's eyes. I've told you before.'

'Madeleine, you're an actress. You . . .'

She cuts me off, jabs at me as if I were another salad leaf. 'I really don't know how you can sit there so calmly and eat. You of all people!'

'Will it help matters if I stop?'

22

'Maybe.'

I put down my knife and fork and fold my starched napkin back into a neat triangle. I stare at it. I am guilty, condemned by implication. I summon up the crimes against women I may have committed and shudder despite myself.

Icy fingers curl round my wrist.

'Sorry,' Madeleine murmurs.

It isn't a word Madeleine uses often. I cover her hand with mine, try to read her eyes beneath the opaque blackness of the glasses.

'I'll come and see you in the play tonight.'

'No! Certainly not.' Madeleine's hand is gone despite my attempts to hold onto it. She leaps up. She pulls on her coat. 'I'll see you at Mémère's. On Christmas Day. It's agreed, isn't it?' She pauses uncertainly. 'You'll come? I'd like you to come.'

I nod, make to rise, but Madeleine shakes her head. She doesn't want my company. A tremulous smile which doesn't quite curve her lips, a weary half-wave, and she is out the door before I can retrieve my coat. I don't have time to say the 'don't be so frightened' which is on my tongue.

That evening, despite Madeleine's command to the contrary, I go to the theatre. I can't stay away.

I wait until the lights have dimmed and slip into a seat at the back of the stalls. I keep well down. The place is half-empty and I am afraid that even at this distance, Madeleine may somehow decipher my silhouette.

She has never played Hedda Gabler before. It is a

23

role that has always intrigued her and I know that it is the challenge of playing Hedda that has tempted her back to the stage. But it is clear from the moment that Madeleine steps on that something is very wrong.

The fire – that wildness, unleashed or contained, which has so often made her a mesmeric stage presence, that magic of glamour in which we all bathe – is simply not there. She moves woodenly, as if afraid that Hedda's matchless witchery will rebound on her. Instead of delighting in Hedda's small, everyday acts of manipulative spite, she holds back, a reluctant bitch. When it comes to the charged bravura of playing with pistols or burning the manuscript and ruining the life of the only man she has ever loved, she advances in an unwilling trance, her hands on the midriff where an unwanted child lodges.

Only at the very end, when her pale, already dis-embodied face appears through the curtained door to announce, 'Never mind. From now on, I promise to be quiet,' do her words emerge with an uncanny force – a herald of that pistol shot which within moments disrupts the quiet respectability of the stage.

Despite my earlier desire for invisibility, I find myself rushing backstage. I flash an old press card, dash towards Madeleine's dressing room. Inside, there is a murmur of voices. I knock insistently.

Madeleine opens the door a fraction. From the whiteness of her creamed face her eyes stare at me without a flicker of recognition. 'Not now,' she says in a dull tone. 'I'm too tired.'

I barely stop my fist before it can inflict a pounding on the slammed door. Instead, I walk slowly to the front of the theatre and prowl the emptying street. When Madeleine emerges, she is with another woman. I hesitate for a moment. Too long. She is already inside a waiting taxi. As it lurches away, her gaze skirts over me. Her eyes grow wide, but I cannot quite read her expression. She does not wave.

Later, as I speed north along the darkened autoroute towards Ste-Anne, I force myself to concentrate on Madeleine's performance and realize how oddly unnerving it has been. She has given the proudly inviolable Hedda, who relished playing with pistols and with lives – even if she hadn't the courage for sex and scandal – an aching vulnerability, made her forcibly into a woman trapped by whatever amalgam of circumstance and nature. What her suicide lacks in the more usual defiance, it gains in emotion. It is a driven and snared creature's exit from an impasse.

In the mirror above the sink, I meet my eyes for the first time that day. Against the foam of the shaving cream they look unnaturally dark. Liquid, Madeleine used to tell me in the old days.

She would stand there, secretly, invisibly, in the corner of whichever bathroom, and watch me until by some accident of angle our eyes met in the mirror and I would shoo her away. She always went recalcitrantly. Perhaps she was so fascinated because she had never had a father to watch when she was small.

Shaving, she told me, was my most intimate act. The taut concentration with which I presented cheek and chin to the mirror, the intensity of my gaze, the surgical precision with which I wielded the razor, the unconscious tension of my movements as if danger had to be averted at every stroke; and then the happy lap of water, the smile, boyish and stern, a little smug, yet undeniably attractive – in all this she claimed she saw my essential being.

Once, she showed me. She gave me a rendition of myself so unnervingly correct in its accumulated detail that sometimes now, in the act of shaving, I think I am enacting my double rather than engaging in an everyday routine.

Madeleine is a voracious observer. She observes obsessively, ferociously. She doesn't think about it. She does it with her body. And then she can play it all back. In the flow of that instinctual mimicry, she loses herself completely. She becomes that friend or acquaintance, that politician or animal. Yes, those too. I remember once, when we were still very young and lazing about in the field, she lifted herself on her haunches, stuck out her chest, did something with arms and face, and suddenly she was that preening robin on the branch. It's an uncanny talent.

I wash my face and wonder whether my smile is still smug and boyish. The rest hasn't changed all that much. I am thirty-nine years old and my hair is thick, my stomach firm . . . I stop the inevitable catechism of vanity and find a hum on my lips. I am happy in anticipation of seeing Madeleine. I will convince her she is not the flop the newspapers have proclaimed. Far from it. She is a Hedda for our troubled times.

On the landing, I pause to look out the window. The sky above the valley is almost colourless, as pale as the frost that ices ground and trees. In the distance, the horizon has a steely charcoal tinge. The snow is coming.

Downstairs, I deliberate between a turn to the right or the left. The house is too big for me. My father's thoughts turned on grandeur when he had it built, as if he had at last, my mother dead and a new younger wife in tow, attained the desired status of a seigneur. A turn to the left means the leap and crackle of a fire to accompany my solitary breakfast. A turn to the right promises freshly brewed coffee sooner.

I find myself in front of the fire. I sweep out last night's ashes, pile logs and twigs and newspaper into a haphazard pyramid, watch paper curl and twigs catch flame, before replacing the ornate metal guard with the sweeping R at its centre.

Apart from the bookcase and sound system lodged in a far corner, this room is just as my father left it. Overstuffed floral sofas face each other across a low table of old honeyed pine. In random groupings, there are armchairs and rockers and rounded tables topped by pottery lamps and vast silken shades. There is even a curiosity of a nineteenth-century bench which unlatches into a rock-hard bed. The floor is solid shining birch, covered here and there by a blazon of rag-rugs.

The heritage bug, which hatched with Québec's quiet revolution and proliferated at an astonishing rate during the noisier end of the sixties and seventies, had bitten my father early, had made him into a collector. With a truck bought for the purpose, he scoured the habitable length and breadth of the province, covered a distance greater than that of Western Europe. In search of 'authentic' Québecois furniture and bric-à-brac, he travelled the Gaspé Peninsula and the banks of the Saguenay, the streets of the capital and the farms of the loyalist townships, not to mention the northernmost tips of the Laurentian range. He acquired enough furniture to keep an auction room happy for a year. He also collected a mountain of sacred hearts and maple-sugar moulds, cushion covers embroidered by Ursuline nuns and butter dishes sprouting Gallic cocks, as well as the inevitable array of carved crucifixes.

They all still lodge in an accumulation of moulded cabinets and panelled chests. I have even left his unfinished history of the region safe in the centre of his eighteenth-century éscritoire – though I'm not sure this last mightn't be a French import.

Across the front hall from the salon is a dining room which would do justice to a small conventual order. Indeed the long refectory table comes from just such a site, as do the uncomfortable assortment of chairs, though the elegant diamond shapes in the two cupboards suggest a different provenance. So too does the bronze chandelier with its array of candle holders now carefully replaced by bulbs.

I tiptoe through this room like a stranger. It is not that I don't like what is here. But living alone in a museum makes one behave a little like a ghost, unsure whether one inhabits past or present. Unsure, too, whether one should touch anything or simply tear it all down.

Thankfully, the kitchen is modern. It has all the signs of human negligence – unwashed teacups and mugs and glasses, heat stains on the table, the lingering aroma of last night's bacon and eggs and one too many cigarettes.

I switch on the radio and listen for a moment to the unfolding of the Christmas story, then quickly redial. Bach plays over the coffee grinder. The cat leaps through the hatch, bumps into a pair of old boots I don't remember having left here and rubs herself against my legs. I empty out a tin for her and watch her concentrated lapping, the thrusting back of dainty head as she chews a large morsel.

I butter some toast and carry a tray to the fireside table. I have a pleasant sense of lazy hours stretching in front of me. At the same time I am restless, impatient for the time that separates me from Madeleine to pass. I wonder if she has arrived yet. Yesterday's newspaper sits in my hand, seen but unread.

After breakfast, I pull on the old boots, my raggedy fur-lined suede jacket and lumber out with the excuse of a search for firewood. There is a ready supply of logs in the shed, but twigs are more scarce and always useful. I have gone through my hoard over this long weekend. Monday is a lame day for

Christmas, though it has meant that Madeleine can come here where I want to see her so much. Today I will find the opportunity and tell her. I must tell her.

The air is still and moistly cold. Not even the usual distant rumble of cars disturbs it. My footsteps crunching over frosted ground sound unnaturally loud.

I look back at the house and, through the mist of my breath, see it in all its sentimental habitant splendour – a sweeping colonnaded terrace, walls of neatly pointed local stone, an old- fashioned sloping roof with a row of mansard windows, the timbers, like that of the wide door, painted a deep blue-green to match the most resplendent of the firs.

The wood stretches behind the house, up and over the hill. Birds twitter and swoop from gnarled oak to birch to maple to wild cherry, their branches dark and brittle. In the autumn, everything here is ablaze with colour, the maples an incandescent red, the birches golden, the ground a burnished carpet of leaf, as if in the act of dying the woods gave of their best, a soaring climax before the long emptiness of winter. Now only the solemn green of the pines reminds one of the existence of colour.

At the top of the incline I stop for breath and through the bare trees glimpse the distant grey of the river. I am tempted to make a detour just to see whether Madeleine's car really has arrived in her grandmother's drive. I restrain myself, note instead that the wisps of smoke in the air can only be coming from her chimney.

My burlap sack laden with twigs, I return to the house and like some renegade Father Christmas empty the contents in a shapeless heap on the floor of the shed. For the sheer joy of the sound, I splice some logs with the old axe which hangs on the wall. It still surprises me that I take pleasure in these mundane tasks. Until I came back here, I had always thought of myself as fundamentally an urban being.

As I carry a second load of wood to the house, the stillness is suddenly pierced by the barking of dogs. Excited howls, angry yaps and yelps and growls. I can't quite distinguish the mood, but I recognize the animals. Mme Tremblay's two collies. Perhaps Madeleine has decided on a walk and a visit.

I hasten into the house, deposit my load and nervously brush chips and splinters from my sweater. I survey the living room. It is a long time since Madeleine last came here.

A glance at my watch tells me it is already eleven o'clock. I gaze out the window. The dogs are still barking, their excitement unabated. But they don't seem to be coming any closer. Madeleine is probably playing with them, stirring them into a frenzy in the way she likes to do. They're lazy mutts, she thinks, will grow old before their time with all their genteel strolls and lying about in front of the fire.

To still my impatience, I brew more coffee and pour it into a Thermos flask. I prepare a fresh tray, add some biscuits, and bring it into the living room. The dogs have gone quiet now. As I stand in front of the window, I hear only the occasional muted yelp.

I hide my disappointment in a book, then

remember that I still haven't wrapped the Christmas presents. By the time I reach my bedroom, the yapping has begun again, closer now. At first, from the height of my window all I can see is a fine dusting of powder like flurries of talc trapped in the air. The snow has started.

Then I make out the dogs and a lone figure, half walking, half running, a little way behind them. They race ahead of her, then pause and race back, their golden coats streaming. I rush down the stairs and out the door, skidding a little on the freshly powdered steps of the porch.

But it is not Madeleine I see coming towards me.

'Get your coat,' Mme Tremblay says. She doesn't bother with French, nor a greeting. Her hair is wild, her long scarf trails the ground behind her. She is panting, seems barely capable of speech, though she rasps out again, 'Get your coat.'

'Wouldn't you like some coffee?' I ask. The words sound inane as I meet her glazed eyes. I fetch my coat and am back in an instant.

Her gloved hand grips my arm. She leans heavily against me. She has never done this before.

'Don't ask me any questions.' Her voice chafes. 'Just come. Quickly.'

We follow the dogs, skirt the side of the house, walk down the path which cuts through the field and up again through the small apple orchard and round. It is the quick route to the old farmhouse.

I don't allow myself to think. I am busy holding up Mme Tremblay's weight, matching my steps to

32

her erratic movements. The dogs are ahead of us, their barking hectic again. It surprises me when they fail to stop at the white clapboard house with the wrap-around porch which is their home. I glance at Mme Tremblay, but there is no expression on her ashen face. She is all grey pallor. Even the customary line of burgundy which outlines her lips so neatly has disappeared. It has smudged and gathered into a pink welt on her cheek.

Madeleine's car isn't in the drive, nor do I spy its metallic glint beneath the trees which spread their twisted branches over the ramshackle outhouses. We don't stop at these either, but carry on downhill. At last our destination is clear.

The dogs are running in circles in front of the old barn where Madeleine used to stable her pony. Mme Tremblay points a shaking finger at the rickety door and turns her back on me.

It takes a few moments for my eyes to accustom themselves to the gloom. I see a stack of firewood, some old chairs, their backs or legs missing. The earth beneath my feet is hard and bumpy. Light glints in through a knee-high crack only to expose a small heap of blown snow.

I don't know what I am looking for and when I see it, I don't want to look. The chair appears first. It is behind the makeshift stall where the horse was once kept. The small scattered bale of left-over hay makes no sense. Neither, initially, does the tumbled chair.

Then the feet, neatly shod in their soft lace-up boots, come into view, swinging slightly. The deep pile of a golden fur bristles with spots and synthetic life.

I step backwards, stumble over a ladder and suddenly she is before me. Madeleine. Suspended by a rope from the thick beam which props up the old hayloft. Her pale face tilts to the side and catches an arc of light from the window above. Her eyes are rounded in surprise. She looks like some larger-than-life marionette, abandoned by her puppeteer.

My gaze clings to her. I am waiting for that head to right itself, for that sweet smile and slight bow, for the applause which signals the end of the performance. I am waiting for the darkness of a screen, the roll of credits, the murmur of voices and the shuffle of feet leaving the cinema.

But this is no theatrical spectacle. Madeleine does not move. She is dead. She has performed that ultimate act and taken her own life. I was not there to prevent her.

All around me there is the sound of moaning. It takes a moment for me to realize that it is coming from my own lips and in that moment I sense Mme Tremblay next to me. Her arm is on mine. I don't know who holds up whom but together we stumble towards the house. My leg is tangled in her long scarf so that I trip up the stairs. She lurches behind me and I half carry, half drag her in, deposit her on the sofa.

From the corner cabinet I unearth a bottle of whisky, force some through her lips. I hear her cough which is also a sob as I pick up the telephone. The police take a long time to answer. Maybe the station is as firmly shut as my office. When at last a grumpy voice blurts an '*Allo*', my own sounds inordinately distant. I announce a death.

Mme Tremblay and I wait in the living room. She hasn't spoken yet, but every time I make to set out for the barn, she holds me back with eye and gesture. As if to warm the dead, I stoke and fan the fire into blazing heat.

Next door the table is already set for Christmas dinner. Four settings on a starched white cloth, gold-wrapped crackers and candelabrum in place, glasses gleaming. In the corner there is a Christmas tree. Old wooden ornaments and silver streamers dangle from its branches. An angel with gilded wings and halo perches at its top. I remember that angel. Madeleine made it.

That thought tempts me again, more seductive than the serpent in the garden. Yes. Madeleine has just been rehearsing one of her parts, playing a prank. She will race through the door any second now, laugh at us and demand a good glass of Bordeaux.

Then the image of her hanging in the barn cuts across my vision. I see her stillness, her skin, bleached of colour. I sit down and cover my face. Guilt scalds me and with it a sense of utter helplessness. I think of that phone call I didn't manage to answer. I remember Madeleine's despair when we last met, my inability to stir her out of it, my stubborn reasonableness. I remember the last scene of the play, her pale Hedda face eerily haloed by the curtain, already a rope.

A fierce voice slashes the stillness of the room.

'She didn't do it.'

Mme Tremblay has been reading my thoughts. Two bright circles illuminate her cheeks, as if all her blood has gathered there.

'She didn't do it,' she repeats.

I don't understand what she means.

'You don't believe me.' Abruptly she flings the blanket I have covered her legs with to the floor and starts to pace. 'My girl wouldn't do that. Not my Madeleine. You should understand that. You of all people. Not suicide. Never suicide.' Her voice scratches at me, taut with anger.

I have never seen her so angry. And I feel I am somehow to blame. To blame for everything. 'But Mme Tremblay—' I stop myself. I understand that the notion of suicide may be anathema to her.

'Let me get you another drink,' I say lamely. 'It will do you good.'

'Nothing will ever do me any good. Not now. Not again.'

Her eyes are savage, then suddenly blank and listless. She crumples into a chair.

The crunch of tyres on the drive together with the renewed barking of the dogs is a relief.

'The police at last,' I murmur.

'You tell them. Tell them what I said. Then bring them in here to talk to me.'

Two pink-cheeked constables stare up at me when I open the door. They look young enough to have their mothers scrub their faces.

The smaller, plumper one addresses me politely. 'M. Rousseau?'

I nod. I think I recognize him. He must be one of the Miron sons. Guillaume, perhaps.

'*Venez, c'est par ici.*' I lead them towards the barn. The dogs sniff at their heels, then run ahead of us. They have barked themselves into silence.

Snow has begun to leave a thin coating on the ground but in the air it is just an icy moistness. It wets my hot face like the tears I haven't yet found.

Inside, I can barely bring my eyes to gaze on Madeleine. Maybe if I don't look, she won't be there. But the splutter of the taller policeman tells me otherwise.

'*Mauditcriss de tabarnak!*' he curses by Christ and tabernacle beneath his breath and runs his hand through a tight mesh of dark curls. '*Et c'est Noël . . .*'

'*Qu'est qu'on va faire?*' The other is at a loss.

'*Rien. Faut téléphoner.*'

They shrug their shoulders at me, order me not to touch anything, order me out in fact, since they want nothing more than to get out themselves.

I still my trembling hands and force myself to look up at Madeleine's face. Her expression hasn't changed, but now I notice a certain wistfulness in it. The rope around her throat is heavy and too coarse. Not a necklace she would have chosen. I think of her grandmother's words and then notice that under her coat Madeleine is wearing only the briefest of blue nighties. She looks so frail. Frail and beautiful. I touch her hand. It is cold and waxy and the pressure of my fingers seems to leave an imprint.

'Heh.' Young Miron urges me on and I turn away with a shiver.

'We're going to have to ring headquarters. Don't know who we'll be able to get out here today. The photographer's on holiday. Dr Bertrand's probably gorging himself at—' He clamps his lips shut. 'I'll just get some tape from the car. We can rope off the area at least.' He says this as if struck by divine inspiration and then chides me, 'No-one's to go in there, you understand?'

We've reached their car and I hear the curly-headed one muttering into the phone. He throws his hands up in the air as he clambers out of the car. 'No-one. Only Lucie. She's going to ring round.'

'I know where I might reach Dr Bertrand,' I offer.

'Ya?' They glance at me with momentary suspicion, then follow me to the house. Miron changes his mind after a moment. 'I'll do the cordon,' he says self-importantly.

Mme Tremblay is in the kitchen when we come in. She has composed herself. Without a word, she pours out two steaming cups of tea and hands them to us. She won't meet my eyes as I ask her for a telephone directory.

The mayor's home number has flown out of my head, but it is there, clearly listed, as befits an apparently unblemished civic official. It takes at least ten rings for a voice to answer and then it is muffled by a dozen others in the background.

'Mme Desforges?' I apologize for disturbing her

Christmas gathering, but make it clear that I need to speak to her husband.

The mayor chides me as soon as he comes on the line. He rebukes me for not offering my Christmas greetings in person.

I can see him, glass in hand, swaying slightly, his face beaming, then tightening in irritation as, tersely, I explain my business.

'Madeleine Blais! *Ah non*. What a drama.' He is imagining the headlines, wondering if they can be deflected, making a quick calculation of how the episode might be turned to the town's advantage.

Desforges is a shrewd man. He keeps up with things. He has even managed to make an advantage of Ste-Anne's being off the map. Concessions have been granted to antique shops along the old highway, picturesque now that the through traffic from Montréal is concentrated on the autoroute. Artists and artisans have been courted, wooed away from the city with the promise of space and country quiet. With a display of nationalist fervour, he has wheedled provincial funds and had an old barn converted into a plush exhibition hall. Like a little de Gaulle, a president whose name is often on his lips, Desforges understands the importance of culture, even if he is blind and deaf to art.

'Yes, Bertrand is here,' he says to me after a pause. 'I'll send him over. And I'll rouse our beloved chief of police.' Old Gagnon is not his favourite official. 'He should just about manage to find a camera. But listen, Pierre,' he says after another hesitation. 'This is too big for us. Madeleine Blais' home address is in Montréal now, isn't it? I think I'll just make a call to the metropolis.' He chuckles, then offers as an afterthought, 'Terrible business. Heartbreaking. Give my condolences to Mme Tremblay.'

Two hours later and the area round the barn looks like the parking lot for an open-air spectacle. Dr Bertrand has arrived, growling with ill-humour or indigestion, manoeuvring his belly with less dexterity than his black bag. Old Gagnon, the chief of police, is here, with some kind of assistant wielding a notebook. The two constables hover round them waiting for orders. Another man carries a metal ladder which glints at every camera flash.

A lean, tousle-haired photographer clicks away at Gagnon's instructions. As I watch him, I have the distinct impression that he is in fact the new man our local paper has hired. There is a woman at his side. She may be a girlfriend, but she displays all the avid curiosity of a budding journalist.

The ambulance is here too, its light still flashing. Thickening snowflakes turn blue then white and blue again, as it traps and releases them into the gathering dusk. The uniformed paramedics stand to the side and stamp their feet on the ground while they wait impatiently for the order to carry Madeleine away. Even Mayor Desforges has just turned up in his new municipal Mercedes.

He takes Mme Tremblay's hand in a perfect semblance of mourning. She averts her face and he turns towards me. 'Tragic,' he murmurs. 'She was so young. So talented.'

I nod. I cannot speak or make myself believe in the reality of all this.

The photographer's sidekick has no such difficulty. She approaches us with a smile and a shake of long hair. 'What do you think of all this, Monsieur le Maire?' she asks obsequiously. A notebook appears magically from her bag.

Never one to alienate journalists, Desforges clears his throat in preparation for a suitable statement.

Mme Tremblay interrupts with sudden force. 'I need to speak to the police chief. Right now. It's urgent.'

'Of course, of course.' Desforges is solicitous. 'He'll be with you in a moment, I'm sure.'

'And you are . . . ?' the girl asks sweetly.

'Never mind who I am.' Mme Tremblay gives her a withering look. She stomps off in the direction of the barn, the dogs trailing her.

I run after her. I am afraid for her.

'I'll make sure Gagnon talks to you as soon as he's finished in there.'

She stares at me as if she has forgotten who I am.

'Look, he's coming out now. Why don't you go back to the house? Keep warm. I'll bring him to you.'

'No, I'm staying right here. Then I'm going with them,' she says. She has already seen Gagnon gesture to the ambulance men. 'Going with Madeleine.'

I catch old Gagnon's eye and wave him over. He

walks with a kind of careful belligerence. He is not a man who likes being outdoors. An old protégé of my father's, he prefers paperwork and hides his craftiness behind a sullen indolence.

'*C'est Mme Tremblay,*' I introduce them. 'Madeleine Blais' grandmother.'

'Yes, I know.' He assesses her from watery eyes, then bows his head in respect.

Before either of us can say anything more, Mme Tremblay blurts out, 'It's not suicide. Madeleine didn't do it.'

'But madame . . . all the signs.'

'I don't care about the signs.' Her voice rises, shrill now, so that everyone turns. 'She didn't, I tell you.'

'The autopsy will—'

'Never mind the autopsy. She was happy last night. She was laughing.' Her face twists. Her eyes wander.

The men are carrying the stretcher out of the barn. On it there is a bleak zipped sack.

My knees don't feel right. There is a sudden pressure inside my head so that my skull grows too tight. I take a deep shuddering breath. Before I can move, Mme Tremblay has launched herself towards the ambulance, propelled herself through the open doors. The collies are barking again. One of them leaps in after her.

'*Ah non!*' Gagnon exclaims. He lumbers towards the car. I half see him talking to her, gesticulating. But my eyes are on that sack. I put my hand out as it passes close to me. There is something silky and

42

firm beneath the thick polythene covering. Yet it resists my touch. Madeleine behind a screen, I think. A screen filled only with shadows.

A high-pitched cry comes from the ambulance.

'*Pierre, viens ici,*' Gagnon orders me out of my dream. 'Explain to her. Tell her she can't go along. Tell her we'll take good care of the body. Of her granddaughter,' he corrects himself. 'Tell her in English.'

'I'll give her a sedative.' Dr Bertrand has come up beside us. With an effort, he hoists himself into the ambulance. 'You know me, Mme Tremblay.' He whispers something to her and after a few moments, she emerges. Bertrand is right behind her.

Gagnon's relief is palpable. 'I'll remember what you said, Mme Tremblay.'

She gives him a cold stare. 'It was that man. That man who came with her.' Suddenly she spits. The gesture is so out of character that we are all transfixed.

'A man?' Gagnon finally mumbles.

'Yes. With a ponytail. And a black leather jacket.'

'What's his name?'

'That's just it. I can't remember. It was so late. I didn't think ... I didn't pay attention. I didn't know ...'

Her face is so white that I fear she may faint. I put my arm round her.

The stretcher-bearers make a detour round us and lift the body into the ambulance.

'Paul or Pierre or—' She glances at me. 'No, something foreign.'

43

'Tomorrow. You'll remember tomorrow.' Gagnon has stopped paying attention. His constable is at his side, carrying a large bag. His hands are milky sheaths of transparent plastic.

'That's all the clothes, the rope, everything you said,' he says.

'Angelo or . . .'

'You'll have to stay with her, Pierre,' Bertrand says. 'Keep her warm. Make her eat something. Don't leave her alone.' He lowers his voice. 'She's a tough bird, but these things, eh, they take their toll.' He shakes his puffy face. 'You too. You look as if you could use a drop of that old firewater. What about it, Mme Tremblay?' He fixes her with his pale blue eyes. 'Have you got something to warm these tired bones?'

His arm through hers, he edges her up the path towards the house, waves me along, but Gagnon holds me back.

'Was Madeleine Blais ever mixed up with drugs?' he asks in a lowered voice.

'What do you mean?' The question startles me.

'Oh no. It's nothing. Forget it.' Gagnon ambles away just as Mayor Desforges arrives at my side.

'I got rid of that pesky journalist.' He licks pursed lips.

'Heh, join us in a drink,' Dr Bertrand calls over.

'Don't mind if I do. A quick one. I'm colder than a stiff,' Desforges announces, then quickly clamps his hand over his mouth.

In the house, Mme Tremblay makes straight for the

kitchen. With the clumsy movements of a robot, she puts out three glasses, fetches a bottle from next door, pours whisky, then looks about her at a loss.

Her eyes alight on the counter. The uncooked turkey is sitting there, its stretched white flesh moist and topped with thick slabs of bacon.

Silently, she lifts the heavy oven-tray. She gestures at me to open the door for her. She whistles for the dogs.

With a great heave, she flings the pale dead bird out onto the snow.

2

A single lamp casts shadows over Mme Tremblay's living room. From somewhere a wooden door clatters in the wind. It is the only sound to have punctuated the silence of all the hours we have sat here, apart from the 'no' she uttered when I made to stoke the fire. This has long since burnt to ash.

I would like to put an end to our wordless vigil. She is waiting for me to leave and I know that I must stay, though I wish her in bed. Her anger and intensity have usurped my emotion. I cannot think in her presence, cannot feel what I want and need to feel – which is the state Madeleine was in during those last days or hours or minutes leading to her decision to take her own life. For I am as blindly convinced of that as Mme Tremblay is of the opposite. I don't know why. The story she blurted out to Gagnon about a nameless man with a suspicious ponytail and malevolent eyes makes no sense to me. But then nothing makes any sense. I need to be alone and prod that numbness which sits where feelings ought to be.

Red and blue and grey threads weave through the arabesques in the worn carpet. I have memorized their pattern as I have now memorized the place and shape of all the objects in this familiar room – the silver-framed photographs of Madeleine at different ages and in different roles, the blue and white china on the dresser, the animal etchings on the walls, horses and sheep and mallards and robins, the scratched and polished mahogany of the piano in the corner.

The old clock in the hall chimes the half-hour. I glance at my watch and note that it is already twenty to twelve. I don't know why the pills Bertrand gave her haven't taken effect.

'Perhaps you ought to eat something,' I say. 'I can make you a sandwich, a cup of tea. Then we really ought to go to bed.'

Her eyes focus on me with difficulty. 'You help yourself. There's everything in the fridge. After that, you can go home.'

'Dr Bertrand said—'

'I know what he said.' She shrugs and suddenly there are tears on her cheeks, luminous, silent. She wipes them away. 'Pierre,' she murmurs to me in a different tone, the tone she used to use when she still trusted me. 'You don't really believe it, do you? Madeleine wouldn't. Not Madeleine. She loved life too much. She wasn't like that.'

Her voice breaks and she sobs aloud, once, a loud uncontrolled cry. It seems to surprise her, for she puts her hand to her lips.

'Let me see you up,' I say.

She shakes her head. 'You go. The guest room is made up. You know the one. Last door on the right.'

'Please, Mme Tremblay. You need to rest. Rest for tomorrow.'

At last she lets me take her arm. On the stairs I feel how much she needs my support. But at Madeleine's room, she stops and pulls away from me with sudden, surprising force. She throws the door open.

'Stupid. How stupid of me!'

Light glares over a bed so rumpled I can't take my eyes from it even though I don't want to see. A black dress in some soft angora wool seems just to have landed on the bedpost. Its sleeve sways slightly. The fluffy white carpet is dotted with black – knickers, a lacy bra, stockings. The odour of sex lingers in the air.

'Have you remembered the name of the man with the ponytail?' I hear myself ask, my voice unsteady.

Mme Tremblay isn't listening. Her attention is elsewhere. She is scouring the corner table, the desk, the chest of drawers. Objects move. Sheets of paper fly. Every item in Madeleine's capacious handbag is flung out on the bed. She bends to Madeleine's open case and heaves out trousers, skirts, sweaters, underwear, adding to the litter on the floor.

'Nothing!' she announces after a moment, an edge of triumph in her tone. 'Nothing!'

I know what she has been looking for. There is no point my saying that a suicide note could be any-where – in the house or out of it, in the post, in Madeleine's apartment.

All I want is to get out of this room, but I find myself folding the garments Mme Tremblay has tossed out of Madeleine's bag, replacing them one by one, gathering, touching, in a mute rite.

Mme Tremblay is watching me, so I put back everything, even what wasn't originally there. Even though I would like to steal something away with me, so that I can keep the scent of Madeleine's skin close to my nostrils.

The bed in the guest room sways and sags in the middle and smells of lavender. It is impossible to lie in it without rolling downhill. Madeleine and I slept here together on occasion and laughed at the squeak of the springs and the dangerous incline. A long time ago.

Outside, the old beech creaks in the wind. Snow fringes the outer window. Its whiteness creates the illusion of dawn. Memories crowd in on me, preventing sleep. I want them. I need them. In her death, I need to separate, all over again, the woman from the icon she became.

When did I start to love Madeleine? Was it when I realized that with her days had the intensity of weeks, weeks of months or years? Did I already love her before I knew what love was?

Easter 1964. I was fourteen years old and home for the holidays from the *collège classique* in Montréal where I boarded. Not that home was where I had left it.

My father had moved out of the turreted red-brick house in Ste-Anne which was the only

49

home I had ever known. We were now positioned on the hill in a brashly new and to my eyes pompous structure, as yet unshielded by trees and landscaped only with the cloying mud the builders had left behind. Visiting friends was hardly easy. I had to beg lifts or trudge three miles into town and three miles back. By the time my bicycle made it through the drive and out onto the narrow road, it was so caked in mud that the wheels refused to turn.

Worse than that. Ensconced in the glaring house, like the mistress of the manor, was my equally glaring stepmother of two years. She had a piercing laugh and blond bouffant hair and spectacles winged with rhinestone. She only wore bright red or equally bright pink and her nails always matched. Her conversation did too. It was as loud and inane as it was endless.

I couldn't understand how my father could so quickly have forgotten my mother. Nor could I understand how he could have replaced her with this contemptible woman. My mother had been beautiful, her voice and hands always gentle with understanding, her hair as dark and sleek as a blue-jay's wing, her bearing, even in that last long year of her illness, always graceful and proud.

I couldn't forgive my father.

To get away from my invasive stepmother, I spent as much time as I could locked in the room designated as mine but in which the only familiar objects were my books. I read and I stared out the window and dreamed until an excess of energy propelled me out of doors.

The woods behind the house were splendid – I had to give my father that – and I roamed their length and breadth, my boots thick with mud. Late one afternoon, I was at their highest point when I heard a crackle behind me and turned to see a boy swinging from a branch. He leapt and landed on the ground with a laugh and a thud.

'B'jour,' he greeted me. He was wearing a thick oversized lumberjacket and one of those peaked brown hats with ear flaps, and as he came up to me I noted that he was smaller than myself. But I was used to that. I was tall for my age and a boy of any size was a welcome relief.

'You live around here?'

I pointed downhill.

'Oh ya? Great. Where d'you go to school?'

'Jean Brébeuf. In Montréal,' I said self-importantly.

The boy whistled.

We walked side by side for a few minutes and then he asked, 'D'you like music? Cause we could go and hear some.' He gestured towards the other side of the hill. 'Come on, they're probably rehearsing now.' He started to run, swerving in and out of trees, leaping over fallen branches as if he knew the whereabouts of each twig by heart.

I followed more slowly and concentrated on my feet. I had no clear idea where we were until I heard the rush of the river swollen with the winter's ice. At its edge and bordering the old highway stood a whitewashed inn with a big neon sign. It was already flashing out the pink and purple letters of its name into the gathering dusk: Point Ste-Anne.

My new friend put a finger to his lips. His posture took on stealth, his face an intrigue which locked us in daring complicity. We slipped silently between the cars in the open lot and stole behind the building. Crates of empty beer bottles loomed high amid old tyres and junked furniture. From an open door came a whiff of frying onions and moist burgers. We clambered up a fence and leapt onto sodden grass.

As if to announce our landing, drums set up a whir and rumble. Electric guitars whined and twanged. A keyboard picked out a melody. By the time we had perched on the slope and brought our knees up to our chests for warmth, the very walls of the inn, the ground itself, had begun to vibrate with sound. His face striped with the colours of the neon, my new friend beamed. 'Wait. Just wait until they really get going.'

I don't know how long we sat there, lost in amplified sound and an acute sense of the forbidden. The bar, of course, was closed to children. We wouldn't have been allowed indoors. But out here, as night fell, we had free and privileged seats. We rocked and swayed and crooned along with the band until in a pause between numbers my friend peeled back a mitten and suddenly sprang up. 'Jeez, it's late. Got to get back. Come on.'

In a flash, he vaulted the fence and was running up the hill, pausing only for a second to urge me along. Half-way up, he stopped. I was panting and ashamed to see him hardly breathless.

'D'you know your way back?' he asked.

I nodded, despite my uncertainty.

'See you round, then.'

He was off before I could wave.

I blundered along, unsure of my direction until I saw the house approach me from an unexpected angle. I snuck in, deaf to my father's roar, until it occurred to me that I was starving and the prospect of a night without food was a worse fate than his anger.

The next day was Saturday and we were scheduled to go to the seasonal recital at the seminary in Ste-Anne. It was a ghastly event with performances by recalcitrant boys and graceless girls, many of them tone-deaf, all of them wishing they were out chasing a hockey puck rather than sitting in the comfortless hall under the vigilant eyes of nuns and priests. I knew it all too well, and from the inside. Up until my move to Jean Brébeuf in Montréal, I was one of the performers, my half-hearted renditions of Bach or Mozart enough to make even the most doting parent squirm.

My ingenious excuses had no effect on my father, already disgruntled by my behaviour. I had to don a white shirt and blue blazer grown too small. I had to listen to my stepmother's mindless chatter in the car and, in the hall, the withering hypocrisies of local acquaintances about my strides into manhood.

The hard seats near the raised stage – pride of place for Monsieur le Notaire and his family – came as a relief. I stared at the slightly smeared mimeographed programme and watched the blue ink form blobs on my sweaty hands. It was hot in the room, that sudden heat of spring which catches us unawares so that we don't remember to take off the coats that a day before were essential. I shed mine, then stared at the crucifix above the stage and wondered whether Christ's writhing had anything to do with the shrieks of the violins which had just begun.

Quartets were followed by solos, violins by piano by cello, all of them interspersed by clapping so violently enthusiastic that I imagined even Glenn Gould would have been flattered.

It was the turn of the dancers next. Four little girls in white tutus padded onto the stage. Bewildered eyes gazed out at the crowd in search of familiar faces. Pink-shoed feet missed a beat, then the bravest one started a plump-legged twirl and brushed against her neighbour, waking her from her daze, and suddenly they were all leaping and twirling and rushing about the stage and waving surreptitiously at dewy-eyed mothers and fathers. The applause which met this display was deafening. One of the girls was so entranced by it that she forgot to leave the stage and had to be fetched by an embarrassed teacher.

And so it went on, up through the ages and colours of tutus.

Towards the end, despite my new big-city boy's contempt, my attention was riveted. I had rarely been so close to girls of my own age, let alone girls showing such an expanse of bare flesh. One of them, in a blue leotard and tutu, moved with particular grace, her long legs arching, her leaps as light and effortless as a gazelle's. Her skin was honey-gold and flawless and, as my gaze moved up her curved arms towards neck and face, I realized I was sitting at the very edge of my chair and tilting precariously. I sat back with a scrape.

From the end of the row I caught my former father confessor's eyes on me. I flushed painfully but my attention flew back to the girl. She was almost directly in front of me now, her face raised in a dreamy expression towards some distant heaven. I could make out the separate strands of thick, tawny hair which sculpted her profile, the pins which kept her topknot in place. There was something about that face which made my spine prickle in discomfort.

For a moment, my thoughts winged to the centre-fold in the prohibited magazine one of my friends at Brébeuf had snuck into the dorm. I was glad the applause drowned the remembered snickers of my mates, less glad when I felt Père Xavier's eyes on my neck again. He had always been able to read my mind.

I didn't watch the next number. I stared at the floor instead. And then the music changed. A stronger beat took hold of the room. There was a clacking and tapping of feet above and I looked up to see a figure in top hat and tails, a diminutive Fred Astaire, crossing the stage in an easy rhythmic lope. Beneath the hat, I suddenly recognized the face and this time my flush was so hot that I thought it must be visible across the hall.

The figure in the top hat, the girl in the blue tutu were both my friend of the previous evening –

the boy I had sat with outside the inn.

In the vaulted dining hall next to the auditorium the ritual post-recital drinks and cakes were laid out. I shuffled along the far edge of the room, hiding from my embarrassment as much as from the crowd. But there was no corner dark enough to shield me from my father. His hand firmly on my shoulder, he prodded me into the fray.

'There's someone I particularly want you to meet,' he said, leading me towards a cluster of people amongst whom I could already hear my stepmother's raised voice. 'Thérèse,' he shushed her and urged me forth. 'Pierre, I want to introduce you to our new neighbours, Mme Tremblay and her granddaughter, Madeleine.'

I raised my eyes from my shoes. A sombrely dressed woman, her hair pulled back in a tight bun like a schoolteacher's, was stretching out her hand to me.

'Hello, Pierre.'

I mumbled something. I was acutely aware of the smaller figure at her side, whose hand was now similarly outstretched.

'Hello, Pierre,' she echoed.

I noticed white stockings, the slight flare of a kilted skirt, and then I was looking into heavily fringed eyes, vast and tawny-yellow against smooth skin. One of them winked at me roguishly, right there under Père Xavier's gaze.

Was it then, as I gauged the reality of that wink and tried to find a voice adequate to a 'Hello', that I first began to love Madeleine?

* * *

The next day we went to Mme Tremblay's house for tea. It was not a meal I had ever heard of. Nor had I ever visited a house that was at once as ramshackle and inviting as Mme Tremblay's. We sat in front of the fire while she poured first milk, then steaming liquid into our cups from a slightly chipped china pot decorated with birds and flowers. She passed around hot buttered cakes she called scones and urged me to smother them in the cream and jam on Madeleine's tray – something I just managed to do without upsetting tea and tray alike.

Mme Tremblay spoke French to us and had a French name, but I realized from what my father had said that she was in fact English or Scottish. I didn't know the difference. I had never met anyone English in the town before. The only English people I had any contact with were Montrealers who worked in the stores on the Côte-des-Neiges not far from my school.

I could speak English of course. Speak it more or less. From the age of eight I had been taught. But not taught well enough according to our English teacher, who wasn't a Jesuit like the others but who managed to tweak our ears just as assiduously when we made mistakes. And like all of my generation, I had sat glued in front of American television and imbibed *Howdy Doody* and *Disney Time* and *Father Knows Best* with my mother's milk – alongside the homegrown pap of *La Famille Plouffe*.

The oddity of Mme Tremblay, her careful French and her careful manners, intrigued me, though it didn't altogether allay my suspicions. Like a superstitious believer in the creed of stereotype, I watched for signs of contempt and distaste, for any gesture which might reveal that she secretly despised these lowlife Frenchies.

But even the prickly, over-sensitive teenager that I was could find nothing to fault in Mme Tremblay's manners. And towards my father, at least, she showed genuine warmth, enquiring about the new house, asking after my older brother, who had been away in Rome for some time training to be a Jesuit. The fact that she knew this surprised me. It seemed to imply that my father was an older friend than I had surmised.

Strangely enough, I didn't even begin to think of Madeleine in terms of the great Anglo-French divide. I had met her in French after all, even if in a different sex.

The fact was I was so acutely aware of her presence that I tried very hard not to think of her at all.

Only when my stepmother started in on her 'Oh, how cute' this or other bit of china was did Mme Tremblay evince the slightest shudder of distaste. I could hardly blame her here and I almost shouted my approval when she cut her in mid-flow and asked Madeleine whether she might like to perform for their guests, provide a little entertainment.

Madeleine had none of the hesitation I would have had. She neither hummed and hawed nor pretended not to have heard. Instead, with a mysterious little smile, she said, 'What do you think, Mémère, a little Shakespeare?'

'Why not? Though perhaps the language . . .' Mme Tremblay turned towards my father, who waved away her hesitation with a 'No, no. It will do Pierre good.'

Madeleine stood in front of the window, a beam of late afternoon light playing over her long loosened hair. In a dutiful little girl's voice she explained to us that she was going to do a speech from a play called *A Midsummer Night's Dream* in which the queen of the fairies, Titania, at war with her tyrannical husband, Oberon, speaks of the havoc his jealousy has caused.

I have to admit that I found all this talk of fairies faintly ridiculous. Nor had Shakespeare ever troubled my intelligence. I had just about heard the name. But there was something in the way Madeleine then turned her back on us, the growing silence in the room, that forced my attention.

When Madeleine confronted us again, I was startled to find that she was no longer altogether Madeleine. Her shoulders thrown back, her head high, she paced the makeshift area of the stage with a regal air, her hands busy with some flowing gown we could feel if not see. The voice which came out of her was deeper, no longer a girl's voice, but a woman's, and it seemed to taste the words which came out of her throat.

After the first taut exclamation of 'These are the forgeries of jealousy', I followed few of them. Somehow it didn't seem to matter. I could touch the

59

anger that had filled the room, sense discord and disappointment, and I was enthralled by the gestures and expressions of this Madeleine who was not Madeleine. So much so, that I forgot to clap until my father poked an urgent finger into my back.

By this time Madeleine was a girl again and was asking her grandmother whether she mightn't now take me to visit her pony. A moment later we were outside and she was laughing gleefully.

'Your mother hated that, didn't she?' She set up a flapping of jowls and hair and looked like nothing so much as an irritated Pekinese. It was a startling imitation of Thérèse.

'She's not my mother,' I grumbled. 'My mother's dead.'

'Oh.' Madeleine stopped in mid-gesture. 'I'm sorry. I didn't know.'

'No.'

We walked in silence towards the barn. 'And your mother?' I asked, still irritated.

'Not dead, no.' She flashed me an odd, angry look, then started to run. 'Mémère's my best mother,' I heard her call, her voice trailing, distorted in the wind.

I turn over in the sagging bed and, unsure whether I am awake or asleep, hear that voice again, like a keening in the air.

Pale, milky light casts a faint strip across the room. It does nothing to dispel the sound. I stumble over to the window and throw open two sets of panes. The cold attacks me, forces me into wakefulness. But the wail has only grown louder, buffeting the sides of the house, rising from the snow. I shiver and then, with a start, pull on shirt and trousers and rush from my room.

I pause at Mme Tremblay's door, but the sound isn't coming from there. I hurry to the end of the long corridor and with only a second's trepidation push open the door to Madeleine's room.

Mme Tremblay is standing at the open window. She rocks back and forth, clasping herself with her hands. Lank hair falls over shoulders covered with a knitted shawl. Under the length of her nightgown her feet are bare.

I put my arm round her, try to turn her away from the window, try to blot out the sound which issues from her lips and the sight of the barn in the distance with its circle of flapping tapes.

'Please,' I whisper. 'You'll make yourself ill.'

I pull the window to and suddenly she stops. The face she turns on me is haggard, streaked with tears, more fragile with its years than I could ever have imagined. She doesn't seem to recognize me.

At last she says in a strange little voice, 'Madeleine spoke to me. Yes. Spoke.'

I try to stop the shudder which has taken me over. 'Come,' I urge her away from the window. 'You must get dressed. You'll catch cold.'

'I tell you she spoke to me.' Her tone is firmer and she resists my direction.

I cannot think what to say. I have never known Mme Tremblay to be superstitious, to commune

61

with her dead. Even her Catholicism seems to have a tersely matter-of-fact, puritan cast, unadorned by ritual objects or Marys-full-of-grace. But now she is staring at me with the raised eyes of a New Age convert, insisting on an impossible communion.

'She told me she was in pain. Great pain.' Her red-rimmed eyes are wide and gaze through the door into the middle distance.

What I feel with sudden acuteness is Mme Tremblay's pain. It sits on top of my own like a great juddering bird.

'We must make amends. She told me. She cannot rest. We must exact vengeance.'

Despite myself, I shiver again. The intended soothing sound turns into a gasp as it issues from my dry throat. I steer Mme Tremblay from Madeleine's room towards her own. 'You get dressed now and I'll make some coffee. All right?'

She focuses on me directly for the first time. 'I'm not mad, Pierre,' she says and then blurts out, 'Children should not die before their grandparents. It turns the world topsy-turvy.'

I squeeze her hand and nod my assent.

Downstairs, I pat the dogs and pour fresh water into their bowls. With numb fingers I extract cups and saucers from a cupboard, find instant coffee, cut thick slabs from an untouched loaf. I feel anaesthetized, unable to think. I have an odd sense that I am in a tunnel where the light is too bright for sight and at either end there is a welcoming darkness I cannot quite reach. I do not notice that I have cut my finger on the sharp knife until I see the blood brightening the white bread. I stare at the patch of red and then chuck the slice in the bin.

Mme Tremblay and I sit opposite each other at the kitchen table. She is dressed. Her hair is pinned into its customary bun. But she makes no pretence of eating and speech has deserted her.

In a flat voice, I tell her that if she is to have the strength to carry out the vengeance she spoke of, she must eat.

She probes me with eyes that have suddenly taken on a sharper cast. 'So you agree with me now?'

I shrug. 'It's certainly possible,' I say, though I don't believe my own words. But somewhere in the preceding silence I have decided that the notion of retribution may be good for Mme Tremblay. It will give her a purpose, a narrative by which to order her days. I almost envy her.

'I spent half the night trying to remember that man's name.' She scowls. 'Madeleine didn't say it very clearly, just threw it off, like an aside.' She lowers her voice to a mumble. 'I think she may have picked him up. A hitchhiker. I won't tell them that.'

The wood of my chair cuts into my legs. I get up testily and boil more water. The coffee tastes of soiled laundry. It reminds me of the rumpled sheets on Madeleine's bed.

'And they were in such a hurry. It was already late by the time they arrived. I had half given Madeleine up. I was dozing by the fire. Asleep when they came. Vague with it. Yes, such a hurry.'

She broods and I don't want to follow her

thoughts. I know she is censoring them for me. She doesn't want me to see Madeleine rushing upstairs with her hitchhiker in tow.

'You should never have abandoned Madeleine, Pierre.' Her voice reaches me from behind. 'You loved her. You were the only one for her.'

Boiling water splatters out from the mug with its small heap of instant coffee, sprays my shirt with scalding liquid. Mme Tremblay has never said this to me before. I veer round to face her. 'I didn't abandon her. She—'

Mme Tremblay cuts me off. 'Yes. They were in such a hurry. To get to midnight mass. In town. It was Madeleine's idea. She was laughing. She just wanted to change first, out of her jeans. She asked me whether I wanted to come with them. That man didn't speak much. Maybe he couldn't. Italian or Spanish he was. Yes, that's it. I didn't really get a good look at him. But he was dark. If only I could remember the name. Sandro or—'

I interrupt her. 'Was there a second name?'

'A second name?' She looks up at me with a blank expression. 'No. I don't think she said. I . . .' She covers her face with her hands. 'I'm too old. I forget things. Stupid little things.'

'It doesn't matter. It'll come back.'

At a loss, I switch the small table-top radio on. A few bars of music are followed by a weather fore-cast and the news. I don't listen to the blunt tones of the announcer, until I hear: 'The actress, Madeleine Blais, was found dead yesterday in Ste-Anne . . .'

Mme Tremblay gasps. I turn the radio off with

64

so violent a gesture that it hurtles across the table.

We sit in silence again and suddenly I can't sit any more. The house has become a trap, filled with the voices of Madeleine and her hitchhiker which I have no right to hear. I push my chair back with a scrape.

'Look. Why don't I take the dogs for a quick run? You'll be all right for a few minutes?'

Mme Tremblay nods, then calls after me when I am already at the door, my boots on my feet. 'Gagnon said not to let them go near the barn. Remember.'

Outside, a pristine blanket covers the ground. Yesterday has been wiped out, its traces eradicated.

I plunge towards the woods, the dogs at my side. My boots are heavy with the snow, but there is not so much of it as to make running impossible. I run. I run until I can run no further and suddenly I am lashing out. From nowhere there is a stick in my hand and I am flailing it, battering the trunks of trees and the bunched thickets, hitting out again and again with savage abandon as if beating could provide answers, as if rage and the whack on wood and ground and the solid, impassive resistance of nature could tell me why. Why Madeleine? Why now? Why?

I howl. I hit and beat until snow topples from the boughs and the stick in my hand is reduced to nothing. My mind is a void. My legs crumble. I sprawl against bark. Around me there is the slow drip, drip of snow melting from topmost branches. It makes a little pattern of indentations on the ground as it falls. I look up and the cold moisture hits my face. Only then do I notice that my face is already wet with too many tears.

The whimpering of the dogs rouses me. I don't know how long I have been sitting here but my trousers are stiff with cold, my toes icy. I brush the snow from my clothes and move slowly back towards the farm.

In the distance, tyres squelch. As I reach the house, a car skids to a stop. Dr Bertrand emerges from it slowly, balancing his weight. He waves a gloved hand at me.

'You haven't left her for too long?' he says by way of greeting.

'Hope not.'

He gives me a critical look, then shrugs. 'Bad business.'

'Very bad.'

A sweet acrid smell pervades the kitchen. Mme Tremblay is chopping onions. She looks back at us and wipes her hands and streaming eyes hurriedly on her apron. Onions are a good cover.

'I thought Pierre should have some lunch,' she announces. The glance she casts in my direction is consoling and tinged with guilt.

'Is there enough for three?' Bertrand pokes his nose towards the counter.

She nods. 'Do you have some news?'

'Just the barest details. That's what I came about. Thought you'd want to know.' He gestures her towards a chair, pulls up a larger one from the corner to fit his ample frame.

'Well?'

'Don't be in such a hurry, Claire,' he chastises her. It is the first time I have heard anyone but my father call her by her first name.

I pour him a drink and he looks at me gratefully.

'Well, the good news is that Madeleine died instantly. No pain, I imagine. Her spinal cord was severed, the first three cervical vertebrae fractured. The coat helped, undoubtedly. Made her heavier.'

Mme Tremblay is staring at him as if he were her own executioner.

'Is that what you've come to tell me?' she murmurs at last.

'Heh. I can't tell you more than I know.' He has taken hold of her hand and is rubbing it, as if to restore its warmth. 'The only other thing is that she probably died between two and four in the morning. Maybe a bit sooner. I've allowed for the cold. The lab reports will tell us more. If the police decide to do them.'

'What do you mean, if they decide to do them?' She springs up, fired by some new energy source, and she is suddenly by the telephone, screaming into it, demanding to speak to the chief of police.

When she comes back, she tells us with steely calm, 'Gagnon's not in. He's ringing me back.'

I clear my throat. 'If you don't mind, since you're going to be here, I'll skip lunch and just pop back to my place to get some fresh clothes.'

'You run along, Pierre. I thought you might need to. I've arranged for one of my nurses to turn up at

67

three. And she can stay. If Claire doesn't take the broom to her, that is.'

We both wait for Mme Tremblay's response. But she has her back to us. She is chopping onions again with a clatter which speaks more of frenzy than precision. Her goodbye to me is barely audible above the noise, which must also mask the sound of the bell. When I open the door, I am surprised to find Constable Miron and his partner standing there.

'Gagnon's sent us to do a search of the house,' Miron stammers.

I lead the two men into the kitchen and steal away. The desire to be gone makes me furtive.

From the crest of the hill, my house looks as serene as an old hand-painted picture postcard. Snow covers the huddled pines in a graceful swoop. The cat, like some vigilant sentinel, is poised gracefully on the eaves. Smoke curls thinly round the weather-vane and disappears into a sky which has turned crisply blue.

Madeleine will never taste this sight again, I think, and suddenly I would like the house to show some sign of the devastation which has occurred: a scar of graffiti, a gaping wound in its side. But the only change I can see as I slip down the incline is a car parked in the drive.

My heart sinks. As I open the door, the rumble of a vacuum cleaner emerges from the far room. I consider sneaking upstairs, but no sooner have I put my foot on the first creaking step than the noise stops.

Maryla Orkanova appears through the arch of

the doorway. She has a starched white apron on over some blue swirling dress more appropriate to dancing than cleaning and she stands there, her pinned-up hair slightly dishevelled, her grey eyes wide in a thin face whose expression I cannot read.

'Pierre,' she breathes, her voice husky. 'I—'

'I'd forgotten you had said you were coming today.'

'I told you. Stefan's out with his friends and . . . But I'm not surprised you've forgotten. I . . . Pierre, I'm sorry.' She is fumbling for words and suddenly she races past me and reappears a moment later, a paper in hand. She waves it at me. 'I bumped into Françoise. She told me. Then I read about it. I'm so sorry.'

I grab the newspaper from her and unfold it clumsily. The local rag has rarely worked so quickly. A special edition, no doubt. On the front page there is a large photograph of Madeleine in the high-necked gown she wore as Hedda Gabler, in her hand one of the general's pistols. Above the photograph the headline blares, '*SUICIDE D'UNE STAR*'.

The eager glossy-haired reporter has had no trouble in reaching a verdict on Madeleine's death.

My eyes skim the story. There are the barest of details – the site, the manner of death, a bio which manages to hint at salacious details amongst a list of films and plays, all culminating in a resounding quote from our beloved mayor: 'A tragic death has befallen one of the greatest of our own. We can only join with the relatives, the friends, the many fans of Madeleine Blais, to mourn her passing.'

I crumple the paper into a ball and pass it back to Maryla.

She is staring at me, her eyes frightened. 'You knew, yes?'

I nod. Is there anyone by now who does not know? I consider ringing Mme Tremblay's and telling Dr Bertrand that he must keep the paper out of her sight. But I know the protective measure would be pointless. This is a small town and gossip travels with the speed of light and with more excited insistence.

'Can I make you some coffee?' Maryla's eyes are still glued to my face.

'Yes. No. I'll do it.' I make for the kitchen, hoping that she'll leave me on my own, but she is right behind me.

'It's so sad. She had everything, had so much to live for. So why? Why?' She is wringing her long-fingered hands, pausing at the wedding band, twisting it. 'Life is too precious to be wasted like that. An act of will. Why did she do it?'

'We can't interrogate the dead,' I mutter. It is a stupid thing to say. All I want to do is interrogate Madeleine, force her to answer my questions so that I can bully or cajole her into hope, prevent that act which is too definitive for the living to bear.

I don't know why my thoughts won't accede to the possibility of murder, despite Mme Tremblay's conviction. Nor do I know why I refrain from mentioning this to Maryla. My mind won't tolerate a terror which is somehow worse than despair.

'She was spoiled. Too rich and famous and

70

spoiled.' Maryla's face is suddenly all angry passion. She turns her back to me and starts scrubbing at the cups stacked by the sink, one by one, fiercely, as if she wanted to remove their colour. 'It is a sin. A violation.'

'Maryla. Really! That's enough.' My voice is steely.

'Yes.' Her outburst isn't over. 'By damning herself she has damned God. Cursed all of creation. Denied it. Disfigured it for the rest of us. Selfish. A selfish woman!'

She is facing me and suddenly my hands are on her arms and I am shaking her, shaking her so hard that she winces and the cup flies from her hands, shatters on the tiled floor.

I step back, aghast at my abrupt surge of violence. I bend to pick up fragments, stammer out an apology.

Tears flood Maryla's eyes. 'There is enough death,' she says.

Death is no stranger to Maryla. Some months before I returned to Ste-Anne, her husband died. They had only been in Canada for a matter of months. What accident of circumstance had led them from Poland to settle here remains a mystery to me. Maryla doesn't like to talk of it. More deaths, I suspect. Jerzy worked at the plywood factory at the other end of town, Legrand et Fils. It has been there for ever. And one day he simply didn't come home from work. When they phoned Maryla, she didn't understand what they were saying to her. Her French was still rudimentary then.

She rushed over to the factory to find Jerzy dead. A stroke, the doctor told her.

She was left with a three-year-old son and a cousin of her husband's in Toronto who had arranged for their immigration and then promptly abandoned them to their own devices.

When I arrived in Ste-Anne she was still stunned, a lonely soul stranded in a strange land. Her confessor asked me whether I might have work for her, part-time, something, anything. She came to the house, her son in tow, and before I had really arrived at a conscious decision Maryla had become my housekeeper. We tried to bring her mother over from Poland after that. But before the papers were in place, there was news of her mother's death.

Maryla worked for me until Stefan was of an age for school. Her French, by then, had improved greatly and I found her rather better work as a receptionist in a doctor's office. But she has refused to give me up altogether. She is both grateful to me and feels I need her; wishes, I know, that I needed her more. The fact that I don't she blames on Madeleine.

Maryla is staring at the remaining pieces of blue and white china on the floor. I put my arm round her shoulders. She is still trembling slightly.

'Forgive me,' I say. 'The cup doesn't matter.'

'It matters. I shouldn't have said all that.'

I shrug, unable to come up with the appropriate lie.

'You would rather be alone.'

I nod without meeting her eyes, gesture at my

trousers which are still damp from the snow. 'I need to change.'

When I am already out of the room, she calls after me in a hard little voice, 'Perhaps some man made her desperate.'

I pretend not to hear her.

My bed is neatly made. Its heavy blue spread displays not a single crease. The scatter cushions have been plumped into rectitude and symmetrically aligned. Maryla's attention to detail is scrupulous.

Like a pampered child I throw the cushions on the floor. I tear my carefully hung robe from the door, fling it round myself and plunge down on the bed. The anger is unnecessary, but Maryla's comments and speculations echo in my ears. I recognize that similar words are probably already on every pair of lips. The noise robs me of Madeleine, scatters her into a hundred alien fragments which blow back into my face and refuse to coalesce.

There will be no genuine tears shed over Madeleine Blais in Ste-Anne. She has always been seen as an outsider here. Lightly veiled envy dogged her every bid for freedom, attended her every achievement. It will now be transformed into gloating malice. The town has never judged her kindly and it will not forgive her suicide.

All my ambivalence about the place suddenly rises up and chokes me.

I see beams of satisfaction settling on every face. 'It was inevitable,' Mme Groulx says with lowered, pitiless eyes. 'What else was there for her, eh?' Serge

73

Dufour leers as he jingles the keys in his trouser pocket. 'After that wild life, there could only be suicide.' My brother stands at the pulpit and intones, 'Sin leads to sin . . .' He transforms Madeleine's death into an exemplum: better settle for mediocrity than risk the fate of Madeleine Blais. The tyranny of opinion takes over and obliterates dissent.

Madeleine's wild laughter suddenly rings in my ears. It blots out the stampede of voices. She has her teasing face on, all pouting lips and innocent eyes. 'Maybe if you understand them so well, you're becoming just a little too much like them. *Eh, mon Pierre?*'

I focus on her smiling face, and abruptly I see her stretched like a purring cat on some sofa. In Paris, is it? The upholstery is striped and she is running her hand over the fabric. 'I'm so glad you still want me, Pierre,' she murmurs. 'When no-one wants me any more, I'll curl up and die.'

I touch my finger to the smooth warmth of her cheek and tell her that I want her still. Always. That someone wanted her on Christmas Eve, if her bed is proof of anything. But Madeleine has already dis-appeared, faded into that swinging marionette with its cold deathly pallor.

I burrow under the covers for warmth and force the image away and try to make sense of a world without Madeleine. For the tenth time I re-enact our last meeting, then remind myself that that wasn't the last time I saw her. Or spoke to her. Could I have done anything? Crabs scuttle and claw at the murky

74

edge of my consciousness, scrabbling for something which won't take shape. I chase them away only to stumble again on that cold, cold body wrapped in its icy sheath.

A knock at the door forces itself to my attention and I see Maryla opening it tentatively. She is carrying a stack of freshly ironed shirts. She walks on tiptoe and places them carefully on my dresser. Then she turns to look at me and steps back.

'I . . . I thought you were sleeping.'

I shake my head.

'I'm going now.' She comes towards me and bends to kiss me on the cheek. Her loosened hair brushes my face. It smells of tart green apples and something muskier and suddenly I am pulling her down on top of me.

'Pierre!' Her voice is startled.

There is no need for that tone of surprise. It is hardly the first time that Maryla has come to my bed, though perhaps it is now longer than I remember.

Her lips are warm and slightly bitter with coffee. I like the bitterness, like the warmth more. It is there in the fingers she curves round my neck, there in the cleavage her dress leaves bare. I unbutton it and find her small breasts. They are warm, too, and as I put my face to them I can hear the rapid beat of her heart. I kiss the life of her, lick at it, trace the heat to its source and pray that it can warm both of us.

Afterwards Maryla is happy. She doesn't instantly spring up to scrub herself clean in a way that I have long guessed is a prelude to the confession she will make the next day. Latterly the confessions have been to my brother, which may be one of the many reasons our love-making faltered.

No, today she lies peacefully in the crook of my arm. I am grateful to her for that, grateful too for her warmth and the caress of her fingers on my chest, which remind me that I may still be alive.

'Perhaps now that—' she begins and I put a stilling finger to her lips.

I know she is going to say that now that Madeleine is dead there may be hope for the two of us. I don't want her to say it. I don't want her to tell me again that she loves me, that she loves my goodness and my beauty and my dark eyes and darker hair. That I am the best man apart from Jerzy she has ever been fortunate enough to meet. I know she is mistaken and I kiss her to ensure her silence.

From a distance I hear Madeleine's laughter gathering again and, with all my being, I wish her here.

Both act and wish make me feel like a criminal.

3

'Pierre Rousseau?'

The man at the door wears a trimly belted soft grey coat which squares his shoulders to perfection and an elegant matching hat. Sitting incongruously beneath it is a boxer's face, complete with a mash of a nose and a stubborn jaw. His steel-dark eyes protrude slightly and are on a level with my own. They examine me with sullen curiosity.

'Pierre Rousseau?' he repeats. His stance has a hint of belligerence, despite the hands casually hidden in the recess of his pockets.

I hesitate. The morning has already brought two phone calls from curious acquaintances and three from journalists. I am not prepared to confront another in person, certainly one whose feet are so solidly planted on the ground.

The man brings a wallet out from the depths of his pocket and flashes it open for me.

'Detective Contini. Sûreté du Québec.'

I stand back to let him in. Mayor Desforges has pulled in his contacts. But for the provincial police to take over, the circumstances of death have to be suspicious.

'Your police chief, Emile Gagnon, recommended that I see you early in our investigation. You were one of the first on the scene of Madeleine Blais' death . . . And he thought you might be able to help me. Orient me in Ste-Anne as well. You come highly recommended.'

His voice is smooth and he throws me a complicit smile as I take his hat and coat and usher him into the living room.

'So the matter is no longer in local hands?'

'Let's say we're all working together. Big name. Big pressure. Too bad they didn't get us in here on day one, eh?'

He gauges my reaction on some unknown scale of civic loyalty, then looks round the room with an appreciative murmur and settles into the sofa. There are newspapers scattered on the table. The Montréal papers. All of them featuring Madeleine's death on the front page. I wish now that I had tucked them away.

He gestures at the papers. 'You can see why.'

'Yes, I guess I can. And the autopsy?'

He doesn't answer. He is staring at me. 'We know each other, by the way. You may not remember . . .'

I study his face and he laughs, points to his nose, to receding hair and solid girth. 'Before all this.'

'Oh?' I cannot place the features.

'You haven't fared so badly. Look much the same in fact, bar a few lines. Jean Brébeuf, it was. You were a couple of years ahead of me and I didn't stay

78

the course. The parental money ran out.' He grimaces. 'Nor was I really cut out for all that classical education.'

The smile is back on his face, tugging at full lips. He is waiting for me to remember, teasing, as if it were some kind of test.

'Richard Contini,' he prods.

'Can I get you some coffee?' I point at the flask. 'Should still be hot.'

'Sure. Black. You were Père Lévesque's favourite. Our great historian, remember? He had you help out with us slower ones. On one occasion, I recall, you read out what he told us was a model paper, all about the Parti des Patriotes and the grievances which led to the rebellion of 1837 against the Brits.'

He gives me a smirk, as if he has just triumphantly recited a piece of homework.

'Ya. It was full of calls for real democracy and independence for the French. And gory details about British reprisals. Villages burning. Women and children thrust out into the cold. Deportations. Executions. Hangings . . .'

He pauses dramatically. The coffee I am pouring spills over the edge of the cup.

'Yes, I do remember that.' I banish Madeleine's body and compose myself. 'Towards the end of that term, Père Lévesque took us out on a separatist demo. Queen Victoria Day, 1964. It was the first time I saw the Union Jack burnt. We were marching towards the Monument des Patriotes where the hangings had taken place. There were police

79

everywhere.' I look at him pointedly. 'On foot, motorbikes, horses.'

He coughs. 'Yes, well, that day I was right beside you. You were supposed to make sure I didn't get into trouble.'

I stare at him. A little boy's face comes into focus, dark eyes gazing up at me in fearful respect, a tuft of light brown hair, a hand clinging to my jacket.

'Riccardo Contini,' I murmur.

'That's me. But let's get back to the present. Madeleine Blais. You knew her well apparently?'

I nod without meeting his eyes. He has reached into the bowl of walnuts on the table and is cracking two of them against each other in the palm of his hand. The gesture seems unconscious, but the crack is loud, brutal. With an air of surprise, he looks at the mangle of innards and shells, then starts to pick at them delicately.

'Had she talked of suicide?'

My 'No' wavers, a visible hesitation. 'Maybe once or twice. In the way that everyone does.'

He looks at me sceptically. 'You don't seem too sure.'

'I didn't see her all that much. Of late.'

'When did you last see her?' He takes a notebook from his pocket and waits for my answer.

'So you're treating it as suicide?'

'We have an open mind. Despite these.' He points contemptuously at the papers and I gather them up, place them to the side of the hearth.

'When did you last see her? What kind of shape was she in?'

I keep my tone even and tell him about how troubled Madeleine was over the killings at the Université de Montréal. 'She was afraid. Men hate women, she told me.'

'Nothing more specific?'

I shake my head. 'She was depressed.'

'So who isn't?' he grumbles.

From his pocket, he takes out a pack of du Maurier and a square gold lighter, flicks it over and over on the table in a series of slow somersaults.

'Nasty affair that. Got a lot of people down. But hardly enough of a motive. On its own.'

'Madeleine took it very hard.'

He nods sagely, lights up and inhales with visible pleasure. 'What about other things? Her personal life. Love affairs? Career? Last reviews weren't wonderful.'

'Did you see the play?' I ask with too much disbelief.

'*Hedda Gabler?*' His look is judicious and I wonder whether he is about to lie. Then he grins and his face becomes wholly amiable. 'No. To tell you the truth, I have no stomach for theatre. Too much out there.' He waves dramatically towards the window where there is only the gloom of gathering clouds. 'Still, my wife keeps me in touch. And I know it's about a woman who kills herself.'

He sips his coffee thoughtfully. 'Don't get me wrong. I've seen Mlle Blais in a film or two over the years. A beautiful woman. But depressed despite it. Love affairs not going well, I imagine?'

I shrug.

'No, why should she tell you, eh? Still, there was that man with the ponytail. We'll have to check on him. He left lots of prints. In the bedroom. They're dusting for them now.'

'You've been to see Mme Tremblay?'

He laughs. 'I'm not twelve years old any more. I know my job.'

His hands are busy with the walnuts again. That casual cracking, like a threat.

'And the lab reports?'

'All in due course. Short-staffed over the holidays. It's the car we need to find.'

'What car?'

He looks at me in surprise. 'Madeleine Blais' car. It's not where her grandmother claims she left it and your guys haven't traced it yet. Apparently . . .' he flicks pages in his notebook, 'Mme Tremblay heard it revving and driving off at about two in the morning. Which proves nothing, of course. Still . . .'

He tucks the notebook into his pocket and looks up at me candidly. 'I'd like you to come with me. Give me a hand with things. In town.'

'Sure,' I say, though I feel oddly reluctant. I don't want to confront people, don't want to hear them speculating about Madeleine. Yet at the same time I sense I have been blessed with an unparalleled opportunity. With Contini, I will be at the helm of the investigation. He will help me make sense of things. Put me in possession of facts.

Somewhere in the midst of these facts and my knowledge, I will arrive at some kind of truth about Madeleine. Madeleine, the mistress of illusion.

A north wind is blowing and the police tape flutters around the old barn like festive streamers at the launching of some ancient ship. A television crew is in attendance. At the side of the barn, a man points a camera through a window. People cluster round, chattering with animation and stamping their feet against the cold. A red rose has been tossed across the barrier. It lies like a gash of blood in the snow.

'Damn!' Detective Contini mutters. 'Just what we don't need.' With loud authority, he urges the onlookers away, shouts at the cameraman.

A man shoves a microphone towards his mouth.

Contini pushes it aside. 'There'll be a press conference. Soon. You'll be notified.' He urges me under the tape.

'Damn intruders! Fools, tramping everywhere. No sense. How am I supposed to reconstruct anything? And this confounded snow! Even if there was anything to find, we wouldn't now.'

He crosses his arms and pounds his shoulders with gloved hands. 'Fucking cold. Heh, you know the joke? An old Québecois is asked what he does in summer and he takes off his toque, scratches his head, and answers, "On that day, I go fishing."'

He guffaws. He is trying to put me at ease, but as we trudge into the barn, I can barely lift my eyes from the ground.

'So, Mme Tremblay brought you in here and what did you see?'

I start to fumble with words. I don't want to remember. 'Didn't you look at the pictures?'

'Sure, I saw the pictures. But pictures are selective. Like memory. Put the two together and I might get somewhere. So she was hanging here?'

I nod.

He is looking around, examining the assortment of broken chairs, the beams, the bits of hay, dispersed now, calibrating the height of the pony's stall with his arms.

'How tall would you say Madeleine Blais was?'

'Five foot six. A little over.'

'She was wearing heels?'

The lace-up boots spring into my mind and I shiver and nod.

'Was she an acrobat?'

I stare at him. 'No, an actress.' This is not the time for more jokes. 'Oh, I see.' I follow his upward gaze. The beam is high. I would have trouble reaching it. But I imagine Madeleine, her lightness, her feline grace. 'Yes, she was agile. She was good at all that.'

'Still. It's pretty damned high.' He looks up and then starts to scrabble round the barn.

'How'd you get up to the loft bit?'

Suddenly an image coalesces. Madeleine and I, children, shimmying up the two swinging ropes which hung from the thick beam and launching ourselves into hay. Was it one of these same ropes that Madeleine used? It is so long since I have been in the barn that I have no idea whether one of them was still in place. And now, there are no ropes at all.

I say all this to Contini as he scours the space, prods open an old wooden chest.

His response is grudging. 'Possible. She must have been very determined.'

'Despair is an odd motor,' I hear myself saying.

'Mmm. OK. Her lover's run off in the middle of the night . . .'

I grimace, but he carries on.

'Abandoned her. So she's depressed. She puts her coat on over her nightgown. Maybe she's had a little too much to drink. She goes for a walk. Ends up here. Decides she's had enough. Is that how you see it?'

I weigh the complexity and unpredictability which is Madeleine and say, 'Maybe.'

'So this thirty-seven-year-old woman wearing a heavy fur coat shimmies up a rope, launches herself into the loft, ties a perfect noose, places it round her neck and jumps. So what are the tumbled chairs doing beneath her?'

My mind is like a swamp of quicksand, refusing precision. But my fists are clenched. I would like to land one of them on Contini's placid face. 'Maybe the noose, the chairs, were already there,' I mumble. 'I don't know. We'll have to ask Mme Tremblay.'

'Hmmm,' he grunts sceptically. He doesn't understand the mixture of impulsiveness and persistence which is Madeleine.

He is darting round again, peering into corners with the agility of a far lighter man. He bends to pick something off the ground and drops it in his pocket. The flick of his wrist is oddly elegant.

'You don't trust our local police then?'

'It's not a question of trust.' He meets my eyes in

the gloom. I cannot read his. They are opaque.

'What does Mme Tremblay use this place for?'

'Not for much these days. In the summer there are chickens.'

'Right. Let's go. We're going to drive into town. I want to find out if anyone noticed Mlle Madeleine Blais on Christmas Eve.'

On the way back to the car, I see two uniformed Sûreté officers combing the area. They bend to examine bare, craggy shrubs. They peer under firs. They run their boots over the ground, their necks stiff in concentration. Contini leaves me for a moment and goes off to exchange a few words with them. One of them digs into a bag and shows him something that glistens.

When he comes back to me, he rubs the flattened arch of his nose. 'You didn't by any chance lose something out here, did you, Rousseau?'

His look makes me edgy. 'No. Don't think so. What is it?'

'Oh, nothing. Don't worry about it.'

As his car's tyres turn uselessly for a moment in the soft snow, he swears again. 'You know what Montréal spent last year on snow removal? Forty-seven million dollars! Forty-seven! Jeez! That's the entire national revenue of Zambia!'

The church of Ste-Anne straddles the centre of town like some slumbering dinosaur. On a bright day the gleam of its vast sheet-metal roof blinds motorists within a twenty-five-mile radius. Around it and dwarfing all neighbouring houses stand the solid stone structures of seminary and school.

This is my brother's domain and in the normal course of things I rarely set foot here any more. But today is not like any other day. Detective Contini is urging me through the central door, his impatience with my halting steps evident in look and gesture.

The smell of incense floats through the air. A mass is in progress. After a moment, the detective crosses himself. He has a slightly furtive air, as if he doesn't want his friends finding him out, but the alternative of God finding him out poses a worse threat. Out of atavistic habit, I almost follow suit, then stop the hand that has raised itself to my brow.

This is the church of my childhood. It was in these chairs that I strained to think of the sins I would blurt out in one of the confessionals on the left. The sins were sometimes real, as often imagined. My head bowed beneath the level of the grate in that oak cubicle, I would confess to anger against my father or my brother, to gluttonous chocolate excesses and, on occasion, when led on by the softly sonorous yet exacting voice of my confessor, to strange and exciting stirrings in my evidently not so very private parts. This last type of confession always exacted the greatest toll of Hail Marys – a litany we had all learned to recite at such speed that the only discrete word within it was 'entrailles', 'womb'.

To be fair, confession was not always a burden. The priest's probings could sometimes shed light on tangled feelings, on classroom tensions or play-ground viciousness, on the obscure fears and desires which parents and teachers were all too often wilfully blind to.

But they also instilled in us a habit of inquisitorial vigilance and a hovering shame. Only miraculous somersaults of the personality or total white-out permit escape.

The detective and I perch on wooden chairs, well behind the small congregation. In the distance I see a gold-clad figure, who can only be my brother, raise the chalice above the altar. He is an iconic presence, I tell myself, not my brother at all, yet the throaty voice I hear echoing over the microphone is distinguishably my brother's and I don't like the sound.

It is not altogether clear to me why beneath our well-mastered surface civility my brother and I should still bear this rancour towards each other. After all, for many years our age difference meant that we hardly knew each other: by the time I was eight he had disappeared into the cloistered shadows of the Jesuit order.

Perhaps it was simply that my father would repeatedly report the progress of his vows to me with the kind of curdling respect which hurled my own haphazard trajectory squarely into the devil's court. Indeed, throughout my childhood and adolescence my brother was constantly invoked as a moral authority, a saintly double. In the pure light of his mirror, all my rebellions, big and small, took on a depraved cast. I began to relish the difference.

When I was growing up and the church's

stultifying effect on the social development of my province became a point of common knowledge amongst anyone who wanted to launch Québec, a little late, into the twentieth century, I could never analyse the mantle of backwardness the Church had shrouded us in without thinking of my brother's black robes. It gave an added fervour to my denunciations. Ignorance, superstition, prejudice, underdevelopment, passive acquiescence to the oppressor – all these could be laid at the door of the Church, which had increased its own wealth and status and power at the expense of the rest of us. And behind the door of the church stood my brother with his stern countenance.

In this image I have of him, it is always a large gold key, not a cross, he is swinging. The key turns the lock to all the precious things which, until the mid-sixties, were forbidden to us: not the obvious things like guiltless pleasure, but all those other things such as access to a philosophy which wasn't only Aquinas; to science; to books. Even maps had to be approved by the Catholic Commission for use in class. In the schools of Québec, the Papal Index had burgeoned to forbid ordinary French classics. Discussion of Flaubert was prohibited. Reading Baudelaire was equivalent to an act of black magic. When I bought my first copy of *The Flowers of Evil*, I kept it hidden in brown paper covers, under my mattress.

Detective Contini tugs at my sleeve. The sparse congregation, largely made up of elderly women, has begun its slow shuffle towards the door.

89

'Any regulars who knew Madeleine Blais and who would have been here on Christmas Eve?' he whispers to me.

I spy Mme Groulx arm in arm with Mme Préfontaine and hasten towards them.

Mme Groulx is encased in a mink which thirty years ago must have been the envy of Ste-Anne. It sits around her as voluminous as the Cadillac her son used to drive. At the two traffic lights in town, he would pause for exaggerated lengths of time and puff away at a cigar which was only slightly shorter than his car in order to give anyone who was watching the extended pleasure of his opulent presence. Even by then the piano factory the Groulx had long owned was in financial difficulties. A few years later, it burnt to the ground, taking everything but the insurance papers with it. On the advice of my father, Mme Groulx made a few shrewd investments. She has been threatening her numerous offspring with their proceeds ever since.

She puts a wrinkled hand on my arm now and gives me a soulful look from her sly eyes. '*Mon p'tit Pierre, mon pauvre*,' she murmurs. 'What an ordeal. For all of us. Still, perhaps it's better this way.' She crosses herself quickly. 'She can do no more harm now.'

I swallow and try to keep my voice even. 'Mme Groulx, Mme Préfontaine, this is Detective Contini. If either of you were here for midnight mass, he'd like to ask you some questions.'

Mme Rossignol has joined our little huddle. Her eyes are vast and watery beneath the thick lenses of her spectacles. This doesn't deter her from instantly proclaiming herself a plausible witness. 'You want to know about that stuck-up Mme Tremblay's granddaughter, is that it?' she asks in the loud voice of the partly deaf.

Mme Préfontaine hushes her to no avail.

'I saw her here. Indecent. She was wearing next to nothing.' She gestures towards her thighs and makes a movement which takes on greater obscenity because of the inappropriateness of her bulk. 'No hat, nothing! And she and that friend of hers. Whispering, giggling. Touching each other. No respect! That's what it is. No respect. She'll learn now,' she adds ominously.

'Her friend?' It is the first time Detective Contini has had the opportunity to throw in a word.

'Mafia,' Mme Groulx says with irrefutable authority. 'Not one of us. Some Hollywood gangster.'

'Don't be silly,' the quiet Mme Préfontaine interrupts. 'He was just an ordinary young man.'

'A lot younger than her, that's for sure.'

'You don't know that.' She turns towards Detective Contini. 'He had a black leather jacket and one of those ties, you know like a string, with a gold badge or something under the collar.'

'And he had his hand on her bottom when they were kneeling. I saw it. I was right behind them. Poor old Michel, who was sitting a few seats away, couldn't take his eyes off them. And that oaf Georges, not to mention Pascal Mackenzie – all of them, staring.'

91

'Michel who, Mme Groulx? Georges who?' Contini interjects.

'Michel Dubois. Georges Lavigueur.'

'So, did you hear Madeleine Blais and her friend say anything to each other?'

'Plenty.'

'Well?'

'I don't like to repeat it. This is a holy place.'

He gives her the first look of impatience I have seen cross his face. 'Shall we go outside then? You can join us in a moment, ladies.'

Mme Groulx looks suddenly lost without her cronies. She casts them a backward glance, then, seeing us watching her, raises her shoulders in stubborn defiance.

I want to follow them, but Mme Préfontaine has her hand on my arm. She is murmuring something which I take to be condolences. Even though I like Mme Préfontaine, I don't want to hear Madeleine's name any more on her or anyone else's lips. They are ripping her away from me.

I block my ears and nod and focus on the wispy white hair beneath the knitted grey beret. Mme Préfontaine has been white ever since I can remember. Story has it that she turned white the day her daughter gave birth to a black baby. During the war it was. Mme Préfontaine put it round that the child was the son of a black prince from Haiti whom her daughter had met in Montréal and who had then gone off to war and been bravely killed. But everyone knew he was really the child of one of the American soldiers who had been briefly stationed at the base some miles out of town.

It didn't matter. By the time the child was three, everyone half believed her, such was the quiet dignity with which she and her daughter brought the boy up. And after a while, the truth grew obscure. The town preferred the illusion in any case. The son of a prince brought more credit on us.

My father told me all this when we were having one of our arguments about what with my adolescent severity I judged as the appalling hypocrisy of Ste-Anne. He was trying to show me that there were gradations of untruth and some of it was to good purpose.

In the midst of Mme Préfontaine's speech I hear an authoritative clack of footsteps behind me. I know that tread. I turn and see my brother coming slowly down the aisle. He has shed his glittering robe and is now black-suited and collared, his long, bony face a beneficent if austere mask beneath his steel-grey hair. Something in the way he nods at the women makes them bow their heads and take flight.

From a certain angle, my brother is the exact replica of my father, right down to the working of the muscle in his cheek when he is repressing his anger. It is working now above the thin lips set in sympathy and I imagine my own face, which is like my mother's, taking on a quiet impassivity.

His hand rests on my shoulder. 'I'm glad you picked up my message so promptly. We need to talk.'

I have had no message, but I don't bother to contradict him.

'Will you join me in my office?'

'Not right now. I'm here with somebody.'

'I noticed. But he seems to be gone.' My brother misses nothing, even as he holds up his sacred vessels and intones the mass.

'He's waiting outside.'

'Who is he?'

'Detective Richard Contini.'

'I see. Well, ask him to wait a little longer.'

'I don't think that would be wise.'

'Oh?' He gives me a look, more gloomy than my response warrants.

'Too late in any case.' I am relieved to see Detective Contini put his boxer's face through the door. He blinks for a moment to accustom his eyes to the dimness, then comes purposefully towards us.

'Père Jerome Rousseau. The very man I want to see. I have just had a back view of Madeleine Blais and now I imagine you can give me the front.'

My brother shudders slightly. He doesn't like the detective's off-hand tone.

'I take it you officiated at midnight mass?'

'I did.'

'Did you happen to notice Madeleine Blais in the congregation?'

'Detective, Madeleine Blais did not have the gift of rendering herself invisible. Quite the contrary. She lived for the limelight, for the spectacle of herself. And now I note she has chosen to die in a similar manner.' My brother divests himself of this speech with dry aplomb.

'Oh yes?' Detective Contini is equally dry. 'So you saw her on Sunday night?'

'She waved to me, detective. Right in the midst of mass. A long deliberate wave.'

'I take it you didn't wave back.' Contini chuckles beneath my brother's disapproving gaze.

'She also had the audacity to step forward to take communion.'

'No bad thing, given what followed that night. You'll agree, I'm sure?'

The muscle is working in my brother's cheek. His eyes are on the floor.

Contini doesn't give him time to answer. 'Though given her gaiety, I'm beginning to find that last act a little difficult to imagine. And the man who was with her. Did you recognize him?'

My brother shakes his head. 'No. I had never laid eyes on him before, though I can't say I had too good a look at him. He didn't take the host.'

'Father, is there anyone in the parish whom you know to be hostile to Mlle Blais? I mean really hostile.'

My brother stares at him for a long moment. 'I don't quite see what you're driving at, detective. But you should know that Madeleine Blais was not universally liked in Ste-Anne, though she was on occasion admired from a distance.'

'I'm not trying to pry into the secrets of the confessional, Father, but if anything should come to mind, something more than generalized dislike or envy—'

'I shall think on it. And now, if you'll excuse

me, I need a few words in private with Pierre.'

'You might wait at Senegal's,' I murmur to Contini. 'The café over the road. The old man has the thousand eyes of a born concierge.'

I follow my brother out the side door, across the yard and up the stairs to his office. It is a pleasant, unpretentious room, clean and ordered. A few books – the main library is in the seminary – a well-polished and immaculate desk, a tolerable oil depicting Sainte Anne teaching Mary to read.

My brother gestures me towards a chair and perches on the one behind the desk. He plays out a rhythm with a pencil for a moment, then gives me a long, hard look. 'I hope you'll put that woman out of your mind now.'

'Gone,' I say flippantly. I lean into the chair and prepare myself for the inevitable lecture. But my mind is not on my brother's words. I am thinking that it is significant, whatever her surface manner, that Madeleine took communion. She must have been preparing herself for death. She wouldn't have done it otherwise. There wasn't much religion left in her, but there was a lot of superstition.

Suddenly I have a clear picture of the two of us that first summer of our friendship. We are lying beneath an old spreading beech and gazing through leaves at the clarity of a sky made bluer by the occasional froth of a passing cloud. Madeleine says, 'I almost wish myself up there. Wish myself dead. I can see myself walking through the portals of heaven. There are two shimmering wings waiting for me and a wonderful white robe, soft and flowing. And a deep voice calls to me, our Father's voice, and says, "Try it on, Madeleine. Welcome to eternity."'

She was still at school with the nuns then. The following year, her grandmother took her off to Europe, six months in England, six months in Paris. She came back with wonderful accents and without religion. But occasionally, when things got her down, even when we were living together, she would sneak into a church and make a rapid confession. It made her feel better, she said with an apologetic smile.

'I warned you, didn't I?'

Jerome's face moves slowly into focus.

'You haven't heard a word I've said, Pierre. Listen for once, will you. Vice is infectious. And malignant. It spreads through the community more quickly than a virus.'

I am wriggling in my chair like a guilty schoolboy who has been caught with a friend in the toilet and I have to remind myself that Jerome is not a bad man, that he means well. Yet he suffers from institutional deformation. He has spent so much time in schools and seminaries that his vision of evil is askew. Wars, exploitation, political terror are not in his purview. Instead, he has a heightened sensitivity to sex, to rebellion against authority, to pride. He is as alert to these homely transgressions as a medieval inquisitor.

Madeleine was never a model pupil and he has always disapproved of my association with her. The brother of a respected cleric should not be linked to scandal, however remotely.

'We're all sinners, Jerome,' I say softly. 'If we weren't there would be no job for you to do.'

Anger hovers over his face and is instantly banished. It is replaced by pity. My brother has decided to pity me. It is an emotion he enjoys.

'Listen, Pierre. I want you to go off for a few weeks, longer if necessary. Get away from this whole sordid business of Madeleine's suicide. I don't want you gushing to the press. You're not to be mixed up with it all.'

'What on earth are you talking about?'

'Don't you know what I'm talking about?'

'I haven't the faintest idea.'

He examines my face, shifts uneasily in his chair. 'I did try. I tried to warn you about her years ago. You refused to listen. It really is time that you woke up.'

I am about to lurch out of the room, but there is something about the gravity of his face which makes me pause.

'All right, tell me then. What is it that I'm supposed to listen to?'

My sudden and unusual acquiescence unnerves him. He passes a finger under his collar as if it has grown too hot in the room. For a moment, he scans my face. Then he lowers his gaze to his desk and takes a deep breath. 'Madeleine was illegitimate.'

'You amaze me!' Irony drips from my voice. 'Illegitimate. It's not a word we use much these days. Not in the real world.'

'You knew?'

'It hardly takes much intelligence.'

'Madeleine, too?'

His childlike naïveté surprises me and I quiet myself into patience.

'Madeleine always knew that Blais was her stepfather's name. Her mother married him in Maine, when Madeleine was tiny. It wasn't hard to work out the rest . . .'

I have the sudden urge to explain Madeleine to him. 'Look, Madeleine realized early on that she was an unwanted party in the new marriage. During the time that I knew her, on the single occasion she went to visit her mother, she came rushing home after two days and said she would never repeat the experience. She hated the disorder of the household, the squabbling heap of children, her sullen heavy-drinking stepfather. She even talked of changing her name. Somehow she never got round to doing that. But it was because of the turmoil in the household, because Madeleine had no place there, that Mme Tremblay took her over. You must have known that . . .

'She took her right away. They spent a year together in England then came back to Ste-Anne when Madeleine was about six. Later on, Mme Tremblay officially adopted her. The line was that Madeleine's natural father was dead. Maybe by the time I met her that was true. Maybe not. It didn't matter to Madeleine. Mme Tremblay was quite enough parent for her.'

Something in my brother's face makes me stop.

'You didn't know about the adoption?'

He doesn't answer. His hands are clenched in front of him, the fingers very white. 'So her mother won't come rushing back here for the funeral?' he asks after a moment. 'She won't want to share in the spoils?'

I shrug. 'I'm not a clairvoyant. I don't remember her ever asking Madeleine for very much.'

'Frightened of her mother, probably. Of old Mme Tremblay.'

'What is it that *you're* frightened of, Jerome?' I ask, for I suddenly have the distinct and uncanny sense that he is. 'You didn't by any chance have a fling with Monique Tremblay some time in the dim and distant past?'

'Certainly not.' He is all virtue now, despite the sudden flush of his face. 'But I remember . . .'

He scrapes his chair back from his desk and starts to pace. 'I didn't really want to talk about this, but . . .' Memory etches his frown into deep grooves. I have to strain to hear his voice when it comes.

'You know that Father and Claire Tremblay were friends from way back. Her husband was Father's oldest boyhood friend. They enlisted together during the war, the only two from Ste-Anne to do so. The town didn't much care for the war. It was European business, had nothing to do with us, people said. There was even a demonstration against conscription. I remember that. It made Mother very nervous. We didn't go to church for three weeks, for fear of being singled out, though by then I could barely remember Father. He was just a picture in uniform on the mantelpiece.'

He pauses, but I don't interrupt the flow of memory. This is a time before my birth and what I know about it comes from history books and the brief wartime episodes in my father's journal.

'Mother used to say that they had enlisted for Claire's sake, both of them, because she was British. Mother was very anxious in those days and Claire Tremblay used to come round and try to comfort her. I think she was lonely too. In any case, she was very solemn. I can still see her back then – a very tall woman with honey-gold hair coiled into a thick plait at the neck. She wore men's trousers. Maybe she didn't have money for dresses. But she always brought a cake with her and she and Mother would sit and drink tea, while Monique, the daughter, bullied me into stupid games. Monique was only about five years older than me. But that's a lot when you're small.'

He has stopped to look out the window and for a moment I think he has policed the flow of his own thoughts and imprisoned them. But he begins again, even more quietly now, as if there might be some eavesdropping cleric at the door.

'And then, Guy Tremblay didn't come back. Killed in Normandy. Father did, though, and when I was little we used to see a lot of Claire and Monique. Sometimes I had the impression he felt guilty about being the sole survivor and he wanted to make that up to them. Anyhow, then the decade turned, 1950, and you came along and Mother got all involved with you, didn't want to do anything.'

He glances at me. It is a glare and in it I suddenly sense a burning childhood jealousy of the mewling intruder that was myself. I remember a family photograph, the four of us, myself a plump presence in my mother's arms. My gawky brother doesn't look at the camera. He is staring at me with naked hatred, as if he wants to take the cushion from the sofa and squash it down on my face with obliterating force.

His voice continues. 'As a family we stopped seeing the Tremblays. But Father carried on with his visits. I knew that. Mother complained of it. Then too, on a number of occasions on my way home from school, I saw him coming out of his office with Monique. She was already big then.'

He hesitates, makes a curving gesture with his hands, blushes slightly, and I see him as a boy on the cusp of puberty, hormones beginning to rage. The gesture makes me feel oddly close to him. I daren't move for fear of rupturing the mood.

'Developed, pretty. Maybe sixteen. I think she had left school. Was doing some part-time work for Father. Anyhow, they were together. And he had his hand round her shoulder, casually, paternally. But there was something about the way she sidled up to him while they were walking, the way she looked at him. Then, in the car, she sat very close. Presumably he was taking her home. Or maybe not.' His voice cracks. 'Once I approached them and Father shooed me away, sent me running. He didn't want me there.'

'I don't understand what you're saying, Jerome.' I wade through the muggy heat of adolescent imaginings which have mired us in silence. 'Are you really implying that our father was also Madeleine's? I suggest you've been listening to too many confessions. You've grown prurient.'

He doesn't rise to the bait. He is staring out the window at the snow-clad maple in the yard. Its branches cast shadows over his face.

'Maybe. But he was, after all, only thirty-nine or so then. Not an old man. Your age. It was soon after that that Mme Tremblay took Monique off and by the time I was up in Montréal it was common knowledge that she had given birth to a girl. Then, too, Father left a healthy bequest to Mme Tremblay in his will. And a separate one to Monique.'

My mind races over the times I saw my father with Madeleine. I search out little telling gestures, hidden caresses. I remember Madeleine performing for us, stroking the keys of the piano and crooning a song. I see her looking up at him, seeking approval. My father's expression is fond. But not overly so. No. I reassure myself.

But the seeds of doubt are sown and, like rampant weeds, they don't need much watering. In order to trample them, I tell myself that Mme Tremblay would never have allowed my closeness with Madeleine had my brother's version of history been true. Yet I have to acknowledge that we didn't give her much choice.

'So you see why I always wanted you to keep away from her. And now, now . . . The last thing we need is a bunch of snooping reporters digging over the past.' He shudders. The dirt has already found its target. He is sullied.

'Madeleine's birth certificate lists her father as Alexandre Papineau,' I say with a notary's precision, though the note of triumph in my voice is not as firm as I would wish it.

'Are you sure? I thought it was Père—' He stops himself, but I have caught him out.

'You thought it was one of your lot? A priest?'

He has the decency to look shamefaced. 'He wasn't a priest then,' he mumbles. 'But it's not the named father that matters. We just have to stop the local tongues wagging. There were not a few of them way back then. I heard Father and Mother arguing over it. Over the gossip about Monique spending so much time in his office.'

'What did he say?'

'I think he said he owed it to his dead friend.'

We look at each other, both of us bowed down with our separate thoughts. Any rancour I may have felt towards him has dissipated. Even his vocation appears to me now in a new light. I have a sudden sense that he rushed with troubled and unseemly haste into the safety of sanctity in order to protect himself from the sins of the family. To expiate them, he became an expert in sin.

'So you'll go? Go away for a while. Go to Europe, perhaps, until all this blows over.' The edge of steel in his tone takes me by surprise, cuts through the aura of complicity which existed just a moment before. Jerome is not posing a question. He is ordering.

'No. Of course not.' I am again the rebellious younger brother.

'You should, Pierre. You really should.' He scrutinizes my face and in his look I suddenly sense that there is something he is holding back, that everything that has gone before was of secondary importance.

His features crystallize into a mixture of suspicion and distaste. 'It will be far better if you go. Trust me. It's for your own good. I need to protect you from yourself. There are rumours.'

His voice flutters like his hand, but his gaze remains insistent. Beneath it, my skin turns clammy. What is it that he knows about me?

'Rumours?' I ask.

'Things I can't repeat,' he says solemnly. 'But take my advice, Pierre. Otherwise . . .' He fingers his cross in a gesture which makes me feel I am the evil he is warding off.

As I turn on my heels, my spine prickles in disquiet.

A smell of old grease mingled with the sickly sweetness of some canned fragrance floats across the threshold of Senegal's diner. Potato plants droop and twine from the window ledge. The chequered linoleum floor is wet and gritty with boot tracks.

Huddled in their coats, a few old-timers sit at the plastic-sheathed tables. Slowly, they spoon up what could be soup or coffee. This is not the most fashionable restaurant in town.

Detective Contini looks like a sleek seal who has

mistakenly blundered into the scruffy harbour of a forgotten fishing village. He is working hard at impersonating a minnow, but no-one is fooled. Every eye and ear is attuned to him.

He waves me over and pushes a plate of fat, perspiring chips towards me.

'Hungry?' he asks hopefully.

'No. Coffee will do me.'

'Can't really recommend it.' He glances at the murky liquid in front of him, then smiles as a plump young dungareed woman comes bouncing towards us.

'*Bonjour, M. Rousseau.* Can I get you anything?'

'Maybe not, Martine. Just came to fetch my friend here. How's your grandpa?'

'He went up to have a nap.'

She is staring at me, her eyes sparkling. She opens her mouth, then shuts it. She wants to tell me something, but can't quite bring it out.

'Yes, Martine,' I encourage her. I am glad that she has not run off to Montréal like so many others and joined the crowds of pallid drugged youth who grow prematurely old in the less salubrious parts of the metropolis.

'Look!' She points at the scarf coiled round her neck and starts to unwind it so that her dungarees are suddenly ablaze with russet and orange and gold. 'Look what Madeleine Blais gave me. The other night. Isn't it pretty?'

'Beautiful.' Despite myself, I finger the silk. I would like to bury my face in it.

'She just took it off and gave it to me. Right

106

there in front of the church. Because I said I liked it.'

'That was very kind of her.' My voice feels hoarse.

'Yes. Very.' Martine's eyes grow blurry. 'And then . . . It feels so strange. She was very beautiful,' she adds with a note of defiance.

'Did she look unhappy at all?' Contini asks quietly.

'Oh no! Well maybe, just a little. Around the eyes.'

'Hmmm. Did you see her leave?'

'No. Maman dragged me away. It was cold.'

Contini puts some bills on the table.

'I think she was wonderful,' Martine murmurs, as if she is still carrying on an argument with someone.

'Learn anything?' Detective Contini asks me as we cross the street.

I keep my eyes on the ground. 'Not really. Nothing useful. You?'

'A few things. None that make sense. Yet.'

In the car, he says casually, 'Your brother didn't like Madeleine Blais much?'

'Not much.' I can feel his eyes on my profile as I pull away, and I add, 'He thinks she got people worked up, excited. Frenzied. He prefers calm, as you can imagine. It's better for the soul.'

He makes a sound which is neither negation nor acquiescence. He is looking round the streets, the few desultory shops, the garage by the bridge, the shiny funeral parlour where the cinema used to be, the smattering of passers-by.

When we stop at the traffic lights, he seems transfixed by the windows of the Bon Marché, the one remaining general store in town not yet to have succumbed to the competition of the shopping mall. The single mannequin with her out-of-date bob and bright, unfocused eyes wears a gold lamé dress. It hangs limp and too large over her pallid frame. Slung awkwardly over her extended arm is a matching purse and a mismatched shawl. At her feet a tubby Santa Claus slews shirts and pyjamas onto a cluttered floor.

The detective makes that sound again and I pull away quickly, veer into the Rue Turgeon with its row of what were once fine houses. I feel defensive, as if I don't want Ste-Anne negatively judged by outsiders.

Maybe he senses that, for he says, 'Nice old porch, there.'

We drive past the new development of Identikit duplexes where the younger people live. There is a skating rink here. Above the wooden frame, children's hats bob, brightly coloured. A group are rolling a huge ball across the ground, the base of a snowman.

'You haven't got any?' Contini asks me.

I shake my head. 'You?'

'Two. We considered a third, but my wife said she wanted to get back to work. Now she's wondering. Heh, you know what the old gals told me?' he says with no transition. 'Madeleine Blais was busy signing autographs after mass. In front of the church. A whole crowd of local fans round her. Preening and smiling and sprawling against a shiny motorbike as if she were posing for some fashion magazine. Like some Jezebel, according to Mme Groulx. Apparently even young Père Gaucher wasn't immune.' He chuckles. 'Are those old ladies reliable witnesses?'

'They can more or less see what's in front of them, I guess. I can't vouch for the commentary.'

'What about the motorbike?'

'Don't know. I've only ever seen Madeleine ride one in movies.' I refuse the images which leap into my mind and focus on the road. We are in the countryside now, the roads slippery. 'I doubt it was hers.'

'Not likely to be the boyfriend's either. Old man Senegal is certain he saw her drive away in a silvery car.'

'That would be hers. Was she alone?'

'He couldn't tell me that. Still, hardly the demeanour of a woman on the verge of suicide.'

'No. But then she is an actress.'

'Was.' Contini corrects me. He is staring at my profile again. I can feel his eyes as acutely as if they were surgical probes.

'Right,' he says as we pull into the drive. 'Time to check in and see what the boys and girls have come up with.' He slides out of the car and then sticks his head back in. 'By the way, who stands to benefit from Madeleine's death? She must be worth a few tidy pennies.'

The query flusters me. 'I don't know,' I stammer.

'She didn't come to you for her will?'

I shake my head. 'Madeleine never thought about such things. I can't remember her ever mentioning—'

'Come, come. A rich woman like that. Didn't you advise her?' His expression accuses me. He doesn't believe me.

'You can ask Mme Tremblay.'

'Yes . . .' He muses for a moment, then is suddenly in a hurry. 'Right. If you see or hear anything, get in touch.' He hands me a card. 'And why don't you make up a list for me? All the dark, pre-geriatric men in and around town who sometimes sport leather jackets and might have had a crush on Madeleine Blais. Or nurtured a grudge.'

'I don't think that would—'

'Don't think, Rousseau. Just do what I ask. And while you're at it, note down any priests under your brother's aegis who might have had or fancied a little fling with the great lady. It's been known to happen. And that might account for your brother's venom. Who knows what he's heard!' He gives me a wink and slams the door hard.

As he plunges towards his car, he turns back and waves. There is an odd little grin on his face. It may have taken the passage of years to tilt the balance, but now he knows he has the upper hand. Next time we meet I will remember exactly who he is.

110

4

The house feels as bleak as a cemetery on a windy November night. Even the lights I switch on do nothing to dispel the gloom. Nor does the music.

There is only one place I want to be and I can't allow myself that. Not now. Not yet. It is too unpredictable. There are things I cannot allow myself to think about.

Despite the earliness of the hour, I pour myself a hefty drink. My brother's words mingled with Contini's have insinuated themselves into my mind and set up an unstoppable babble. In my search for distraction, I half wish that I hadn't prevented Maryla from coming back today, as she had wanted to. I stare at the telephone, wonder if I am going to ring her against my better judgement, when I notice the flickering of the light on the answering machine.

With a fierceness I don't like in myself I prod the message button. Voices, even displaced ones, are better than echoes.

Janine Dupuis asks me to dinner, whenever I can manage. An open invitation. Her tone is soft, seductive, reeks of sympathy. Perhaps she can help me, the way I helped her, she suggests.

Maryla masks her nervousness. She has only rung to see how I am, but if I'd like company, she could arrange to be free.

Danielle Leblanc, a sometime friend of Madeleine's and mine, has just heard the news. She wants to talk. Should she come and visit or will I drive up to Montréal and see her? Her voice fades into a murmur of condolence which is also an invitation.

I stop the cynicism which flickers through me. Over these last years of my apparent availability, women have offered themselves to me at every opportunity. They seem to find me irresistible, my presence compelling, my meagre achievements Napoleonic.

I have come to realize that their desire is rarely specific. It is not directed at me but at that rare breed of which I form a part: reasonably attractive unattached men, in work, and approaching middle age with no visible scars.

Returning this diffuse desire is often difficult, since it owes little to chemistry. It is compounded of loneliness and fear. A fear that life is slipping irretrievably through one's fingers.

The fact that I might prefer my solitude or even a solitary bed is incomprehensible to them. They are sad and angry by turn and both emotions seem to evoke cruelty. I don't like this cruelty in myself. I have known too much of the kindness of women. Often I feel the lesser cruelty is to keep myself to myself.

The next voice is not a woman's. Louis Debord, a friend from *Le Devoir*, suggests we meet up and drown sorrows in whisky. His tone is frank, friendly. He offers comradeship. Eagerly I jot down the number he leaves. Even though I know journalists and their mixed motives too well, I tell myself *Le Devoir* has always been a serious paper. Louis is not interested in gossip.

When I hear Mme Tremblay's voice, I realize this is the one I have been waiting for. She stumbles a little over her words, as if there is someone in the room with her and she can't say what she means. Yet her veiled urgency is clear. She wants to see me as soon as possible.

I don't bother with the rest of the messages. I dash for the door without even rehearsing a diplomatic way of putting the questions my brother has so poisonously seeded. Only the sight of the spare housekeys hanging on a hook by the door's side give me pause. The monogrammed rectangle, another relic of my father's time, is missing from the thick silver ring. Where could I have lost it? The memory of Contini's casual query sidles into my mind. I prod it away. I have more important matters to consider.

Three cars are parked in Mme Tremblay's drive. As I come close, a man leaps out of one of them and adjusts the lens of a camera. More journalists waiting to feed off Madeleine's dead body. My one-time profession saddens me.

With a sharp twist, I pull off into the lane which

leads towards the barn. Half-way down it, I park and make my way through the trees to the side door of the house. From the kitchen, I can hear voices. I hesitate for a moment, then knock. Mme Tremblay's outline is visible through the flowered curtain. She lifts a corner of it and peers out with the gestures of a woman under siege. When she recognizes me, she unbolts the door quickly.

'Good of you to come so quickly, Pierre.' She touches my arm. She looks composed, her hair tightly coiled, her clothes neat. Only the pouches under her eyes and her trembling fingers betray her inner commotion.

Standing at the counter and pouring out tea is a figure I don't recognize.

'Mlle Solange.' Mme Tremblay introduces me to a buxom black woman who smiles at me so brightly that the room seems to shed its mourning. 'Dr Bertrand sent her. She's been struggling to keep me in order. And to protect me from the vultures.'

'They do keep coming.' Solange flaps her arms as if they were wings. 'But I don't suppose they're night birds.' She grins. 'Like a cup?'

'Please.'

'And then you'll leave us for a few minutes, Solange. I need to have a private word with Pierre.'

'As long as he doesn't upset you.'

'I'll try not to,' I say, and wonder if I'll be able to keep my promise.

Mme Tremblay waits for her to leave the room then motions me towards a chair.

'Have you seen the television news today?'

'No. Was it unbearable?'

Mme Tremblay squares her shoulders. 'No. It was perfectly correct. Far better than the papers. An appropriate obituary.' Tears spring into her eyes and she wills them away. 'Nothing salacious. No sensational hints. But Pierre, look. I'm ... I'm just a little worried. You know Madeleine, how she always leaves things lying about. Well, I'd like you to go to her apartment, just check things out. Bring me anything that ... you know—'

'I know.' Mme Tremblay doesn't want scandal. There are so many things in Madeleine's life which couldn't bear the weight of prurient eyes. Do these include what my brother has told me?

'Before the press get their hands on them. They're very persistent. There might be journals too. She kept them sometimes. Erratically, I think. I'd rather sift them first. Before the police ... you understand. I'd know what to make of them. Madeleine will forgive me.'

From a canister on the dresser shelf, she unearths a pile of keys and places them in front of me. 'I think you should go quickly, Pierre. Today. Now.'

She stands in front of me and I nod, but I don't move.

'You're tired?'

'No. It's not that. I ... You see, Jerome ...' I stumble and look at her and in the rectitude of her presence Jerome's words take on all the unreality of hothouse flowers, perverse, exotic blooms, forced into aberrant life. 'No, it's nothing.' I shake free of their tendrils and get up.

'Tell me, Pierre. Go on. It's about Madeleine, isn't it? Jerome saw her that night.'

'No, no. It's not that.'

'Tell me.'

'It's about Monique,' I falter.

'What about my daughter?' She gives me a sharp glance.

'It doesn't matter.'

'It matters. I can see that in your face.'

I shrug, try a grin which feels like a grimace. 'Jerome has this mad idea that Monique and my father . . .'

'Monique and your father?' She stares at me in incomprehension. 'Go on.'

'That they were . . .' I wave my hands, unable to find the appropriate word.

Suddenly her mouth drops open. 'Pierre, really. Not you! And Jerome! He's as bad as these snoopers I've got around here. No. The answer is a categorical no. There was never anything between my daughter and your father. It was Jerome.' She laughs. The sound is so startling that she seems to realize it herself and stops mid-way. 'He was infatuated with Monique, never knew where to put his hands when she was around. It wasn't his fault, of course. She used to tease him mercilessly. But your father! Jean-François. No. That's pure projection. Not Jean-François.'

Something about the way she voices my father's name makes me feel it with a hot suddenness. It was she who loved my father. Loved him like a brother perhaps, but loved him all the same. I have no way of knowing and I certainly will not ask.

'No. Your father was always extremely kind to us. Even when Monique disgraced herself with that scoundrel of a Papineau. Too handsome by half he was, that piano teacher. At the seminary, too. And when I confronted him, he packed his bags and ran. That very day. I have no idea where he ran to. I didn't try very hard to find out, I have to confess. Maybe I already knew I wanted Madeleine for myself.'

She is wringing her hands. The knuckles are white, bloodless.

'I'm sorry. I shouldn't have—'

'No. It's my fault. I ought to have told you. But I never thought about it. All so long ago. Monique wanted an abortion, you see. She was only seventeen. But I wouldn't let her. It was too dangerous. And wrong. I told her I would help her with the baby. We fought. Then and afterwards. I didn't handle my own daughter very well.'

There are tears in her eyes.

'You don't have to tell me all this.'

'No, no, I do. I should. When Madeleine arrived, Monique made a volte-face. It was partly to spite me, I guess, but in any case, she said I was to have nothing to do with Madeleine. She could manage perfectly well without me. So she stayed in Hull, which was where we'd gone for the last months of the pregnancy. Monique couldn't bear being in

Ste-Anne – all the gossip – and I had a cousin in Hull, dead now.

'Then she met Arthur Blais and she lost all interest in the child, though she wouldn't admit that to me, not at first anyway. When I went to visit them in Maine, I was distraught at the way they treated poor little Madeleine. I started working on her again slowly, more tactfully. Eventually I even offered Blais money . . .'

She peers up at me sharply as if she has heard a rebuke I haven't made.

'I was desperately worried for her,' she says in apology. 'And Blais said, yes, sure, take the brat. Raise her. I don't want anything to do with her. Monique wasn't prepared to make it so easy. We arranged for visits, all that . . . The intervals between them grew longer and longer. Madeleine didn't like staying with them.' She throws up her hands. 'You know the rest.'

'Have you contacted Monique now?' I ask softly.

She shakes her head. 'We haven't seen each other for more years than I care to remember. But I guess I'll have to. For the funeral.' Her voice catches and she sobs once, harshly. 'Probably she won't come. And if she does, she'll tell me it's all my fault. And she'll be right. If I hadn't asked Madeleine to come up here for Christmas . . .'

She scrapes her chair back from the table and stands on visibly shaky legs.

I put my arm round her shoulders. 'Don't think like that, Mme Tremblay. You mustn't.'

'You all right in there?' a hearty voice calls from the hall.

'Yes, fine. Fine.' Mme Tremblay presses the key-ring into my hand. 'Go, Pierre. Come and see me as soon as you're back.'

The autoroute into Montréal is quiet – a stretch of flat monotonous grey flanked by white. The grey seeps into my mind, inducing trance. I curl into it with relief, barely aware of my foot pressing down on the accelerator. Cars on my right vanish into oblivion. Saplings rise in the distance, grow into dense huddled pines and disappear into mirrored specks. A shaft of sunlight breaks through cloud. It dances over the chrome of a truck, splits into radiant shards, dazzles. I speed past and suddenly remember the medallion. I haven't thought of it for years.

The sun found it, picked it out of a grassy verge near the college chapel. Spangles of heavy silver shaped into a sun, the signs of the zodiac dotted round its centre. The object sparkled and glinted like temptation itself. I picked it up and held it in the palm of my hand, felt its satisfying weight, then whipped it into my pocket. The medallion became my talisman.

I must have been about fifteen then, by turns a gregarious and solitary boy. In my solitary moments, daydreams would besiege me. All of them had to do with women. Those holiday meetings with Madeleine apart, I had never been close to a girl, let alone a woman. Never held a conversation with one. The college was a male fortress. On our rare forays into the streets of the city, we would glance furtively at those alien creatures. Sometimes, if a gust of wind or a stride up the steps of a bus accidentally exposed a forbidden expanse of smooth female skin, a throttled sound would emerge from the throat of one of our cohort with all the force of a collective gasp. The teacher's rebuke was always swift and aimed at all of us.

My medallion became my magical pathway to women. Its leather thong around my throat, I would fantasize myself into bold escapades. A mere flick of my shirt, and its silver dazzle would catch the eye of the most beautiful passer-by and hypnotize her into my power. She would follow me obediently to the ends of the earth, past the last bus stop, to some remote fog-bound castle where my pictorial imaginings ceased, but where the words 'fruit of thy womb', repeated daily in our Hail Marys, took on a throbbing resonance which had not a little to do with the blood rushing into my penis, its trembling more intense, since I knew with doomed certainty that this pulsing, sinful pleasure condemned me to the fiery ravages of hell.

It wasn't just one woman. It was any woman, all women – blondes, brunettes, redheads, small and curvaceous, tall and lithe. At the sight of my sun they grew as docile as robots, attended my every wish, were more compliant than Mary Magdalene faced by Jesus. More obliging than my hand on my wilful adolescent cock.

That summer, it must have been just before she went off to Europe for the year, I showed my medallion to Madeleine. We were in the small apple orchard beneath her house. The buds on the trees were plump and dappled with pink. The stubby grass beneath our backs was warm and fragrant. Maybe it was the medallion, maybe it was simply the warmth that made me brave, but I touched Madeleine, let my fingers caress the downy softness of her arm.

We were fast friends by then, but we had never touched. We had spent all of the previous summer gambolling in the fields together or, when it rained, listening to music on her transistor radio in the loft of the barn. Or sneaking into the local cinema and watching whatever double bills were on offer.

That in itself was an adventure. We had to pretend to be sixteen. Some perverse accord between church and provincial government had decreed that, special showings apart, movies were closed to children. So we dressed up. Madeleine donned lipstick and piled her hair on top of her head. I pulled on a jacket, and with butterflies in our stomachs we braved the cashier and half ran into a darkness of mouldy smells and rough plush seats and flickering images. The illicitness cemented our bond, but it had nothing overtly physical about it. Maybe it was because Madeleine hadn't yet sprouted breasts.

The next summer, as we stretched lazily beneath the apple trees, I noticed the marvel of these new curves beneath the thin cotton of her shirt and my hand strayed of its own accord. She didn't stop it. She let my fingers wander – up her arm, across her neck and then with a breathless sense of destination arrive at her bosom. I touched, I stroked. I felt ripe peaches in the palm of my hand. And then I felt something else. Madeleine's fingers. They were on my shirt, my jeans. They curved round the bulge at my crotch, rubbed. My vision grew furry. My ears rang.

I think it was then I showed her my medallion. I don't know what I thought it might do.

She held it in the palm of her hand and contemplated it, then lifted it up and let it swing like a pendulum, so that light flickered and spun through the branches.

'*Tu me le donnes?*' she asked, and without waiting for an answer, she lifted the medallion over her neck and patted it where it lay between her new breasts. Then she kissed me quickly on the lips and raced off.

I was so startled, I couldn't move. I simply stared after her, stared for a long time after she had disappeared.

It was my first intimation that women weren't simply distant and enticing machines set into motion by some superior magician. They had a consciousness of their own. An unthinkable independence. Far from following the scenario of my fantasy, Madeleine had just run off and taken my precious talisman with her.

She never returned it. She should have returned it.

The mountain which gives Montréal its name looms out of flatness. Astride its rounded, ancient volcanic mass, the university tower rises like a pale sentinel.

I smile to myself and think I will tell Madeleine how she taught me a crucial lesson the day she ran off with my boyhood medallion. Then, as I join the snarl of rush-hour traffic at the junction with the Boulevard Métropolitain, the realization pounces upon me, brutal in its sudden vividness. There is no longer a Madeleine to speak to.

Tears crowd my eyes. I do not wipe them away. I do not want to be lulled into forgetfulness again. Yet I no longer have the courage for Madeleine's apartment. The direction I need to follow grows blurred in my mind. Which is the best route to take?

In the dying light, the office and factory buildings which border the road look deserted – grimy façades opening onto nothing. All life is concentrated in the stream of vehicles moving like lazy waves up and over the crest of the road's elevation. I could stay in this sea for ever, a willing captive to a flow which has nothing to do with volition.

But the car behind me hoots impatiently when I fail to move with sufficient speed into the five-foot gap in front. I do so with a lurch and find myself veering dangerously towards the next exit.

Rows of well-tended ranch houses fringe silent streets. There is less snow here, just a sprinkling through which the knobbly grass of extensive gardens is still visible. I wake up to the fact that I am in the Town of Mont-Royal. This used to be a WASP enclave. But the city has changed now, old demarcation lines between French and English have shifted. Strongholds have been scaled. An illuminated crèche, complete with three wise kings and shining star, adorns a lawn which in the past might only have sported a discreetly lit pine.

Closer to the old railway yards, affluence gives way to a terrace of brick triplexes. Winding exterior staircases complete with ornamental railings relieve the box-like flatness of the buildings. Each staircase leads to a separate apartment containing a regulation six rooms.

After 1911, the city made exterior staircases illegal. Too many children and old people hurtled down their icy winter treachery. Now these oddities of cheap local architecture have taken on a historic sheen. While the working class and the immigrants move out to the newness of the suburbs, the young and rising colonize the past.

South of Van Horne lie the tree-lined streets of Outremont with their comfortable two- and three-storey houses. A mere century ago, this north side of the mountain was an area of market gardens and orchards. Then, sniffing the wind of change as shrewd clerics in our city have often been known to do, the St Viateur religious order bought up all the land and fostered development. Outremont was transformed into a prosperous suburb, the first neighbourhood in Canada to be interested in its own beautification. A far-sighted mayor had the utility companies agree to lay telephone and electricity wires underground. Trees and bushes were distributed to citizens at cost price.

When I was a boy, Outremont was to the French what Westmount was to the rest of Montréal's population – the most desirable of residential enclaves. To us, the WASP fortress of Westmount was impregnable, even in wish. And we French were '*outre*', other, never the centre. The granite barrier of the mountain straddled our imaginations, separating us out on either of its sides more decisively than it divided the topography of the city.

Two of the founding fathers of Québec nationalism lived within a street of each other in Outremont, though the differences between them have over time mapped out a rift wide enough to drop a country into.

Henri Bourassa was an MP, a champion of French language and culture and also, it goes without saying, of French Catholicism. He battled for a strong, united Canada which respected its two separate cultures equally. An anti-imperialist who opposed Canadian participation in British wars, he nonetheless favoured a link with Great Britain. Britain was Canada's bulwark, he thought, against absorption by the United States. It was Bourassa with his pebble-bright eyes and drooping moustaches who, at the turn of the century, founded the newspaper I used to work for.

Walking towards me past the one-time home of the Abbé Lionel Groulx are two Orthodox Jews, tall hats perched regally over ringlets, faces pale above long black beards. The abbé would not have been pleased. His evocation of a separate state called La Laurentie, an independent Québec ruled by an élite of well-spoken French heroes, had a distinct bias towards racial purity. Around the abbé and his radical dreams of independence, the nationalists of the twenties and thirties congregated.

With varying inflections, Québec continues to vacillate between the positions voiced by these two men: equal and different within a Canadian federation; or valiantly independent, a French-speaking island dyked against the waves of the North American sea.

Why am I thinking about geography and politics? Is it the influence of these streets so close to the sites which mapped out my political education? I know myself better. I am avoiding thoughts of Madeleine and the ordeal that awaits me.

With a sense of impending panic, I make a detour into the Rue Laurier. The brightly lit cafés and restaurants remind me that I have not sat down to a meal in days. I need the fortification of food. That is why I have come here. Of course. It all makes sense now. I must have been planning this all along.

I pull into the first available parking space and walk into Luigi's where I know the food is good and plentiful and the tablecloths are always starched to glistening perfection.

I sit at a table at the back, away from the fashionably dressed couples in the window seats. I order the first items that spring out at me from the menu. Spinach and ricotta ravioli in a pesto sauce, a pan-fried slab of veal buried in mushroom. Without thinking, I ask for a carafe of house Chianti. This is not a night for gourmet reckonings or fine decisions.

I swallow wine and wolf down food without pausing to taste it.

Only as my eyes rise from my plate do I realize that I have made a mistake. Luigi's is too well-liked a haunt within my one-time circle for me to emerge from dinner unaccosted.

A woman in a trim black trouser suit is already upon me, her hand covering mine. Her face is a battleground between beauty and ugliness. Somewhere between the dramatically hooked nose and the liquid eyes, beauty wins out.

'Pierre,' she says. 'What a disaster!' She runs long, knobbly fingers through a thatch of short, dark hair. 'We're all devastated. Everyone at the theatre. We can't believe it. I wish you could tell me it wasn't true.'

I find myself returning the pressure of her hand. 'I wish I could, too, Gisèle.'

She gestures towards the empty chair opposite me and I nod, wave the waiter over for another carafe, a second glass.

'I knew Madeleine was upset. But I never thought . . .' Gisèle's hand finds her hair again, as if reassurance lay in its bristling texture. Her wide mouth trembles, settles in an expression which would like to be a smile but doesn't quite make it. 'You know how you retell yourself stories once you know their end. So you can make some sense of them. Exonerate yourself, maybe. Well hell, I've been trying with Madeleine. Ever since I heard. You live down there now, don't you? In Ste-Anne. Where she did it.'

127

I nod. 'Did you see a lot of Madeleine these last weeks?'

'Not so much at the very last. I'm the publicity director. My work's all at the beginning.'

'And the beginning wasn't exactly propitious this time round—'

'Not exactly.' She scowls. 'The bastards had it in for her. I think they wrote their features, even their reviews, before they saw the play. I warned her. We laughed about it. Madeleine and I go way back, you know that. She even scribbled a mock piece for me, told me we should publish it ahead of time, anonymously. A pre-emptive strike, so the bile would be puked up early. It went along the lines of "Madeleine Blais returns to the Montréal stage. Perhaps she shouldn't have bothered to honour us with her fading presence. All those years in the movies have made her forget . . . blah, blah."'

'But she was hurt, nonetheless.'

'Yes. No. I don't know.' Gisèle pulls out a cigarette and lights it with a shaky hand before I can locate the matches. 'She didn't really seem to care, that was the odd thing. Not really. At first I thought she was just putting on a brave front. But then . . . I changed my mind. She really wasn't thinking about the reviews, even about the play.'

'Only about the killings.'

'So you know?'

I shrug. 'We talked about it briefly. Once. What did she tell you?'

'It's not so much what she told me. It's what she did. Not only did she go to the vigil, to the funeral

128

mass, she went to the hospital to visit the wounded. She thought she could give them something, cheer them perhaps, with her presence – the famous star and all that. She even tried to see the parents of the dead girls. One of the fathers talked to her at length, wept in her arms for hours. I know about that, because she was late back to the theatre and we had to postpone the curtain for fifteen minutes.'

Gisèle shivers, stubs out her cigarette. 'She looked me in the eyes and said, "It should have been me. That poor girl was just a child. She had her whole life in front of her. They all did. I've already had more than my share."'

We stare at each other.

'I should have suspected then. I should have said something. Done something.'

I squeeze her hand. 'We all feel like that.'

Silence covers us, an airless capsule. The voices of the other diners, the clatter of glass and silver, seem to come from another galaxy.

At last I say, just to say something, 'Would you like to eat, Gisèle?'

She shakes her head. 'I'm with friends. I should get back to them.'

But she doesn't move. She frowns. 'Maybe you don't know, but on the day of the assassinations, Madeleine was over there. At the university. Not at the polytechnic. But next door. In the main building. She was going to see someone. I don't know who. But when she came out the ambulances were already there. The police. Maybe that's what it was.

Maybe because she saw the stretchers, the bodies . . .'

She reaches for another cigarette, then changes her mind. 'She didn't want to talk about that. But I've been thinking. Maybe she also saw something beforehand. Maybe she saw the killer. Maybe she felt guilty.'

'We're all shrouded in guilt, Gisèle.' I cut off her speculations and she nods sagely, like a dutiful girl who has just been reprimanded.

'Did you see her? See the body, I mean?' she asks after a moment.

The wine I am pouring spills over the edge of the glass.

'I can't talk about that.'

'No.' Her voice is small, but her eyes hover over me insistently. 'I . . .'

'But I wanted to ask you something. Was she seeing anyone? A man?'

'Oh, Pierre!' Gisèle squeezes my hand again, mistakes the motive for my question. Maybe it is only half-mistaken.

'Was she?' I press her.

'I'm not sure.'

There is something in the way she says it, her eyes on her wine glass, her fingers tapping its edge nervously, that makes me think she is trying to protect my feelings. I want to rephrase my question, but a spectacled man I vaguely recognize interrupts us.

'The food's come, Gisèle.' He looks at me and pauses. 'Pierre Rousseau? I'm sorry. I didn't realize . . .'

'It's all right. I was just going.' I extricate myself from social discomfort, give Gisèle a peck on the cheek.

'Ring me,' she calls after me. 'I haven't got your number.'

A thin spray of frost coats the car window. Restlessly, I wait for heat and windshield wipers to do their work. With a bare wedge of visibility, I race towards the Chemin de la Côte-Ste-Catherine. Something in the meeting with Gisèle has fuelled my impatience. I don't know what it is. But I am avid now for what Madeleine's apartment may reveal.

Perhaps my speed is simply a way of outflanking ghosts.

I don't slow down to glance at the imposing bulk of Jean Brébeuf, my old college. Yet I find myself veering left and then left again to make a slight detour along the Boulevard Edouard-Monpetit. Even if from the distance of a slope, I want to see the site of the tragedy which so disturbed Madeleine.

The area is deserted. A lone man walks down a path and pauses beneath a streetlamp. In the light his face is like finely wrinkled parchment. Behind him the university buildings are shadowy, pale coffins unlit from within. The lack of chattering, hurrying students makes the place feel ominous.

I stop the car and get out. I walk and breathe in cold, crisp air. Wedged in the snow, a stark reminder

131

of horror and grief, is a clump of carnations, as red as blood. I shiver.

I try to imagine that fateful afternoon, try to imagine it as Madeleine must first have seen it – the milling students, the raised voices, the nervous anticipation of exams. And then, the scene when she emerged from her meeting, the scream of sirens, the panic in the air, the sobs, the bodies. I taste her fear, the distress she communicated to me. The taste is foul, bitter. It settles in a rancid unswallowable lump in my throat as I stare at those smudges of red in the snow.

I tell myself Madeleine's inconsolable grief is enough of an explanation for her decision to take her own life. I do not quite believe myself. I know too much.

Back in the car, I make a U-turn and find myself at the corner of the Rue Fendall. It was here I lived during one of my years as a law student. Lived well. I was house-sitting for a professor on sabbatical. It was here, too, that my adult life with Madeleine began.

I race past the house, suddenly afraid of the memories its innocent façade conceals, and make my way past the cemetery, up and over the hump of the Côte-des-Neiges and down the steep crest of the south side of the hill. But there is another memory waiting to pounce on me here. I cannot avoid it, can never avoid it. Now, it controls my limbs, forces my foot to the brake, whether I want to slow or not.

Dawn. A low milky sun finds crevices between

buildings, throws slats across the road. We are hurtling downhill in an old car, a 1950s Dodge with razor-sharp fins, painted in unbelievably tacky tones of pink and purple.

I am in the back, my elbows planted on the front seat, my face visible in the rear-view mirror, where I can also see Madeleine's profile. She is wedged against the driver, a broad-shouldered, square-jawed hunk, whose thick fingers grasp the wheel. Nestling on his crotch, its nozzle pointed towards the floor, lies a gun. One of his hands moves repeatedly from the steering wheel to the gun and back again. Madeleine's fingers are on his thigh. They grip and fondle by turn. Her face is alight with a kind of soaring excitement.

Crowded against the door in the front seat is the cameraman whom I don't watch, whom I am not allowed to see. Not that I would want to. Between Madeleine's hands and face, between the gun and the speed, my attention is more than fully occupied.

We repeat this race down the hill six times. The cameraman isn't always with us: on three occasions, he sits in an open-backed van which precariously matches our speed. And though Madeleine's expression is meant to replay itself each time, I can feel the shifts in her, her mounting exhilaration.

I clutch the back of the seat and wonder why I am doing this and wait for the crash I know must come at the intersection of Guy and Sherbrooke, where fate and script coincide to provide us with a red light to run.

The film is a very low or no budget operation and

Madeleine has railroaded me into playing a bit part. For free, of course. The director is a friend, a former teacher at the theatre school. Madeleine is thrilled. It is her first movie role and the plot, which has been cursorily explained to me, is good enough – a loose mix of new wave and B-movie.

We are in the tail-end of the Duplessis era. Duplessis was our local, second-rate Franco. He ran Québec like his own feudal fiefdom. For sixteen long years between 1944 and his death in 1960, if a town voted in numbers usually larger than its population for his Union National party, it got new hospitals, new bridges, new schools, new roads. And a few dollars on top for individual pleasures. If it didn't, too bad.

Under Duplessis, Montréal boasted an exemplary underworld, full of small- and bigger-time hoods who doubled, when necessary, as strike-breakers. Full, too, of strippers and drugs and clubs. A liquor licence went for as much as $30,000. In 1961, when a new government finally came in, the price went down by $29,900.

Duplessis collected an estimated hundred million in graft. The powerful English community remained silent throughout this corruption. In exchange they were allowed to run the province's economy – the trust companies, the banks, the insurance and brokerage houses.

Yes, Duplessis was our very own despot. And like an African dictator, his authority was maintained by the complicity of the colonizers – or so a later generation of commentators would analyse his regime. In the early sixties, after his reign was finally over, whenever we saw a road being dug up, we would laugh and say someone was looking for Duplessis' buried treasure.

The movie which had us racing down the slope of the mountain was to give us a critical take on the era. Its hero was a hood who was also a strike-breaker; Madeleine the floozy who makes him see the wrong of his ways.

So, initially I wasn't averse to playing a bit part as a fellow gangster. All in a good cause. And, of course, I was curious. But no-one had prepared me for the dangers, both physical and mental, of film-making.

Madeleine's hand on our hero's thigh, the excite-ment in her face seem to me to have little to do with play-acting. Nor does the blare of the car we miss by centimetres at the junction of Guy and Sherbrooke. Certainly, the police who minutes later pull us over to the kerb have taken their lines from a different script. It requires rather a lot of explaining from our director and a great deal of tearful pouting from Madeleine – though this indeed does bear the authentic stamp of acting – before we are sent off with a reprimand and a ticket for running a light.

The day's filming is at an end. All of the crew have other jobs to go to. Madeleine refuses a lift and together we hop on a bus back towards my place. She is utterly unaware of the inquisitive stares the early morning workers cast at us. Amongst them, she looks less like an off-hours fifties floozy than a girl dressed up in her mother's cast-away clothes.

Yet the striped pedal-pushers above high-heeled sandals, the fluffy turquoise angora sweater and equally fluffed-up hair suit her wonderfully. She is radiant. And as taut as an electric wire. Madeleine likes danger, thrives on risk.

'I saw you,' she says, as we edge into a back seat. Her tongue moistens the bright pink of her lipstick. She looks at me with golden eyes. 'That was clever. Stashing the gun under the seat before the cops could notice it.' She presses close to me, puts her fingers exactly where they had been on that other man's thigh. 'Very clever. Alain thinks you're good, you know. He told me. "Musing and muscular" were his words. Good combination for the screen.'

She laughs that teasing laugh of hers, as if she knows more than she is saying, then runs her nail along the inside of my leg, so that I have to imprison her caress. I no longer wonder at the actor's speed. In fact, as Madeleine's excitement seizes me, I no longer wonder at all.

My hand is on her nape. It is slightly damp with the heaviness of her hair. I touch it with my lips and feel her hand climbing higher.

'Come on,' she whispers. We leap off the bus and she starts to run. I am right beside her. We run the two blocks to my house and before I have closed the door behind us she has kicked off her shoes and unzipped the pedal-pushers. Her panties are wet, as moist as her mouth. I cannot say we make love. We are too hungry. As if it were the first time.

It is always the first time with Madeleine and always, potentially, the last. We fuck. Against the door, my hands on her buttocks, her taut breasts pushed against me. On the plush carpet, her hair streaming over my face so that I lose my sight as I arch against her, abandon myself altogether to the frenzied pulse of our desire.

Afterwards, she strokes my hair and my chest and my groin and looks at me with that gamine smile, which is a mixture of surprise and shyness and impish delight. 'You know, Pierre, I've been thinking. Now that divorce is so easy, we should get married. What do you say? It would please Mémère.'

I am so startled, I don't answer right away. I have never thought about marriage, but now its romance envelops me as surely as Madeleine's scent. A Madeleine to have and to hold in a formalized forever. A wife who is Madeleine to be conquered anew every day in the intimacy of familiar places. A Madeleine to be claimed and tamed in a large marital bed. A Madeleine in the morning shower, putting on make-up, parading new dresses for me, laughing. A joint pattern of meals and washing up and arguments and truces. A Madeleine to introduce to colleagues as 'my wife'.

As this fantasy of the quotidian plays itself out before me, I find we are making love again. There is a kind of solemnity to our movements, a slow tenderness, as if the event, once spoken, had already occurred. I marvel anew at the curve of her hip, the tawny perfection of her skin, the surprising weight of her breasts, the perfect marriage of our movements. I groan under the pressure of her lips and fingers and as I move into that warm, secret space, I murmur a yes and think I am the luckiest man in the world.

I should have known that Lady Luck is the ficklest of women.

5

The apartment Madeleine took over some three years ago when she decided she wanted a more permanent base in Montréal stands half-way down the hill which marked our first and only joint experience in film. I never dared ask her whether she had chosen it because of that.

Now it is too late.

The building is a large, modern, mustard-brick block with a drive and a colonnaded entrance. I fumble with the keys, let myself into the brightly lit, maroon-carpeted lobby and slope towards the elevator. I avoid the inquisitive glance of a tiny, fur-wrapped woman who emerges from its silent doors with a yapping poodle in her arms and quickly press the number eight.

In the long corridor, I cross paths with a bald-headed giant of a man who avoids me as stealthily as I avoid him. Nervousness attacks me. What if Mme Tremblay's intuition is the right one? The thought of murder rears through me and shakes the keys from my hand. A light flickers at the edge of my mind and then goes out, covering everything in blackness. My feet feel as if they are sinking into quicksand. I force myself to breathe deeply, grapple clumsily with the lock. No, not murder.

The third key produces a click which rebounds along the hallway. But still the door won't give.

At shoulder level I notice a tiny new lock and an electronic eye. Madeleine's fear has had concrete consequences. I insert the smallest key and at last, with furtive haste, I slip through the door and shut it softly behind me. To my side the alarm box is open and inactive. In my confusion, that strikes me as strange. Has Madeleine forgotten or simply not bothered to set it? Or has someone been here before me? Some of Gagnon or Contini's men perhaps? Of course. Even Gagnon is not a complete slouch. Mme Tremblay's thought has come too late.

The apartment is a dazzle of lights. They leap through the vast picture window from the streets beneath like intimate stars. The fortress-like structure of the Convent of the Sacred Heart is just below me. To the left the twin stone towers where the missionary Marguerite Bourgeoys once taught Indian children rise out of the darkened grounds of the old Sulpician seminary, now Le Grand Séminaire. If I crane my head to the left I can see the river and the twinkling lights of the Champlain Bridge. Like a harlot, Montréal grows more beautiful by night.

I draw the gauzy curtains and switch on a lamp. For a moment I cannot move. Though I do not know this apartment well, the teeming clutter which is Madeleine's particular stamp is so familiar that it makes me gasp. How can all this chaotic abundance be here and not Madeleine?

There are newspapers and magazines and books piled on every available surface. They all but obscure the television. Near the comfortable bulk of the two creamy sofas, they spill over onto the floor, which also here and there spawns shoes and mugs. On the alabaster coffee table shaped like a generous cello, a great white bowl heaves with a collection of the matchboxes she can never find. Amidst them are stone eggs in every mineral colour. The shelves atop radiators are crammed with the objects of Madeleine's random and altogether unsystematic collections: cheap painted madonnas of folk art and commercial exploitation; tiny china houses, pierrots with white innocent faces and single luminous tears; hand-painted pots in a riot of colours.

Unframed canvases lean against the walls as if Madeleine has forgotten to hang them or simply couldn't make up her mind where they belonged. By the window stands a vast terracotta urn, the gift, no doubt, of some Roman admirer. It is stuffed with every conceivable variety of dried branch and flower.

When Madeleine and I first lived together, what I thought of as her mess irritated me. I like a certain sparseness, a certain order. I like to know where I can find things. But Madeleine never seemed to leave the house without coming home with some object happily retrieved from a tip or a flea market or a junk shop. Her dressers and wardrobes burgeoned with jewellery and scarves and belts and bric-à-brac. She rarely wore or looked at these things. It was simply enough for them to be there, as if her business were the recovery of lost objects.

Sometimes she would remember something that she wanted and set up a frenzied search, only to turn up with a treasure she had quite forgotten. This seemed to make her inordinately happy. Then every so often she would dump random armfuls of things into black bags and we would transport them to charity shops. And the whole process would begin again.

I came to realize that for Madeleine a home was an evolving space, a living environment. It didn't matter whether its basic structure was large or small. Even the regal house in Neuilly on the outskirts of Paris which was the fruit of her stardom and which would have imposed its own bourgeois order on anyone else had no impact on her ways. Her reckless disorder took it over.

She had no predetermined ideal of the way things should look or be. She didn't, in any real sense, care. What she needed was the casual chaos. And a degree of unpredictable flux. It fed her in some indefinable way, charged the motor of her talent.

Since one person's comfortable clutter is another's insupportable mess, my study grew a closed door, a lock and a contrasting clinical precision. So, too, eventually, did my bedroom.

In the shorter arm of the L-shape which makes up

the capacious central space of Madeleine's apartment stands an elegant ash table with six high-backed Mackintosh chairs. The table is covered in Christmas cards. A tall blue-enamelled vase perches at its centre. Lilies, waxy-white and huge, sway from its depths. I touch them and shiver. They are alive. They have outlived Madeleine.

I glance into the kitchen. Two plates stand on the counter. They bear a complement of crumbs, a piece of crust, a smear of jam. The sink contains a couple of unwashed mugs, a few knives and spoons, two long-stemmed glasses. The fridge is all but empty: a sliced loaf, a tub of margarine, a carton of milk, a bottle of Dom Perignon. For Madeleine, it is all surprisingly tidy.

I force myself to interrogate these objects with an objective eye. I want to know the truth, don't I? If the kitchen displays two of everything, there was someone with Madeleine on the day she left for Ste-Anne. But perhaps only someone at breakfast. And the night before, if the wine glasses are anything to go by.

I find myself rushing to the bedroom, then pause to take a deep breath before I open the door and switch on the light. To my astonishment, the bed is neatly made, the white habitant coverlet tucked and seamlessly stretched over its vastness. Which proves nothing, I chide myself. Madeleine is quite capable of making a bed. A partner is capable of making a bed. But if there was a partner, could it have been the man with the ponytail? Or someone else?

With an edge of irritation, I start to rifle through

her commode, her night-table drawers in search of papers, in search of the day-diary which should have been in her bag but wasn't. Perhaps the police have already taken that. Though it is uncertain what it might reveal. Madeleine was never an assiduous planner. She would hardly have noted D-Day.

That thought gives me pause. If Madeleine decided to take her life, it would have been as impetuous a decision as all her others. She wouldn't have thought. If she had thought, she wouldn't have done it. Her grandmother's sorrow would have stopped her. No, it could only have been the organic cumulation of a mood which said, 'Enough!' And a concatenation of events provided an opportunity, a sudden brainstorm.

Emotions swarm through me, crowd out the clarity I strive for. Why does my mind keep thrusting aside the clues Madeleine herself gave me – her depression at the killings? Why does it keep returning to the notion of a lover? Is it a buried desire for vengeance which has me imagining a single hated man who is ultimately responsible for Madeleine taking her own life? As if Madeleine were a fragile and bereft woman. Some lovelorn girl who had no resources to fall back on.

I swat at these thoughts, vexatious wasps, and remember that I have come here on an errand – the journals Mme Tremblay is certain Madeleine sporadically kept. If the police haven't already found them, the study should have been my first port of call.

The room extends along the front of the building

144

and has the same dramatic view as the salon. I have only been in here once before. Perhaps, despite my imaginings, this study was more private to Madeleine than her bedroom.

A desk which is really a long refectory table covers the length of the window which is also the width of the room. But for a tiny cleared space at its centre, it is buried in papers, manila envelopes and a multitude of brightly coloured folders. Two ornate tins hold piles of pens and pencils. There are plants everywhere. Books, CDs, cassettes and thick cardboard box-files line the back wall.

If Madeleine has kept up old habits, I know the contents of these boxes. They are filled with the scripts that have been sent to her over the years. These, for some inexplicable reason, she never throws away. The floor is littered with more of them. And with newspapers. In the far corner, there is a garishly painted rocking-horse, like an old-fashioned fairground animal. A large rag-doll sits astride it. On the opposite wall there is a *chaise-longue* in deep blue velvet.

I sit in the desk chair and start to comb through a heap of papers which bear no visible order. If there was a suicide note, then presumably the police have already taken it away. I thrust aside some bills and find a letter from Marie-Ange Corot, Madeleine's agent in Paris, asking if she might be interested in a medium-sized part in a film that promises well. Attached to this letter is a stack of fan mail which I only glance through cursorily.

These letters puzzle me. At the back of my mind

I'd assumed that Madeleine's depression was linked to a bleak patch in her career. Her last two American films didn't do well at box office. She had told me that she wasn't interested in working in Hollywood any more. It was one of the reasons she had taken on Hedda. But here was a clear offer.

I put aside my thoughts and glance through more correspondence. There are invitations, letters from friends abroad, both male and female. Nothing out of the ordinary, were it not that Madeleine is dead. In this room, so replete with her presence, that fact becomes increasingly hard for me to keep at the forefront of my mind. More and more I feel like a snooper, who will be caught in the act at any moment. I look over my shoulder superstitiously and have to force myself back to the task.

I open an orange folder and a young bearded face leaps out at me. It takes me a few minutes to recognize Marc Lépine, the university assassin. Madeleine has clipped newspaper stories of the event, not only from local papers but from further afield, Toronto, the US, France. The files have the authentic note of an obsession. For one thing, there is a neatness about the clipping and filing – the stories of the victims separated out from accounts about the killer, his family, his schooldays – which is not in evidence in any of her other papers.

It suddenly occurs to me that there might be a practical reason behind Madeleine's fixation. The police never allowed the papers to publish Lépine's hit-list. But perhaps they questioned individuals. Madeleine may have known her name was on the list. Contini will be able to find out about that.

At the bottom of the Lépine file there is a crumpled sheet of paper, a letter, half-written, crossed over. I don't know who '*Mon cher Armand*' is, but my heart pounds with unnerving speed as I scan the first lines. 'I can't go on. I really can't.'

As I read, it comes to me that Armand is the director of *Hedda Gabler* and Madeleine is asking to be replaced. 'I hate to let you all down, but you'll have to find someone else. By Christmas at the latest.'

There is no date on the letter. I have no way of knowing whether a version of it was sent.

I put the Lépine file to one side. Beneath it the bright colours of a magazine catch my eye. Its contents shock me. This is no magazine but a mail order brochure for guns and rifles. A felt-tipped pen has circled all the semi-automatics on offer as well as tiny pistols, the kind that fit easily into a handbag.

Madeleine's fear is suddenly as real to me as if it were my own and an armed marauder had entered the room. I throw the magazine to one side and go in search of a drink. Had she ordered a pistol for herself, I wonder as I uncork a bottle of wine. I swallow a large mouthful without tasting it. Is the pistol perhaps already here, stored somewhere in the apartment, a security shield against women-loathing men? But if so, why didn't she use the pistol?

All the stories I have been telling myself start to unravel. Once more, I force myself to remember that I am here for a specific purpose which is not my own. I am here to save Madeleine from any potential scandal. If they are still here, I must find those journals Mme Tremblay is certain exist. I almost pick up the phone to ask her whether she has any idea what they look like, but a glance at my watch tells me it is already far too late to ring anyone.

Bottle in hand, I trudge back to the study. More quickly now, I rifle through folders, looking only for Madeleine's flowing hand, her black ink. I have just put a publicity folder to one side when a single sheet of paper flutters out from between two files.

It is in her writing and the text assaults me with the steely coldness of a bayonet.

I want to creep into a dark hole and die. I want to become utterly invisible, a heap of ash caressed only by the wind. How could you? I thought it was you. Now I am certain. Perhaps you see it as an act of love. A strange love it is which wants only to fathom and control.

I stare at this text with no date and no addressee for I don't know how long. Then, with a shiver, I fold it into my jacket pocket. I know the addressee. I know him only too well. Quickly, I start on another pile, reversing the order this time, turning the whole thing upside-down. It is then that a small green diary magically appears on a corner of the desk like some precious long-lost ring. The police have hardly been thorough.

148

My fingers grow clumsy. I can barely make them turn the tissue-thin pages. But apart from the 6th, which has been blacked out in thick ink, December holds very little. Lunch with me is marked as P 1.00 and the name of the restaurant. Ps also signal performance evenings. I remember this coding from way back.

What I have forgotten is the excellence of Madeleine's memory, for which the diary is an almost unnecessary prop. There are a few other dates with letters of the alphabet I can't be certain of. And then on the 20th a letter, it could be T, it might be F, 'arrives!' After that there is nothing. The diary is blank. Because it has nothing to tell or because Madeleine willed it so, I don't know.

With sudden fury, I crush my fist against the desk and fling the diary to the floor. Why is Madeleine being so obstinate? Why won't she yield any of her mystery? Why can't she simply tell me what all this is about?

I do not realize I am sobbing her name until the walls hurl it back at me. I steady myself. The wine bottle is almost empty. A glance at my watch shows me it is half past two. Where have the hours gone? I am in no state to drive home. Nor have I accomplished my mission. Despair threatens. I can feel it paralysing my limbs.

Before it takes me over completely, I open each of the box-files on the shelf in search of something that might be a journal. As I replace the final one I tell myself that here, at least, the police have succeeded. Or, alternatively, that Madeleine has left her purported journals in the house in Neuilly, perhaps even in Los Angeles. Or that she has thrown everything significant out, has accomplished another of her periodic purges. For there are other things missing, too. Things that should be here, but that I can't find. Things that I don't want to think about, but that I need to locate. Yes, need too.

In the bedroom, I start again. I am not a good detective. Madeleine robs me of the power of clear-sightedness. I am too interested. Stray objects keep usurping my attention. A pair of shoes I remember because of the way they make her foot arch. A crumpled silk-velour scarf in which her fragrance lingers. I read these objects and they give me clues to Madeleine's life, but not her death. There is a crucial final chapter missing.

I lie on the bed and try to cast myself into her mind and body.

The sliding wardrobe door is half-open and an assortment of dresses peeks out at me. Shoes too. And one of those large glossy hatboxes I didn't know still existed.

The hatbox. My eyes return to it. It seems to speak to me. A low, throaty voice.

With shaky hands, I lift the box onto the bed. I edge off its shiny lid. Colours assault me – the deep yellow of sunflowers, the lush green of art nouveau vines, the blues and reds of delicate Indian silk prints, faded watery pastels like ink blots streaming down a porous surface. One by one I place the note-books on the bed and stare at them.

The need to open them, to read, is overwhelming.

Yet I hesitate. It is a breach. Would Madeleine forgive me the transgression? Perhaps if the books are dated I can pick out only the last, the final chapter. I lie back on the pillows and finger the texture of their covers. I have lain here before. Madeleine and I slept here together once. It was the first time in too long. Just after she had bought the apartment. I handled the transaction for her.

The day the bed and the sofas arrived, she invited me over, invited me into this room. It was summer and she was wearing some kind of clinging dress which left her back and shoulders bare. The deep gold of the California sun was on her skin and her voice had a husky resonance as she murmured, 'Let's.'

I had forgotten the nature of passion. I don't know if it died an ordinary death or I killed it off. In any event, Madeleine reminded me of its fierce beauty. It was only ever like that with her. Perhaps it had to do with her laugh or her acrobatic grace or her generous, almost gratuitous desire which asked for nothing in return. Or simply the fact that we go so far back. But we both felt it. And recognized its impossibility.

Afterwards she curled into me and told me I was her earth. She had to keep coming back to me. I grounded her. She laughed her mischievous laugh then and added, 'But generally, I prefer flying.'

I pick up one of the notebooks, the shiniest one with the sunflowers, and open it at random.

Back from Europe. The farm is lovely. Star is happy to see me. And Michel and François and Mme Laporte. But Ste-Anne is deadly. A dump. A year is a long time. I rode for hours this morning then stopped off for breakfast at the Rousseaus. Pierre doesn't want to know me any more. Too bad for him. I'm not going to give him the present I bought. I'll give it to Michel instead.

I have chosen badly. There is no date here, but I can supply it. August 1966. We were still children, but I thought I was a man.

The thudding of horse's hooves reached me in my room. I looked out and saw Madeleine tethering Star to the porch. Her presence made me unaccountably nervous and if my father's voice hadn't insisted I would have remained hidden.

As it was, I could barely make myself meet her eyes. All I could focus on were her legs, which looked inordinately long in her riding boots. And her voice, which was distant, formal, too Parisian as she shook my hand.

I squirmed uncomfortably and looked out the window while my father plied her with questions. The weather was unbearably hot. August mug had set in, the kind that barely lets the sun break through the clouds. Perspiration gathered in my armpits. My fresh shirt was already sticky. I didn't want to hear the marvels of Paris and London chanted by a girl with a stuck-up voice.

Maybe I was simply guilty. Earlier that summer

the miracle had happened. With Annette, a waitress in a local diner, I had finally made my way to that mysterious place where 'the fruit of thy womb' resided. As a result, Madeleine felt alien to me. She inhabited the innocence I had so recently left behind that the fragile reality of the distance between us had to be established with an almost brutal coldness. Also, I knew I had only a week left with Annette before the walls of Jean Brébeuf closed round me once more.

Madeleine and I effectively lost touch after that. Mme Tremblay had determined that there had been more than enough of nuns and convent education. And the ordinary French state schools in the area were simply not good enough for her granddaughter. She sent Madeleine off to board with acquaintances in Montréal who had a daughter her age. Together the girls went to an English-language high school in the west of the city.

When our two families met that Christmas Madeleine and I were cool with each other. The following summer I had a job at *Le Devoir*. It was the year of Expo '67 and the city had spawned a whole new island of wonders – national pavilions containing every kind of invention. The Americans had built a vast Buckminster Fuller geodesic dome. The Russians had included a miniature hydro-electric dam in their exhibition. Visitors poured into the city. Theatre troupes arrived from every corner of the world. The whole thing proved so engrossing that I didn't bother going home to Ste-Anne. Then university took me over. Between work, the occasional articles and the stimulus of the decade's politics, I rarely if ever thought of Madeleine and a childhood which I felt I had left behind.

I skim Madeleine's notebooks. I have found the one that follows on from the sunflowers. I am not really reading. I am only capable of looking for my name. The rest can come later, if Mme Tremblay allows it.

Went to a demo today. Thousands of people, waving banners. *Vive le Québec Libre* and *Maître chez nous* and the fleur-de-lis and all that. I can't tell whether I really care about the politics or only about the thrill of the crowd.

I bumped into Pierre Rousseau. I think he cares . . . About the politics that is. He's turned very handsome and very revolutionary. All he talks about is the class struggle and the French being the white negroes of the continent and cultural and economic oppression. Forty-four nations have declared their independence since the Second World War. Why not Québec? He used to speak proper French. Now he slips into joual. It's quite seductive. I wanted to prove something to him. I think I did. I really think I did.

What does she mean? I skim subsequent pages but my name has vanished.

The book slips from my hand. I am back there. Back with Madeleine in search of an explanation. June 1970, it must have been. I was well into law school, heading our deputation for the march. Maybe I had already joined the Parti Québecois.

The crowd was huge. Ever since de Gaulle had proclaimed his '*Vive le Québec Libre*' from the height of the garlanded town hall and effectively blessed the movement, the crowds had been huge.

This occasion was a particularly raucous one. The chanting and cheering of the gathered mass already a celebration of an event that was still a dream.

At first I paid no attention to the tug on my sleeve. When I did, I turned to see a woman of astonishing beauty. Beneath the fringe and the lazy flutter of hair, I recognized those gold-flecked eyes. Madeleine. She was wearing a scruffy T-shirt and tight jeans. Her thumbs were hitched into their waist and she walked with a kind of coltish sexuality, an animal grace which made me think of Brigitte Bardot. I hugged her. Speech was all but impossible, but I shouted and mouthed above the crowd. 'If we lose each other, let's meet up later. About eight. At the pizza parlour on the corner of the Côte-des-Neiges and Lacombe.'

She squeezed my arm and walked off. Had it been possible to follow, I would have.

Later I sat among my friends in the pizzeria and sipped bad wine and glanced so often at the door that Guillaume, my closest mate, reprimanded me for not paying attention to the conversation. When Madeleine finally came in, I think he understood. A momentary silence fell round the table. She sauntered towards us, slipped into a chair. I swallowed hard and introduced her, put my arm a little possessively round her shoulders.

While we ate, she was quiet, attentive in a languid way. At one point, in the midst of our heated emphasis on separatism, she said, 'But what's wrong with Canada?'

'What do you mean by Canada?' I grilled her, and when she failed to answer, did so for her. 'You mean that family romance, that peaceful, loving, co-operative federation made up of two ethnicities, French and English, coexisting happily from sea to glorious sea? But that's never been there, Madeleine. That's always and only ever been a fantasy, a myth. What we really have are two separate entities. English and French.'

I went on and on, lecturing passionately, loading her with statistics, evoking justice, the pride of a people who had lived too long with bowed heads. I was trying to impress her. I must have been insufferable. My only excuse is that I was still a mere twenty. Political passion is the province of the young.

Soon after that I asked her if she'd like to come back to my place for a quieter drink. She surprised me by saying yes.

Alone with her on the streets, I was suddenly gripped by shyness. I could hardly believe that this exquisite woman was my old friend Madeleine.

Madeleine, however, came into her own. Released from the dreams and quibbles of politics, she started to tell me about her courses at the theatre school – how one of their teachers had them sing 'God Save the Queen' in English in order to practise their diction, how another could barely get his lips round Racine, so that the rhymes never rhymed. She mimicked and pranced and by the time we had reached the house on the Rue Fendall we were both laughing so hard we could barely stand up straight.

'Nice place.' Madeleine caught her breath as she looked around. She peered up at pictures, tried lamps, touched objects with avid curiosity.

'Not mine. I'm house-sitting.' I uncorked a bottle of Bull's Blood, which was about the only wine we drank. 'And you, where are you living?'

She didn't answer. Her silence made me think she must be hitched up with a man. I didn't want to press her, but I suddenly couldn't think of another thing to say. I handed her a glass and she curled into the sofa and sipped it with a serious intentness.

'Do you have some music?' she asked abruptly.

'Sure. What would you like. Mozart, Brahms, Debussy, jazz, rock, *chansonniers*, Gilles Vigneault, Jacques Brel?' I was sounding like an idiot again and I shut up.

'Vigneault, why not. Since you're such a patriot.'

I met her eyes for a second and I had the impression that any moment now, she would launch into an imitation of me I wouldn't like.

'Vigneault it is.' I put on an LP. I could feel Madeleine's eyes on my back and I only dared turn round when the guitar was already well into the mournful chords of 'Mon Pays' and that dry, broken voice had begun to dissect our condition.

Madeleine patted the seat beside her. I sat down and we gazed at each other. There was a crackle in the air, like fire licking at wood. Then suddenly our lips met.

I don't really remember anything else. It was the first time loving, sex, passion – whatever it was – had extinguished that watchful inner eye. With Madeleine there was nothing except the music of our limbs, the percussion of desire, the melody of discovery.

Afterwards, our bodies entwined, I felt I had come home to a home I had never really known, like heaven, or a sea that lapped at one continuously, bracing and embracing, all at once. Madeleine's luminous eyes told me she felt the same way. Or so I thought.

I must have slept with inordinate heaviness, for when I woke she was no longer there. Not in the bed. Not anywhere in the house. A chasm opened inside me, as if I had been split in two. And with it a sense of disbelief. Had I dreamed the whole encounter?

The tell-tale splash of blood on the bed suggested otherwise. But it filled me with a secondary disbelief. I hadn't noticed, hadn't imagined, could still not imagine that it was Madeleine's first time.

I lay there, smoking furiously, one cigarette after another, trying to make sense of things, and then I lunged for the telephone. She hadn't left me a number, so I tried Enquiries with no success and then the theatre school. I left a message, left a number at the paper where I was doing a summer stint again, left my home number. All day and the next and the next I waited for her to ring. Nothing.

Swallowing my discomfort and my pride, I finally contacted Mme Tremblay. She told me Madeleine had just left for Connecticut where she had a small summer stock job. She gave me an address.

I didn't write. I wouldn't have known what to say. I felt too hurt and, at the same time, I had the sense that I had failed somewhere, whether through lack of tact or something else I didn't know. Women were so incomprehensible.

I made myself forget. It didn't take all that long. Work, youthful spirits, the pace of political and other passions – everything then moved with the blurred speed and raucous enthusiasm of a Rolling Stones concert.

Our group at the university knew the enemy in intimate detail. We had analysed his component parts. We knew the size and scale of his assets, the tentacles of his power. We hated him and the Jews who were his cohorts and the complicit clerics who had kept the province locked in the nineteenth century. We had managed in a few brief years to extricate ourselves from the choking grip of the clergy and to restore some pride in our French identity. A great deal remained to be done.

All this was fine and well in the abstract. The trouble was few of us had ever met any English people face to face, let alone any Jews, those ogres of the Catechism we had imbibed with our mother's milk. For centuries, we had managed to inhabit two separate and neighbouring solitudes and make monsters of the other.

I had the bright idea of forming a discussion group with our equivalents at the law faculty of McGill, the English university on the other side of the mountain. Five of us and five of them. The only stipulation was that the language of discussion had to be French.

We met on a Wednesday evening in a room at the university. They arrived in a group and for a moment we all stared at each other in embarrassed silence. They didn't look any different from us. They were young, casually dressed, polite as we shook hands and introduced ourselves. The only difference was that one of them was a woman. Anne Davies. She was tall and self-composed with wavy copper hair and a smattering of freckles, and her French, unlike the others', sounded just like my own.

I talked through the points of a prepared statement which detailed the kinds of issues we wanted to discuss with them in the coming weeks: economic and political discrimination, the charade of bilingualism, the need for the universal use of French as the official language of Québec and so on. They threw in a few more. We grew a little heated over our Prime Minister, Pierre Trudeau's policies, which we felt reduced the French to just another ethnic minority. But all in all, things progressed with a degree of friendly civility and concluded with my invitation to retire to my place for drinks.

It was in the informality of my living room that things began to go awry. My friend Guillaume started on one of his anti-Semitic riffs, blaming the Jews for this, that and the other, for their disproportionate share of resources.

Anne interrupted him sharply. 'Look, I'm Jewish.'

One of the men echoed her. 'Me, too.'

He stood up to leave, but Anne stayed in her place. Her face was fierce, her posture suddenly that of a street kid, poised to fight. 'The trouble with you Québécois is that the whole history of the twentieth century seems to have passed you by. Where've you been hiding? Do you know where nationalisms based on racial homogeneity have led to? Have you heard of fascism, Nazism? The Second World War?'

Guillaume cleared his throat and I butted in, saying the first thing that came to my mind before he brought further shame on us: 'My father fought in the Second World War.'

She met my eyes. Hers were green, the pupils huge. I hadn't known Jews could look like this.

The absurdity of the thought, the fact that it had leapt into my mind, the sense that I was trapped in stereotypes, made me burble on. 'Look, this is obviously something we need to discuss further. Next week, maybe you could, I don't know, throw it all at us, give us your list of prejudices. We'll give you ours.'

Anne laughed. 'Sounds like fun. Think we'll come out of it alive?'

As the others left, I asked her if she could stay behind for a few minutes. I wanted to apologize in some way. I was also interested in her – the way she argued, the things she had to teach me, the mixture of wit and fire. Within a few weeks we were engaged in an affair, which had as much of mutual

161

curiosity and the pleasure of argument about it as passion. The affair outlasted the discussion group. It also deflected my thoughts from Madeleine.

Anne and I are still friends, though she left Québec for New York, where she teaches at Columbia. It was she who helped me keep my intellectual balance through the terrible days of the FLQ crisis which finally shattered the collective dream of a harmonious Canada. The bombs in mailboxes and armouries had begun the process in the early sixties. The kidnapping in October 1970 of James Cross, the British Commercial Attaché, and then a week later the kidnapping and murder of Québec Labour Minister, Pierre Laporte, by a terrorist cell of the Maoist Front de Libération du Québec finished it.

The federal government sent in the army, instituted the emergency War Measures Act. Our civil liberties were suspended. I and many of my colleagues found ourselves marched off to police headquarters for days of interrogation. It was difficult to disentangle our hatred for these abusive measures and our sympathy for the ultimate aims, if not the means, of the terrorists. Anne helped. I may have wanted independence, but not at any cost.

In the midst of all this, a postcard with a picture of flaming autumn leaves arrived from Madeleine, saying nothing more than 'Hope you're well. See you some time.'

The some time stretched into two years. It finally arrived in the form of an invitation which reached me at the newspaper. A single sheet of paper

162

depicting a circus scene and announcing a new production of *Lulu* by a theatre group I had never heard of. On the back Madeleine had scrawled, 'Come to the opening night. There's a party afterwards.'

I went. Even another woman or a political meeting couldn't have kept me away. Though I felt a little like a well-trained dog who would have liked to chew at the leash.

The theatre was in the old town, a few streets up from the harbour – an area of beautiful grey-stone houses which were just beginning to be reclaimed from dereliction. This one still hadn't quite made it, though a bright banner hung over the doors and the woman at the ticket desk beamed good humour as she gestured us down the stairs into a basement room that had been decked out with ramps on three sides. A spangled light, like a great balloon made out of mosaics, swung over what served as a stage.

A brass band dressed in a madcap array of circus tat and glitter started to strut across the stage and boom out a cacophony of sound. In its wake came three larger-than-life puppets, bulging caricatures – a humble, leering priest, a bewigged judge, and a cigar-smoking politician. The puppets bowed and bobbed and lined up at the back of the stage. Suddenly a grate clattered down in front of them, encaging them. They growled like wild beasts, thrust themselves against the bars of their prison.

A whip lashed the air. The puppets growled more savagely. From somewhere a pistol rang out and a circus master's voice welcomed us to the show. The fury of the beasts increased. Then a silver sylph of a dancer appeared. Her face was that of an angel, her first steps as sinuous as a serpent's. With astonishing abandon, she leapt and shimmied and threw herself about the stage. Half-goddess, half-fiend, her presence bewitched beasts and audience alike.

It took me a moment to recognize Madeleine. In the next I forgot her. I was as prey to Lulu's magic as the series of men and women who entered her sway and fell victim to her unleashed sexuality. Her sheer physical vitality captivated and entranced. Like a force of nature or of the unconscious, she lived above and beyond any social or moral conventions.

I later realized that the troupe had played fast and furious with Wedekind's original turn-of-the-century plays. Gone were the doctor and artist and newspaper owner to be replaced by more contemporary figures of establishment hypocrisy. The music, too, was wholly of our time, as brash and loud and pulsating as a rock concert, so that it was almost impossible to sit still. Lulu never did.

As a reviewer said of Madeleine Blais the next day, she embodied that true, savage, beautiful beast who was young Québec. He didn't bother with the play's end where Lulu lies prone, her fast and free life ravaged and ended by Jack the Ripper, a modern serial killer before his time.

With a start I realize where my thoughts have taken me. My hands are clammy, my throat dry. Was Madeleine's end already written in her flamboyant beginning as Lulu? And if so, in which of her male leads am I inscribed, victim or killer?

I hurl off my clothes as if they were responsible for the straitjacket of my thoughts and plunge between the sheets. The pillow retains the scent of Madeleine's hair, a fresh fragrance composed of I don't know what flowers. I bury my face in it. Three nights. Only three nights have passed. I force my mind away from death and find the living Madeleine again. Find her as she was in that first vibrant performance. I see her perched on the bar in the centre of the stage, swinging her legs, back and forth, randomly to the side, always in motion, a little girl who has woken to the power of her sexuality. Was it then that I said to myself, if I had been the first, I had certainly, in those two years that had passed, only been the first of many? When I approached her at the party afterwards, I was intensely aware of the fact.

She was standing in the midst of a group of admirers. Her eyes were radiant. A simple black triangle of a dress, sleeveless and very short in the style of the time, did nothing to mute her presence. I hovered at the edge of the group, uncertain about how to behave with this new Madeleine.

But when our eyes met the sexual magic between us was still there, more potent than ever. Trapped in its taut lines, we didn't move for a moment. Then she took a step towards me and in a blink I was at her side, effusive with congratulations.

Her tone was sceptical. She drew me towards a quiet corner. 'You really liked it?'

'Really. Very very much.'

She began to anatomize the production and her performance with the seriousness of a practised critic, telling me where she had failed, where she could do better.

'You were wonderful,' I reiterated.

'That isn't, I hope, just a comment about my legs.'

I allowed myself to examine her legs. 'No.' I laughed. 'Though they're not bad either.'

Our eyes locked again. I don't know what she read in mine, but she turned away, was about to be swallowed by an exuberant group. I touched her shoulder, held her back.

'Can we see each other, Madeleine? Perhaps even later tonight? I looked for you, you know. After . . . after . . .'

'Maybe.' Her face took on an enigmatic cast. 'Let's see how things go.'

I waited. I don't think I could have done otherwise. I watched her raking in the congratulations. I watched the hugs and kisses and instant intimacies which make up theatrical life. I chatted and drank and mingled and never took my eyes off Madeleine. Maybe it was simply the persistence of my attention, maybe she had always intended it, but eventually she did come back home with me. And once she was there, I never wanted her to leave again.

Oddly, it was as if no time had passed. We didn't speak about the intervening years. No explanations were given. Perhaps we were still too young for them. The present was enough. It was flushed with desire. It enveloped us in its generous heat.

I dream of Madeleine. She is sitting on a swing in the apple orchard. But she isn't a girl. She is Lulu. Her legs arch and beckon. She waves to me and I run towards her, stumble on a root and when I look up again she isn't there. Only the swing creaks a little in the wind. I hear her voice in it and I follow it, up and into the house. My house. My childhood house. The old one with its red brick and wrap-around porch. I climb the steep stairs in search of the voice. My legs have grown shorter and my knees are bare.

Madeleine is in the bed. It is very white and very high off the ground. She stretches her arm out to me and I take it. Her hand is hot and dry and very thin, but larger than mine. I look up at her. Her face has changed. It is soft and pale and distant and the eyes are vast and dark. Not Madeleine, no.

My mother's voice is tender. '*Au revoir, mon Pierre*,' it says.

But I don't want to say goodbye. No. No.

'*Maman*,' I call. '*Maman*.'

I tug at the sheets and scramble and pull myself up onto the bed. As I climb towards my mother the bed tips, up-ends itself so that it is hanging in the air. My mother is hanging in the air, high, high up above me. I don't want to look, but my eyes reel upwards, tugged by the rope round her neck.

'No! No!' I shout. I stretch my hand towards her feet, towards the blue silk of her nightie, but I cannot reach. I cannot reach and my scream won't scream.

Pain swirls round me, clutches at my throat, invades my stomach, coils and heaves through me, crushes. My mother has abandoned me and run off with Death. He wears a doctor's white coat, but beneath it he hides a tail and his eyes are red like the devil's. I retch. The retching won't stop.

Light invades my eyes. Morning. I struggle for a sense of my whereabouts, try to calm the heaving of my stomach, this dry gagging.

It is then I hear the noise.

6

One by one the locks on Madeleine's apartment door click and give.

Who else has access to her keys? A cleaning woman who is oblivious to her death? A lover whose existence I am unaware of?

Fear pricks at my confusion. With an effort at balance, I edge towards the greater shelter of the bathroom.

The intruder is not interested in silence. The slam of the door reverberates through the apartment. It is followed by voices. I listen, but the walls muffle sound.

One of the voices is coming towards me. 'The bedroom must be through here.'

Quickly I run a hand through my hair, tuck my rumpled shirt into bed-creased trousers, try to still my stomach. Eradicate the horror of that dream image of a double loss – Madeleine and my mother, one death reinvoking another.

I force myself into composure. I listen. I recognize that voice.

'Detective Contini! Why didn't you ring the bell?'

My attempt at startled privacy isn't altogether successful.

'What the hell are you doing here?'

His bruiser's face is vivid with irritation and censure. Blatant suspicion follows. 'Heh. You tell me you hardly see Mlle Blais, yet you've got a key to her condo?'

'Mme Tremblay asked me to . . . check on the place.'

He is staring at the disordered bed, the scatter of notebooks. 'You've been going through things, messing everything up. Great. Just fucking great! Not bad enough we've had one of Gagnon's incompetents here, we've got you to deal with as well.' He paces disconsolately, then his gaze settles on me and he guffaws. 'Bad night, eh? Well, sort yourself out, cause we're going to have to run you down to headquarters and get you fingerprinted.'

'Whatever for?'

'Because we're carrying out an investigation here and you've left your pawmarks everywhere, that's what for.' He lifts one of Madeleine's notebooks and flicks the pages. He is still wearing his outdoor gloves and the clumsy carelessness of his gestures makes me want to tear the book from his hands.

'So the great Madeleine Blais kept a journal. Lots of journals by the looks of it. Found anything revealing?' His manner is suddenly conciliatory.

'Not really.'

'Well go and wash the grit out of your eyes and come and tell us what you did find. You've

170

obviously been making your own feeble attempt at detective work.'

I splash cold water on my face. It does nothing to neutralize the haggard eyes that stare at me from walls which are all mirror.

When I come back into the bedroom, Contini is standing there with a woman. They are bending over the open drawer of Madeleine's night table. The woman looks little more than a girl disguised in a mannish striped suit. Her hair is short, a spiky helmet hennaed in an outlandishly playful orange. In contrast, the face beneath it is evenly featured and set in a sternness which gives away nothing. But it is what the woman holds in her transparently gloved hand which makes me take a step backward.

The pistol is small and delicate, like a clockwork toy or a piece of jewellery.

The woman cocks it. 'Loaded,' she says. She removes the bullets and drops the gun unceremoniously into a plastic sack.

'Rousseau, meet my partner, Ginette Lavigne.' He doesn't give me a chance to register my surprise at the pairing. 'Did you know about the gun?'

I shake my head. 'But I told you. Madeleine was scared.'

'Hmmm,' Contini grunts. He is shuffling through the books in the night table. 'I'm not surprised, given what she'd been reading.' He flings a couple of paperbacks towards me and I see the imprint of a True Crime series. 'She talk to you about murder?'

'A bit.'

'What did she say?' Ginette Lavigne asks, a little

171

breathlessly, as if she wants to know for more reasons than one. I have the distinct impression she doesn't like my face.

Suddenly I need to get out of the room, out of the apartment. The air here is too thick to breathe, viscous with Madeleine's fear. I don't want to confront the aphrodisiac nature of that fear. It has no part of the man I am now. No part.

'Look, I could use some coffee,' I mutter. Right now I feel I could mainline it.

'Good idea. Get some for us too. We want you back, remember.' There is the steel of an order beneath Contini's breeziness. 'A double espresso for me. Ginette here prefers cappuccino. With a dash of cinnamon. And a couple of Danish would go down nicely.'

I flee the apartment. Outside it is so cold that the hair in my nostrils freezes over with the first deep breath. An icy wind gusts up the hill from the river. It jars me into wakefulness as I push my way down towards Sherbrooke Street.

There is a coffee shop at the corner of Guy. Not that coffee shops are difficult to find in Montréal. Oblivious to recessions or depressions or political rifts, they flourish across the city and sprout ever-increasing gourmet blends. In this one, the board above the glistening chrome of the counter lists some twenty variations on a theme. I choose the first and the waitress throws me a reassuring smile as she passes me a giant cup of froth. Maybe she can tell I need it.

I go and sit at a shiny corner table and wait for

the jolt the coffee will bring. By the time it comes, I have leapt to my feet again, my eyes and ears glued to the television set which juts from the height of a side wall.

Mme Tremblay confronts me from the screen. She is standing in her living room amidst the pictures of Madeleine. Her hands are tightly clasped in front of her. They betray more emotion than her face or steady voice. She is speaking English. She is saying, 'My granddaughter was not a woman to take her life. Of that I am as certain as I am of the camera in front of me. The police, the press are being blinded by appearances. I will not rest, I will not allow the police to rest, until the truth is out.'

The newscaster's face fills the screen. He says something about the investigation continuing, but I am no longer listening. I pick up Contini's order and race out. At the front door of Madeleine's building I pause. A thought, at once perfidious and tantalizing, has crept up on me. Perhaps it would indeed be better if I disappeared, went off right now to some place wholly untouched by Madeleine's presence. As my brother recommended.

Too late. My hand is already on the bell.

Contini is talking on his mobile phone when I come in. He paces. With his free hand, he picks invisible fragments of lint from his grey jacket. His face does not look friendly.

I take the paper cups and Danish from the bag and place them carefully on the cluttered coffee table. As he tucks the phone into his jacket pocket, I say, 'I just saw Mme Tremblay . . .'

'Ya. I heard. She's putting the heat on.' He sinks into the sofa, carefully edges the cover from his cup and takes a sip, before roaring, 'Ginette. Coffee's here.'

When she comes in, he prods the cup towards her and asks, 'Find any drugs yet?'

She shakes her spiky head.

'What is it with you and Gagnon?' I grumble. 'You're obsessed with drugs. Madeleine didn't . . . well, maybe occasionally, a little coke to get her through a long shoot, but nothing . . .' Contini's pitying look makes me falter.

'OK, OK. Forget that.' He bends towards me, lowers his voice. 'So what do you think? Was Madeleine Blais the kind of woman to take her own life or the kind of woman to be done in?'

'What do you mean "kind of woman"?' I don't like the look on his face, the way the eyes have turned into narrow slits.

He rides over my question. 'Bit of a slut, wasn't she?'

I give him a venomous stare, but he carries right on. 'Maybe she deserved to die. Doesn't make it legal, mind. But some women, they take you by the balls and just wring them, until POW, the man explodes. Heh, maybe they're all a bit like that? What did our Latin master used to say?' He quotes pompously. 'Woman is a temple built upon a sewer. *Templum aedificatum super cloacam.* Tertullian, isn't it?'

'Sounds like pure Continian to me,' Ginette Lavigne mutters. 'Men score. Women are sluts.'

Despite her words, her features are free of insubordination. What challenge there is in her eyes is aimed only at me.

'Got it in one, Ginette.' Contini guffaws. 'You also got one hell of a lot of work to do. So get busy.'

With a smile, Ginette ambles towards the study.

'Talented cop, that one. Meticulous,' Contini confides, loudly enough for Ginette to hear. 'But she's got a little something to learn about men. So what do you say? Ginette, I should tell you, is convinced Madeleine Blais was murdered.'

I have a sudden sense that this whole scene has been laid out as bait. The voice I manage to find in response is astonishingly cool. It is the voice I use with difficult clients. 'Have you had the lab reports yet? They should tell us more than these wild speculations.'

He chuckles. 'Don't like your Madeleine being called a slut, do you?' From his pocket he unearths a pack of du Maurier and offers me one. 'We have actually. Not much help. That's the problem. She was definitely killed by the rope. Whether she put it there, or someone else, we have no immediate way of knowing. Probably she was roughed around a bit before that.' He touches his neck daintily while his shrewd eyes follow my every gesture.

'Suicide? Assisted suicide? Murder? Can't tell yet. But they discovered she'd bedded someone not so very many hours before her death. Trouble is, the sperm on the inside was not the same as the dried bit they found on her coat.' He shrugs. 'It's like I told you.'

I mask my flinch with a cough. 'Anything else?'

'Not much. A black hair; a bit of dark blue woollen fluff beneath a fingernail. You got a blue coat? A blue sweater?'

I gape down at my sleeve. 'You don't really think I . . .'

He lets out a short, sharp laugh, almost a growl. 'I'm a cop. My suspicions are democratic.'

I am about to protest when the phone rings. It is not the phone in his pocket and he leaps up, walks quickly towards the study. I am right behind him.

Ginette Lavigne moves to pick up the phone, but Contini waves her away. He points at the answering machine where the tiny red light is already flashing. Why didn't I notice this last night? Why didn't I listen to Madeleine's messages? The machine was sitting there, right next to the desk, only slightly obscured by the leaf of a ficus.

I hear Madeleine's disembodied voice, warm, light, humorous. First in French, then in English, eliciting messages. My hand trembles. I hide it in my pocket. When the beep comes, Contini leans forward tensely. But there is only silence, followed by a click.

'Damn!' he mumbles.

It occurs to me that perhaps Mme Tremblay is trying to reach me, impatient to hear what I may have found, as troubled by Madeleine's voice as I am. I don't bother to say any of this.

'Have you listened to the other messages?' Contini addresses his partner.

'Gagnon's man listed them. But we need IDs.'

Contini gestures to me. 'Maybe you can help us.' He presses the button and I hear Manou's silvery tones wishing Madeleine a very happy Christmas. The message is repeated by other voices, two unnamed women whom I don't recognize and two men, one of whom identifies himself as Armand.

The final message has nothing to do with Christmas.

A male voice speaking heavily accented French. I can't locate the accent. Greek perhaps, and the French it goes with is French, not Québecois. There is no name. Like some of the others, the caller assumes proximity and recognition.

'Spoke to our producer,' the voice says, then pauses, audibly uncomfortable. 'He's not keen. It's like I told you. Let's talk later. Maybe we can still convince him. And thanks.' The voice swallows. 'Thanks for everything. Ring me.'

I don't like the sound of this last thanks, but I have no time to reflect on it. Contini is quizzing me. I tell him what I know.

'Manou is a friend of Madeleine's in Paris. Armand is the director at the Nouveau Monde. The others I don't know.'

'Not even the last?'

I shake my head.

'This is obviously a machine one can ring into to pick up messages. The last one sounds like a brush off. A part she didn't get? Did she mention anything to you?'

'No.'

177

Contini scratches his head. 'Right, Ginette. Let's run a check on Bell Telephone. Get a list of the numbers Mlle Blais dialled most frequently. And where the hell are the crime scene team? I want to get this place dusted.' He curls his hand into a fist and with the other, cracks his knuckles. It is as if he missed the nuts on my table.

'So what'd you find in here, Rousseau? Anything that'll help us? We could be here for days sifting through all this junk.'

'It's not junk.'

'No, no of course not. Sorry.' He turns a smile of sudden and angelic sweetness on me. 'I forgot myself. Tell me about it.'

Before I can open my mouth, the bell rings. Contini strides towards the answerphone. Moments later a man and a woman come into the apartment. The woman is stocky and pertly pretty and greets us with a 'Hi'. The man has the grey skin of a creature who has rarely seen the open air. They each carry a metal case.

Contini takes them aside without bothering with introductions. 'Concentrate on the kitchen and the bedroom,' I hear him say. 'Prints, any blue woollens, and check the bed.' He ushers them towards the kitchen and lowers his voice, but I can imagine his instructions.

When he comes back to me, he grins like an old friend. 'Where were we?'

'Look, I really should get back to Ste-Anne.'

'You working today?'

'It's not that.' I decide not to lie. 'It's Mme

178

Tremblay. I should look in on her.'

He picks another piece of invisible lint from his jacket before his eyes fix on me again. 'She gave you the keys, right?'

I nod. 'And where did you get yours?'

'Gagnon, via Mlle Blais' coat pocket. It was considerate of her to leave them there for us, since Mme Tremblay wasn't forthcoming. So what did the old lady want?'

'The journals,' I murmur.

'Well, she can't have those. Not if she's so keen on this truth she talks about.'

'She's afraid . . . of the press. You know. There are private things in there. Things that—'

'Wouldn't look good,' he finishes for me with a salacious twist to his lips. 'Well we won't tell if you don't. You report that back to her. Tell her it would be obstructing the law. In fact you can ring her right now and explain you have to take a little trip to HQ. Then pass her over to me.'

He hands me his mobile and I do as he asks.

Mme Tremblay sounds resigned. 'At least they're doing something,' she mutters.

When I pass the receiver over to Contini, he is at his most polite. 'Mme Tremblay? I hope you're feeling just a little better today. Yes. You know that man with the ponytail you were talking about? I'd like to get a photofit done. Do you think you could get someone to drive you up to Montréal? I can arrange for the local constable, perhaps? No? Whatever you say. Yes. At headquarters. With the computer. Perhaps you can come to Mlle Blais' apartment and we'll go together? Yes, we'll still be here.'

He presses a button and beams at me, then glances at his watch. 'You know what, I'll just sort out a few things with HQ and then you and I can leave these people in peace and get ourselves some lunch with our chat. There's a nice little place just off Crescent. My uncle runs it.'

He goes off to have a few words with Ginette in the study. I walk casually towards the kitchen. The woman is brushing silver powder onto every available surface. It floats through the air like talc. With a latex-gloved hand, the man carefully deposits a glass into a plastic sack.

I look away. It comes to me that Madeleine's dying knows even fewer intimacies than her living.

Despite the cold, Sherbrooke Street is busy with lunchtime pedestrians. They walk as quickly as we do. No-one pauses to glance at the antique shops or galleries which crowd this golden mile of the city.

'Through here.' Contini's hand is firm on my shoulder. He leads me down a narrow lane by the side of an antique shop where grey stone gives way to a new internal structure, a small hidden mall, with a restaurant encased in its glass frontage.

He greets everyone in effusive Italian and discusses the menu at length with a white-shirted waiter. He is in his element and relishes it. His eyes flash. He lifts his fingers to his lips and mimes a kiss and orders for both of us with a gourmet's precision. Only then does he lean back in his chair.

'So tell me. What did you find?'

'Not much. A heap of material on the university assassin. Some fan mail. A diary which you'll see. Not much there.' I fill him in best as I can. Even when the tagliarini in clams arrive, he listens intently.

'And the journals?'

'I fell asleep before I got very far,' I manage to say honestly.

'Hmmm.' He stares at me and lets it go.

We talk for a while about the trajectory of Madeleine's career. I give him the names of her agents in Paris and Hollywood, the names of some friends. I even dig out numbers from my address book.

'Lovers?' he prods me.

'We didn't talk about that.'

'No, no. Of course not.'

Over the stewed figs, he shakes his head. 'You know, part of me really thinks the grandmother is barking up the wrong tree. Getting us all to bark. It's just a simple suicide. Not that they're ever simple, I'll give you that. But from the police point of view . . . We're just going to waste a lot of time and taxpayers' money. You think that too, don't you?'

I shrug. I no longer trust my voice. Beneath the casual conviviality, Contini follows my every word and gesture with an acute attention I only want to escape.

By the time we finish our far too leisurely lunch and get back to Madeleine's apartment, Mme Tremblay has arrived.

She hasn't taken her coat off yet. She hovers against the expanse of window and sky like a wounded bird, too stricken to take flight. Ginette Lavigne's vivid colouring bleaches her into frailty.

'You must sit down, Mme Tremblay.' I gesture her towards the sofa. 'Please.'

'No, Pierre, thank you. I have sat for too long.' She looks at me but I notice she isn't looking at anything else. She holds herself tautly rigid, as if she is afraid her eyes will stray. I understand. These objects, this space of Madeleine's are filled with too much emotion. If she allows herself to take them in, to relax for even a second, her hard-won poise will disintegrate.

'Detective,' she greets Contini. 'How long will you need me for?'

'We should be through by five. A little later, perhaps.'

'It's just that I need to tell Michel.'

A figure emerges from the bathroom, his face half-hidden by a sooty beard. Michel Dubois was once one of two hired hands on Mme Tremblay's farm. These days he helps out with odd jobs, occasionally chauffeurs her. He is a taciturn man, at times even surly, who prefers being outdoors. I have rarely heard him utter a full sentence.

Now, he hangs back from us, his inky eyes darting round the room, only to settle on the floor.

'I can take you back to Ste-Anne, Mme Tremblay. It'll be simpler, since I have to come along to HQ as well.'

'Could you, Pierre? That's fine then.' She reaches

into her purse, takes out a few notes and folds them into Michel's hand. 'Eat something before you start back, Michel. And if you've got time, put something out for the dogs when you get back.'

'Ya, you do that, Dubois, and while you're at it keep an extra special eye on the place. You never know who might turn up.' Contini winks at the man with surprising familiarity. He must already have interrogated Michel, who now nods without meeting Contini's eyes.

'Can I just get your opinion on a few things before we head off, Mme Tremblay?' Contini is all politeness. 'Do take off your coat.' He helps her with it, then urges her towards the study.

Curious, I trail behind her. Michel comes too. Maybe he feels he needs to protect her.

The study shrinks with our numbers, becomes too close. Mme Tremblay must feel it, for she waves us away. Or perhaps it is just Michel. We linger by the door.

Ginette Lavigne digs into one of her plastic sacks and pulls out Madeleine's diary. I am glad it is not the pistol.

'Do you know anything about these initials?'

Mme Tremblay looks at the pages Contini holds open for her. Her lips tremble a little as she mumbles a series of 'noes' in response to his pointing finger. And then she exclaims, 'You see! Pick up shawl from T for M. That's Tanya for Mémère, me. My Christmas present. Hand-woven. Beautiful. I opened it last night.' Tears fill her eyes. 'And there's something for Pierre, too. Under the tree. Though

183

it's not noted here. But there are other things. A whole list of presents. Look.'

I hurry to her side and read over her shoulder. In my fraught state I missed the list on the final blank page of the diary. What else have I missed?

'She never intended to die.' Mme Tremblay stares at Contini.

'So you keep telling us. Telling everyone.' His voice suddenly takes on an edge of menace. 'What is it in your granddaughter's journals that you didn't want us to see, Mme Tremblay?'

'What do you mean, detective?'

He shrugs. 'Perhaps there are things in there about you. Maybe your relations with Mlle Blais were not quite so cosy as you make out? You discovered her body, isn't that right?'

Mme Tremblay exhales a long ragged breath. 'Really, detective! What are you suggesting?'

'You're so certain it was murder. Perhaps you know more than you're telling us.'

The coolness in his voice sends a chill through me. Simultaneously I have the feeling I could easily punch that smug face.

'You're being dumb, Contini!' I find myself exclaiming.

He doesn't respond. His eyes bear down on Mme Tremblay.

'What do you know about Mlle Blais' will?' he asks her.

'Her will? This is poppycock, detective. Are you trying to tell me I murdered my granddaughter for her money?'

'It's not an unusual motive.' A smile scuttles across his face and disappears as quickly. 'You will show us Mlle Blais' will.'

'If I had such a thing, I would gladly do so. I said the same thing to Monique and her son last night when they suddenly appeared.' The face she turns towards me is taut with distaste. She brushes a stray hair from her neck. 'Did Madeleine lodge a will with you, Pierre?'

I shake my head.

'You see, detective. There would be a will if Madeleine had intended to die. She was a practical woman.'

But Contini has already changed tack. 'Monique . . . I take it you mean your daughter, Monique Blais – Madeleine's mother. And the son would be . . . ?'

Mme Tremblay is staring mutely at the floor.

'Madeleine's stepbrother?' Contini prods her.

'Marcel Blais,' she replies in a flat tone. 'Apparently he lives in one of those South Shore suburbs now. He alerted Monique to . . .' Her words peter out into breathlessness. 'In any case, Monique came hurtling up to see me.'

'And they're both staying with you in Ste-Anne?'

She looks at him askance, but her voice when it comes is steely. 'No, detective. I told them I wasn't ready to play hostess.'

Contini whispers something I can't hear to Ginette Lavigne, who edges out of the room while Contini, casually polite now, asks, 'Can you help us by naming any of these voices, Mme Tremblay?' He pushes the button on the answering machine.

185

We listen to Madeleine's voice in a silence so hushed it could already be a memorial service.

In the pause before the beep, a clatter of keys dropping to the floor ruptures the stillness. We all turn to look at Michel Dubois. He picks them up with a whispered apology and stands there solemnly, at a loss, his large frame filling the doorway, his eyes focused on his offending fingers.

'*Pauvre Michel*, I know how you cared for her,' Mme Tremblay murmurs. 'Since she was a child. I know.' She squeezes his hand. 'Go now. It will be better.'

Contini flicks on the answering machine again. 'Please listen, madame.'

This time, among the voices, I hear a series of clicks I hadn't registered before. People who hadn't bothered with messages.

Mme Tremblay seems confused. 'I don't know. I think one of the women is Marthe Ducharme. The actress.'

'And the men?'

She shrugs, shakes her head. 'Please, can we leave now?' Her lips are clenched, her face too white. I take her arm and lead her from the room.

She slips into the sofa and hides her face in her hands. After a moment, she looks round her with a dazed expression. 'Has Michel gone then?' she asks.

I survey the room. 'I guess so. I didn't notice.'

'He's taking it very hard. I worry about him. You know he's been with us since he was fifteen. I rescued him when he was expelled from school.'

Her attention strays and then she says, 'Pierre, I

186

think . . . I think . . .' She stops herself and, in a louder voice, calls out, 'Detective Contini!'

Contini emerges from the study. 'Yes. We're going now.'

'It's not that.' She is wringing her hands. 'I think . . . That last message, it could just be the man with the ponytail.'

'Oh?' Contini's eyes light up.

'Yes. I'm not sure. But the accent . . . Maybe.' Her gaze is on her skirt. She smoothes one of its pleats, then looks up at us in visible bewilderment. 'That means he wasn't a hitchhiker. Madeleine knew him.'

Contini sits down and takes Mme Tremblay's hand. He holds it between his own. His tone is warm with concern. 'And you'll agree that message contains bad news. About a part, perhaps?'

Mme Tremblay doesn't answer immediately. Her thoughts flit across her brow and leave their traces in new furrows.

'I know what you're suggesting,' she says at last. 'You think Madeleine got this bad news, decided to take this man down to Ste-Anne with her in order to win him over. Thought she had failed. And took her own life.' She exhales with a moan. 'But she seemed so happy.'

'She was an actress,' Contini says softly. His glance at me is rueful as he echoes my response to him. 'A great actress.'

Mme Tremblay doesn't move.

'We'll find him. I promise you. In a day or two. As soon as we get this photofit done. My men will take it round to all Mlle Blais' theatre friends. Then we'll know. One way or another. The name hasn't by any chance come back to you?'

She shakes her head.

'I think it may begin with an F or a T,' I mutter.

Contini stares at me.

'From the diary,' I explain.

'Right. Let's get over to HQ. Your car's here, I presume?'

I nod.

'You take Lavigne then. She'll direct you. Mme Tremblay, you come with me.'

In the lobby, Contini pauses. 'We should check Mlle Blais' mail. There might be something there.' He strides towards the rows of boxes and after a moment comes back with a small sheaf of envelopes.

The writing on the top one gives me a jolt. I stare at it. I want to tear the envelope from his hands.

'We'll look at these later.' Contini winks at me with something like relish and stuffs the letters in his pocket. 'By the way, Rousseau, did you note those names for me?'

'I'll do it at headquarters.'

Outside the afternoon is already growing dim, but the lights haven't come on yet to brighten the city. Everything looks dirty from the grit beneath our feet to the sooty grey of the sky.

Mme Tremblay's hand is on my arm. 'I'll drive with you, Pierre,' she says with sudden decision.

'Is that all right, detective? We'll follow you. Hold on here while I get my car.'

Contini shrugs, throws me a meaningful look. 'OK, but don't get lost.'

Mme Tremblay is silent as we make our way up the steep hill. Beside us, as a car beeps from behind, I notice a lumbering Chevy, so overlain with grit and dirt its colour has been wiped out. It crawls up the slope at our pace. Only as we turn into the street where I have parked does it shift gear and speed away. Mme Tremblay waves and from the back I recognize Michel Dubois' bulk.

'He worries about me too,' Mme Tremblay murmurs.

We drive east along Sherbrooke, keeping Contini and Lavigne in view. They move slowly, pull over any time they make a light before we do, as if they suspect I might deliberately lose them and slip away.

Mme Tremblay still hasn't spoken. I don't prod her but I wish she would ask what I know she must ask, so that I can report my failure. At last as we turn south, she says, 'Did you get a chance to look at the journals, Pierre?'

I nod. 'But I didn't get very far. I fell asleep. Stupid of me. Contini promises the press won't get hold of them.'

'I've stopped worrying about that,' she snaps.

'He'll give them straight back to you.'

'What if I've been wrong, Pierre?' Her voice fades into baffled misery. 'What if Madeleine did it? To herself. Did I really know her so little?' She buries her face in her hands.

No words which might dislodge her pain come to me.

189

'She wasn't hiding a terrible illness, was she? That's the only thing which might make sense of it. She was terrified of illness. If there were that on top of disappointments with work, perhaps . . .' She shifts in her seat, waits for me to confirm her speculations.

'Madeleine wore so many different faces,' I say at last.

'Yes.' Mme Tremblay's tone is blunt. 'But I thought I knew a great many of them.'

She is silent again. Only when we approach our destination does she speak, in English, now, her voice straining over the words. It takes me a moment to realize she is quoting, though I don't know the source.

'So proud she was to die
It made us all ashamed
That what we cherished, so unknown
To her desire seemed –
So satisfied to go
Where none of us should be
Immediately – that Anguish stooped
Almost to jealousy.

Is that how it is, Pierre?'

I taste her anguish. It is acrid. She envies Madeleine her defiant death.

I cast her an anxious glance. The blue of her veins has grown dark in her taut, mottled hands. I cover them.

'You mustn't even consider it,' I say quietly.

The provincial police headquarters is big and squat and imposing. It dwarfs us as we swing through its doors. Contini, though, swells with its authority. Like some Roman emperor, he waves us along with an imperious hand. Perhaps he would like the lions to finish with us quickly so that he can retire to the sumptuous peace of private quarters.

I am suddenly acutely aware of the resources he has at his disposal. The thought should please me. Instead it fills me with a bewildering anxiety. I watch the elevator swish shut behind Mme Tremblay and wish I could wrench it back open again.

Ginette Lavigne is left in charge of me. Without Contini there, whether to shield her or to cow her, she is coldly officious. She leads me to a windowless room where a uniformed man unceremoniously grasps my hand, tips my fingers into an inkpad, then presses them onto prepared squares on a sheet of paper. First right, then left. Lavigne lurks, watching my every gesture. Maybe this is what causes me inadvertently to move my left hand and smudge the thumbprint. Lavigne tsks. My hand is gripped with steely firmness and we start again. When we are finished, Lavigne briskly orders me to wait for Mme Tremblay in the lobby.

The wait is long, but the momentary anonymity as welcome as an evening breeze after an overheated day.

Uniforms slip in and out of the doors. Voices argue and disappear. A woman in a lab coat taps her foot impatiently then glides into the elevator. A harried-looking man in a frayed jacket asks me for directions and I point him towards a reception desk. Sirens wail.

I decide to shorten the wait by making up the list Contini has asked of me. It shouldn't take long. The younger men I know in Ste-Anne aren't numerous. But I pause over each one, trying to imagine him with Madeleine, pause over each of the priests, too, their features shadowy. I have only managed to jot down a few names when Mme Tremblay reappears.

She is accompanied by a woman with a doughy, humourless face who hands her over to me with lightly veiled relief. It is past five o'clock. She is dreaming of home and a hot bath, but I delay her departure by handing her my list for Contini.

As we climb into the car, Mme Tremblay's words take me by surprise. 'I want to go back to the apartment, Pierre. Drop me there, please.' Her shoulders are rigid, her woollen hat slightly askew.

I hesitate. 'Are you sure?'

'Altogether sure.' Her eyes fix on some distant point beyond the busy streets we crawl through. Beyond Chinatown and its array of steamy restaurants. Beyond Ste-Catherine where the prostitutes and pushers are already gathering for the business of the night.

'I need to reacquaint myself with my grand-daughter,' she eventually offers in taut explanation. 'And I don't want Monique and that hulking Marcel of hers hanging over me. You can stay, too, if you like, Pierre.'

She doesn't mean it. Nor do I want to. As I drop her by the door of Madeleine's apartment and hand her the keys, I suddenly realize that all I want to do now is to be away . . . from everyone. I can't think straight any more. I feel buffeted by winds from opposing directions. They push and pull and batter at me. And at the Madeleine who inhabits me. So that we are both left in tatters. I need to escape to reconstitute the two of us, singly and together.

I drive. I retrace yesterday's route. At some point I notice that I have gone past the exit for Ste-Anne. Where am I heading? Heavy-metal rhythms blare from the radio, the hard-rock sounds of Voîvod, followed by another Québec group, Vilain Pinguoin. I switch off and listen to silence.

The hills of the Laurentian range rise like ancient slumbering dinosaurs out of the darkness. I race past the lights of the ski resorts which twinkle from their haunches. Mont-Gabriel, Ste-Adèle, Val-Morin, Val-David, Ste-Agathe des Monts, I know these slopes and the myriad lakes which nestle between them as well as I know my back yard.

At St-Jovite, I find myself turning off the main road. I realize where I am heading now. I drive past the cluster of small chalets and inns which make up the village of Mont Tremblant, the mountain which according to Indian myth once shuddered and trembled. Tonight, the only movement on its slopes is that of the evening skiers, as bright as exotic beetles in their luminous gear. My melancholy rejects their hurtling brightness.

I cut across the base of the hill towards the small lake to its east, Lac Supérieur. There are no lights here, only the shimmer of ice through trees. One-fifth of Québec's terrain, I remind myself, is now frozen water. The frozen water of vast rivers and 400,000 lakes, vestiges of a glacial age.

Heading south, I drive slowly for about a mile and pull over where a tree bears an old weathered board marked 'Privé'.

After the heat of the car, the cold claws at my face with icy fingers. It rouses me as painfully as the loud cracking of the trees in the woods. Like gunfire leaping from stillness. The sounds cover the crunch of my boots. I walk carefully down the rutted drive. Its state tells me no-one is here, but I tread slowly until the continuing darkness confirms my solitude.

In the pale moonlight, the house with its steep roof looms out at me like a yacht from the mist. I walk round its expanse and meet my own tracks coming back at me in the untouched snow. The windows are shuttered. As stealthily as a thief, I try the door. Everything is solidly locked and bolted. I didn't really expect otherwise. I traipse down to the edge of the lake. On the opposite shore, the lights of the village flicker and dance.

This is the house Madeleine and I came to on our wedding night. We weren't alone. My friend Guillaume, whose father's house it was, and her closest friend, Colette, were with us. They had served as witnesses at our utterly unemphatic wedding ceremony in Montréal. Madeleine wore white, one of those flowing Indian cotton dresses which looked like a nightie and turned her into the slightly wistful flower child she had never been. Mme Tremblay was the single other guest. We dropped her off at Ste-Anne, drank and ate far too much at her urging and then carried on north. To arrive here.

It was summer. The sky over the mountain at our backs still glowed faintly pink and tinged the fluttering surface of the lake. In its depths, the trees scattered in the wind, then slowly reassembled themselves. We were laughing, playful. We dipped our toes in the eternal chill of the water and like children, screamed and scampered away, only to try another and then another inch of skin.

Madeleine was the first to plunge. She let out a wild hoot and thrashed towards the dock, her feet kicking out more foam than an outboard motor. I was right behind her. Groaning and laughing, we heaved ourselves onto warmed planks and rolled into each other's arms.

She gazed up at me for a moment, her eyes round and serious. 'Man and wife,' she murmured, and then intoned it again in the ringing cadences of the marriage ceremony. We erupted into giggles. They merged into a kiss, the first real kiss of our married state.

In the sudden racing of my pulse, I can still taste that heady mixture of passion and promise. The potent brew of youth. In the early seventies, the air itself was intoxicated with it. It was a good time to be young.

The wedding took place a mere three weeks after our breathless film chase down the Côte-des-Neiges. It was only a little over a year since I had seen Madeleine as Lulu. The months in between had raced past, their pace as tempestuous as Madeleine herself. We loved hard and we worked hard. Each day was an adventure brimming with the newness of discovery.

Sometimes, I had the uncanny feeling that I wanted to step out of this rush of time so as to list and hoard the sensations Madeleine stirred in me – not only when our bodies were entwined, but at breakfast when she might cup a warm egg in her hand and stare down at it in silent wonder. Or when I saw her coming towards me, her walk altogether different from the one she had left me with, a mincing gait or a mannish stride, an unconscious rehearsal for whatever part it was she was brooding over. Or when she stopped me in mid-sentence, her fingers on my arm, her face grave, and asked me to take it a little more slowly, to explain exactly what I meant. Yes, I wanted to store each and every one of those moments.

Perhaps, somewhere, I already knew that my life with Madeleine would find its permanent home in memory.

We didn't live together that first year before our wedding. Madeleine shared an apartment, just off the Rue St-Denis, with Colette and I had my own place in Outremont, a few streets north of the university. She was in her final year at the theatre school, a year punctuated by performances with the troupe that had put on *Lulu*. She also had a sporadic part-time job as a waitress. Her clothes-money job, she called it. I was working at *Le Devoir*. But we would see each other three or four times a week, sometimes more. In this, like everything else, Madeleine was unpredictable.

I loved her impulsiveness. It took me out of myself. I loved the way she would say she couldn't see me the following day and then suddenly turn up late after a performance. Looking a little forlorn, she would stand at the door and throw her arms around me and whisper that we must be good, as quiet as two exhausted kittens – sleep the night through so that we could be blissfully fresh for work.

Or she would phone me at the office and ask whether I fancied a late night drive. We would end up at some auberge in the mountains or in Quebec City, alone in deserted night-time streets which had grown glistening ice sculptures amidst which we danced like butterflies released from the cocoon of the overheated car.

If the pressure of a deadline prevented my frolicking, she would curl up in the sofa behind me with a book or a text to be learned. For all her mercurial energy, Madeleine knew how to be quiet, so quiet that sometimes I only remembered her presence when I rose from my desk.

That Christmas, Madeleine played a part which demanded quiet of her. It was a role diametrically opposed to her Lulu and I was awed by her ability

197

to find its dimensions within herself. She appeared as Teresa of Avila, the Spanish nun who survived the torments of temptation and the Inquisition to accede to sainthood. Black-gowned, wimpled, her scrubbed face as pure and serene as the most godly of novices, Madeleine floated across the stage listening to the conflicting voices which raged about her, watching a war enacted by shadowy shapes and lights.

Needless to say, the drama was hardly a conventional exposition of Saint Teresa's life. The text made of her an exemplum of a woman hounded by hostile, hidebound priests for the heresy of speaking directly to God, for speaking, too, in her own voice. She was a prototypical feminist.

When Madeleine rose mysteriously above the stage to levitate, the sweet pain of her rapture made me think achingly of our love-making. I longed to bring that ecstatic expression to her face in the privacy of our twosome.

I was able to do so only twice.

The first time was right here on our wedding night when we lay on the rustling ground beneath a sky alight with stars.

The second time it was already too late.

7

I don't want to go home. Something awaits me there that I am not ready to confront. Something vital which crackles with temptation and dread. The electricity in the crisp, cold air alerts me to its presence.

I head back to the car and drive in no particular direction. Escaping is one of the things I do best. Like an alcoholic, I know how to disappear, from myself as well, and forget that I have done so. It's a useful art, though tonight its practice eludes me. Images of Madeleine haunt me as assiduously as troubled ghosts and force me into myself. She won't leave me in peace. But she isn't there.

The road in front of me wavers and grows misty. I rub my eyes. They are wet. A sense of loss lashes through me threatening my hold on the steering wheel. I press my foot savagely down on the gas. I could careen now into a darkness without end. The world without Madeleine blurs into indistinctness. It holds as little interest for me as the fleeting shadows which bank the road.

A swirl of lights flashes in the distance, blue and red and green. As I draw closer, I see that they illuminate a thick, dusky pine. The words 'Auberge Maribou' come into focus. Without thinking, I brake and skid into the drive.

There is no-one behind the polished teak reception desk, but from beyond a curtained door I hear voices and laughter. Soft, cadenced music which has none of the piping blandness of muzak emerges from some invisible point. A sign beside an old cowbell instructs me to 'Ring this' for attention. I do as I am told.

The resulting clatter would be enough to wake the dead. It produces a sturdy, corduroy-jacketed man with greying temples and the startling good looks of an Italian film actor.

'*Bonsoir*,' he greets me with a softly intent gaze.

I ask him if he has a free room.

He shakes his sleek head a little mournfully. '*C'est plein*. If you'd like some food, though . . .' He points towards the door from which he has emerged.

'I'd better carry on,' I say. Yet I hesitate, unwilling to leave the warmth of the room or perhaps the reassuring solidity of his presence.

'Wait.' He strides through the door and returns moments later. '*C'est fait*,' he announces with a diffident smile. 'The attic room. We'll have it ready in fifteen minutes.'

He slides a register towards me. As I scrawl my name, I can feel his eyes on me.

'Pierre Rousseau.' He barely glances at my

signature as he says it. 'I thought so. But I wasn't sure.' He holds out his hand. 'Giorgio Napolitano. You don't remember? It's the collar.' He traces a semicircle round his neck with a stubby index finger and laughs ruefully.

Suddenly I see a darkly beautiful young man in casual black trousers and sweater, a dog collar just visible at his neck. He is at once passionate and shy. An Italian lilt to his voice, he is saying to a group of us, 'The trouble with you Québecois is that for too long you were a servile race. You trusted in the revenge of the cradle. Power through numbers, through population growth. Good Catholic tactics. Our fault. We priests. And it just wasn't good enough. Equality has to be won by other means.'

Père Giorgio. Fresh from Italy and as radical as they came, even though he was working as secretary to the bishop. Madeleine introduced us. Her theatre troupe were consulting him for their Saint Teresa of Avila project. And despite the conjuncture of our politics, I wasn't altogether sure I liked him.

But now I return his firm handshake. 'So you left the priesthood?'

'Not so long after we met.' He grins, as if the act still has the power to astonish him. 'In Bolivia. My posting after Montréal. Then I got married. I was never too sure whether politics were at the root of my defection or women.' He seems to be about to say something more, but changes his mind and instead asks me to join him for a drink.

Through the curtained door, there is a small,

well-appointed restaurant. Green and white chequered cloths cover the tables. Sprigs of holly decorate grainy timbers. Fat white candles flicker and glow and cast dancing shadows. Diners sip brandy from large tumblers. They look sleepy and satisfied, like well-fed cats.

'Would you like to eat something? It's pot-au-feu night, so there's always plenty. And Paloma is a wonderful cook.'

In Giorgio's expression I see myself as a lone famished wolf who needs to be placated if he is not to disturb the order of things. To please him, I acquiesce. He places me at a table near the fireplace and disappears into the kitchen, only to re-emerge a moment later with a bottle of red wine and two glasses. He pours and sits down opposite me. His scrutiny is slow and steady.

'So, how are things with you?' he asks at last. 'I used to read your articles, but no more . . .'

'No. I've gone back to my original profession. Notary. In Ste-Anne.'

'Oh yes.' He pauses. I can feel the name struggling to his lips before he pronounces it. 'Madeleine mentioned that I think.' Our eyes meet. 'Yes, I know about her death. Of course, I know.'

He rubs his temple, as if to eradicate a sudden pain. 'The world will be poorer without her.'

I swallow a mouthful of wine. I cannot think of anything to say.

He tilts his chair backwards and stares towards the darkened windows. 'I've thought about her a great deal since I read about her death. You know, she was the first woman who ever tempted me. Really tempted me. Perhaps it was because of her . . .' He traces a semicircle round his neck with the backs of his fingers, and I have a sense of that stiff collar still there, still chafing.

Madeleine's words float towards me, playful, flirtatious, but the discomfort I felt then is as acute as if someone were, even now, standing next to me and grating a serrated knife against the base of a saucepan.

'It's a waste,' she says to me with a laugh. 'Such a waste. This beautiful man trapped in celibacy. If it weren't for you, I think I'd make a concerted effort to woo him into life.'

I stare at Giorgio Napolitano. He is still rubbing his phantom collar. Perhaps Madeleine did make her effort. Or maybe she didn't need to.

A slim, trousered woman with the unmoving face and matt skin of a *métis* deposits a shiny copper pot on the table, spoons meat and carrots and potatoes and leeks and turnips onto my plate and disappears into the kitchen. Giorgio doesn't seem to notice her. He is leaning towards me. I have the odd feeling that the world has grown topsy-turvy and I am about to hear a priest's confession.

'Madeleine always made me feel she was living at a pace that was twice as fast as the rest of us,' he says in a hushed voice. 'At an intensity, too. As if she always knew she had to double up on experience. Pack twice as much into the time allotted her. As if she knew she would die young. There are people like that. You know what I mean?'

I nod.

'So that when I read about her death, though I was shocked, though I mourned, still am, nonetheless I had this blasphemous feeling that perhaps it was right. That she had had the best life has to offer, was replete. And now it was enough.'

'A handy consolation,' I mumble.

He chuckles in self-deprecation. 'Yes, that too. I'm not sure I mean it in the small hours of the night. Then I think . . .' He pauses, muses over his wine. 'Then I remember how vulnerable she was when I first met her. Had so little skin and so much imagination. She so desperately needed looking after.'

This portrait startles me. I do not recognize it. Another of Madeleine's many faces, this one created specifically to meet the needs of the young priest Giorgio was. It was not a face I saw, until the end perhaps.

'So, in the small hours it occurs to me that maybe, if only one of us – you, me, someone else – had been brave enough to marry her then . . .' He lets the words hang and I sense that for him marriage is still resonant with sacral meanings.

I don't know I am going to say it until the words are out of my mouth. 'I did marry her, Giorgio. Didn't she tell you?'

His face is all embarrassed astonishment. 'Forgive me. I had no idea.'

'No. Yet it wasn't a secret. Simply a failure. And long ago.'

I can feel the questions rushing through him. But

unlike him, I am not ready for a confession. Even with a former priest. I deflect him.

'Had you seen Madeleine recently?'

'Some ten days ago last. She drove down here to visit regularly. When I recognized you, I thought maybe she'd mentioned this place to you. And that's why you were here. She told me we needed publicity. Others have come on her recommendation.'

I try to remember whether Madeleine did indeed say something. Memory eludes me. Madeleine had so many acquaintances, was so profligate with her gossip and her favours. As a survival tactic, I had half trained myself to let her words flutter over me and leave as little trace as a butterfly's wings. Yet, perhaps, subliminally I took the information in.

'So you were in touch over all these years,' I say.

'No, not all. But when I was in Bolivia, my second year I suppose it was, I saw her. In a movie. It was so bizarre. It was as if she was right there beside me and I could speak to her.' He gives me a whimsical look. I recognize the emotion it hides. Giorgio and I wear the same mark on our brow. Brothers linked by Madeleine.

'Yes,' I murmur.

'I wrote to her. Wrote to the studio, that is. In France. It took some time, but eventually, miraculously, she answered.'

I want to ask him what she said. I want to know the details of their correspondence. Instead I prod at a turnip. 'Delicious.'

'Hmmm. We kept in touch after that, sporadically. And when I came back to Montréal, she paid us a visit. It was Sylvia she fell in love with, I think.'

'Your wife?'

'No, no, not my wife. Nor me.' He chuckles again. 'Our daughter. Sylvia.' Tenderness illuminates his face. 'I don't blame her. Sylvia was, is, eminently lovable. Madeleine sent her presents. Every year. At Christmas. On her birthday. And when it was possible, she came to visit. It made me think she was hungry for a child.'

I weigh the thought and wonder at its density. 'She never mentioned a child to me. Never.' It comes out with a disgruntled harshness and Giorgio casts me an uneasy look.

'No, well . . . Were you close in these last years?'

'We were friends.'

Perhaps I don't say it with the right intonation, for silence falls between us, thick with the tangled creepers of memory and melancholy and yes, suspicion. When I can peer through them, I notice that the other guests have left and we are alone in the room. Giorgio's mood, too, has shifted. I lean towards him and he arches back abruptly as if his thoughts had coalesced into mistrust.

I search for an ordinary voice. 'How was Madeleine when you last saw her?'

He doesn't answer for a moment. He seems to be choosing his words, gauging my reliability. 'Not at her best,' he says at last. He stands. 'I had better let you get some sleep. Your room's at the very top of the stairs. It'll be open.'

I hold him back. 'Did she say anything . . . anything that led you to suspect . . .' My words trail away.

His eyes glint in the candlelight. Shadows leap across his face. I have the sudden sense that Madeleine has told him something about me, confided too much, even if she omitted to mention our marriage. 'Did she?'

My hand is tight on his sleeve. I only notice it when he shrugs me off with surprising force. I fold my vagrant hands into stillness and insist again, 'Did she?'

Giorgio rubs his arm, considers me. 'Not much more than the papers reported. Her distress at the assassinations.' He hesitates and in that hesitation I know that he is hiding something. Mme Tremblay's words about an Italian or a Spaniard, a foreign accent, bound into my mind. Sandro or Giorgio. Why not? A desperate affair with a renegade priest. No. My imagination is running away with me. Nonetheless, I am about to press him when he announces with a cold clarity, 'She was thinking of hiring a bodyguard.'

'A bodyguard!'

'Yes. To keep the more invasive fans at bay. You know what it's like these days. The boundaries have gone. The boundaries between private and public. People just don't recognize them. It used to be so clear. There used to be one's mind, one's nearest and dearest, the confessional for the intimate, and the rest was a separate sphere. Public. Formal. Now it's all mixed up.'

He studies me with unnerving intentness and when I don't answer, he elaborates. 'People see someone like Madeleine on the screen, see her in their own living rooms acting out intimacies, and they get confused. They think they know her, can phone her, intrude on her. No boundaries.'

'Yes.' I gulp the last of my wine.

'In any case, Madeleine was thinking of getting a bodyguard. Apparently her stepbrother had been trying to convince her for months that she needed one, had offered himself for the job since he was out of one. Had been pestering her.' He shifts uneasily, starts to place glasses and plates onto a tray. 'Madeleine told me he made her feel creepy. She didn't like him and she was wondering whether she might hire someone else without getting him too worked up. She couldn't make up her mind.' He frowns, gives me an edgy look. 'I should have persuaded her, instead of joking that she wasn't her stepbrother's keeper.'

With an air of embarrassed apology, he adds, 'Madeleine liked it when I made unpriestly jokes. But we really should go up. Have you got a bag?'

I shake my head. 'I stopped on impulse,' I offer as explanation.

Giorgio's eyes are suddenly moist. 'Like Madeleine.'

The room is small and sloping with a scrubbed-pine ceiling which dips right down to the narrow bed. A child's room. I open the window to the stars, gaze at the brushy outlines of the firs and take a deep scented breath. Somewhere an owl hoots.

I think over the things Giorgio has said and

wonder about what he has omitted. The fact that Madeleine failed to tell him that we were married comes back to plague me and I chase it away. After all, outside our closest circle, not so very many people were aware of it, even way back then. Shortly after the wedding, Guillaume moved to Chicoutimi and Colette went home to Quebec City. And Madeleine and I left for France. Perhaps, if we hadn't gone, everything would have been different.

The theatre troupe had been invited to the Avignon Festival. Madeleine was as thrilled as if a beaming Santa had appeared in her room with a bagful of lavish toys. She wanted me to come along. She wanted me to give her courage for what she imagined as an exacting and sophisticated public. It would also be our honeymoon – though when I initially arranged to take my holiday to coincide with the festival, the notion of marriage hadn't yet occurred.

We set off before the others in order to spend a few days alone in Paris. It was my first trip abroad and I was as excited as Madeleine. France, after all, was my mythical home – home of the language I spoke, of the literature and ideas I had imbibed.

I bought a pile of guides and scoured the Plan de Paris. I read *Le Monde* and *Le Figaro* even more assiduously than usual for months beforehand, as well as any number of Paris magazines and journals, so that I became as familiar with the disputes in the Chambre des Deputés and President Pompidou's utterances as I was with the political scene at home.

We arrived in Paris on 30 June 1973. The airport bus deposited us at the Invalides. We left our cases and walked. For three days, we did little more than walk. Arm in arm under a deep blue sky limpid with fluffy clouds, we drank in the delights of the city. For some inexplicable reason, neither books nor films nor Madeleine's enthusiasm had quite prepared me for the beauties of Paris. Everything astonished me – the curling sweep of the river and the changing vistas each and every bridge provided; the clustered zinc roofs; the bustle of the streets with their dance of flirtatious glances; the theatre of the cafés where we were both spectators and spectacle.

The rest of the world disappeared. There was only the miracle of Paris with Madeleine: the tiny fifth-floor room of that hotel in the cinquième from which, if we craned our necks, we could see a streak of river and the spires of Notre Dame; the breakfast tray poised between us on the bed – flaky croissant and crisply fresh baguette and large bowls of café au lait, consumed so greedily that they seemed to augment our appetite for each other; the forays into boutiques where we pretended to be rich tourists and Madeleine paraded frisky dresses and serious suits and exotic hats before my supposedly discerning eyes.

On the fourth day, we took a train to Avignon. Our hands clasped, we watched the French countryside unfold before us like a series of ever-changing tableaux, their pigments deepening as we moved south.

'Happy?' Madeleine asked, curling into me.

'Blissful.'

'So you won't be bored when I have to abandon you for work?'

It hadn't occurred to me in those terms and I bristled a little. 'How could I be bored in the midst of all this? And I have my articles to do, remember? I'll be scurrying to performances.'

'Ours as well, I hope.'

'Yours first of all.'

I had contracted with my paper to do a series of letters from the festival. My initial thought had been that this would help to cover expenses. In the event, it helped to cover other things as well. From the moment we walked through the walls of the old city and found our hotel, Madeleine was immersed with her troupe. They were opening in two days' time and, since they worked on a near co-operative basis, there was everything to do – check out the theatre, make sure all the props for both shows had arrived safely, do a run through in the new space, make some time for publicity and interviews.

I didn't like to be a hanger-on, so I kept myself busy. I read through the sheaves of material the festival office presented me with and did some necessary boning up. Cultural journalism was not my usual beat. I noted press conferences and performers and directors available for interview. I made appointments and scoured the city and attended events, as many as three a day. I learned how to write in the thronging cafés on the Place de l'Horloge. Our airless room was too small for any activity which didn't take place on the bed. Apart

from the theatre, that was the only place I saw
Madeleine. I didn't mind. Every day was an
adventure.

The reviews were as ecstatic as Madeleine herself.
They talked of a new discovery from their plucky
sister province. They raved over the daring
approach of the troupe, subtleties of interpretation
none of us had ever properly considered. Madeleine
was fêted and grew more beautiful with each
deserved compliment. Both shows were sold out.

On the last night of *Lulu*, she tumbled into bed
with a euphoric smile on her face.

'Look.' She flourished a card towards me.

I read a name I didn't recognize. 'Who is it?'

'He's a producer. He's produced Chabrol, a host
of others. And we're invited to a party. Next week.
At his house. About forty minutes from here. In the
country. He'll send a car.'

'We?'

'Yes, we.' She tickled me. 'I told him about you.'

'And?'

'And . . .' She romped and bounced on the bed,
once again the little girl from Ste-Anne. 'He says
there might just be a part for me in his new film.'

I can honestly say that at that moment, I was as
happy as Madeleine. The magical word 'film' –
uttered not by a provincial like ourselves, but by
someone resonantly called a producer – catapulted
us into a world that was far bigger and richer than
even our imaginations had dared to draw. The
colours in it were at once brighter and more subtle.
The voices had more gradations of timbre and

texture. The fragrances were more intense. We were no longer bound by the mundane limits of home. Suddenly our domain had become the mythical arena of the movies, boundless and varied, grand in action and heroic with excess.

That night we made enchanted love under a canopy of our own stars – Godard and Truffaut and Vadim and Fellini and Hitchcock. Anouk Aimée, Jeanne Moreau, Brigitte Bardot, Belmondo, Brando, Taylor and Beatty. On and on, we invoked our constellations until, exhausted, we slipped into triumphant sleep.

On Tuesday evening, a Rolls-Royce of creamy vastness awaited us at the door of the theatre. We grinned at each other and like two practised cons sashayed towards its open door and leaned with pretended languor into the smell of leather. We drove under a star-encrusted sky through a mysterious landscape of cypress and entangled vines. When we stopped we thought we might already have arrived on a film set.

Set half-way up a promontory, the burnished-ochre walls of the house glowed softly in the night. Voices drifted from the illuminated paths of the sculpture-studded gardens, mingled with the sound of water plashing into fountains. Vast urns of geraniums and pansies and lavender scented the air.

We walked silently towards an elevated terrace where people lounged and clustered. At the base of a steep set of stone steps, we paused in momentary trepidation. Madeleine squeezed my hand. Then, taking a deep breath, she walked up ahead of me, her gait deceptively relaxed, fluid. She was wearing a brief white slip of a dress which set off the perfection of her tawny legs, the grace of neck and shoulders. As she stepped into the light of the gathering, I watched her as if on a stage – watched the swing of her hair over her shoulders, the shy, sensual flicker of a smile, the outstretched hand which found its way instead to the arm of a thickset man who bent to kiss her. An anxiety I couldn't give a name to tugged at my entrails. I leapt up the stairs two at a time.

Madeleine introduced me to Roland Martineau, who surveyed me from lazy, hooded eyes, as if I were rather smaller than him, though in fact I towered above him. We exchanged a few words. A glass of champagne found its way into my hand. Gestures were made in the direction of a buffet table. And then with smooth urbanity and without my having quite noticed that it had happened, I was effectively handed over to two women who lazed in wicker bath chairs at the far corner of the terrace.

Natalie Barret and Micheline Renault were both jet-haired and doe-eyed and as elegant as fashion plates. Their bracelets jangled over bronzed, bare arms as they spoke. Chains of looped gold swayed with their gestures. They drew me out and in with cool charm.

But at first I didn't pay much attention to our conversation. I watched Martineau. He was showing Madeleine off, introducing her here, there, and everywhere. I could feel him gauging her value in people's responses. I saw Madeleine throw her head back and laugh her rippling laugh. Her eyes sparkled. Her skin glowed in the mellow light. There was a quality about her which wasn't only beauty. It drew the gaze and held it.

'Yes, she's not bad, your compatriot.' Natalie must have been reading my mind. 'I think our little Napoléon may indeed have made a find this time.' It was said humorously, without malice.

'You work in the movies?'

'I run a casting agency. And Micheline works for Gaumont. Script department.'

'Are you interested in film?' Micheline asks.

'Of course. But only as a spectator.'

'The industry's very small in Québec,' Natalie offers, as if that were the only conceivable reason.

We begin to talk about Québec and I begin to feel increasingly patronized, as if I inhabited some remote, underpopulated terrain in the vicinity of the North Pole where igloos were the main form of architecture and trapping the primary activity. Perversely, as we move towards the buffet, I slip into slang and they titter over my locutions, point out the English and wholly unFrench structure of my sentences, the archaic usages.

They introduce me to some friends, make me speak for them and soon I am at the centre of a linguistic sideshow, amusing the natives. Although I have partly brought it on myself, this makes me angry. I wonder why I have spent so much of my adult life making a case for the French language, struggling for its pre-eminence, when our cousins across the Atlantic can only snigger when I open my mouth.

My third glass of champagne finished, I have the irresistible desire to be unpardonably rude. Like some country yokel, I point at the cheese platter and ask in my best *joual* why there is a smell of shit coming from the plate: '*Pourquoi c'a pue comme d'la sacré merde?*'

The faces round me beam with unalloyed contempt, glad of this confirmation of a stupidity they had altogether expected from a backward colonial. My fists, I notice, are clenched.

Suddenly Madeleine is at my side, her hand on mine.

'There's a wonderful pool,' she says. 'And a closetful of bathing suits. Shall we have a dip?' She smiles her ravishing smile. She speaks her unaccented Parisian French.

Natalie stares at her. 'So you're not from Québec?'

'Oh yes, just like Pierre. We're neighbours.'

Madeleine tugs at my arm and we walk beyond the crowded terrace, down a fir-banked path. It abuts on a glistening pool of pale green. In the soft breeze, the water laps and sparkles like a bed of illuminated crystals.

To the side there is a small white cabin. Madeleine pulls me inside. She gives me a teasing smile and plants a soft kiss on my cheek. In less than a moment, she stands naked before me. My blood races. I reach to embrace her, to touch the soft golden thatch which suddenly seems to me to hide the centre of the universe. But she eludes me. With a pout, she slips on a white bikini bottom, edges her

216

breasts into a top which might as well not be there. And then she is gone.

I follow more slowly, find a pair of black trunks on a hook and lumber out of my cream suit. I hang it up carefully. It is the only one I have brought with me. My head feels a little fuddled with the champagne. I tuck my socks into the jacket pocket and when I hear voices approach, hide my underwear and hastily don the trunks.

I come out just in time to see Madeleine perform a perfect dive. Her body arcs and cuts into the water, disappears into froth, only to re-emerge a few steps from me. Her head is as sleek as a seal's. She waves me in and I plunge. We swim a few lengths side by side and only when I resurface at the far end of the pool do I notice the man stretched on the deckchair. His arm behind his head, he is staring at Madeleine with a dark, silent intentness. His absorption makes me realize he has been there for some time.

From the way Madeleine shakes out her hair, I sense that this whole spectacle has been enacted for his eyes. Not that she looks at him. She pretends obliviousness to his presence, even as she hoists herself gracefully from the pool and sets out for a second dive.

When she is back in the water, I put my arms proprietarily around her. I kiss her. She kisses me back, coyly, playfully. I don't know how I know this is part of the game. Maybe my skin tells me.

This time when Madeleine emerges from the pool ahead of me, the man comes towards her. He has a hawk nose and mobile lips which are curled now in an ironic smile. In his hands, he carries a large striped beach towel. He wraps it slowly round Madeleine, whispers something I can't make out in her ear and walks away. His movements are brisk, spry, in contradiction to his earlier concentration.

Madeleine stands there, looking into the middle distance. There is a serene but enigmatic smile on her lips. When I take her hand, she shivers, then starts to run past the pool into the darkness of a leafy copse. Under its cloak, she topples breathlessly to the ground and pulls me after her.

'Now,' she murmurs. She licks the moisture from my face, arches against my weight. 'Now, neighbour.' She laughs.

I have the odd sensation that somewhere those intent eyes are still watching, perched in a tree perhaps, or behind a shrub, or perhaps simply there, hidden within Madeleine's own tawny gaze or my darker one.

Madeleine's skin is cool and hot at once. She shudders beneath me. In the pleasure of that, I lose both those eyes and myself.

Cold air gusts through the small attic window and chills my skin. I am lying naked on top of the narrow bed and staring up at the knots in the sloping pine ceiling. I don't remember having got undressed. I don't remember lying down here. I don't remember the roughness of the woollen blankets beneath my back. How many other things are there about my life that I don't remember as I tune into Madeleine?

With a shiver, I get up to close the window, secure the double pane, and crawl beneath starched sheets. To console myself, I imagine Mme Tremblay lying in Madeleine's bed and conjuring her up in exactly the way I am doing, though her Madeleine will be different from mine. For a moment those differences engross me. Where I see a playing with fire, Mme Tremblay will see dedication. Where I see an inability to distinguish between work and life, Mme Tremblay will see a genuine actor's temperament. She is not wrong. Neither am I. Truth, where Madeleine is concerned, is never a simple business. Tangled in the thickets of mourning, we both need to constitute Madeleine in our own way, so as to eradicate that rope around her neck.

So as to make sense of it.

It is the thought that there might not be any sense which makes me plunge into the past. If I lie very still and don't force the pace, don't allow future knowledge to contaminate prior experience, the full sweetness of our early life together is still there within me, like a flower untrammelled by later storms.

Yet the work of memory is not easy for me. Men in love are always tainted with the ridiculous. More absurd than heroic. The abasement, the blurring of critical faculties, the sense that our equilibrium is in thrall to another though we can hardly explain what it is that constitutes the loved one's uniqueness, what singles her out as the sole repository of our happiness – all of this unmans us. We become blind, snuffling infants, searching for the breast.

There is a searing contradiction here. Women want us to be manly and they want our passion. Yet the second desire attained destroys all the characteristics of the first. Can a woman still love the abject person who is the man in love?

The only male passion in our culture which is heroic is Christ's. And he too is feminized, passive in his suffering. Or infantilized, a child calling on an absent parent.

Throughout my lifelong passion for Madeleine we struggled with these things. Sometimes I thought she preferred me feminized, loved me as a woman. Homosexual love, it occurred to me, does not have to be tied to gender.

Sometimes I knew she hated me and I made myself withdraw, shored myself up, made myself hard with defences, indifferent and manly and desirable.

Sometimes I hated her, too, for the abyss she thrust me into, though I must have been half in love with that easeful death.

But I don't want to think of that now. I don't want to run ahead of myself. I am still on that first journey to France. It is early days.

Madeleine's Napoleonic producer offered us a room at his villa for what remained of the night. The next morning, Natalie Barret announced she would be driving us back to Avignon. She had good news to convey to Madeleine.

I listened to the good news from the back seat of

the car as Natalie zipped carelessly round bends. I learned that the man with the brisk pace and intent eyes was the director of the film Martineau was producing. I learned that late the previous night he had signalled an interest in Madeleine. Natalie's agency would now take Madeleine onto their lists. They would arrange for a screen test, for a necessary series of photographs. Madeleine was a fortunate young woman.

Madeleine sits very still as if the bright southern sun has lulled her into a half-sleep. She doesn't let out the whoop of elation I expect.

At last, she runs a hand through her hair and says coolly that she will consider Natalie's proposal. She would like to do the screen test, of course. But it would have to be arranged quickly. She has a commitment to a play in Montréal on her return. So the timing of the film, too, would have to be right. And she needs to know a little more about the part. Martineau has been vague.

Natalie throws her a curious glance, taps a Gauloise out for herself and passes the pack round to us. We drive in silence for a few kilometres and then she starts to talk about her agency, about the famous clients she handles.

Madeleine asks her sweetly whether she has a sister agency in Hollywood. We listen to a slightly obfuscating answer. By the time we reach the centre of Avignon, Natalie is vigorously promising Madeleine any number of parts, telling her she is certain the screen test can be arranged for the day after tomorrow.

'You can leave a message for me at the theatre.' Madeleine gives her a lukewarm smile as we wave goodbye.

I find myself chuckling. 'Yesterday, I thought you were over the moon about this film.'

Madeleine beams, drags me towards a café on the Place de l'Horloge and curls into a seat. 'I am.' She giggles.

'So?'

'I didn't like her manner. Yesterday either. No-one does me favours.' She studies me, her face suddenly serious. 'I'm not a poor provincial relation. I'm good, Pierre. When I saw the rushes of that shoe-string film we did in Montréal, I knew I could be very good.' She stirs her coffee reflectively. 'And that woman hasn't even taken the trouble of seeing our productions. I may be hungry, but I'm not starving.'

I squeeze her hand. When Madeleine behaves like this, I am in awe of her. There is a focused certainty about her, a professional pride. Unlike so many of my Québecois compatriots, unlike me, she has none of the bloated over-sensitivity, none of the timber-sized chips on the shoulder, none of the excessive gratitude for crumbs which make up the character armour of those long nurtured in second-class citizenry. Madeleine knows the exact measure of her value. She has coolly assessed its circumference and extent. No first-class citizens phase her. It reminds me how much I love her.

'I didn't like her manner either,' I confess.

'I couldn't help but notice.' She tweaks her nose and makes a face which is all disgust.

We burst into unstoppable laughter. We get up and, arm in arm, amble through the town. The sun beats down on red-tile roofs and heats the giant stone slabs of the papal palace. Pigeons peck away at invisible crumbs and flap their way up to turrets. We listen to a busker twanging out the nasal lyrics of a Bob Dylan song. We throw each other complicit smiles and gaze across ramparts at the lazy course of the river.

We are young. We are free. We will not be compromised.

That night after the show Madeleine triumphantly thrusts a note in my hand. It is a message from Natalie. It contains effusive congratulations on Madeleine's performance of Saint Teresa. It also names a time and place for a screen test the day after tomorrow.

I don't go with Madeleine. Instead, I write an article into which I weave news of this latest success of Madeleine Blais, certainly an actress destined to go far. When I tell Madeleine of this she is unaccountably angry. Superstition grips her. One doesn't count, let alone publicize, one's chickens, until they are hatched, she tells me.

I take her out of the piece and she softens, makes me promise that I will come to the cast party that night. It is their last performance and I must be there to celebrate. What she doesn't tell me until the next day is that she has arranged to have dinner with the director on what was to be our last evening and one of our few alone together in Avignon.

It is my turn to be unaccountably angry. I know

that this meeting is necessary and important, yet I feel betrayed, resentful. Not that I say anything. I bury my sullen mood in work and pretend good cheer. There is a performance by a Québec *chansonnier* in a small club and it will be useful for me to cover that.

Yet when I sit at the marble-topped table in the stuffy room which smells of sewage, I can barely bring my eyes to focus on the spot-lit stage. Nor can I concentrate on the plaintive ironies of lyrics which evoke the little people of Québec, who have nothing to console them except the dance of the snowflakes and the flow of the river and their unrecognized language.

I force myself to sit through two sets. My watch tells me it is not quite late enough to return to the hotel. I invite the *chansonnier* to my table, share a few drinks with him, conduct a half-hearted interview and then head off into the crowded night-time streets of the city.

The atmosphere is festive. Music and voices thrum through the summer air. They do nothing to infect me with their evident pleasure. I wander into emptier streets, find myself by the ruins of the Church of the Cordeliers, where Petrarch's Laura was interred in the mid-fourteenth century. The melancholy of that unrequited love pervades me. I brush it away, an unwanted omen, and hurry on. At last, at midnight, I tell myself Madeleine will be waiting for me and I slope back to our hotel.

The room is empty. I throw myself on the bed and wonder what business there is that can be talked about at this late hour. Then I tell myself in the same plaintive tones as the *chansonnier* that just because I desire Madeleine, it hardly follows that every man in the world shares my desire. After that, I lie there for I don't know how long and force myself to formulate phrases for my last article from France.

When I hear Madeleine at the door, I pretend sleep. She curls next to me. Her breath is soft on my face. For a moment, I think she has dozed off, then I feel her fingers on my chest, smoothing my skin, curving round my neck. She wants me awake. I refuse to open my eyes, refuse her touch. I keep my breathing even.

Suddenly her hand coils round my penis. That doesn't know how to feign sleep. It surges to her touch, frisks and bounds like an unleashed animal. Her mouth encloses it, laps and sucks. The pleasure is unutterable, yet somehow cool, detached, anonymous. I want it to go on and on, yet I also want to rebel at her power over me. I have an odd desire to punish her for my passion.

With a moan, I tug at her hair, pull away from her, lift her towards me so that we are face to face. The streetlamp casts a faint yellow glow through our window. In it her eyes look huge.

'I have the part,' she chortles. 'I have it.'

My answer is half grunt. 'I hope you didn't have to do this for it.' My hands are tight on her breasts, my cock inside her. I turn her over and fuck her hard and even before that violent blind shuddering takes us over, a great sadness brushes me with its wings.

When I look at her again, tears blur my sight. Her face is reflective. She runs her fingers through my hair. 'Would you rather I had let you sleep, Pierre? Or not come back at all?'

The force of that makes me shiver despite the heat. I shake my head, try to gather my daytime self together. From somewhere within it I find a smile.

'Congratulations. Tell me about it. Tell me everything.'

She bends towards the table where there is an open bottle of wine. I watch the cello of her back, the dip of her arm as she pours two glasses. The brief distance between us suddenly seems too great. I reach to touch her, trace the wonder of those curves and lines, the ripple of movement.

Madeleine smiles. She hands me a glass and lifts hers. 'To movies,' she says and falls back on the pillows with a laugh.

The director was enamoured of her screen test. He wants to augment the part they had in mind for her. Shooting will probably start in January in Morzine. The fact that Madeleine skis is a definite plus. The film is a love story, older man, younger woman, with a bitter-sweet ending. The man doesn't get the woman. Her youth is watchable, lovable, but inviolate. It is a time for youth. He doesn't want to sully it with his age.

Or so Madeleine tells it to me. She also tells me that she is doubly pleased, because it will mean she can do the run of the new Québecois play which begins in September.

* * *

The next day we don't head back to Paris. At dawn I steal out and surprise Madeleine by returning with a car. We're going to celebrate properly, I announce to her. We do.

We drive south along leafy roads. The light dazzles as it leaps through the crests of giant planes and skims along mottled bark. We climb the Alpilles and play tourist. We scale the outcrop of Les Baux and meander along the streets of Arles and cavort in the Roman amphitheatre and head east to Aix where we spend the night in a small shuttered hotel where the air smells of lavender.

The following morning, the windows of the car open to the wind, the radio blaring, we head for the Mediterranean. The rocks and the earth are honey pale and then ochre red, the sea deep blue, then turquoise, then blue again. There is the purple of bougainvillaea, the crimson and orange of geranium. Her eyes as wide as a child's, Madeleine speaks only to chart colour.

We sit amongst the sophisticates of St Tropez and sip cool white wine and gorge ourselves on langoustines and watch the boats in the harbour. We buy the bathing suits we don't have and miraculously find a tiny deserted cove where we swim and lie side by side and let the sun beat down on us. We are still lying there when the sea turns pink, then silver with the shimmer of moonlight. Wrapped in our sweaters and jeans and each other's arms, we spend the night on that oval of grainy sand and somewhere in that night, Madeleine says to me in a soft, serious voice, 'Whatever happens to us, Pierre, let's never forget we've had this.'

I have never forgotten. I don't really think Madeleine did either.

8

A rectangle of ashen light at the window signals dawn. My throat feels like sandpaper. My neck creaks like an old hinge as I bend to the sink and let water pour over my face and into my mouth. I shun the features in the small square of mirror.

I stare out the window at the dark clustered green of pines and wish the day would tell me what to do with myself. It occurs to me that I could ring Contini and offer my services to him. Perhaps he would like me to accompany him in his interviews of Madeleine's friends. Or I could offer to read through her journals for him.

The idiocy of these thoughts only strikes me once I am dressed. I make my way quietly down the stairs. There is nothing for me to do but go home or to my office.

The idea of the office beckons to me like salvation. Even if there are no clients to see, there are papers I can immerse myself in, tortuous details which will annihilate memory, stifle emotion as surely as heaped earth obliterates breath.

From the dining room, the aroma of brewing

coffee wafts up the stairs. But the notion of making breakfast conversation with Giorgio Napolitano holds me back. Yet I will have to face him, pay my bill sooner or later. I hesitate.

A rack of snowshoes gives me an out. I pick out a pair and head for the door. The frosty air is more bracing than a cold shower. I head round the side of the chalet towards the hill behind. Where the path ends, I position my feet on the rackets and buckle the ties round my boots.

The snow has a thin covering of ice and I have to pound down hard to prevent the rackets from slipping beneath me. The violence my tracks inflict on the virgin landscape is oddly satisfying.

A pale lemon-yellow sun surfaces above the crest of the hill. Birds twitter and flap at my noisy approach. A white hare bounds from the cover of trees. I hear him before I see him. He hears me too. He pauses in utter stillness. We both hold our breath. Then in a flutter of ears, he leaps away and vanishes into whiteness.

Madeleine kept rabbits in the barn that first summer. Two fat white bundles of fur with pink ears and pink quivering noses. We fed them lettuce leaves and cabbage and carrots.

'Mémère says "They breed like rabbits" is what the English used to say about the French. About them having lots of children. But I've never seen them breed. The rabbits, I mean.'

She is looking at me earnestly and I have the distinct impression that she doesn't altogether know what this act of breeding entails and would like me to tell her.

We watch the rabbits assiduously for the length of a morning and nothing happens. 'Are you sure you've got a man rabbit and a woman rabbit?' I ask her.

'Can you tell the difference?'

I hem and haw. 'Not with rabbits,' I finally manage to say. We look at each other and burst into giggles. We laugh so hard that the rabbits take fright and cower into the straw in the far corner of the cage.

After Madeleine made that first film in France, I never laughed with her quite so freely again. I don't know exactly what changed things and it didn't happen all at once. It was a gradual progression.

First there was the separation. Madeleine flew out to France just after Christmas. A week passed and then another and another. I worked like a demon, but nothing I seemed to be able to do made the time pass. Each day I would wake to her absence with an acute sense of loss.

By the third week, I began to make arrangements to join her. There was work I could do in France, I convinced my editor. I phoned and wired and by the next week indeed there was.

As soon as I arrived in Paris, I hired a car and drove out to Morzine. It occurred to me as I covered the slow mountain kilometres that I would have been wiser to fly to Geneva, but that wouldn't have fitted in so easily with work. By the time I arrived in the small mountain town, it was already dark. I congratulated myself on that. The day's shooting would be over and Madeleine would be free. For me.

I spotted Madeleine from outside. She was sitting in a window seat of the hotel restaurant. I stared at her for a moment with a lump in my throat. I was certain she would turn and see me. I could feel her so palpably I couldn't understand why she couldn't feel me. I stood there stupidly waiting for her to look my way. But she was deep in conversation with her director and at last I gave up, made my way inside and forced myself, despite a second's hesitation, to march right through to the restaurant.

I murmured a hello and Madeleine looked up at me with momentary abstraction as if my features wouldn't coalesce into a face she could recognize. When they did she stretched out her hand to me and squeezed my fingers. 'Pierre,' she breathed with a smile. 'Give me five minutes.'

It came to me then with a resounding thud that the time of separation had passed very differently for Madeleine than it had for me. She hadn't actively missed me, hadn't felt as if a limb had been wrenched from her body. All the hunger and tenderness of our love-making later that night couldn't make up for that difference.

The next day, as I stalked the shoot like some intruder on a closely knit family, I realized I shouldn't have come. It wasn't that the crew weren't perfectly polite. It was simply as if I didn't exist. I was as invisible as a servant in a Victorian household and far less useful.

There was no place for me in this household. Its

inward-looking intensity was total, even more pronounced than the theatre troupe's. Perhaps it was because its members didn't come home to a different home than the working one every night. Perhaps it had to do with the presence of cameras. I don't really know. All I know is that they inhabited a world utterly removed from the rest of us.

When I told Madeleine that night that I would leave the next day, she studied my face in grave silence. 'Yes, that would be best,' she said. 'You do understand, don't you, Pierre? This thing,' she waved her hands, 'it just takes you over.'

I nodded.

'Hold me.' It was a whisper edged by breathlessness, as if she was slightly afraid that she had already flown away in the balloon of her artificial world – even before I had gone.

I held her and while I held her she told me they would be shooting interiors in Paris next week and perhaps, there, it would be better. If I could hang on. If I could stay. She also told me that her director had broached the possibility of another film. After Cannes. After the festival. She said it all tentatively for my sake, but I could feel her excitement.

On the drive back to Paris, I did some serious thinking. I told myself that if I really couldn't live without Madeleine then I would have to learn to accommodate myself to her absences either from a distance or from closer to hand. There was no question in my mind but that this film wouldn't be her last.

About that, if about little else, I was right.

In Paris, I worked. I interviewed politicians and diplomats and officials in the Quai d'Orsay. I made contact with journalists at *Le Monde* and with members of various delegations. I stayed in a flat which belonged to a friend of my editor's. I think it was the flat which by the end of the week gave me the impression I was already a Parisian. I couldn't wait for Madeleine to arrive there.

It was tucked into a tiny alley of a street just off the Boulevard Saint-Germain and as one walked up the curving staircase to the fifth floor, a magical vista opened out from the windows. The building opposite was small, Balzac's old printing house. I could see beyond it into tree-filled courtyards, gaze on roofs, the spire of Saint-Germain and the dome of the Panthéon. Inside, everything was white and freshly painted and simple, two rooms with a mezzanine and a kitchenette tucked away behind louvred doors. But it was the view that counted. A view with two rooms. I pounded away at my type-writer and looked out at the view.

When Madeleine came, she loved it. She loved me better too. Maybe it was simply that the rooms and the view were mine, if only by referral. She was in my space. I was no longer an intruder.

'Pierre. There you are.' Giorgio Napolitano waves at me from the bottom of the hill.

I walk my clumsy snowshoe walk towards him, a penguin with big net feet.

'I was a little concerned when you didn't turn up to breakfast.' He casts me a quizzical look, but he is too courteous to turn it into words.

'I wanted some exercise.'

'And now some breakfast?'

'Coffee will do me.'

As we near the hotel, he pauses. 'I had a phone call this morning from a Detective Contini. He wants to see me. About Madeleine's death. Does the name mean anything to you?'

I nod.

'I don't know how he came across me. We ... Madeleine and I hardly moved in the same circles.'

Partly in order to gauge his reaction, I say, 'Could be through her journals.'

'I see.' Do I imagine the muscle fluttering in his cheek?

'So nothing is settled yet about the manner of her death.' He pushes open the door so hard that it hits the wall, ushers me towards the dining room and disappears.

A moment later he comes back with a jug of coffee. Close behind him is a woman with the darkly dramatic looks of a flamenco dancer. She is all voluptuous curves, from the waves of her hair through the sweep of nose and lips, to the arch and sway of hips beneath a full skirt. She carries a tray brimming with croissants and rolls and jams and fruit and once she has placed it on the table, she candidly examines me for a long moment.

'My wife, Paloma,' Giorgio says.

'I am pleased to meet you, M. Rousseau, even if it is in a time of great sadness.'

I sense that Giorgio has told her I was once a

husband. What else can he have told her to elicit this frank scrutiny?

'We all loved Madeleine. She had a particular flame. Perhaps it can still warm us a little. But I know from your face, it is not the time for small talk.' A look I can't interpret passes between her and Giorgio. 'You will come back to us, I hope.' She places a sudden kiss on my cheek and with a wave vanishes into the kitchen.

I drink my coffee which is strong and hot and for a moment can't meet Giorgio's eyes.

He laughs. 'You're thinking that now you know why I left the priesthood. Well you are at least three-quarters right.'

I have an uncanny certainty that the other quarter is to do with Madeleine.

The narrow road is made narrower by its banks of snow. Cars, topped with skis, whiz past me heading in the opposite direction. On the hills, the lifts have already creaked into motion dragging or hoisting their eager passengers up to the cold peaks.

Perhaps that's where I should be, out on some tricky slope, the wind biting my face and whistling in my ears, the danger of speed, the battle between gravity and skill voiding my mind of thoughts.

Madeleine skied far better than I did, but it was not until I saw that first film of hers that the sheer miracle of her grace came home to me. She pooh-poohed this when I mentioned it to her, told me the grace was all in the camerawork, told me I was an innocent to believe in everything I saw. But that was really one argument cloaking another. By that time our arguments had become more frequent. Not that they were necessarily voiced. They were an atmosphere which inhabited us and didn't let us rest.

But I am getting ahead of myself. I don't want to think about that. There were a few more relatively unsullied months before all that began.

After the shoot in France, Madeleine came back to Montréal to do another play, Racine's *Iphigénie* this time. She wanted to try her hand at the classics.

They were good months. We moved into an apartment on Sherbrooke near the Main. Perhaps, in memory of that week in Paris, we chose to live high up in the air, our own eyrie, buffeted only by wind and sky. A place to be private in away from the turmoil of the streets below where we lived our adamantly social and often separate lives. We were kind to one another in our eyrie, solicitous, tender.

Later it occurred to me that Madeleine was making up for something, either in the past or perhaps in the future. But that was later.

It was in those months that I grew close to certain key figures in the Parti Québecois. My articles had begun to cause a stir. I was invited onto platforms. I spent time in the provincial and federal capitals. I took part in media debates. One night, after she happened to see me in one of these, Madeleine looked at me with shining eyes and told me she was very proud of me.

I think I managed to say the same to her after the

première of her film at the Cannes Film Festival. I am no longer sure.

In May, we flew to Cannes together. Though I wanted to, I wasn't sure I should go. But Madeleine insisted. We were put up in the turn-of-the-century splendour of the Carleton. Through our window we could hear the beating of the waves on the shore and gaze out at that wondrous sea. But its magic wasn't that of the previous summer. It was simply a scenic backdrop to the mad whirl of activity we were caught up in. I say we, but I mean Madeleine. There were parties and cocktails and breakfast and lunch meetings, on yachts, in grand hotels and tiny restaurants on the steep streets of the old town. There were countless interviews and countless flashing cameras. Madeleine was a star in the making and by the end of the week she had been made.

I still distinctly remember that moment when, flanked by her director and male lead, she slowly emerged from a white convertible and climbed the stairs of the old festival building.

There was electricity in the air. The crowd, among which I hovered before going into the cinema, pushed against the police who had cleared a path for the celebrities. Television cameras rolled, bulbs flashed, and in the midst of it all, Madeleine played the star. She did it well. She did it naturally, as if she had been born to it – the extra swing to her hips, the glowing skin, the erect carriage in that long gown which shimmered like moonlight on water when the bulbs flashed. The enigmatic smile, the lowered lashes which raised themselves to reveal shining eyes whose gaze only ever rested directly on individuals, somehow making them feel larger, singled out.

I watched every inch of her progress and sensed the magnetic force of her glamour. I didn't envy her the limelight. I was excited for her, happy. The problem between Madeleine and me was never one of competition, though the fact that we both led frenetic working lives could cause logistical difficulties, as eventually did her fame. No, the problem was elsewhere, less tangible.

I began to sense it the moment she appeared on the screen. Maybe it had something to do with the sheer size of her, the extra huskiness in her voice, the hint of tragedy in the curve of her lips.

Each gesture, each tantalizing movement of the eye took on mythic proportions. Yet at the same time, each was intensely intimate. The touch of her hand on another's shoulder, the shimmy of stockings as she pulled them up her legs, the reflective glance in the mirror, the flurry of her hands as she worried over something – I recognized each of these movements and yet didn't recognize them. They were strange, removed. I had seen them, yet never altogether registered them, not in this way. They were mine, they were meant for me as myself and as a spectator, yet they no longer had anything to do with me. They were public.

It was as if our intimacy had been plundered, stolen away, transformed into an act which floated uneasily between the brazenly public and the deeply private. To add to my visceral confusion, there was

Madeleine herself, sitting beside me in the dark, nervously gripping my hand, wanting the comfort of mine.

Maybe I only began to feel all this when that first screen kiss came, that slight raising of her head, those half-closed eyes. I could sense the pleasure on both sides. I was bewildered, beside myself. I was watching my wife perform intimate acts with another man.

And the images haunted me, well after the uproar of applause, the speeches and flowers and more applause, the party which lasted the length of the night. The images hovered and endured, appeared to me when I least wanted them, took me over, so that even when the living and breathing Madeleine was beside me, they would intrude, public, intimate, unwanted, inescapable.

I didn't know or think all this at the time. I only knew that I had never felt like this when I watched Madeleine on the stage. Had never sensed either this disturbance nor this odd and occasionally rapturous dislocation. For she was very good. She was that young guileless woman she played. For long stretches of time I forgot and yet knew she was Madeleine.

I didn't confess any of this to her. What was there that could be said? I had no words for anything except the congratulations that were her due and these I made with what I hope wasn't a false enthusiasm. After that, I moved into the sidelines where I belonged.

It was already dawn when we returned to our

hotel room. We looked out at the glimmering expanse of sea, the stretch of pale sand, the rows of umbrellas, still neatly folded, and we kissed.

Those other kisses floated into my mind and I held Madeleine more tightly to whisk them away. When we stretched out on the vastness of the bed, I asked her, 'What was it like kissing Luc?' I stumbled over the name of her lead.

She gave me a curious glance, then laughed lightly. 'Have you ever tried kissing with a camera hovering at your right nostril?'

I chuckled, hiding my unease. But I couldn't let it go.

'And lying beside him? Touching his skin? Having him touch yours?'

I touched Madeleine and she moved away.

'Pierre, if you're asking me whether I was aroused, the short answer is no.' She laughed again, more nervously this time. 'When you're asked to repeat a gesture for the fifth take, arousal is not what you feel.'

'No?'

'And the lights are beating down on you and you're worrying about your forehead growing shiny with perspiration. Or about your next line which has vanished into the ether. Or your leg has suddenly seized up because of the odd angle you've had to force it into. And then the make-up woman suddenly appears to powder your cheek or your shoulder or some technician drops a coil and you have to start all over again . . . It's not sex, Pierre. It's cinema.'

'It looks like sex.'

'That's the idea.'

She turned away from me, gave me her back.

'You believe what you want, Pierre.'

'I want to believe you.'

I do want to believe Madeleine. I really do. But somehow I can't control those images. They intrude themselves, place themselves between Madeleine and me at the most delicate moments. I touch her and I see another man touching her. I kiss her and feel her responding to someone else. Sometimes it stimulates me to passion. At other times it turns me cold. It always troubles me.

I know that men sometimes fantasize about other women when they make love to their wives. But my fantasies are of my wife as another. Of myself as other too. I do not know what to do with these ghosts. I do not allow myself to talk about them to Madeleine. It is too demeaning. Instead, I struggle to put them out of my mind.

At first I am almost successful, but as the toll of Madeleine's films mounts, so does my predicament. Her face and body leap out at me seductively from hoardings in the streets and in the metro. They leap out at everyone else too. Her latest film has scenes of such graphic and felt passion that I cannot believe her earlier humorous descriptions of the jokes and pitfalls of filmed sex.

We are living more or less consistently in Paris by then. It is 1977. Madeleine has chosen a large court-yard apartment in the Marais and from the outside our lives seem more than enviable. Mine too. I am a correspondent with a wide brief – European trouble spots, France, French-speaking Africa. I have a desk at France-Presse who also use my services. I have learned to live with the jokes about my accent and I spend some of my time lobbying the Quai d'Orsay on Québec's behalf. We are on the select guest list for the historic reception at the Palais Bourbon for the new Québec Premier, René Lévesque, a man of integrity and one I have long respected and championed.

Madeleine and I are successful, busy, affluent, privileged.

I repeat this litany to myself as I steal away from work early one afternoon to watch Madeleine's latest film quietly on my own in a small cinema near the Odéon. The notion has taken hold of me that I can verify the reality of the flow of filmed sex by counting the number of cuts in any given scene. The fewer cuts the more reality.

The cinema is all but empty for this first of the day's screenings. I find a seat towards the far end of a row in the middle of the hall and wait impatiently for the run of trailers and publicity to stop. As the film starts, I try to keep myself vigilant. But the story sucks me in.

It is the end of the first year of the German occupation of Paris. Madeleine plays a shop assistant, a rather severe, coolly self-sufficient woman whose life centres around the repetitive routine of work and the care of her invalid father. A Nazi officer falls in love with her. Madeleine resists, resists ferociously for the added reason that her father is Jewish. Yet the play of attraction between them is evident. One day, because of her fear of his greater power, because of their mutual desire too, Madeleine allows herself to be spirited away into the countryside.

I watch the sequence which begins with the officer pulling a grip from her hair with taut fascination. The rich golden strands break free. Madeleine's face is transformed. Like a daffodil just opened to the sun, her head sways languidly. The camera lovingly, slowly travels up the distance of her arched neck. As the officer bends to kiss her, I lose track of the camera. I lose count of the cuts as well. I cannot see any. The painfully charged sensual play of skin and limbs and clasped, rolling bodies goes on in unendurably real time.

From along the row beside me, there is an audible release of breath, a low aching moan. In the flickering light I see a lone dark-suited man. His legs are splayed out in front of him. For a moment I think he has been taken ill and then I notice his hand in his pocket, the rhythmic jiggle of his trousers.

Rage takes me over. My fists clench. I want to beat him to a pulp.

'*Cochon*,' I hiss. '*Sale cochon*.'

He turns white startled eyes at me as I stumble towards him. 'Dirty pig,' I repeat.

A pleading hand reaches out to fend off my assault. The man whispers a 'shhh'. Suddenly, he looks so ordinarily respectable that I restrain my hands, rush past him instead into the blinding brightness of mid-afternoon.

244

I walk. I try to still myself. I tell myself that I cannot really blame that man for the terrible impact of the visual. I ask myself for the hundredth time what Madeleine felt for her lead man. For feel something I am now certain she did. As certain as I am of the effect her sexuality had on the man sitting near me. Or am I?

For the first time, I acknowledge that I am jealous. Painfully, hopelessly jealous. It is an invidious emotion and a humiliating one. I feel sullied, ashamed. I cannot think straight. I am of the generation which doesn't believe in jealousy. Women are not property – possessions to be kept and controlled. They are free. I have always loved Madeleine for her spirited freedom.

My jealousy feels doubly insidious. I am not even certain that there is a basis for it in the real. It is a phantom jealousy, jealousy directed at an illusion made up of the play of shadows and light. I am a reasonable man, I tell myself. And I talk to myself reasonably. There is no need to feel any of this.

But the tortuous tangle of emotions and suspicions persists. I cannot face the office. I go home instead and lie on the bed where I wish Madeleine was, so that I could grill her, interrogate, fume. But she is away until the weekend. Away doing what?

It occurs to me as I close my eyes that in fact my jealousy is in no way particular. Why am I bothering to distinguish an inevitable tawdriness? All jealousy is embroiled with phantoms. It doesn't need the spur of the real. It only needs the sense that we are losing something we had. Something we do not wish to lose.

Yet Madeleine doesn't belong to me. Has never belonged to me absolutely. I know that, know too that I didn't fall in love with a nun. The knowledge doesn't help. Nor does the grim recognition that in certain ways Madeleine now belongs to everyone. That horrible little man in the cinema as much as myself. The realization cuts more sharply than a knife.

My thoughts go round and round. I find myself picking up the telephone just to break their treacherous circularity. I am dialling the office. I hear myself asking Christiane Dumont whether she would like to go out to dinner tonight. She says, 'Yes' in her clear crisp voice. Christiane has made it plain often enough that she likes me, that she would be interested, if I were so disposed. She is a tall, angular, intelligent woman with jet-dark hair and a wide mouth, a divorcée and older than I am.

As I shower and try to wash away the grime of the afternoon, I wonder for a moment what it is that I am doing. But I don't allow myself to think too hard. I plunge into my meeting with Christiane and astonish myself with my verve and occasional wit. It doesn't flag, even later in her bed, even though I know that if I make one slightly mistaken gesture, Madeleine's image which I have been keeping at bay all night will overwhelm me.

No sooner have I congratulated myself on what I choose to call my act of homeopathic medicine and I am out on the streets than the thought of

Madeleine comes crashing back. She is in bed with someone else. I know it. Or she is being filmed in bed with someone else for all the world to see. The democracy of her passion annihilates me. It destroys my uniqueness, my very sense of individuality.

As I turn the key in the lock, my hand trembles, already the hand of a man touched by death.

There is light coming from the kitchen where I don't remember leaving it. A typescript lies scattered on the living-room sofa. On the corner table a bottle of Perrier emits a soft hiss like a child's snore. I tighten its top and peer into the bedroom.

In the half-light, I make out Madeleine. She looks so utterly innocent as she lies there asleep, her hair fanned out against the pillow, her cheeks slightly flushed, her arms akimbo. I tell myself I am mad, as deranged as Othello perched over his blameless Desdemona.

Then she stirs. A long bare leg peeks out from beneath the duvet, curves and nestles against its softness. An image from the afternoon's film lunges into my line of vision. The duvet takes on the muscular contours of a man's back. The temptation to cover Madeleine over, to destroy the sight of her is so great that I rush into the bathroom and lock the door.

The water scalds and freezes me by turn. I am grateful to it.

As I stand under its erratic stream, I suddenly remember a terrifying hellfire sermon one of my priestly teachers delivered on the sin of concupiscence. It was full of the burnings and lashings of the flesh, of horned devils pricking and prodding at tender parts, of the torments of the mind chained to lustful desires whose satisfaction was always out of reach.

I silence the exhortations of that haranguing voice. Quietly I slip into bed. Madeleine turns over, places a warm hand on my chest.

'Working late?' she murmurs sleepily.

'Mmm.'

She doesn't ask me any more. She nestles into the pillow and is asleep again within seconds.

Though moments before I wished for nothing more than that she stay asleep, now I feel that her unconsciousness is a crime. It is the sign of her dis-interest in me. Her lack of passion here is a signal of its surfeit elsewhere.

The clatter of dishes in the kitchen rouses me in the morning. Above their sound, Madeleine is singing. Her voice rises in a false soprano trill then cascades into that androgynous timbre she likes to imitate. There is the smell of coffee. For a floating drowsy moment I am happy and then I remember. My limbs take on a painful rigidity. I keep my eyes firmly shut.

'Morning, sleepyhead.' Madeleine plants a kiss on my cheek. I turn over with a grunt and she ruffles my hair. 'I've made coffee,' she says in her most seductive voice. She pulls open the curtains.

Light bounds into the room and she bounces onto the bed. She is as bright and playful as the light. 'Drink it. It's right beside you. Just the way you like it.'

I sip the sweet, milky café au lait and gaze at her. 'You came back early?' My voice doesn't sound quite right.

'Olivier developed laryngitis, so they're shooting some other scenes first.'

Madeleine has been filming a small cameo part for a television drama.

'Aren't you pleased to see me?'

I nod and look away, then say with what I hope is a teasing voice, 'I saw you yesterday.'

'Oh? Were you out in Le Mans?' Her expression betrays more confusion than I would like.

'No. I saw you on the screen.'

Madeleine laughs. 'Did you like it better this time? No, no, don't protest. I know you loathed me as Julie. I could feel the waves emanating from you. Big black waves of dislike.' She wriggles her fingers like a voodoo magician.

I shrug and sip my coffee.

'There was a man sitting down the row from me. He was masturbating.'

Her face crinkles. She bursts into giggles, falls back on the pillows in hilarity.

I cannot understand her reaction and sit there in rigid silence.

'You don't think it's funny?' she asks, wiping tears from her eyes. She represses another giggle. 'Not even a little bit?'

I shake my head.

'That poor man,' she says in a solemn voice.

'Poor man! What about you?'

She casts a quick glance at me, then stares at her

toes. 'Let's talk about something else. I've got some news.' Playfully, she walks her fingers up my chest. I stop her hand.

'Good news. Very good news.' The golden flecks in her eyes dance as she looks up at me. 'There's been an offer. From Hollywood.' She snuggles into me, strokes, intersperses her narrative with little nips of kisses. 'A good, fat part. An ultra-modern take on the golden-hearted whore. And mega bucks. Maybe we can buy a house. I'm going to fly out and meet the people. Week after next. I thought I'd stop on the way back and spend some time with Mémère.'

Madeleine's fingers work their magic on me. We make love. But in the midst of the images which ransack the space of my imagination, I no longer know whom I am making love to. My anger at this spurs my passion. I delve and probe. I am searching for a Madeleine prior to this chaos. I want the smell and touch of her flesh to eradicate the jumble of flickering betrayals which succeed each other in my mind.

At last, in the blinding whiteness of orgasm, there is a momentary respite.

'You're pleased,' Madeleine whispers as we lie clasped in each other's perspiration.

I nuzzle against her. I cannot contradict her. There is no ready translation for what I feel.

Later, before heading off in our separate directions, we pause for coffee and a cigarette in the breakfast room. Madeleine has her bottle-green Chanel suit on and her hair is wound into a smooth coil in readiness for her meeting with her agent. I have always liked that efficient smoothness, the way it sets off the structure of her bones and veils her sensuality.

I touch her hair. Her neck curves towards me. Her eyes catch the light in a particular way and suddenly I say it.

'As Julie, you did it, didn't you? With Bruno. There were no cuts.' My voice is peculiarly flat.

Madeleine takes a long puff of her cigarette and stubs it out. She meets my eyes and gets up. She doesn't deny anything. Her face has that tragic cast which works to such effect on the screen, grounding her characters in a tangible if unspoken emotion.

Only when she reaches the door does she speak. 'I'm a free agent, Pierre. I always have been and I always will be. I didn't come to you with a guarantee. A guarantee from heaven that nothing would ever change. You've changed too.'

'Have I?'

'Yet I'm here with you.' She slams the door behind her.

In that moment, as she confirms her betrayal, Madeleine feels very real.

PART TWO

PART TWO

9

The coil of my thoughts is so tight that again I miss the autoroute turn off for Ste-Anne. I force myself into attentiveness, loop round at the next exit and retrace the kilometres.

The sky has turned a deep crystalline blue, the kind of cloudless electric blue that only comes with the freezing temperatures of winter. In the distance, the vault of the church sparkles and shimmers like a thousand polished blades. I avert my eyes from it, am grateful for the dip and curve of the slip road.

At the next crest, I see a thick black stream of smoke tainting the sky. I wonder where it could be coming from; the plywood factory perhaps.

The wail of a siren fills the air, grows louder and louder as it approaches from behind. I pull over and a fire engine screeches past. It is not our local one. I watch it hurtling away, see the cloud of smoke again billowing from the valley and suddenly a twist in the road rights my perspective.

I push my foot down on the accelerator and follow in the wake of the engine. I wish I could overtake it. My father's house is burning.

Apocalyptic images rush through my mind, punctuating the speed with which we take the bends. I have a hazy sense that I should have been in that conflagration. Not here in the cocooned safety of my car, trying to rewrite the course of my life with Madeleine in order to give it a different end.

When we rise out of the scoop of the valley, I realize my mistake. The smoke is not coming from my house, but from behind it on the other side of the hill. A new kind of terror pulses through me.

It takes another few minutes to whiz round the bend and climb the narrow road on the hump of the hill. I can smell the smoke here, despite my closed windows. It seeps round the edges and attacks my nose. Mme Tremblay's house is cloaked by it. But the blaze is not here.

The fire engine bumps down the drive and squeals to a halt. Four men leap out of it and unwind the thick hoses at its side. Through the grey-blue clouds of smoke, I can see the flames now. Orange and gold and red, they leap and prance from what was once the barn. The roof is gone. Supported by a beam, part of it leans drunkenly on the ground.

I think of Mme Tremblay and am relieved that she spent the night in Montréal.

Smoke clutches at my nostrils as I leave the car. I raise my scarf to my nose. All around me voices shout above the heave and crackle of burning timber. Through the acrid haze, I see the outline of a second fire engine on the other side of the building and the flashing lights of police cars. I try to make my way towards them. A looming hulk of a man emerges from the smog and waves me away with a giant's gloved hand.

I wend my way round to the side, but I have chosen the wrong direction. Two of the outhouses have given way to the flames. The branches of Madeleine's favourite beech are charred. The wind carries sprays of water from the thick jets towards me. I turn away and arc round to the other side.

In the distance, coming out from the first copse, I make out a thin gangly figure in uniform. It looks like Gagnon. He is flanked by two men, one of whom pushes a slighter, stumbling person before him. I run towards them, my feet clinging to the thicker snow of the field which has grown sticky from the heat.

'Where's Mme Tremblay?' Gagnon asks as soon as he recognizes me.

'In Montréal as far as I know.' I fall in beside him.

'Can you get hold of her?'

'I'll try. Shall we radio from your car? It'll be quicker.'

He nods. 'Damned bloody mess.' He gestures towards the blaze. 'But just look what we got ourselves here.' He prods the arm of the man who is walking in front of his constable. 'Stupid bugger.'

I look at the man properly for the first time and notice that he is handcuffed. His hair is long and black, his face thin and as beautiful as a woman's with its full lips and high cheekbones. Above them, his dark eyes are vast and vacant. He looks young and confused, as if he didn't know what was happening to him.

'Dumb bugger,' Gagnon repeats. 'But they all do it, don't they! Come back to the scene of the crime. Like lemmings. Or moths to the flame.' He cackles at his own joke.

'You mean—'

'Damn right, I mean. This is our man. The very man Mme Tremblay described. Leather jacket and all. Just need to tie his hair into a tail. And we found him right here, sniffing round the blaze. You bet your bottom dollar he started it, too. We can tell that sneering ponce of a Contini where to get off now.' He snorts with derision.

We are close to the blaze. The flames lick and spit and lurch under the jets of water. The youth stares at the fire with rapt, empty eyes.

'What's his name?' I ask Gagnon as we veer to the side and give the firefighters a wide berth.

'Hasn't told us yet. Hasn't said a word, in fact.' He taps his forehead. 'He's a bit slow.'

One of the constables shoves the boy forward in the direction of the police car.

I move to the youth's side. 'What's your name?' I ask him in English.

He gazes at me from those blank eyes.

'What's your name?' I repeat.

There is an answering flicker in the vast pupils. He moistens his lips and forms a single syllable. 'Will,' he says.

'He doesn't speak French.' I fall back with Gagnon.

'Heh, who cares what he speaks? This is not a case for the language police. We leave that for the guys in Montréal. Leave that for Contini's boys.'

Gagnon is more garrulous and happier than I have ever seen him. Contini has got to him.

'He's also on something.'

'What do you mean "on something"?'

'Drugs. Heroin, I imagine.'

His eyes tighten into slits. 'That's Miron's domain. He's off today.' He seems to be about to say something else, but changes his mind. 'Never mind. *Mauditcriss*, we can get the bastard on three counts.'

We have reached the car and the constable prods the youth into the back seat and gets in beside him.

'You stay here,' Gagnon orders the second one. 'We'll go back to the station. So what's that number?' He turns to me and I give him the number of Madeleine's apartment.

The radio sputters and crackles as he calls into the station and gives them instructions to ring and get straight back to him.

'Not that there's any real hurry.' He grins at me. 'That one's not going anywhere.'

'You better let the Sûreté know.'

'In due course. All in due course. You want to come down to the station with us?'

'I'll come in my own car.'

The radio leaps into sound. He picks it up. 'No-one there? Never mind. We'll try later.' He turns to me. 'Mme Tremblay's not there. Only an answering machine. Lucie left a message.'

259

I swallow hard as I think of the voice on that machine.

Gagnon glances at the back seat where the youth sits, his eyes fixed on the fire. 'Still, as I say, no real hurry. And better to have the blaze out, before we get Mme Tremblay down here. Good thing she stayed in Montréal last night. It's not going to make her very happy.'

He suddenly pats my shoulder with a paternal gesture. 'You don't look too happy either, Pierre. I'll have Martine bring some hot soup round from Senegal's when you get down to the station. God-awful Christmas this! But at least we got him.'

As I make to leave the car, a flash goes off in my face. When my eyes refocus, I see the youthful pair who were first at the crime scene on Monday. This time, there's a television news crew right behind them. I slip round the back of the car and make my escape.

The air is thick with smoke, but the fire seems calmer now, less hungry, the tips of the flames an iridescent blue. Beneath my feet, where tyres and water have ousted the snow, the ground is cloying and muddy.

By the time I reach my car, my boots are clogged with it. I watch the flames from my window for a few minutes and think of the youth with the vacant eyes and imagine him in Madeleine's bed and then in the barn, but I can't see it. I can't rouse any rage. Maybe my mind and emotions are as clogged as my boots. Or maybe Gagnon has got it wrong.

* * *

260

I decide to stop at home before heading down to the station. It won't take long to shave and change.

No sooner do I emerge from my car than the cat leaps down at me from the roof and miaowls emphatically. She is hungry. I have forgotten to leave her food out. Nor does she like the dense smoke the wind has brought. It hovers in the air like a bad omen.

I pick her up and stroke her and carry her into the house. '*Pauvre minou,*' I console her, and only stop to take off my boots before filling her bowl to the brim. She rubs herself gratefully against my leg and then abandons me for her food.

The light on the answering machine is flashing red. I avoid it. There is something gnawing at my mind which I can't quite bring to the surface. I shave quickly, don fresh clothes and a blue workaday suit and stare out the window where the dingy smoke has obscured the brilliant blue of this morning's sky. The something still won't quite materialize. Impatiently I press the button on the answering machine.

Maryla again. Out of fairness, I will have to ring her later. Then two more of my lonely women friends. Then the political editor of *Le Devoir* asks whether I would consider doing some think-pieces on the constitutional crisis. Then my brother. He wants to know whether I've left yet and if I check into my machine, could I just let him know where I'll be – in case he needs to find me. I take a deep breath and try not to let his tone irritate me.

After that comes a voice which identifies itself as

Marie-Ange Corot. I haven't seen Marie-Ange in years. She is Madeleine's agent in Paris, the one who took over from Natalie. Madeleine and she became fast friends. On the answering machine, Marie-Ange is both hesitant and tearful.

'Pierre, I'm so sorry. I didn't know who else to ring. I've just managed to locate your number. Mme Tremblay hasn't been in. I only heard on Wednesday. It's tragic. I need to speak to you. Please call.'

I jot down Marie-Ange Corot's number, then listen to Contini. He is abrupt, slightly angry.

'Where have you got yourself to, Rousseau? You're supposed to stay in touch.'

The tone intimidates. It sounds as if my finger-prints have turned up in inappropriate places. Or maybe he has some news.

I search for his card, but before it comes to hand, I find I am dialling Madeleine's number. I listen breathlessly to her voice, then hang up, wait a few moments, and dial again. That nagging feeling has returned. It clutches at the pit of my stomach. I glance at my watch. Mme Tremblay would have had to phone Michel Dubois at the crack of dawn for him to get his old jalopy through Montréal's rush hour and carry her away.

The telephone is engaged. The loop on the answering machine hasn't found its way back yet. I wait and as I wait I see Mme Tremblay's barely restrained misery when she left me yesterday evening. I see her pacing Madeleine's apartment, touching things. I think of my own state these last days and her suffering whips through me, a familiar demon.

I have to sit down. I try the number again. A line from the poem Mme Tremblay quoted to me resonates in my ear above Madeleine's voice, something about anguish stooping to jealousy.

I lunge up the stairs and retrieve yesterday's jacket. Contini's card is in the pocket. Hastily I dial his number. A woman's voice tells me he isn't in, but she's expecting a call from him soon. I ask her if his partner, Ginette Lavigne, is available, but the answer is the same.

The urgency of someone getting to Madeleine's flat at last impressed upon her, I leave the woman both my office and my home number. Then, without allowing myself to think, I dial emergency. Better to put them to trouble than to be sorry.

Would it help if I were to race up to Montréal?

My legs answer for me. I am already back in the car, bumping down the hill, accelerating away from the lingering smoke into the cloudless blue of an afternoon which refuses the shadows of my fear.

On the hill leading down to Madeleine's apartment building, I hear the wail of an ambulance. I veer into the drive and almost collide with a parked police car.

'Heh!' A uniformed officer leaps from its interior. 'What the hell do you think you're doing?'

'Have you been up to the eighth floor?'

'What's it to you?'

'I reported it.'

I make to go past him, but he stops me.

'They've just taken the old lady away.'

'They?'

'The ambulance.' He takes a notebook from his pocket. 'You Pierre Rousseau?'

I nod.

A professional air of condolence settles on his meaty face. I cannot find any words with which to put the question.

'We found her slumped over the table, a row of pill bottles in front of her. The medics pumped her, took her to the Montréal General.' He points up the road.

I am already in the car and backing up when he shouts after me, 'We had to break through the door. We don't want any complaints.'

The Montréal General is at once cavernous and busy. Voices echo and rebound, hushed, officious, plaintive. I am told to wait. The chemical reek of antiseptics attacks my nostrils, brings in its wake a dizzying vision of my mother on that last hospital visit I made to her. I am suddenly a helpless, hopeless ten-year-old, unmanly tears pricking at eyelids that don't want to acknowledge their existence.

Feet move along scuffed tiles. White-shod, crêpe-soled, booted, healed. I cannot bear to meet anyone's eyes.

A second time, I am told to wait. A toddler comes up to me and leans against my knees. She has a white woolly hat on, a fluffy pompom at its tip. Dark curls peep from its edges. She stares up at me with serious eyes, then from her mouth she takes a half-chewed sweet and places it in my hand.

'Catherine!' A woman's voice calls her away.

The candy stays in my hand. It is sticky and white with stripes of faded pink. I should throw it away, but somehow I don't want to. I look round surreptitiously and pop it into my mouth. The tang of peppermint explodes in its dryness. At the same time I hear my name called.

Mme Tremblay's face is as white as the pillow she rests on, but with far more creases. Her eyes flutter open as I approach, their focus uncertain. She doesn't speak. It is not clear that she recognizes me.

The stickiness is still there in my hand, when I touch hers.

'How are you feeling?' I murmur.

'Pierre.' Her gaze rests on me. 'Pierre, I wanted to talk to you.' Her voice feels sore. 'Your father so wants to come to the wedding. He's too proud to say. Ask him, please. It doesn't matter about your stepmother.'

It takes me a moment to realize that like some time-traveller in search of a happier epoch her mind has landed her in the weeks just prior to Madeleine's and my wedding.

'All right,' I say. I don't want to lurch her out of that better place.

Her lips struggle with a smile, her lids droop and close.

I wait and think how odd it is that she has said to me now what she never said before. My father, whose presence I rebelliously shunned in those

265

years, did not come to Madeleine's and my wedding. I never invited him. The thought saddens me now. I am glad that Mme Tremblay has reinstated his presence.

Her eyes are closed, her breathing light and regular. She is asleep.

The nurse who has shown me in pokes her head through the door and waves me out.

'Let her rest,' she says. 'That's what she needs. Quite a shock to the system, all this, when you're her age. Lucky, she fell asleep before she took too much.'

'Will she be OK?'

'We'll keep a close watch on her.'

She looks at me curiously from dark, forthright eyes. 'Do you know why she tried it?'

I shrug, reluctant to offer any information.

She prods at the watch pinned to her bosom and walks me towards the desk.

'You'd better fill out these forms for us. You're her next of kin?'

'Not exactly. But I'll have to do.'

She watches me from the other side of the counter as I fill out what I can of the forms.

'Jeez, it's just come back to me. She's the grand-mother of that movie star who killed herself, right? Madeleine Blais?'

I nod.

'OK, we'll take good care of her.' Her voice is suddenly hushed with respect. 'Come back tomorrow. You've left your number just in case . . .'

I point to the form and she beams a shy smile at

me as if my presence were already one step in the direction of limelight.

Night has fallen by the time I leave the hospital, that half-darkness of hazy refracted light which is the night-time of the city. I speed away from it. If I hurry, I won't be caught in the snarl of rush-hour traffic. It is only four o'clock.

It occurs to me as I drive that perhaps my instincts have done Mme Tremblay no favours. But I cannot allow myself to think that. No. I will not.

A narrative I have read somewhere springs into my mind – about a hospital in which after the first patient has hanged himself from a hook, fifteen others follow suit. Only once the hook has been removed do the suicides cease. Suicide is contagious.

It was Contini's subtle yet bullying insistence that Madeleine committed suicide which led Mme Tremblay to swallow those pills. When she was intent on revenge, anger carried her along. Perhaps it is a good thing that the barn has burnt down and re-focused our thoughts. I, too, felt the pull of suicide's fatal charm.

For the first time in hours, I think of the beautiful youth with the vacant eyes. Will. William. Bill. I remember the bad joke I made to Madeleine about all her killers being called Bill and I press my foot down on the gas. Is Gagnon right? Could Will be Madeleine's murderer? Did she know him, already have him in mind when she spoke to me those three weeks back? Was he one of the reasons she wanted a bodyguard? I put a tape of Bach's Toccatas into the deck and force myself to concentrate on the movement of Glenn Gould's hands – as if the solution to Madeleine's mystery could be traced in their counterpoint. I don't know why I don't feel more vindictive anger.

The centre of Ste-Anne is more animated than usual. Maybe it is the effect of the Christmas lights. They swing across the road, define trees, curve and twine round rotund angels and plump Santas to people the dark. Couples saunter slowly round the church square. Through the frosted windows of Senegal's, I can see a gaggle of old-timers crowded round the tables and, at the counter stools, a couple of younger people, perhaps attracted by Martine Senegal's presence.

As I push open the door, I hear Mme Groulx's voice raised above the rest. She holds forth with irrepressible authority.

'Yes. It was him. Definitely him. I recognized him. The same one who came with her to midnight mass. Same hair, same jacket. You know what? I think he's part of that gang of scum who hang out in that Jew's summer house. Down by the river. I've seen them before. They come into town in their four-wheel drive, radio blaring, no respect for anyone. I see them from my window.'

Mme Groulx's second-floor window on the corner of Rue Turgeon is the outpost of rumour in the town. From this strategic front line, news spreads more quickly than brush fire.

'Ya, I know the ones you mean,' old Senegal chips

in, wiping his hands on his flecked apron. 'They've been in here once or twice. No respect. Don't even try and speak French. And their attitude! Heh, I bet they're responsible for all the thieving that's been going on here of late. You remember, at the Bon Marché, someone cleaned out the till one day when Mme Ricard was in the back room. Then—'

'Yes! Of course.' Mme Groulx's creased cheeks flush enthusiastic pink. 'I always suspected that Jew doctor.' She lowers her voice to the level of conspiracy. 'He carried out abortions in that house. The lights stayed on well into the night and all kinds of women came and went and—'

She stops as she sees me.

'Pierre! Have you heard? Gagnon's tracked him down. Madeleine Blais' murderer. Imagine. It was murder. Not suicide at all. Brutal, barbaric murder. Poor little Madeleine. Poor, dear girl. How she must have suffered! So talented, everything to live for. I only hope it was quick.'

For a moment I have the impression I am hallucinating. Just two days ago, Mme Groulx described Madeleine as a brazen hussy, unworthy of an ounce of her pity.

'Join us for a coffee, Pierre.' She points regally towards a chair and insists that I squeeze it in beside hers.

'And a piece of apple pie.' Senegal puts a plate in front of me before I can say anything.

I swallow a wedge of apple, gluey with some cinnamony artificial syrup.

'Terrible times,' Mme Rossignol pipes in. 'Poor,

poor Claire Tremblay. Her granddaughter gone. Her daughter at odds with her. Her barn burnt to the ground.' She shakes her pink-white head in genuine grief. 'I'm going to bring her one of my meat pies.'

'Her husband must be writhing in that Norman grave of his,' a gravelly voice proclaims from the corner. 'None of this would have happened if he hadn't gone off to be a hero. He was my friend, you know. Guy Tremblay. The best man round these parts.'

I turn to stare at old Godbout. It is the longest speech I have heard him make in years. He must realize it too, for he wipes his toothless mouth now with the back of his hand, as if he needed to touch his sunken lips to ascertain their existence.

'We've never had anything like it around here. Never. Not since that business out in the barracks during the war. But no fear, Gagnon won't let the villain get away with it.' Mme Groulx is adamant. 'Poor, dear, beautiful Madeleine. Ste-Anne's most famous daughter. Killed by a madman. What do you know about him, Pierre?' Her eyes fix me with their eager guile.

'Less than you, I imagine.'

'It's too horrible!' a voice from behind the counter erupts with soft terror. I notice young Martine Senegal. She is fingering the scarf Madeleine gave her.

'Don't worry, Martine.' Mme Groulx is as fierce as a Trojan woman. 'He'll be locked away in the pen until he roasts in hell. For myself, I only wish that could be tomorrow. And we'll get his sidekicks, too. All of them.'

'All of them,' a voice I don't recognize echoes from a counter stool.

'Yes, hang the killer and good riddance to him. To them all.' Senegal puts a protective arm round his granddaughter. 'We have to avenge Madeleine.'

It comes to me in a flash that Madeleine as the victim of a murder has re-entered the magic circle of community, a status she has long been excluded from. Her suicide only confirmed her as an outsider. As a murderee, she can be embraced. There is a new and more intolerable figure to cast in the role of outsider, one who can meld both the young and the old in the town together in justifiable hatred.

I push my chair back from the table.

'Going already, Pierre?'

'I have to see Gagnon.'

'Of course.' Mme Groulx pats my hand. 'Come back and tell us if there are any developments.'

The police building is a solid square of brick just round the corner from my office. Its doors are thick oak and as they open, a buzzer sounds somewhere in the interior. Young Miron is sitting at a desk behind the counter.

'I thought you were off-duty, Miron.'

'The chief called me back.' He averts his eyes, presses a button and waves me through to Gagnon's office.

Gagnon is on the phone. A scowl hovers over his face without quite settling. He scribbles a note on the pad in front of him. It is the only visible paper on his uncannily tidy desk.

'We'll see you about ten tomorrow then,' he says and puts the receiver down with a bang. 'That was Contini. You heard. He'll be here tomorrow. Where d'you go off to? I still haven't been able to get Mme Tremblay here. Not that it matters. Mme Groulx made the identification.' His thumb moves unwittingly over his badge, polishing it.

'She told me. I just bumped into her.'

'Hmmm. Made a meal of it, did she? Never mind.' With a sly grin, he points to a corner of the room. Next to a filing cabinet, I see a transparent plastic sack. Inside it sits a large can.

'Kerosene,' Gagnon says triumphantly. 'Michel Dubois turned up the can near the barn.'

I tell him about Mme Tremblay, tell him too that, for her sake, the information had best be kept quiet. His gaunt features furrow into grimness. 'Can't really blame her for trying, can you? I hope you didn't add to her misery and tell her about the fire.'

I shake my head. 'And how is your suspect keeping? Has he made a full confession?'

Gagnon lets out a growl. 'Not a squeak. Miron's had a go too. The bastard just lies there. And there's no ID on him. No credit cards. Only a wad of bills.'

'Can I see him?'

He hesitates. For some reason he is no longer as keen on my presence as he was earlier. Maybe Contini has given him orders.

'I might be able to get him to talk.'

Gagnon shrugs. 'OK. What the hell . . .'

Through the peephole in the bolted door of the cell, I see the youth, but he is not stretched out on the narrow strip of a bed. He is pacing. The distorting glass makes his head inordinately large, a dark, wavering blob on a shaky stick of a body.

Gagnon pulls open the door and the reek of vomit attacks our nostrils. I can see its source in a flecked yellowy-green heap in a corner of the room.

'*Maudit cochon!*' Gagnon swears, and with a savage thrust pushes the youth onto the bed.

He stares up at us with his vast red-rimmed eyes. The hand he lifts to push his hair back from his face starts and trembles.

'I gotta get out of here,' he mumbles. 'Gotta get out.' His fingers twitch convulsively.

'Bring him some water. Lots of it,' I say to Gagnon. 'And rouse Dr Bertrand. Or better still, Bergeron. He's only five minutes away.'

He doesn't move.

'Go on. Or you'll have a hospitalized suspect on your hands and a family complaining of police brutality.'

'Brutality! After what he's done! All he needs is a fix and Miron's promised him one – when he confesses.' He winks at me.

I refuse the assumed complicity. 'Go on, Gagnon. This won't look good.'

He gives me a hard, assessing look, then hollers for Miron down the corridor.

'Where's your family, Will?' I ask softly. 'Can you give me a phone number?'

The youth stares at me from his vacant distance

and rubs his arm. 'I gotta get out of here,' he repeats.

'Tell me where you live.'

His expression focuses into sudden canniness. 'Oh no. No way. You're not gonna get me that way.' A shudder takes him over. Retching follows in its train.

I try again as I hear footsteps approaching. 'You're in big trouble, Will. Big trouble. Just tell me where you've been staying.'

'Staying,' he echoes. 'Staying.' His eyes are out of kilter again, scurrying round the room in jerky motions. 'The river . . . water. I need water,' he mumbles just as Miron appears with a pitcher and a paper cup.

Will drinks in great noisy gulps, the water trickling down from the corners of his mouth, and sticks out his cup for more.

Miron pours without once taking his eyes off him, as if the youth were some wild animal who might claw and bolt.

'Fire's made him thirsty,' he mutters.

'Has Gagnon tracked down a doctor?'

He collects himself with an effort. 'Bertrand's not around. And Dr Bergeron's line was engaged. He's still trying.'

'It'll be simpler to run over there.'

'I can't leave here,' Miron says, a sullen stubbornness in his tone. He exchanges a look I can't quite interpret with his prisoner.

'OK. I'll go.'

Relief fills me as I leave the nauseating smell of

the cell behind and step out into the crisp cold of the evening. I walk quickly towards Dr Bergeron's office.

Only as I hear her voice over the answerphone do I remember that this is one of Maryla's late days at the practice. It is clear from her smile that she thinks I have dropped round especially to see her.

'Pierre. How nice.' She smoothes the collar of the white uniform she wears for office hours, then lowers her eyes guiltily. I notice a neatly dressed young woman sitting in the corner of the room, a baby in her lap.

'I should only be another twenty minutes or so,' Maryla says in a formal voice. 'There's just Mme Chrétien and baby Yves to go.'

'In fact, Gagnon's sent me, Maryla. We need a doctor over at the police station. Can you ask Bergeron if he'll come, as soon as he's through here?'

Maryla's posture takes on the rigidity of a chinkless wall.

'Is it for that man the police have caught?' the woman in the corner asks, her question underlined with a tremor.

I nod. Her shudder is visible.

'I said to my husband when it all happened that a woman like Madeleine Blais had no earthly reason to do away with herself. I'm no feminist. But you can't help get the impression that these men are out to do us down. What's to become of you, Yves?' She gives the baby on her lap an uncertain glance, then to make up for her betrayal bounces him too vigorously.

'Dr Bergeron says he'll be over as soon as he's finished here. Yves' shot won't take long.' Maryla turns a frosty face on me.

'Thanks. Be seeing you.'

I am already at the end of the corridor when she comes up behind me. 'Pierre.' She puts a hand on my shoulder. 'I'm sorry. It was wrong of me to say all those things about Madeleine Blais. I've been feeling terrible about it, ever since I saw Mme Tremblay on the television.' Her lips quiver. 'And scared. A killer loose in the area! Thank God, they've got him now.'

'Yes.'

She gives me a beseeching look. 'Would you like to come and have dinner with Stefan and me later?'

I squeeze her hand. 'I've got things to do, Maryla. And I'm preoccupied at the moment. You understand.'

She nods mournfully and I rush away. I cannot cope with Maryla's sadness. If only I could find her a suitable man. I run through the possibilities for the hundredth time as I make my way back to the station. I am just about to push the door open when I change my mind. There is little more I can find out here for the moment.

Just as I skirt the town hall a Mercedes pulls up and I hear my name called from the window.

Mayor Desforges eases himself from the depths of the car with remarkable agility. After a moment spent in the necessary polite exchanges, he lowers his voice and complains, 'I don't like this new development at all, Pierre. Not a single bit. Of all places for Madeleine Blais to be murdered. I had just about convinced this collective of ceramicists to take over the old toy factory. You know, the MacKenzie place. But now . . .' He shakes his head.

'There are deaths in Montréal, too,' I mutter.

'Yes, but this is a women's collective. Still.' He taps his leather-gloved fingers on his belly. 'It can only be to the good that a local man got the murderer. Who would of thought it of Gagnon, eh? And the villain's not from Ste-Anne. An Anglo, Gagnon tells me. Mme Tremblay must be relieved.'

'Relieved that he's not from here?' I find myself saying.

'No . . . no. Just . . . Convey my regards to her, Pierre. I've got to dash to a meeting.'

He propels his sturdy form through the doors of the town hall and vanishes with a wave.

For a moment my old anger at all the inhabitants of Ste-Anne and their bigotry overtakes me. I don't stop at my office as I had intended. Instead I get into the car, back up with a lurch and head to the right away from the main street.

As I drive, I try to imagine Madeleine with the beautiful spaced-out youth. Why won't the pictures coalesce? It's not as if I have ever had any difficulty in imagining Madeleine with other men before. And this time I have the evidence of her bedroom. I saw the rumpled sheets. I have her grandmother's word. I position myself at her window and look in, but all I can see are blurred shadowy shapes. Nor can I force my mind to take the next steps, to follow the pair down the hill, towards the barn, into it. The boy is simply too vacant, too young, his thin limbs too weedy.

But what if my premises are all wrong? What if this Will in the omnipotence of an 'up' is altogether different from the Will I have seen – in a daze in front of the fire, retching weakly in a stinking cell? Or what if both he and Madeleine were on something together, some potent chemical concoction? Not heroin, no, but some other cocktail. And if she decided to perform the ultimate act for his eyes alone?

Something in me still refuses the picture. Is it simply that Will's voice is not the voice on the answering machine that Mme Tremblay identified as Madeleine's guest? She could easily be wrong.

The picture shifts and suddenly hovering in front of my eyes is an image of Will setting the barn alight. He is swaying on those long, thin legs of his, the wind blowing through his black hair. He turns his back on the gust and shelters the match with his hand, stares at the magic of the leaping flame, watches it billow and grow.

That I can see clearly. Yes. Whether he did it accidentally or on purpose is for the moment almost irrelevant. I edge myself into his skin and, as I do so, I notice that I am not following the route home. Yet I know exactly where I am going.

10

The stars are hidden above a charcoal wash of cloud. Behind a gnarled beech hedge, the house stands out squat and white against the darkness. It has a dilapidated air. The paint on the clapboard bubbles and curls. The gutter hangs loosely from the roof and slopes precariously where it has rusted away from the pipe. Each fresh gust of wind brings a yawning creak.

A faint light flickers from the edges of a single curtained window. It helps me follow the path where the ground slopes gently towards the river. The door is to the side, through a covered porch which bears a worn mat. On it the word 'Welcome' is still distinguishable in English.

From inside raucous music reverberates, the fast, pounding beat of techno. The bell I press makes no dent on the noise. I wait and then bang my fist and bang again and wish I had some police badge to flash.

After what feels like an eternity of pounding, there is a pause in the music. I press the bell again and for good measure, knock.

'Ya?' A voice calls out, just as the music comes on again.

'Open up,' I shout.

The door squeaks open to the width of a chain. A young face appears, rust-coloured dreadlocks, staring eyes, a sharp yet flaring nose. For a moment in the thin gleam of light I don't know whether the features are male or female. Then the 'What d'you want?' makes it clear.

'Does Will live here?'

The youth's eyes narrow. 'You a cop?'

'No, a lawyer.' I cheat a little. 'Pierre Rousseau. Look, why don't you open the door and let me in. I just want to ask you some questions.'

'I haven't got any answers.'

The music has been turned off and in the background I hear a woman's voice: 'Who is it, Charlie?'

A wisp of a girl appears behind him. He slams the door in my face.

I press the bell again. Through it, I can hear them arguing. I wait. 'Open up, Charlie,' I shout after a moment.

The door swings open. The girl stands there, swaying a little, wispy strands of hair half obliterating her face. She smiles a wide smile which makes her pretty, an elf in skin-tight leggings and a baggy sweatshirt.

'Charlie doesn't like visitors,' she says.

'I'm sorry to disturb you like this. I didn't have a number to ring.'

'You're cute,' she lisps. 'Charlie,' she shouts suddenly. 'He's cute. He won't be any trouble. Come on in. Have a drink.'

She leads me into a living room which still bears traces of what must once have been rustic holiday comfort. There is a wide arc of a fireplace, an L-shaped sofa, a scattering of tables. Striped Mexican blankets hang from the walls. But around them the paint is mouldy. The fabric on the sofa has worn thin and is splotched with wine stains. Balls of dust fly at my tread. Dirty dishes clutter the tables. A row of Russian babushka dolls stands atop a radiator shelf. The largest of the dolls is open, its upper half swinging slightly.

The light comes from an assortment of candles. They flicker and gut from floor and mantel. Everywhere there is a stale smell of embedded nicotine and the higher, sweeter whiff of marijuana.

From the next room I hear cupboard doors slamming, the clatter of objects hastily hidden. I imagine needles being stashed, bottles of pills, strips of powder.

The girl pours some wine into a blotchy glass and passes it to me. 'Charlie's just cleaning up,' she giggles.

The giggle goes on until Charlie reappears and then stops abruptly. His sweatshirt has Crash written on it in big letters. His jeans are strategically punctuated with holes. He pats his pocket. There is something hard and angular in it. He thrusts his hip forward and sneers.

'Don't try anything.'

Fear tickles at my nostrils. The girl bursts into giggles again.

'Shut up,' Charlie says to her. 'OK, what d'you want?'

'You got a licence for that?' I hear myself saying.

'What's it to you?'

I shrug. 'Look, all I want to know is about Will. He's in trouble.'

'Will who?'

The girl laughs again, then clamps a hand across her mouth.

'You tell me that. It's one of the things it would be useful to know.'

I hear the sound of footsteps behind me. I veer round to see a large, slightly puffy youth with dark curling hair and sleepy eyes plodding down the stairs.

'What's going on? Where's the mu—?' He stops as he spots me. 'Who's this?' He looks scared.

'I'm Pierre Rousseau,' I say soothingly, 'from Ste-Anne.' I pull a business card from my pocket for good measure and hand it to him. 'I've come about Will. He's in trouble. Arson.'

'Arson!'

'Maybe worse. Can you tell me about him?'

'We're not getting mixed up in that, man. Shit, my father will kill me.'

'Shut up, Raff,' the dreadlocked youth intervenes.

'Don't tell me to shut up. You're not even supposed to be here.' Raff lumbers down the remaining stairs.

I glance at Charlie whose hand hovers warily around his pocket. The tension in the air increases my own. They are as unpredictable to themselves as they are to me.

Raff pours himself a glass of water from a large

open bottle, drinks. A genial look settles over his pudgy features. 'So you're from Ste-Anne?' He eases himself into the sofa, switches on a lamp. He has the hearty air of a doctor interviewing a new patient. 'Nice little burgh.'

Though I have never met him, I suddenly imagine his father, plump and professionally pleasant, a guise for Raff to fall into in difficult moments.

'Yes.' I return his half-smile.

'We're just down for the holidays,' he offers.

'And Will?'

'Cori picked him up at a party. Last week. Before Christmas.' The elfin girl giggles again and flops down on the sofa beside Raff.

'Idiot,' Charlie mutters.

'Where's Cori?' I ask.

'She went back to the big city.'

'Without Will?'

'Guess so. It was just . . . just a passing thing. He already had a girlfriend. Down here. Rich and beautiful, he said she was. Boasted. That's why he tagged along with us.'

'Shut it, Annie,' Charlie growls.

'Look, Mr Rousseau, we don't really know Will.' Raff has his cordial face on again. 'Don't even know his second name. He was just hanging out here. Bedding down. Just for a few nights, on and off.'

'Who was the girlfriend?' I ask, my voice not quite steady.

'We don't have to answer any of your fucking questions.' Charlie suddenly lunges at me and I find my fist furiously meeting his chest. I would like to

283

keep pounding at it but Raff drags him away with a 'Manners, Charlie,' and heaves him towards the sofa.

'Charlie's a little excited,' Raff says to me smoothly. 'Aren't you, Charlie? Cool it. This man's almost a neighbour.'

'Who was the girlfriend?' I address the girl again.

'Dunno. Don't really believe in her. Cori said Will wasn't much cop in . . .' She flushes and stops herself. 'All we know about Will is that he's American. From Detroit or somewhere.' Her eyes betray fear for the first time. 'Arson, you said. What did he burn down?'

'A barn.'

She giggles.

'Annie!' Raff reprimands her.

From behind me I hear the creak of a door. I turn round and see a wraith-like shape peering at us from a darkened room.

'It's OK, Hal. Get back to bed,' Raff calls out. An edge of nervousness has crept back into his voice. His smile flounders. 'Some more friends,' he says, as if he were already in a courtroom.

'Where was this party you met Will at?'

'Further up north. In a club. In Ste-Agathe.'

'Did he go and see his girlfriend once he got here?'

'I couldn't say. We don't keep tabs on each other. As you can imagine.'

'But Will deals, right?' I say softly to Raff.

His face crumbles. Nothing comes out of his open mouth.

'Never mind. You can tell the police about it. You better prepare yourself.' I say it without a hint of menace. I feel rather sorry for Raff, but as I make to leave, Charlie leaps up and blocks my path. His hand is poised threateningly on his hip just above the bulge of the gun.

'What the fuck are you gonna tell the cops?'

I still myself. 'It depends what they ask me. If they ask me anything.'

'Oh ya? So what the fuck you so interested for? Your barn or something?'

I shake my head.

His look turns querulous. 'You just a busybody then.'

'You could say that.'

He still isn't prepared to let me go. 'I don't buy it.'

'Buy what you like. Buy a newspaper. My wife's been murdered.'

His body goes slack. As he digests my words, I push past him into the cold.

I don't look back. Instead I wonder at myself. In death, it seems Madeleine has become my wife again.

Snow has started to fall. Big blundering flurries flop across the windshield and gather in white banks along the edges of the screen. I drive slowly, my tyres squelching uneasily in the soft new snow, my headlights illuminating only random flurries of whiteness.

After a few minutes, I see the yellow glow of lights through the trees in the distance. The car

285

clock reads 9.40. Not too late. I turn off onto a narrow drive and park a few metres from the sprawling, slightly ramshackle house, with its beguiling row of mansard windows.

'Pierre! *Tiens*. It's good to see you.' Oscar Boileau envelops me in a bear hug. 'We missed you on Tuesday. And I left you a message when we heard, but . . .' He holds up his hand to stop my apologies. 'I know you've had other things on your mind. Miserable business. How're you holding up?' He surveys me speculatively for a slow, silent minute, then ushers me into the warm kitchen.

Oscar is my closest friend in Ste-Anne. We met just after I came back here. A painter, he had moved into the vicinity from his home in Trois Rivières some years earlier. He came to my office because he wanted to acquire a strip of land adjoining his house, together with some outbuildings to convert into studio space. A second child was about to squeeze him out.

Our friendship grew quickly. A big, generous, bearded man with dark laughing eyes, Oscar had everything I didn't have: high spirits, single-minded dedication to his work, a loving and devoted wife, and children. And I had, as he teasingly told me, everything he didn't – experience of the world, intelligence, good taste and money. This shared acknowledgement of our differences and liking came as we were working out how Oscar could raise the funds to purchase the property he wanted. I helped a little by buying three of his canvases. Two of them hang in my office. One, I gave to

Madeleine. She liked it so much she came to meet Oscar on one of her visits and bought two more.

Needless to say, he was enthralled by her. Though he rarely does portraits, he offered to paint her. He told me it would be fascinating to try and render in solid, emphatically material oils a subject who owed part of her magic to that flickering, illusory domain of the screen.

Madeleine said she'd be thrilled to sit for him when time allowed. Time didn't.

Oscar knows that Madeleine and I were once more than friends. He doesn't know much more. Perhaps he's guessed, but there never seemed to be much point in elaborating a past which often feels too intimate even for my own reflections.

'You're not exactly looking your best,' Oscar tells me now as he uncorks a bottle of wine and puts it down on the chequered cloth which covers the large rectangle of a kitchen table. 'Hardly surprising, I guess. How about a bowl of Elise's soup to set you up?'

Without waiting for my reply, he lights a hob beneath a vast copper pot and cuts a thick slab of bread.

'The children asleep?' I ask. Oscar and Elise's brood of three have taken on the status of god-children for me.

He nods. 'And from the depth of the silence, I imagine Elise has dropped off with the babe.'

'Just as well. I've forgotten all the presents.'

'Poor little underprivileged darlings will just have to forgive you,' Oscar snorts and shunts aside the toys which litter the table. 'So tell me. Tell me everything. We've followed the papers, but what with the grandparents here until yesterday . . .' He shrugs with full Gallic emphasis and straddles the stool opposite me.

'In fact, I'd like to do some asking.'

'Oh?'

'Yes. You know the holiday house about a kilometre north of here?'

'Dr Rosenberg's property? Someone interested in buying it?'

'Is it for sale?'

'He had it on the market a few years back. He rarely comes here any more. But no-one wanted to buy. The sign's gone now. I think his kids use it from time to time. Changing bands of them. It's beginning to look like a squat.' He gives me his puzzled frown. 'What's all this about, Pierre?'

'Do you know the kids?'

'Not really. Layabouts from what I can make out. Students maybe. Stoned out of their heads most of the time. Gone are the days, eh . . .'

He gets up to ladle soup into a bowl. It steams in front of me, hot and fragrant. I suddenly feel very tired.

'Have you heard that Mme Tremblay's barn was torched?'

'No! When? We didn't catch the news today.'

'Early this morning. The police think one of those kids did it. They've arrested a youth called Will. Gagnon is convinced he murdered Madeleine as well.'

Oscar stares at me in utter stillness, his cheeks drained of their usual ruddiness.

'*Mauditcriss!* I didn't like to believe that when Mme Tremblay said it. Not around here. Not murder. How ghastly for Madeleine.'

He unearths a pipe from an ornate box on the counter and plays with it absent-mindedly.

'Two nights ago, maybe three, Elise was putting things away in the playroom, you know, at the other end of the house in the back, and she turned and saw this face staring in at her. She came screaming up to me but by the time I got my boots on and went out, there was no-one. I told her she was hallucinating.'

'Did you find anything missing?'

'No. Don't think so. Though someone or something had been into the shed. It was a bit of a jumble.'

'What did Elise say the prowler looked like?'

'Wild. A savage. But you know, when you haven't been sleeping much . . . Anyhow, I didn't take it too seriously at the time. But now . . . I'll have to watch Christophe and Chantale as well. They're always wandering off on their own. Still, the police have got him?' He looks at me for the reassurance I can't altogether give.

'They think so.' I sip my wine in order not to meet his eyes.

'What do you make of all this, Pierre?'

I shrug and push back my chair. Like one of Oscar's canvases, my mind refuses outlines. Everything is a blur of shape and raucous colour.

He puts a staying hand on my arm. 'Listen, why don't you stay here tonight? There's an old misery of a blizzard out there. And Chantale will never forgive me if she hears you've been and gone without saying hello. What do you say?'

I hesitate. But I don't hesitate for long. Though I don't like to admit it to myself, the last place I want to be for the length of a night is home.

Warm breath on my cheek and the murmur of a 'Bonjour' wake me in the morning. I open my eyes to see a small face bending over me.

'There. I told Maman you were awake.' Eight-year-old Chantale's smile is at once innocent and mischievous beneath her china-doll eyes. 'Breakfast is ready, Tonton Pierre, and there's a mountain of snow.'

I kiss her smooth forehead and whisk her off to tell her mother that I'll be down in a few minutes. She hesitates at the door, turns back.

'There's been a murder, Tonton Pierre. A murder!' Her mouth is round with the emphasis. 'Just like on the television. I heard Maman and Papa talking about it.'

'Does it frighten you?' I ask softly.

'*Non*.' She shakes her head. 'They're going to hang him.' Her hand flicks across her throat in a swift arc and with a bounce and a skip she is out of the room.

I stare after her and wonder at the certain precision of her sense of justice. My head is muddy with dreams. Their footprints bog me down, drag me into a murky world where the figures who hang from ropes are transformed with kaleidoscopic speed. Madeleine, the youth called Will, Mme Tremblay, myself. Above and around and through it all, there are words, writing on a page I can't quite read. Madeleine's journals, perhaps. An explanation? Something in me resists the notion of murder, refuses it, balks with all the fury of a rearing stallion. If Madeleine must be dead, I want it to have been by her own hand. Why? Why? I try to shake myself into a semblance of clarity and make my way down the narrow staircase.

The smell of frying bacon curls from the kitchen. Elise glances away from her skillet as I come in and gives me a warm smile. She is a woman of lazy voluptuousness, all generous curves and waving hair and easy charm. Her studio, where she chips away at hunks of stone to reveal surprising shapes, half-animal, half-human, is adjacent to Oscar's. I have seen her working in there, her concentration total, yet somehow alert to the children playing in the corner.

'I've made your favourite,' she says to me now and simultaneously gives the baby's canvas chair a little rock. 'Pancakes. Because you missed the duck on Tuesday. Why don't you call Oscar and the kids? They're outside.'

Oscar is clearing a path between the house and the studio. He scrapes the ground with his large curved scoop of a shovel and heaves the snow into growing mounds at the side. The children pat it into stiff peaks with their spades. Chantale waves to me. I trudge out to join them. It is still snowing, but only a little now.

'Breakfast is ready. But I could give you a hand, if you point me to another shovel.'

Oscar shakes his head. 'You go and get yourself a cup of coffee.' He grins at me. 'Didn't your mother teach you to wear a coat before you came out?'

'Yes, Tonton,' Chantale scolds in a maternal voice. 'It's cold out.'

'Elise wanted to have a quiet word with you,' Oscar says for my ears alone. 'We'll join you in a few minutes.'

'He wants me to tell you?' Elise asks when I report Oscar's words. 'OK.' She scoops a last pancake from the skillet and pops the plateful into the oven. She pours me a cup of coffee, wipes her hands meticulously on a teacloth.

Elise doesn't like words. She prefers gestures, has to make several of them before language finds its shape in her.

'It's the kids. They were playing in that wooded stretch. Pretending they were space rangers or something. Scouting out a foreign planet. A few days back, it was. Last week maybe. They couldn't quite remember. They saw two men. One of them had hair like rope, Christophe said. The other one was dark, in leather. They had a knife. A big knife.' She shivers and grips her mug with both hands.

'They were cutting marks into the trees. Chantale claims they dropped something into them too. Small bags. Bags of jewels, she said. Something small in any case. When the men spotted them, they shouted and chased after them. But my kids run like furies. Or like space rangers. Luckily.' She laughs to cover her fear. 'They didn't tell me about it, cause they knew I'd get mad. What's going on around here, Pierre?'

'Nothing good,' I mutter just as the children burst through the door closely followed by Oscar.

'Don't make a big thing of it now,' Elise whispers. She smiles a little shakily at her brood, squeezes the baby's foot and repositions his chair at the end of the table before calling out, 'Right, how many pancakes can each of you eat?'

'A hundred,' says tousle-headed Christophe.

'A hundred and fifty,' blurts Chantale.

'Three for me,' Oscar chuckles.

Elise dishes out pancakes and bacon and generous splashes of maple syrup. We eat and pretend normality and eventually it settles over us, as reassuring as the baby's gurgle and the soft milky batter in our stomachs.

Maybe because I want to extend my stay in this safe haven, before I leave I ask Oscar if I can have a peek into the studio where I haven't been for some time. He hesitates unusually, but then with a shrug walks me over and unlocks the heavy double doors.

The first impression, as always, is that of vivid colour leaping out from walls and easels. As the colours take on shape, I notice Madeleine's profile emerging from a canvas which Oscar is turning to the wall. His manner has an edge of deliberate nonchalance. He doesn't want me to see.

'So you did make a start,' I murmur.

'I couldn't resist the temptation.' Oscar doesn't meet my eyes.

'Even though she didn't have time to come and sit for you?'

There is a veiled expression on his face. He turns away from me. The way his fist is clenched sets up an odd prickle in my spine.

'Did she?'

'Once. Just once.' He veers back at me, his body poised in challenge, a glimmer of hostility in his dark eyes.

'I see.'

'Drop it, Pierre.' He up-ends a large canvas. 'What do you think of this?'

I cannot think of anything except the meaning of that 'once'.

As I skid along the road in the ridges left by the plough, I try to focus only on the innocent white of the newly fallen snow. But the fluffy blanket which has bleached the world evokes a kind of panic in me. How am I to distinguish the proper outlines of things? How am I to distinguish the meaningful from the meaningless, where there is only nature's impassive whiteness?

Abruptly I take the turn to Mme Tremblay's house and inch along the drive past the parked cars which no longer surprise me. A dark-jacketed man is shovelling snow from the steps. He looks up at me with overt suspicion. I recognize Michel Dubois just as he recognizes me. From somewhere the dogs bark, their excitement drowning the whirr of the heater.

Michel waves me to a halt, lumbers towards me. I lower my window.

'Where is Mme Tremblay?' he asks as accusingly as if I had done away with her.

'In Montréal.' I offer no explanation.

He glares at me from beneath bushy brows.

'Do you need her for something?'

'Her daughter's been looking for her.'

From behind him on the porch, a woman emerges. Middle height, dress just a little too tight, buxom figure, blond hair out of a cheap bottle.

'Has Maman arrived, M. Dubois?' she calls in sugary tones.

Trailing her like a welcoming committee are two men. One of them is my brother, Jerome. The second I don't recognize. He is balding and stocky, his eyes dark smudges half-lost in the flesh of his face. As he thrusts a pugnacious jaw in my direction, I remember Giorgio Napolitano's account of Madeleine's insistent stepbrother.

Jerome beckons me towards them. Reluctantly I leave the shelter of the car.

'I thought you'd had the good sense to take my advice and go,' Jerome mutters and then, his face repositioned into stiff politeness, he clears his throat and introduces me to Marcel and Monique Blais.

Close to, Madeleine's mother has pouchy rouged cheeks which obliterate the structure of her face, a slightly snub nose and mascara-dark eyes which gaze up at me in near-sighted curiosity. There is

295

nothing in her face to remind me of Madeleine. Nor can I conjure up the Monique of my brother's pubescent fantasies.

'Pierre Rousseau!' she breathes. 'So this is how you turned out. Well, well, well. Madeleine never sent me a photo and I haven't seen you in I don't want to admit how long. You were just a baby. You look so like your mother. While Jerome, he's your father through and through.'

Her face abruptly takes on a tragic cast and she sways a little so that my brother puts a steadying hand on her shoulder and then, as if he had been burnt, quickly removes it.

Monique Blais takes a step towards me and buries her face in my shoulder. 'It's too terrible, Pierre. Too awful for words. I still can't believe it!'

I move away from her, watch the tissue come out of her pocket, the dabbing at the eyes, see that my brother is altogether riveted.

'I drove here as soon as I heard, but Maman, she . . .'

'Where is Mme Tremblay, Pierre?' Jerome asks in the steely voice of a knight bent on a mission. 'I wanted to have a word with her. It really isn't right—'

I cut him off. 'Mme Tremblay has been taken unwell. She's had to stay in Montréal.'

'*Pauvre maman!*' Monique exclaims. 'Madeleine was the whole world to her. More than a daughter. Yes, I'm not afraid to admit that, Jerome.'

'Unwell?' Michel Dubois interjects from behind me.

'Yes. She should be back in a few days,' I prevaricate.

'You'll give me her number. Monique really needs to be able to stay here. And Marcel.' Jerome turns a look of sudden distaste towards the man at his side who hasn't uttered a word.

Marcel wears a look of stubborn and impatient dissatisfaction. 'Madeleine would have wanted us here. She told me that—'

'Well, you can't stay unless Mme Tremblay tells me so,' Michel Dubois cuts him off with no attempt at politeness. He trudges into the house and is back moments later bearing three coats.

'What did Madeleine tell you?' I ask Marcel.

'Oh nothing,' he grunts and for a fraction of a second I think he is going to raise one of the large, stubby-fingered hands which swings at his side and hit Michel. But the latter unceremoniously thrusts a thick navy-blue jacket into his arms and without a word double locks the front door.

'I'll drop by to see you later, Pierre,' my brother says with low menace as he passes me on the steps.

I watch Monique get into Jerome's car, watch Marcel stamp towards his and then, grateful for Michel Dubois' decisiveness, carry on in the opposite direction.

There is sheer ice under the snow where the fire engines spilled their stream. My tyres all but lose their grip. Below me, where the barn once was, only an L-shaped wedge of snow inflects the horizon. The site of Madeleine's death has been utterly eradicated.

I step out into the wind. I have the odd impression that its whistling gusts carry Madeleine's laughter.

'You never see what's in front of your nose,' she tells me.

What does she mean? And yet she's right. Altogether right, I reassure the wind. I never saw Madeleine's betrayals until I saw too many of them at once and then I couldn't see for dizziness. But I don't want to think of that now. It doesn't matter now. I stand there and gaze at nothing until the cold becomes as painful as my thoughts and forces me into action.

By a sheer miracle of patience and luck, I manage to turn the car round. I skirt my house and drive into Ste-Anne. Even though it is Saturday morning, the snow has made it quieter than yesterday evening. Then too, most people now do their shopping in the vast mall some twenty kilometres away where piped music and airport air can smooth and encourage their purchases.

At the small-scale *supermarché*, I stop off and buy some instant coffee and a carton of milk to replenish my office supply. For good measure, though I am not sure I want to look at them, I pick up the papers.

The headline in the local rag catches my eye with its sheer size even before I have reached my office.

'BARN BLAZE: SUSPECT HELD IN MADELEINE BLAIS CASE', it blares in its second and now official issue of the week.

My office is cold and smells of a week's abandonment. I turn the heat up and make my way past the front rooms to deposit the supplies in the kitchenette. The back room, which serves as my private space, overlooks a small garden. Despite the cold, I open the window to allow some fresh air in and glance at the pink terracotta Aphrodite which Madeleine once gave me as a present. Shipping it back from Paris was a madness I have not regretted. The warm stone is now capped with a white hat, but the colour irradiates the garden like a touch of Italian sunlight.

Above my desk, Oscar's canvas fills the wall, its gashes of blue as vivid as Aphrodite's earth. The picture, unusual for him, depicts Chantale's nursery. Cribs and chairs rock, mobiles swing around a still centre of mother and child illuminated by the blue sky which pours through the windows. I gaze at the picture and will it to blot out the glimpsed portrait of Madeleine with all its undertones of treachery. It refuses. The papers seem preferable.

Below the local rag's photo of Mme Tremblay's burning barn, a heinous story of arson and murder unfolds. 'An unnamed man is being held in connection with both crimes. Sources close to the police say the suspect is not a local, but was visiting the home of Dr David Rosenberg on the Shore Road.'

I wonder at these sources close to the police. They can only be a loquacious Mme Groulx.

The Montréal paper takes a slightly different tack. Next to a picture of the blaze, there is a photograph of Mme Tremblay which, given the earnest determination of her face, seems to have been reproduced from her television appearance. The story underlines how correct Madeleine Blais' grandmother has been in her intuitions.

Seeing Mme Tremblay brings me to my senses. With guilty haste, I ring the operator to get the number of the Montréal General and then hang on for what feels like hours until I am put through to the appropriate ward. At last a Nurse Reynolds tells me that Mme Tremblay is making good progress. She is aware of her surroundings now, though she isn't talking much.

'The only troubling thing . . .' Nurse Reynolds hesitates, 'is that she keeps going on about the urgency of a funeral. That it isn't right the funeral hasn't been arranged yet.' She sighs. 'The doctor wants to keep her under observation for at least another day.'

I digest this and suggest to the nurse that Mme Tremblay may well be talking of her granddaughter's funeral and not her own.

'Oh, I see. Yes, of course. Still, it will be best to keep her here.'

I concede that. I also stress that for obvious reasons all newspapers must be kept from her. 'And on no account must any journalist be allowed to sneak through to disturb her. Will you make sure of that?'

'Yes, yes. Of course.' Her voice takes on that trill of excitement that a mention of the media always seems to elicit. 'But how will we know whom to let in, if she has visitors, that is?'

'Look, I'll try and arrange for a couple of friends to come and sit with her. I'll ring you back with their names.'

On the spur of the moment I contact Gisèle Desnos, the publicity director at the theatre. She answers on the second ring. She hasn't left home yet.

'Pierre.' Her voice is husky as if she has already been through a day's worth of cigarettes. 'I've just seen the papers. It's too awful. I can't take this murder on board. The police came to interview me yesterday morning.'

'Oh?' I interrupt her nervous flow.

'Yes. An Italian guy.'

'Contini,' I fill in for her and feel a sudden tingle of apprehension.

'That's it. And he didn't breathe a word about murder. But he asked about you. We've got to talk, Pierre. Are you in town?'

'No, that's why I'm calling.'

I explain about Mme Tremblay. Gisèle is aghast and only too willing to help. 'Yes, sure I'll sit with her. The office can go and stew. All I do is answer journalists' questions about Madeleine in any case. And it'll be worse today. Far worse. My assistant can cope. I'll enjoy keeping the snoops away from Mme Tremblay.'

With a small sense of triumph, I ring back Nurse Reynolds and then, despite the unusual silence of the office, try to pretend this is an ordinary working day. Not a Saturday. Not a day five days after Madeleine's death.

I stack the heap of unopened mail in a tray. I

switch on the computer for company. I make myself a cup of instant coffee and carry it back to my desk. Pen in hand, I press the button on the answering machine and listen to a voice which, after a few high-pitched seconds, identifies itself as M. Lefèvre who wants to change his will after the disaster of Christmas with his son and daughter-in-law. Two messages later comes one from his son enquiring about the nature of power of attorney. His ancient father, he says, is definitely losing his marbles.

On impulse, I ring back both father and son and listen to their plaints, soothe them, and give them an appointment for the coming week. The very fact of a named date on which things can be sorted out will, I know, calm their relations.

I scribble down names and numbers of two more people seeking appointments, then pause as I hear Marie-Ange Corot, Madeleine's agent in Paris, again. I have forgotten to return her call.

Glancing at my watch to check the time in France, I dial the number she has left, only to be greeted by another answering machine. Relieved, I convey my apologies and say I will try her later.

No sooner have I put the phone down than it startles me with its ring. I stare at it in fascination, wondering who thinks they'll be able to reach me here on a Saturday morning. On the third ring, I pick it up.

'Mr Pierre Rousseau?' a tentative voice says in English.

'That's me.'

'Oh, thank goodness. Mr Rousseau, this is

Raff. Raff Rosenberg. You came round last night.'

'Yes.' My attention is total.

'We're in trouble here. Don't know what to do. Bricks have come through the windows. Two of them. Horrible messages wrapped round them. And there are these people outside. Lots of them. They don't look friendly.' He swallows noisily. 'We're scared.'

'Have you rung the police?'

'No. You see, that's just it. We don't want the police here. We were going to leave this morning. There's just Annie and me now. The others cleared off in the night. We wanted to tidy up. My - parents . . .' He leaves the sentence hanging, then rushes on in rising hysteria. 'But now, it's a complete mess. There's glass everywhere. Annie's hurt.' A sob escapes him. He chokes it into control. 'We just want to get out of here. We thought you could come and talk to the people outside.'

'Look, Raff.' I put on my most soothing voice. 'You'll have to face the police some time. Better here than at home, no? I'll get them to come straight over. I'll come with them. You go and sit tight in an upstairs room.'

I rush round to the police station. Despite the buzz the opening of the door sets up, there is no-one in the outer office. I hesitate to push open the half-door which leads to the inner rooms. I pause for a moment and wait. Through the glazed window on the side, I suddenly notice Contini's bent head. Facing him is Mme Groulx in her best fur hat. It perches on her hair at a precarious angle.

Contini's voice weaves clearly round the door. 'You're sure that this man we've just seen is the same as the man you saw at midnight mass with Madeleine Blais? Absolutely certain?' Contini sounds exasperated.

'Yes. It's just as I told the man from *La Presse* this morning.' Mme Groulx preens herself like some plump outlandish bird. 'He's one of those types who hang out at the old Jew's house. He—'

'I didn't ask you for his religion, Mme Groulx,' Contini interrupts. 'So now you're telling me that you saw him before midnight mass. You had already seen the youth before you saw him with Mlle Blais?'

For a moment, Mme Groulx looks confused. She adjusts her hat. 'Yes. Yes. I think so.'

'Thank you, Mme Groulx. That will be all.' Contini stands up.

'Don't you need me for anything else, detective?'

'Not right now, Mme Groulx. Oh, just tell me,' he adds as he ushers her through the door, 'do you wear glasses, Mme Groulx?'

'Sometimes. When I need to. My eyes . . .' She glares up at him with swift suspicion. 'You're not going to let him go, detective?'

'We'll do exactly as the law requires of us, Mme Groulx. You can sleep in peace.' He looks up and sees me. 'Rousseau, what are you doing here?'

'Pierre.' Mme Groulx hastens towards me.

'I need to talk to the detective, Mme Groulx. In private.' I open the front door for her and, with a gesture made up in equal measure of unbreachable authority and irreproachable politeness which I must

304

have learned from my father, help her through it.

'So you don't trust Mme Groulx's eyes?' I ask Contini.

'The eyes of one or even two old ladies rarely hold up under cross-examination for murder. You've been eavesdropping.'

I shrug. 'Does that mean you'll only hold Will on the arson charge? It seems he might have known Madeleine before . . . before . . .'

'Oh?' Pebble-dark eyes glint at me. Their irony is uncertain. 'So you've been carrying out your own investigation, Rousseau? That's good. That's good. I need evidence, Rousseau. Hard facts.' He scrunches up a piece of paper on the desk as if it weren't hard enough. 'We're taking Will up to headquarters. We'll do a sperm-test on him. If he complies, that is. You bet he's got a rich daddy somewhere just dying to hire a high-flying lawyer. Did you see that Rolex on him? Either that or he's been making a more lucrative living as a dealer than his nerves would seem to allow for. We'll see. We'll hold on to him for a bit. He's in no shape to go anywhere in any case. I don't know what that local doctor of yours pumped into him, but I wouldn't like it in my veins. His name's Henderson, by the way. Mean anything to you? From Chicago, he says. But that's just what he tells us. Who you been talking to?'

'Damn, I'd almost forgotten! Where's Gagnon?'

'Preparing our charge for his little drive to the big city.'

Hastily I explain about the kids out in the house on the Shore Road.

Contini whistles beneath his breath. 'Getting better and better, this place. And here I was hoping for a quiet Sunday with the missis. Tell you what. We'll all drive out. Henderson, too. See what he tells us when he's among friends. Set the sirens blaring. Make a little procession of it. That should give the heroic local champions of Madeleine Blais something to throw bricks at.'

11

Three police cars precede me along the white strip of snow-banked road. As we weave past Oscar's place, their sirens start to flash and whine and I worry about Elise and the children and the inevitable anxieties the noise will produce. The temptation to stop and explain to them, if not just yet to confront Oscar, is great. I am not looking forward to a second visit to the Rosenberg house.

The curve of the road makes the placards visible before their bearers. 'Go home' one reads and the second follows suit: 'No killers in Ste-Anne'. I wonder if Mayor Desforges would be proud of this instance of civic pride. Certainly he wouldn't approve of the string of cars erratically parked along the stretch of scenic road.

A gaggle of people, maybe twenty-five of them, stand outside the house and stamp their feet as much in cold as in anger. They are shouting, their words incomprehensible, though their mood is as clear as the writing on the impromptu placards. Amongst them I notice Martine Senegal and Noël

Jourdan, a hot-blooded youth whose schoolboy scraps are well known in the town. It occurs to me that it was Noël Jourdan whom I half glimpsed at Senegal's yesterday, sitting at a bar stool and ogling Martine. Georges Lavigueur, a mountain of a man, dull-witted and too strong, stands beside him. Next to him is Gilles Belfort, a bumptious layabout, only and ever cowed by his mother. Some of these names featured on the list I gave Contini.

There is also a teacher from the local primary school. A stickler for the language laws, she once lodged a complaint with Desforges about a missing acute accent from the word Québec in one of his campaign posters and asked him whether he was intent on turning back the clock and rendering the province English once more.

From his gait rather than his face, which is all but hidden between hat and scarf, I also recognize Michel Dubois and realize that, in Contini's words, he can now be counted as one of the champions of Madeleine.

The police cars have ploughed through the snowbound driveway. I pull up alongside and as I get out I hear the jeer of the crowd. A barrage of snowballs whizzes past my ears. One hits Will Henderson on the back of the head. As he turns, a lemon-yellow streak of sun cuts through the covering of cloud. In its light, handcuffs glitter like expensive bracelets. The crowd hoots. More snowballs fly. One of them hits tall, moustachioed Serge Monet, the Sûreté detective who has come down from headquarters with Contini today. With a pitcher's lope, he aims a return shot. I catch myself thinking that I am glad he has replaced Ginette Lavigne.

'Get them out of here,' Contini bellows to Gagnon. 'Tell them we still have trial by jury in this country. Not trial by mob. Book them if you have to. For creating a disturbance. Find out who threw the bricks.' He drags Will towards the house.

Gagnon is distinctly peeved at being ordered about on his own turf and he approaches the crowd with a scowl more determined than any I have ever seen on his face.

'You're not going to protect them!' a woman screams, scandalized. 'We're the ones who need protection.'

'Bloody Jews!' someone exclaims.

'Bloody Anglos!' another echoes.

'What the hell're you doing with that lot, M. Rousseau?' an unrecognizable voice shouts.

'Belt up and get out of here. All of you.' Gagnon hollers as loudly as if he had a megaphone to his mouth. His two constables glance at him in surprise and start dispersing the crowd.

Gagnon puts a restraining hand on Noël Jourdan's shoulder. 'You throw the bricks?'

'Me? Never. I just came along with Martine. Didn't I, Martine?'

The girl nods. 'He's been with me all the time.'

'So who's responsible?'

'We didn't see. He ran away. Round the back. Big guy.' A smirk flashes across Noël's lips.

'Tell me about it later. Now get out of here. All of you.'

309

On the fringes of the crowd, next to fat Georges Lavigueur, I suddenly spy Oscar. I walk over to him and ask him what he's doing here. Despite my better intentions, there is an edge of animosity in my voice.

'Curious about my neighbours,' he says. 'Not that I expected this. Bit of a witch-hunt. The girl at the window looked terrified.'

'Rousseau. Get over here,' Contini bellows from the porch.

I hurry towards him and he glares at me. 'You have a hand in organizing this rabble?'

'Me?'

'You used to be good at this sort of thing. Now get this lot to open the door, will you? Some stubborn lout says he'll only do so if you're here.'

'Raff. It's Pierre Rousseau. Open up.'

The door recedes a crack. Raff peers through, then releases the latch. In the daylight, he looks pale and blotchy and very young, an overgrown kid.

'Will!' his voice erupts with a crack.

'Where's Charlie?'

It is the first coherent phrase I have heard Will utter. The words introduce a certain cunning to his face. He seems nervous but oddly composed, somehow above the fray.

'Charlie's gone,' Raff murmurs. 'Went last night.'

'Charlie who?' Contini is right in there.

Silence meets his question.

Will's dark eyes bear down on Raff in contest with Contini's voice.

'Charlie who?' Contini repeats. He gives Raff a

nudge and moves him towards the front room. 'Look, kid, you're in hot water already. Co-operate.'

'McNeil,' Raff blurts.

'Got a home address?' Serge Monet asks.

Raff shakes his head.

'What's he driving?'

'They all went in Hal's car.'

'All?'

'You don't have to talk, Raff,' Will says casually. 'Get yourself a lawyer.'

For the first time I hear the American twang in his voice and simultaneously, I don't know why, I can picture Madeleine with him. The image momentarily obscures my view of the front room.

When its expanse finally materializes in front of my eyes, I am shocked. There is glass everywhere, on the floor, on the sofa, on the tables. Shards of it crackle beneath my feet. About a metre from the shattered window a brick lies on the corner of a frayed rug. Wrapped round it is a piece of paper on which the crinkled lettering is nonetheless clear: 'Get out and stay out'.

Contini is turning the brick round delicately with his foot, as if it were a kitten to be played with. 'Good thing it didn't hit you.'

'Where's Annie?' I ask.

'Lying down upstairs. She's got cuts on her forehead. I really think we should get her to a hospital.'

'Gagnon,' Contini hollers through the window. 'Get one of your constables in here. We got a hospital case.'

Outside, the crowd has all but dispersed.

311

'Who's Annie?' Contini asks as three of Gagnon's men pour into the room.

'My sister.' Raff looks as if he is about to cry. 'Dad's going to kill us.'

'You deserve it!' Contini growls, then with a change of heart, he puts his arm round Raff's shoulder. 'You speak English?' he asks one of Gagnon's men and when he shakes his head, he orders Serge Monet upstairs with him. 'Check on the girl. See if she needs to be taken to hospital.' His arm still around Raff, he leads him towards the kitchen.

'We speak French,' Raff murmurs.

'Ya, sure. Speak what you like. Just give me a few terse and true facts.' He closes the kitchen door behind them.

In the midst of the commotion, I see Will edging towards the far side of the room with cool nonchalance. Like some male model posed for a shoot, he leans against the radiator. Behind him, the Russian peasant dolls are all assembled today, their bright painted grins macabre in the midst of the surrounding chaos. Will warms himself for a moment, then moves casually away. The largest of the babushkas now lies open. Its top half rolls and falls onto the rug with a soft thud. When I look round, Will is already at the door. I am so engrossed by his bravura that until he has slipped out, I forget to make a sound.

Then I prod Miron. 'Watch your prisoner.'

'*Merde!*' He rushes towards the door, his partner at his heels.

312

I follow in their wake. The two constables are standing on the porch looking from side to side. There is no sign of Will anywhere. One of them points to the prints on the fresh snow and they race off round the corner of the house in the direction of the copse which borders the river. I think of the marked trees Oscar's children talked about and remind myself that I should mention this to Gagnon or Contini.

'Bunglers,' Contini explodes when I come back in. He repeats it to Gagnon who has just stepped into the room. 'Your men are complete bunglers. Either that, or they're up to something.' He scowls at Gagnon.

'Make our job easier,' Gagnon announces tersely. 'Resisting arrest.'

'If they catch him.' Contini is not charitable.

I have the feeling Gagnon is about to say something he may regret, when Monet comes down the stairs.

'And?'

Monet shrugs. 'The girl doesn't seem too bad. More nerves than injuries, I think. Dupuis phoned the local doctor. Said it would be quicker than the hospital on a Saturday. He's sitting with her.'

'OK. Here's the—' Contini stops himself. For a split second, his posture is rigid. Only his ears seem to quiver. Then with a lunge, he makes for the door. Monet is right behind him, his pistol already released from its holster.

'*Mauditcriss*, they're shooting.' Gagnon hesitates.

'Shooting!' Raff's voice screeches into panic.

'You stay here. Go up to your sister. Dupuis will take care of you.'

I follow Gagnon out the door.

Half-way down the wooded slope that leads to the river, angry voices reverberate from the trees. Moments later, we come upon the group of men. Contini is gesticulating wildly, as if he would like to land a punch on Miron's face. The young constable cowers, but stands his ground.

'I don't believe this. I don't fucking believe it. You're chasing after Henderson. You see a gun in his hand. He shoots. Shoots at the ground, mind. You shout. He turns around and you let him have it. But the poor bastard is handcuffed. What did you think he was going to do? Shoot through himself to get at you? And then you aim at his chest. Not his leg, not his arm. His fucking chest. Where d'you do your target practice, Miron? With the SS? In our force, we try to keep our suspects alive.'

'I—'

'You nothing. Look at this. Look, damn you!' Contini waves a tiny pistol in the air. His gloved hands are huge beside it. 'He'd have to get you point blank to do any harm. What did you think it was? A shotgun? A semi-automatic?'

'Take it easy, Contini.' Gagnon steps into the circle. 'He was just scared.'

As the others move back, I see the body stretched on the ground. Will Henderson looks as if he has fallen into a deep sleep. His head is cradled on his extended arms. One leg is bent at the knee, curled towards the other. Only the dark red stain on the snow shatters the illusion.

'The ambulance should be here in fifteen minutes,' Serge Monet announces as he tucks a phone into his pocket.

'OK.' Contini catches my eye for a moment, then rushes on like a general organizing a small army. 'Gagnon, you and your men get back to the house and stay there until the doctor's checked the girl over and they're ready to go. I want them escorted back to Montréal. Meanwhile, give the boy a hand in cleaning the place up. Make sure the windows are boarded. I don't want any more of your brave citizens launching bricks. Is that clear?' He doesn't give him a chance to answer.

'Monet, you stay with Henderson here, then go along to the hospital. Keep your ear to his lips.'

'I'd like to go along.' Young Miron's voice sounds oddly high-pitched.

'You?' Contini glares at him. 'You've had quite enough to do with Henderson for one day. What I want to know is where he got hold of a gun. Got any ideas about that, Miron?' He gives him a rough poke on the shoulder.

Miron steps back.

'I don't think—' Gagnon intervenes.

'I don't care what you think for the moment, Gagnon. I want you to ring Dr Rosenberg and explain things to him in your best goddamn manner. Apologize for the good people of Ste-Anne. If I have a report of even a whiff of impoliteness, I'm going to set up an inquiry, not only into your pink-cheeked Miron here, but you as well. Is that understood?'

This time the chief nods.

'Now get going. And when the ambulance arrives, direct them down here. Fast.'

I fall into line with Gagnon. He is scowling. 'I'm going to have to tell that Contini where to get off,' he mutters.

We walk silently back to the house. Gagnon waves his men indoors and gazes out at where not so very long ago, the jeering crowd stood massed. Now everything is quiet. The only sign of disturbance is the trodden snow, as lumpy and uneven against the surrounding smoothness as if a herd of elephants had been airlifted into the precincts.

'Well, he did commit murder,' Gagnon mumbles beneath his breath as if he has been carrying on an internal argument. 'What do you think, Pierre?'

I hesitate and suddenly find myself saying, 'You might want to check the woods around here for any knife-scarred trees. With hiding-holes.'

'What!'

'Drug caches, I imagine. Nothing huge. But you never know.'

'Have you told Contini?' His thin face has an avid gleam.

'Not yet.'

'O-K. O-K!' He pats me emphatically on the back. His lips crease into a wide smile.

I am my father's son again.

'Hey, Gagnon, you've got things to do. Rousseau

and I are out of here.' Contini has come up behind us as stealthily as a mountain cat.

'Me?' I echo in bewilderment.

'You heard me.' He urges me down the drive, holds open the door for me.

'Any place we can get some lunch in this God-forsaken dump?' He blows his boxer's nose into a monogrammed handkerchief and swerves the car back onto the road without waiting for an answer. Beneath the broad brim of his hat, his face is set in a scowl.

'There's a brasserie a couple of kilometres away that's just reopened under new management. I haven't tried it yet. But I can direct you.'

'If the food stinks, Rousseau, I'll arrest you.' He guffaws loudly and accelerates, drives far too fast for comfort, only slows as the ambulance races past us.

'You in this drug racket, too, Monsieur le Notaire?' he asks after its siren has receded into silence. 'Collecting protection money from Miron and your beloved chief?'

I whip round to gauge his profile. 'You're joking! I don't know what you're on about.'

'I heard you whispering. And Gagnon's an old family friend of yours. He already told me that much.'

'Hardly makes him my buddy. Anyhow, I know nothing about a racket. That stuff about the hiding-holes. It's just a guess.'

'Hmm.' He throws me a sideways glance and takes a curve at breakneck speed. 'Well, there's something amiss. I sniffed it from the start. The laziness. The shoddy way they searched Madeleine Blais' apartment. What are they hiding? Who are they protecting?'

'I suspect it's just a mixture of incompetence and laziness,' I mumble.

'You call shooting down a man in cold blood laziness? *Non, monsieur*. You shoot down a man because you're afraid he'll talk. Corrupt bastards!'

'I could have sworn Gagnon didn't know Will Henderson from Adam. Yesterday. At the fire.'

'Was Miron there?'

I shake my head.

'Well, you can bet your sweet Madeleine's neck that Miron did know him. Knew him all too well. Gagnon may just be turning a blind eye. Two blind eyes in return for a kickback.'

'You're in a foul mood, Contini.'

'Ya? Well cheer me up then. Give me some answers.'

I shrug. 'I think I know where Henderson might have gotten the pistol.' I tell him about the Russian doll.

'So why didn't you stop Henderson before it was too late? Our prime suspect and you let him run? Come on, Rousseau, tell me another one.'

'I was a bit slow,' I say lamely. 'And maybe Miron really was just scared.'

'No. There's a scam of some kind on. I know my cops. I can smell it. OK, maybe it's just small-time stuff. A little payola. They're too dumb for the big time.' He casts me another of his searing looks.

I pretend not to notice. We pass Oscar's house. Chantale and Christophe are rolling a vast ball through the snow. I wave to them. They are too intent on their snowman to see me.

'Ya, I'd rather be playing in the snow, too. Welcome in the new year with the kids.' Contini puffs furiously at his cigarette. 'And here I am. I start off with a simple famous person suspicious suicide and what do I get? Arson, drugs, murder, a mini-riot, a police force that can't even keep its eyes on a handcuffed man! A shot suspect. Dr Rosenberg's not no-one, either. He runs the only Jewish lobby that keeps up a dialogue with the separatists. You of all people should know that.'

'I didn't.'

'Buried yourself away in this dump. What for?'

'It's my home.'

'Sure, sure. And my home's Italy.'

He is quiet while we manoeuvre a slippery stretch of road.

'I dream of it, you know,' he says in a sudden soft tone, 'in these grey, dirty, winter days. Warm sunlit skies, olive groves, terraces, vines twining over a bower. Even though I've never been. Next year.'

'You turn left here.'

'How did you know about Mme Tremblay's suicide attempt?'

'I didn't. I had a hunch. A feeling. After you had that go at convincing her Madeleine had committed suicide, she was very distressed.'

'Sorry about that.'

'And if I were in her shoes . . .'

He nods. 'Lavigne went round to check on her last night. Mme Tremblay was OK, if a bit fuddled. We'll need her to identify Madeleine's supposed hitchhiker and killer, though. Alive or dead.'

Despite the heat of the car, a shudder runs through me.

'That's it. Over there.' I point to the building that used to house the Point Ste-Anne where the boy I didn't know as Madeleine and I sat outside and thrilled to a forbidden band. It has been de-sanctified and renamed Le Lion d'Or. Its roof is bright with new slates. A colonnaded porch decks the entrance.

'Looks OK.' Contini's voice is more grudging than his words.

We are shown to a window table in a large formal dining room, its dark blue walls emblazoned with gold lions. The tablecloths are pale yellow and stiff. Single yellow carnations sit in pencil-thin glass vases. The clients are elegantly dressed, soft spoken.

'You paying?' Contini smirks. 'Out of your ill-gotten gains.'

'Out of my pocket. Sure. Why not?'

He sprawls into the chair opposite me, unfolds his starched napkin and studies the menu with his usual intentness. 'The bouillabaisse sounds promising. If we both go for it. With all the trimmings. Otherwise I'll settle for steak and salad.'

'Bouillabaisse is fine.'

Contini orders from the pert-faced waiter, who seems disappointed not to be allowed to perform the menu. Until the half-bottle of wine he has allowed us arrives, he is silent. But like a doctor probing a difficult patient, his scrutiny is intense. I feel as if my skin might burst into a rash simply to satisfy his need for symptoms.

'OK. Let's try some scenarios,' he says after his first studied sip of wine. 'Madeleine Blais wants to have a good time over Christmas. Will Henderson comes down specially to Ste-Anne to supply it. It's one of his haunts. They know each other. But this time Madeleine won't pay the extra-high-for-Christmas price he asks. So in a psychotic moment, induced by whatever cocktail he's on, he strings her up. Then the sight of the barn offends him, so he burns it down.'

He waits for my reaction.

When it doesn't come, he says, 'No, it's shit. I agree.'

He crumbles a steaming roll and chews on it, bit by bit. 'Let's try it differently, but starting from the same point. Will is Madeleine's supplier. He's also her lover. After midnight mass, they fuck in Madeleine's room. Then they decide on a little more fun, the kind that's too dangerous with Granny around. Maybe he likes things weird. Maybe both of them do . . .'

His eyes never leave my face as he speaks. I struggle for impassivity.

'So they find themselves in the barn and the weirdness gets out of hand. The sadism goes a little too far. Loving becomes abuse becomes death. Well-known phenomenon. But this time, Madeleine Blais is left hanging. And he torches the barn to obliterate the memory. Or some evidence we've failed to spot.'

My hands are so taut on the arms of my chair that they have gone numb. 'Did he say he knew her?'

'He said zilch. *Niente, nada*, nothing. What d'you expect? A full confession? A member of your lily-white police force may already have offered him some kind of deal. Then when I came along, Henderson woke up to the seriousness of it all, got scared and made a run for it. Or maybe he was too blotto to know anything. Whichever way, we'll never prove the police involvement. Even if by some miracle, Henderson lives to talk, all we've got on the surface is an over-ardent policeman trying to stop Madeleine Blais' killer.'

The waiter deposits a large silver tureen on the serving table and carefully ladles chunks of fish and broth into our plates, tops them with croutons and spoonfuls of aioli.

'Not bad at all. Pretty good, in fact.' Contini smiles his gourmet smile. 'The day hasn't been in vain. But back to Madeleine Blais. What d'you make of my second scenario?'

I shrug.

'Feeling squeamish, eh?' He prods a piece of fish with his fork and chews with relish. 'Believe me. It happens. With all kinds of nice people.'

'So you've got your murderer.'

His eyes are so intent on my face that I avert mine. Pale yellow flesh dots my plate.

'Relieved, are you? Funny how everyone in Ste-Anne wants me to declare the case closed.' His chuckle is tinged with malice. 'May not even need a trial now.'

'Not me. I don't believe Henderson and Madeleine . . .' My voice trails off.

'So maybe you're not telling me something I should know?'

He beams, savouring the catch 22 he has trapped me in. 'We found her car, by the way.'

'Madeleine's car?'

'Ya.'

'Where?'

'At the airport. Mirabel. In the underground parking lot.' He gives me a swift appraising look. 'I agree. There are missing links. I have no idea why it was there. The ticket was inside it. It was parked on Christmas Day morning. Around nine-thirty.'

'Someone must have been catching a flight. Have you tried the Identikit face on airport staff?'

'You teaching me my job, Rousseau?'

I shake my head.

'And where were you at nine-thirty on Christmas Day?'

'Me?'

'Yes, you. There's no-one else at this table.'

I close my eyes for a moment. My head is swimming. When I open them Contini is smiling. It isn't a particularly pleasant smile.

'I was at home. Making coffee probably.'

'Anyone with you?'

'The cat.'

'Who can't provide corroboration.' He ladles more soup into his plate, helps himself to aioli.

'How come you never told me you were married to Madeleine Blais, Rousseau?' The question comes with an interrogator's swiftness. I have a sudden sense that I am about to be put on the rack and stretched slowly, each turn of the creaking wheel a malicious delight to my inquisitor.

'You never asked. And it was a long time ago.'

'But you never divorced?'

'The need didn't arise.'

'The need didn't arise,' he echoes, as if it were the punch line of a joke. 'You know that most homicides take place inside the family.'

'We were hardly a family.'

'Well you wouldn't necessarily recognize all these families as families either.' He laughs. 'You're not eating.'

'I had a big breakfast.'

'Oh? Someone cooking for you?'

'I stayed at friends.'

'Yes. I noticed you'd been rather scarce these last few nights. Home not a welcoming place any more?'

'What are you trying to say, Contini?'

'Nothing. Nothing.' He pats his stomach and folds his napkin. 'We've been doing some interviews. We met a few of Madeleine Blais' friends. Not that the timing is brilliant. So many people are away. But we managed a few. Your friends, too.'

'Oh? Have they been maligning me?'

'No, no. Quite the contrary.'

'That's a relief.'

'One of them told me you were completely obsessed with Madeleine Blais.'

'A man or a woman?'

'Does it matter?'

'Maybe.'

'So you aren't, weren't obsessed with her?'

I shrug, though I can feel myself blanching. 'She's a fascinating woman. What are you getting at, Contini?'

'Oh, just fishing. Wondering where you were on the night of her death.'

'At home. In bed.'

'Alone?' he repeats.

'If I'm so obsessed with her, I'd hardly be with anyone else.'

Contini laughs.

I wave over the waiter. 'Do you want some dessert?'

'Maybe just a little something. A tart or a parfait.' His finger moves down the desert menu. 'Yes, a lemon parfait. And a double espresso. Nothing for you?'

I order a coffee and when the waiter has cleared our dishes Contini bends towards me, his voice suddenly low. 'You know, Madeleine thought she was being followed. Stalked.'

I trace the pattern embossed in the tablecloth with my fork. 'Did you learn that from her journals?' My voice betrays more interest and more discomfort than I like and I sit up straight to meet his eyes.

He avoids my question. 'A friend of hers at the theatre mentioned it. Madeleine was scared. Did she ever say anything about it to you?'

My gaze reverts to the hidden pattern in the tablecloth. 'She mentioned it once I think. I didn't pay much attention. Didn't take it very seriously. Actresses are always being followed. Fans, photographers, the curious . . .'

'This was different, apparently.'

'Oh?'

'She bought a gun.'

'Yes. Of course.'

I wait breathlessly but he doesn't follow through with more detail. Instead he takes a spoonful of parfait and tastes it with dainty suspicion.

'Still no will, though. If one doesn't turn up, as Madeleine Blais' husband, you stand to inherit. Quite a tidy estate, I would imagine.'

The thought has never occurred to me. I avoid Contini's gaze.

'I've got a line to Paris. And to Hollywood. Maybe something will turn up there. Had any more ideas about it?'

'No. Afraid not. Maybe she didn't make a will. Madeleine didn't think of dying a lot.' I catch myself in the inanity of the comment. So does Contini.

'So you've finally ruled out suicide, too. You were so convinced to start with.'

'I don't know,' I say with too much nervousness. 'It's just that after the fire and Henderson and all this business . . .'

He nods in sympathy. 'Did you see the fire, by the way?'

'Yes.'

'Where were you?'

'On my way back to Ste-Anne.'

'From?'

'Near Mont Tremblant.'

'Oh yes. Another jaunt. And you arrived just in time to get a good view. And to help Gagnon to Will Henderson.'

'Help him?'

'Gagnon told me you were right there. He said you were the only one clever enough to think of addressing Henderson in English.' He cackles with boyish delight. 'It takes a separatist to recognize an Anglo, eh?'

I avoid the political dig. Contini still has his schoolboy ideas about me. 'I thought you were implying something else.'

'Maybe I was. You want to try some of this parfait? It's good.'

'No thanks.'

'I'm ruining your appetite.' He chuckles, all geniality again.

I say it now in the midst of his good humour. 'I'd really like to read Madeleine's journals.'

'They make spicy reading. I can tell you that. You got any? I wouldn't mind comparing them.'

I feel myself flushing as I shake my head. I take a sip of wine and force myself back into composure. 'And what's next on the agenda?'

'Well, there's the little matter of Mr Henderson's life. Apart from that the boys are going through Madeleine's car. They should be at it right now.' Contini pauses as if he wants the significance of that to sink in. 'Maybe your prints will turn up in it. So don't disappear on me again.'

'Why? Am I a suspect?' I voice the question that has hovered over our entire conversation like some hawk poised for the kill.

Contini laughs cheerfully. 'Everyone's a suspect, Rousseau. That's what it means to be a good cop.'

12

The moon has risen in the darkening sky. It illuminates shafts of cloud, casts scurrying shadows on the
massed snow.

I drive homewards in a grey stupor which owes
far more to Contini than to my single glass of wine.
Our conversation replays itself in my mind like a
tape on an automatic loop. On its third journey
round, I pause it at the question about Madeleine
and my lack of a divorce and wonder how I could
ever explain the tangle of our relations to Contini
since I have never satisfactorily been able to explain
them to myself.

Like a dentist prodding an unanaesthetized tooth,
I force myself into the nerve-centre of pain. I don't
want to be there. It is a part of myself I have split
off, a terrain which exists only as a dull ache, never
to be tongued or fingered. A cautious circling is all
that can be allowed. But now I leap the perimeter
and jab at the cluster of nerves, exposing them. A
howl rises inside me.

When did I begin to hate Madeleine? For hate her
I did, in a hundred ways, small and large. I hated the

way she came into bed at night when I pretended to sleep, her careful silence as loud as the thrashing of drums. I hated the greedy pleasure with which she spooned the froth from her coffee and then left the cup half-full. I hated the casual manner in which she gathered up flowers and chucked them out at the first sign of a yellowing petal. I hated her with a fury which made me sense that what I hated most about her was my very attachment. She had become the stained mirror of all that I hated in myself, my stricken, masochistic dependence.

It took a long time for me to name it as hatred, perhaps as long as it had taken me to name our love. But the naming made things no better. The two emotions coexisted side by side, their passion so equally fierce as to make them indistinguishable.

Maybe it all crystallized when she coolly voiced her betrayal, evinced none of that guilt which might have given me a hold on her. Not that my jealousy needed a confession. It fed off the imaginary as easily as the real. But the voicing gave her an odd advantage. She now had honesty on her side, while I still only had the insatiable beast of my jealousy.

I battled against both hatred and jealousy. I tried to bury them deep within myself and pretend indifference. But the lid on the coffin wasn't tight enough. It rose up and released ranked armies of dangerous emotion. I shot back opposing volleys, tried to negotiate a peace. But the war was interminable. And I was its principal victim.

The dilemma was that intellectually, reasonably, I

could hold nothing against Madeleine. We had never promised each other a dusty fidelity. I had known her passionate nature from the start, intuited its workings that very first time when she had loved me and left me. She didn't confess anything then, nor at any other time, but nor did she particularly hide anything. She was simply and grandly herself. And that self, that self for which I loved her, was unique. Uniquely alive, too, in its disparities, its shifts and surprises, its ever-changing, ebullient masquerade. It was what made her a great actress. I had no right to demand anything else.

And yet that raging, guttural voice inside myself resented everything, demanded everything, was contorted with loathing.

Soon after Madeleine announced to me that she had never come to me with a guarantee, she went off to Hollywood. She came back with a fat contract. She was excited, exultant, living on her nerves. I had never seen her more beautiful.

She was intent on buying a house before the production started. She found one in the leafy suburb of Neuilly, a splendid turn-of-the-century villa with rounded dormer windows and a filigree of vines creeping up the portico and a lavish garden complete with boxed palms. She didn't wait for me to make up my mind and say yes. She purchased it and had it painted out all in white, brought in a modicum of furniture and announced a party, which was to be my welcome to the house, along with everyone else's. The everyone included Mme Tremblay, who was flown over for the event.

Madeleine had a genius for generosity. The champagne flowed. The pâtés and smoked salmon and caviar were unstinting. The guests laughed and glowed, as animated in their chatter as in their dancing. A band played, everything from Edith Piaf to Cole Porter to the latest pop, and the celebrity guests took turns to perform on the small platform. Madeleine, too, sang a number. She was shimmering and teasing, her smile as luminous as her gown. All her leading men, her directors and producers queued up in front of her and paid their respects. Paid them to me, their host, as well. To be fair, all her fellow actresses did too, though I didn't observe them with half the attention. Everyone was unanimous in saying it had been a grand party.

Later, in that voluminous bed which was as yet the only object in the beautifully proportioned room overlooking the garden I was impotent. Madeleine's kisses and fluttering fingers could work no magic. I pretended a cold weariness which seemed to have everything to do with my recalcitrant body and nothing to do with my mind. As I watched Madeleine, infinitely desirable in that nudity she wore like a couture dress, draw the billowing curtains, I felt utterly defeated.

The sense of defeat together with a gnawing shame persisted over the coming months. Madeleine made light of it. Pretended not to notice. Perhaps she really didn't notice. She was too busy and too excited with her preparations for Hollywood. And with the endless stream of rugs and chairs and 'discoveries' which daily found their way into the house.

But I noticed and my humiliation mounted, intensified by the crippling ravages of jealousy. Even while Mme Tremblay was there, I couldn't stop asking Madeleine where she had been and with whom. The lightness I forced my voice into carried a telling burden of inquisitorial despair. It's strange how jealousy can outlast desire.

Just before Madeleine left, like a peevish child I moved a sofa into the room at the top of the house which had been designated as my study and locked the door. Once, at midnight, Madeleine knocked. When I let out a mock growl of sleepiness, she didn't knock again.

On the day before she was due to leave, I made an effort to pull myself together. We lay out in the balmy springtime afternoon of the garden and sipped some lemony concoction of vodka that Madeleine had taken to making. There was something in her manner and demeanour which lulled me into the sense that we were children again in some golden age before sex. Laughing confidants, hidden from the world in the secrecy of our garden.

Madeleine was so consummate an actress she could even slip into herself.

When it grew chill, we walked upstairs still immersed in our pleasurable chatter and before I knew it, we were there, on that vast acreage of the bed I had designated as hers.

'OK, so tell me how many there have been,' I asked playfully. And she took it up in that spirit, replaying the heartlessly romantic scene between Belmondo and Seberg in *A Bout de Souffle*, counting on her fingers one by one, slowly, thoughtfully, then thrusting her hands out again and again in an infinity of repetition. She played it so well that once again I was cast into a no man's land between fantasy and the real.

I don't know why but anger took me over then, a lightning bolt of rage, and I slapped her, slapped her once, twice and a third time so that my fingers tingled. She stroked her cheeks with a bemused air, the tears biting at her eyes, and suddenly I was hard, blissfully, furiously hard. And in that rage, composed of I don't know what storm of hatred and love, I fucked her, fucked her so avidly that not a single extraneous image flew into my mind.

In the morning, she disappeared without waking me. I fingered the pillow and I think I cried. At least it felt like crying.

There was a note for me at the breakfast table. Brief. Little more than an address and a 'come and see me if you feel like it'.

I didn't think I'd feel like it. I was trying to regain some sense of who I thought I was. On and off I met Christiane, with whom everything seemed unproblematic. Conversation, bed, work.

But by the fourth week of Madeleine's absence I felt I would decompose if I didn't see her. The sound of those slaps had set off too many alarm bells within me. And I couldn't seem to get rid of them. They punctuated my dream images of her. Every time she appeared with a different man the slap resounded, until it amplified into infinity, like the fingers of the hand on which she had purportedly counted her lovers.

I flew to LA without telling Madeleine I was coming. I don't know what accident of chance or fate determined it, but I arrived at her Malibu address just as she was leaving it, a blond hunk of a beach boy on her arm – or so my malice characterized him. Madeleine was golden too. Her arms and throat and laugh burnt through me.

They got into a sports car of a red so audacious that it jangled the senses. Like an underemployed Philip Marlowe, I tailed them in my taxi, watched them emerge arm in arm to saunter into some overblown architectural concoction of a restaurant. I followed them in. The following did something strange to my nerves. I felt both humiliated and excited. I wanted to be invisible yet I wanted to be found out.

I hovered by the bar and sipped some sugary cocktail and watched them furtively in the mirror. Madeleine, though her eyes sparkled in my direction several times, didn't see me. Afterwards, I lost them. I couldn't find a taxi quickly enough. The next day I got a flight back to Paris, with a stopover in Montréal to revisit old haunts and to see my father, who had just buried a second wife. I didn't mourn my stepmother. In fact had it not been so utterly inappropriate, I would have congratulated him on a loss which could only be a gain.

When Madeleine returned, things got worse. She was light and breezy and full of the adventure

335

of filming in America, full of new projects, too. Her blitheness only served to fuel my darker emotions.

Over dinner I started to interrogate her. She played along for a while, then got up and turned on me abruptly. 'You would have made a great inquisitor, Pierre. But I have no intentions of qualifying for sainthood. I'm tired. I'm going to sleep.'

I didn't sleep. I roamed the house, pursued by furies, each one of them wearing Madeleine's face. I had stupidly allowed myself to go and see her first film again and its poses and encounters flitted in and out of every room, trapping me wherever I went.

When, towards the middle of the night, I heard noises in the kitchen, I rushed downstairs. Madeleine was pouring herself a glass of juice.

'Jet-lag,' she murmured.

'Shall I come and lie with you?'

She gave me a searching look. 'No, I think not.' She took her drink into the salon, settled herself on the sofa and with an oblivious self-sufficiency, started to leaf through magazines.

I watched her. I had no intention of saying anything and even when I heard that voice rumbling within me, I had no clear realization that I had spoken out loud. 'Who did you fuck this time?' the voice asked.

She glanced up at me for a second then down again at her magazine. 'Genghis Khan,' she said flippantly and carried on flicking pages.

'Who else?'

'Caesar. Oh and Napoleon.'

Suddenly, I was pulling her out of the sofa, shaking her by the shoulders.

'Who?'

'Mark Anthony.'

I hit her hard across the face. She stared at me for a moment, her eyes blazing, and then she hit me back. The slap tingled. I could see that the risk of it had excited her. Her face shone. She launched a kick at me. I caught her foot and she tumbled back on the sofa, rolled over as I came at her. There was an animal smell in the air, a mounting sense of danger between us, more potent than an aphrodisiac.

We stalked each other, thrust and parried. Madeleine was strong, agile too. In a contest which called for more than brute strength, she would easily have been my match. But when she tripped on the corner of the rug and I heaved down on her, the contest was over. Her vulnerability was all in my power.

Our eyes met for a moment over the rasp of our breathing. There was a small ooze of blood at the corner of her brow where she had grazed herself. I licked it clean while we made love or hate, I could no longer distinguish the two.

Afterwards we both slunk away to our separate rooms. We didn't look at each other. We weren't capable of speech. I showered and went out. It was almost time for work, in any case. I didn't go back home that night. I couldn't face her. Maybe I was already afraid.

For a few days we were careful not to be alone together for more than a few minutes at a time. We saw friends. We talked platitudes or business. We slept in our separate beds. I wondered whether our violence had lifted us into a kind of purgatory where the worst was over. But then it surfaced again with its peculiarly shaming mixture of danger and excitement and pain. And again – each time a little more intense, each time with an escalating quotient of anguish and brutality, so that I realized that even during the periods of purgatorial calm, the satanic fires of my jealousy still blazed.

The turning point came with the visit of a friend of Madeleine's from LA.

He wasn't the beach boy, more of a businessman. He was dark with a bronzed narrow face and a slightly receding hairline and he oozed power and wealth. We met at the Ritz, ate in the elegance of the restaurant. He addressed a few questions to me and then focused the full force of his attention on Madeleine. Towards the middle of dinner, he told her in a voice grown husky that he had seen some of the rushes of the film. He eased his fingers beneath his bow-tie and unconsciously loosened it a little as he mouthed a silent, 'Wow'. Madeleine smiled seraphically.

Without thinking, I pushed my chair back from the table, and with a mumbled apology about a story that was about to break, left them.

I walked back to my office. There was no story, but it was a safe place. I wondered as I walked why I had left. Was I performing some kind of ghost marriage rite – giving my wife away to other men as if I were already dead? The thought niggled and I cut short my time at the office and went home. I wasn't dead. Not yet.

I lay on her bed in the dark and waited for her and counted the quarter-hours and then the minutes. At 3.12, she appeared. She was humming a little tune beneath her breath. It stopped as soon as she switched on a lamp and saw me. But she couldn't hide the radiance of her face.

'Where have you been?'

'What do you mean where have I been? I've been at the Ritz.'

'In what room at the Ritz?'

Madeleine didn't answer. She undressed slowly, her back to me, as if I weren't there. She threw her clothes down on the armchair, her dress and then her stockings and her garter belt and her bra. When she got to her knickers, she turned on me.

'I saw you, you know. In LA. Saw you watching me, tailing, spying. You have no right. No right.'

That surprised me. 'I have every right,' I blurted.

'What gives you the right?'

'I love you.'

Madeleine was silent for a moment. Then with the haughty iciness of an examining magistrate, she glanced down at my limp prick and uttered a 'Ha!'

My hands are around her throat. I don't remember putting them there. I don't know how long they have been squeezing and squeezing, but Madeleine is clawing at me, scratching at my arms, my chest, my groin. Her fingers close round my penis, which is hard now and thrusts between us, stupidly looking for a home.

I push her away from me, down onto the bed. She rubs her throat. Rubs and rubs. Her eyes never leave my face. She is staring at my confusion and suddenly she kneels, puts her arms round my waist, nuzzles me, takes my cock in her mouth, softly, firmly.

She loves me. She is saying she loves me. She says it with her tongue. She says it with her lips which meet mine now. She says it with her voice, a whisper in my ear as she pulls me down on top of her. 'I love you too, Pierre.'

We love each other. For the length of that magical night we love each other. There is no-one else. There are no shadowy intruders. Only the two of us. The one of us.

At one point I open my eyes and catch hers, half-closed, glowing. She has that look of rapture on her face. It is the second time I see it. It is also the last.

We lie next to each other and watch the dawn rise. Rosy streaks of light flush the curtains. A soft breeze flutters through the window and cools the lingering heat of our bodies. Madeleine talks to the light, to the wind. Her tone muffles despair with resignation. But her words are addressed to me.

'It's over, Pierre. You know that. I don't really understand what's going on, but whatever it is, we've lost it. We can't live together any more. It's too dangerous. The wrong kind of danger. My

340

fault. Yours. It doesn't matter. It's over.'

I don't know whether she wants me to refute her. In any case, I can't. However much I may want to hold her, she is right.

'Maybe we can be friends. I don't want to lose you. Not altogether. Some time we can be friends.'

My voice seems to have disappeared. I cannot find it. I touch her arm. She pulls away, then gives me her hand.

'Not yet. It's too soon. We need distance. Yes. Distance. Today. I'm going to leave today. For Lyon. Rehearsals will start soon. If you can find another place by the time the play has had its run, that will be fine. If not, I'll sort something out.'

I still can't speak. Something has risen in my throat that prevents words. Maybe it is shock.

Madeleine gets up. She slides open the door of the wardrobe and takes down a case. She throws clothes into it, any old assortment, any old way. She isn't paying attention. Her lips have that tragic cast, as if gravity were pulling at their corners. At the same time, she looks like a child. A child who is hurt from seeing too much pain and is trying very hard not to cry as it tugs on jeans and a sweater.

When she is dressed, she meets my eyes for a moment. 'Will you write?'

I think I manage to nod.

And then she is gone. I lie there unable to move. Only when I hear the door slam does the paralysis end. I am running, shouting, 'Madeleine. Madeleine . . .' But by the time I reach the front gate, she has already disappeared.

The shadows in the house don't want me with them. They bite at me and pursue. They call me brute, killer.

I pack my bags and leave the same day. I move into a hotel. Within two weeks, I am in Algeria. I wander. I run. The hot desert sun burns a hole into my brain. It obliterates the past. When, a little late, I read of Madeleine's Academy Award nomination, I write her a card. I only resurface in the familiar world after several years. And then I go to Ottawa.

The sky has grown dark by the time I reach the turn off at the plywood factory. As I force myself back into the present, I notice a car behind me. It occurs to me that it has been behind me for some time, its lights glinting into my rear-view mirror. I have the sudden certainty that I am being followed, but in the darkness I can't make out whether the car is Contini's or not. A shiver creeps over me. I shrug it away. There is nothing for it but to go home. That is where Contini wants me to be.

As I near my house, the car vanishes. I cheer myself with its disappearance and with the sight of my neatly shovelled drive. I have done well to hire young Bobineau to clear my premises. I must recommend him to Mme Tremblay. Bobineau comes fully motorized, plough in winter, rotor blade in summer, suction hose in fall. Not like Michel Dubois.

The sight of a car in the driveway gives me pause. I am not expecting any visitors. I wind round it to the garage, park, and instead of taking the interior stairs to the house, go round to the front door.

A dark figure waves to me from the porch. It takes me a few seconds to recognize my brother.

'Pierre. It's freezing out here. I was just about to give you up. You'd forgotten I was coming, hadn't you?' There is a querulous note in his voice.

I stop the apology which rises to my lips like a tired tune instantly triggered by a familial push of the admonishing button. 'I didn't think you'd be quite so early. How are Monique and that security guard son of hers?'

He doesn't answer. He waits for me to unlock the door. As I switch on the lights, I can suddenly see his troubled pallor and delayed guilt shafts through me.

'I've been worrying about you. Worrying about Madeleine, too. The awfulness of it.' He searches my face, his lips forming the word 'murder' into a gasp. Then he shakes his head adamantly, as if the gesture could rearrange both his thoughts and reality. 'It's a terrible, terrible thing. Here amongst us. I have prayed for Madeleine's soul. All night I prayed.'

He seems to be about to fall to his knees and enjoin me to do the same. Instead he retrieves the mass of envelopes which litter the floor and hands them to me in a neat pile. The intent look is on me again, my father attempting to probe my boyhood secrets.

'I know what you think,' he murmurs. 'I have been hard-hearted, uncharitable. I have lacked both sympathy and tolerance. It's true. I have asked God

343

to forgive me for that, to help me grow in understanding. I have also prayed that God in his wisdom may be merciful with Madeleine whom I wrongly maligned.'

The self-criticism surprises me. For a moment I envy my brother his religion. It gives him an ability to voice big sentiments aloud and make speeches wholly uninflected with irony. Though from the face he turns on me as he hands me his coat, it seems that for today at least, the communication with forces greater than himself has not altogether provided him with a necessary solace.

'To be merciful with you, as well,' he says.

I want to tell him it is not mercy I think I need. What I need is for the clock to move backwards. But he is already in the salon. He looks around him at a slight loss, settles awkwardly into the stiffest chair in the room. My brother, I remind myself, is not at home here. He has never lived here.

'The parishioners have been coming to me, seeking advice, seeking comfort. All day today, one after another. There is so much fear in the air. Hatred, too. I don't really know how to contain it.' He examines his hands, then quickly folds them into his lap and gives me that probing gaze again. It sets up a nervousness in me.

'Let me get you a drink. Or coffee, tea? Some food perhaps.'

'A little tea would be fine. No sugar.'

'With some brandy to warm you.'

I drop the pile of envelopes on the coffee table and stoop to light the fire before heading for the kitchen.

Jerome's eyes never leave me. I have the uncanny feeling he really can read my unruly thoughts.

He leaps up to follow me. I have done no more than fill the kettle when his hand is suddenly tight on my arm. The face he turns on me is all turbulence.

'Pierre, tell me. I need to know. Did you . . .? Did—'

'Speak to Mme Tremblay?' I cut off his stammer. 'About the circumstances of Madeleine's birth?'

He waves his hand in a dismissive gesture, as if his earlier fears of scandal had grown utterly trifling. 'It's not that.'

'Isn't it? Well, let me put your mind at rest in any case. Madeleine was indeed the daughter of the music teacher at the seminary. Alexandre Papineau. Not our father. Mme Tremblay was quite put out at that suggestion. I guess that means Monique's sins don't have to weigh too heavily on your family conscience.' I turn my back on him, pour hot water into the teapot, slosh it round, measure out the tea, pile everything onto a tray. 'Good thing it wasn't our father. Even I, terrible reprobate that I am, would have found that a little hard to swallow.'

'Don't joke, Pierre. It isn't a time for jokes. But I'm glad you still have a conscience.'

Something in his tone makes the tray waver in my hand as I carry it back to the salon. I don't meet his eyes as I hand him his cup.

'And I'm glad that has been cleared up. But I came about something else.'

'Oh? Don't tell me.' Irritation takes me over. 'You came about Monique. Your great love. Penitent about her past, so you can forgive her now. Well, Mme Tremblay can't quite so easily. She doesn't want her in her house.'

Jerome's face has turned a hot pink. He puts down his cup with a clatter. 'Monique knows she's been remiss,' he blurts out, then with an effort collects himself. 'And in her own way, she's desolate about Madeleine. We must have compassion. Her life has been hard. Three years ago, her husband died. A boating accident of some kind. Did you know?'

I shake my head.

'She's on her own. And I don't think she's very well. She's certainly not very well off. Blais squandered what money there was. The son you met is out of work. The others have nothing to do with her.'

'So it's as you predicted. She's been spurred here by the thought of the will.' A perverse cruelty propels me.

'Did I say that?'

'More or less.'

He looks aghast at his own bad moral taste, gets up and starts to pace. 'Perhaps there's a grain of that. We all have our venality. But nonetheless, that doesn't change the fact that Monique is a sad, disappointed woman. A bereaved mother, even if not altogether a good one.' He stops to face me. 'I've been putting her up in one of the rooms in the school. The boys are almost all away. But they'll be back on Tuesday. And then I thought she could stay here until Mme Tremblay comes round.'

'Here?'

'Yes.' Suddenly he crosses himself. 'Because you have to leave, Pierre. I told you already. That's what I've come about. You must go. Even now . . . even now that the police think they have their man. It may not change anything. Please.'

Beads of perspiration have formed on his brow. They set up a chill in me. A small hammer has taken up residence in my head. It beats against a stone wall, searches for chinks. 'I don't know what you're talking about,' I mumble.

'Don't you?' He surveys me intently. 'It's all bound to come out. All the rot. We'll sink with it. Both of us. You're my brother.' With an abrupt movement, he takes a rosary from his pocket and shifts the beads, his lips formed into a mute murmur.

I pour myself a whisky. For some reason I think of Giorgio Napolitano's story. My brother really does feel he is my keeper.

Jerome clears his throat harshly. 'Don't ask me for my sources.'

As he says it, I have a sudden pungent whiff of the fetid heat of the confessional. All those voices in his ear, pouring out secrets. His own, sanctioned to probe. What has he uncovered?

'Before . . . before her death, Madeleine said she had a score to settle with you. A major score. She was angry. Very angry. She poured vitriol on your character. She said she would see you that very night. Then . . . then just yesterday, I learned . . . Someone saw . . .'

Suddenly, as if we had conjured up the wrong

kind of spirits, there is a loud thud, a booming crash somewhere to the side of the house and Minou comes streaking in, her tail rigid.

With something like relief, I race for the door. Jerome is right behind me pulling on his coat as I unearth a flashlight. We dash in the direction of the noise.

An avalanche of snow has tumbled from the roof of the shed. It lies in broken heaps on the ground.

Jerome's voice punctures the stillness. 'Nothing serious then. Nothing to be afraid of.'

I flash my torch through the door. What was once a neat pyramid of logs is a jumble on the floor.

'It could have been an animal,' Jerome says. 'Not your cat. She would be too light. Something bigger.' He talks on to still his nerves. He doesn't like being out here. He is a man of interiors – churches, libraries, schoolrooms, confessionals. The big dark sky where his heaven might be frightens him.

It frightens me too at the moment. I have the distinct sensation that something is watching us. I remember the car that tailed me. Contini, I thought. But sheds are not Contini's style. I shine the torch on the ground, looking for tracks in the snow. Around the shed, the avalanche has obliterated them. Further afield, speeding towards the house, I can see Minou's prints, partly covered by Jerome's and mine coming in the opposite direction.

I turn the other way and pace towards the woods. It is then that I see it, a fuzzy scattering of snow like an animal's tail dragged over the surface. But no

348

animal's tail could swallow its own tracks. It doesn't make sense. Nor does the fact that my boots now sink so deeply into the ground that walking is nigh on impossible, let alone walking without leaving a trace.

'See anything?' Jerome calls to me.

'Not sure. You need snowshoes to go out there.'

Of course. Snowshoes. But how would one cover their tracks? An image of Noël Jourdan sneering at Gagnon earlier this morning leaps into my mind. Noël would be quite capable of playing some kind of prank on the Jew-lover I patently now am in the eyes of Ste-Anne. Was it he who raced to the confessional and poured suspicions into Jerome's ear?

'We can check it out in the morning.' Jerome's voice echoes my own mounting anxiety.

We trudge back to the house. He pauses at the threshold. 'I'll go now, Pierre. As long as I've convinced you of the necessity of a swift departure.'

I shake my head, urge him in. I don't want to be alone. This time I pour him a brandy.

'Don't ask me to say any more,' he mumbles as he takes the glass. 'Just trust that I know what's best. For once.' His eyes plead.

'Was it one of your priests?' I ask with sudden intuition. I have a vision of an endless ladder of breaches of faith, a priest on every rung, my brother toppling at the crest.

Jerome looks away, his face wretched.

The sound of the doorbell shatters our taut silence. We both jump to our feet, then hesitate, as if our separate ghosts might be coming to visit.

Wrapped in a heavy black coat, his face barely visible beneath his hat, Giorgio Napolitano stands at the door.

'I was in Ste-Anne,' he begins apologetically, 'and Detective Contini told me you might be at home. So I thought I'd drop in.'

'Contini?' I echo in surprise.

'Yes. We had an interview.' He glances round uncomfortably. Remembering myself, I take his coat.

'There is something I need to talk to you about, Pierre. Otherwise my sleep won't be easy.'

I don't know why, but for a moment, I think of the crash in the shed so few minutes ago and wonder whether Giorgio's arrival might in any way be connected.

'Oh?'

'Yes, about Madeleine.'

'Something you told Contini?'

'Not exactly.' His handsome face is rueful.

'Something he told you?'

'In a way.'

'Who is it, Pierre?' My brother's voice intrudes on us. I had forgotten his presence.

'You're not alone.' Giorgio tenses.

'I'm afraid not.'

I usher him into the living room and introduce him to my brother. They exchange desultory small talk. Despite everything, despite the hammer which still pounds away in my head, there is something in this meeting between the renegade priest and my brother which tickles my fancy. Can Jerome guess Giorgio's former vocation just by looking

350

at him? I decide to underline it.

'Giorgio was once one of yours,' I say to Jerome.

'Really?' My brother tries to hide his instant stiffening. He studies Giorgio hard, as if he suspects him of unspeakable acts. 'Did you know Madeleine Blais?' he surprises me by asking.

Something seems to be clicking into place in his mind as Giorgio responds.

'And where do you live now?' Jerome has shifted into an interrogating mood. Whereas a moment before he was on the point of going, he now settles back in his chair and it is Giorgio who declares he must leave. It will be a busy night at the Auberge, he explains. When the telephone rings, he seizes the opportunity and rises.

'You answer it, Jerome.' I gesture him towards the phone and accompany Giorgio to the door.

'What was it you wanted to tell me before?' I ask softly.

He shakes his head. 'Not now.' His eyes stray over my face. He seems to be about to say something more, but instead, he merely grips my hand in a taut shake and hurries down the porch steps.

'That was Mme Orkanova,' Jerome says when I come back into the room. 'She has just finished making a cassoulet and offered to bring it over. Kind of her. I accepted for both of us.'

'What?' I stare at him.

'I thought it was only right that you said goodbye to her before leaving.' He concentrates on some minute spot on his jacket.

With too much commotion, I prod the fire, refill

my glass and slump into the sofa.

'You're wretched,' Jerome murmurs. 'I wish I knew how to offer you consolation.'

When I look up at him, his face is soft with a tenderness I have never before noticed in it.

'Don't worry. I won't preach at you. I would pray with you, but I know how you feel about prayer.'

We gaze at each other and I don't know why but in that hushed meeting of our eyes I have a sense that some tight ancient knot inside me is loosening. I wasn't altogether aware of its presence before, but now I can see each of its thick, hoary coils and their intricate winding as if a spotlight had been focused on them. I do not know when the loops were formed, but I have one of those certain intuitions that the knot grew in thickness and intricacy when Madeleine and I first parted and ever since then its solid coiled presence has cut off one of the paths to my heart. Like an elaborate bulwark, it has guarded against the dangers of emotion, against the hazards of a reliance on anything outside the solitary circle of the self. My brother has forced blood through one of its coils, opened up a passage.

Maybe he feels something of all this, too, for we both look away simultaneously in mute embarrassment.

When he speaks again, his tone is soft, musing. 'You know, all those years ago, when I was in the grips of that delusion about Monique and our father, I had to struggle to pray. Monique's image would interfere with my prayers. She would plant herself in front of the Virgin Mary and I would have

352

to beg Mary to suppress the image of that harlot, Monique.' He laughs.

'It must all have been very hard for you. I can see the confusion. Monique and Mary, both invisibly impregnated. By our father.'

He stiffens and I sense I have overstepped the bounds of spoken intimacy. I start to shuffle aimlessly through the pile of envelopes on the table.

The one at the bottom of the heap, the largest one, forces me into nervous attention.

I know that writing. But I cannot know that writing. I touch the envelope superstitiously to check the strength of my hallucinative ability. It is potent. The envelope feels real. The stamps have serrated edges.

'Documents, are they? Work following you home.' Jerome has seen the packet-sized envelope too.

My voice is gone. I nod instead and touch the ink which spells out my name in that distinctive hand. What is it that Madeleine has sent me from the dead?

Despite my brother's presence, I am about to tear open the envelope when the doorbell rings.

'Shall I get it?' Jerome asks, sensing my dismay.
'Please.'

I pass my finger under the envelope's edge. The glue comes away so easily. Too easily. It has worn thin from the crossing of too many boundaries. A stack of neatly printed sheets slips into my hand.

I glance at the top one and with a shudder wedge the papers back into the envelope. I don't want to see this. I can't see this. Not now.

With the furtiveness of a child caught in an illicit act, I thrust the packet into a corner cupboard. Two of my father's fairground sacred hearts clatter to the floor. With guilty horror I force them back onto the shelf.

Passion comes in too many guises.

13

The old anglepoise casts a yellow pool of light on the manila envelope which lies on the windowside table in my bedroom. I trace the flourish of black ink which spells out my name. I examine the postmark for a date, but all I can make out is the blur of Montréal.

When did Madeleine post the packet which survived her? Why does it take longer for a letter to reach its destination than for a death to occur?

I try to think reasonably. I tell myself the holiday mail is always slower than a tortoise. I tell myself that even though Madeleine knew she was coming here, she wanted the parcel to arrive by post, even wanted it perhaps to precede her – to set a kind of agenda for an overdue conversation.

I breathe deeply. I think of things with which to calm myself. Distract myself, too.

The dinner with my brother and Maryla, which began so awkwardly, ended well. Jerome's presence had initially made her doubly nervous but eventually soothed her; quieted her apprehensions about the murderer in our midst, as well. Then Jerome surprised me by slipping away in a fashion which made it evident that he fully expected Maryla to stay on and that she had his blessing. Perversely, his gesture made me realize that it was time to have that long-delayed discussion with Maryla. I had been selfish and cowardly for too long.

We sat on the sofa and I stroked her hair and her hands and found words which approximated feeling. I told her she was a wonderful woman and far too good for me. Circumstances and need had thrown us together and we had sought consolation in each other. That was good, that could even, if she wanted to name it such, be called love. But the period had passed, for her in particular. She was wasting her hopes on me. I wasn't marriageable, which was what she wanted. I was just her left-over habit. And a friend.

For a while, she didn't say anything. She simply looked at me with her wide grey eyes and unconsciously toyed with the small golden cross she wore round her neck. Finally she nodded. 'Yes,' she said. 'It is best to be clear. Did your brother advise you to speak?'

'In a way.'

We hugged each other and, despite her residue of fear, despite my half-hearted offer of a bed in the spare room, she left. Left proudly. Left me to this.

I trace the black ink on the manila envelope and then slowly open it and pull out its contents.

The odd sensation that someone is watching oppresses me again. It has been with me several times this evening. I glance out the window, but see only my own hazy reflection and beyond that the glimmer of snow. Perhaps it is Madeleine who is watching. Waiting for me to stop procrastinating so that we can at last have the conversation we never had.

The letters lie in front of me, a neat stack of papers – as pristine as a document which has just come out of a computer printer, except for the traces of the double creases they bore when folded into their original envelopes and posted from various locations outside Ste-Anne. Each carries a dateline denoting a month and a year, though no day. Each begins with the salutation, 'Madeleine!' None carries a signature.

What frame of mind compelled me to anonymity I no longer know. I think it began as a joke. An anonymous Orlando posting his epistles to the Rosalind Madeleine had once played. Or maybe it began as a wistful piece of nostalgia, a disembodied, retrospective seduction. To make good my many lacks.

I think I wanted Madeleine to guess the letters were from me. She didn't. Not until the end, I imagine – though now I can never be certain.

The top sheet begins 'Madeleine, or shall I call you Anne, for I have just seen *Winter Spell* again.'

I don't need to read it. The text lingers in my mind, a playful fan letter, full of slightly wicked insight into her role with a dash of hyperbole about her performance.

The dateline is June 1986, the month after

Madeleine purchased the Montréal flat. It must have been the concatenation of her presence in the city, our sudden love-making and its equally sudden end that spurred me.

Not that I hadn't seen Madeleine in the intervening years before this. There was only a span of about two when we were utterly obscured to each other. My desert years I think of them as. When I returned from Africa to Paris at the end of 1981, I rang her. She happened to be in town and she agreed to see me. At her suggestion, we met at the house. So that we wouldn't be bothered, she said. Fame had its penalties.

One of them was a new alarm system which began at the front gate where a woman's voice which wasn't Madeleine's grilled me. The second was the woman herself, a stern matronly figure who opened the door to me and cowed me with her gaze, before ushering me into the breakfast room.

I waited. I allowed myself to look around, a little fearful that I might find my shadow hovering, more fearful that I would not. Through the windows, the garden was wintry, a desolate span of bare black branches and sodden grass which Madeleine had obviously tried to cheer with the addition of some sculptural objects – or that's what I took the strange circle of parking metres to be. They were planted in the centre of the lawn, equidistant from two polished bronze cylinders which evoked without quite replicating human shapes. The palms had moved into a conservatory which now covered one side of the terrace.

Inside, the house had not so much changed as spawned treasures. There were oils on the walls and modernist tapestries and more sculpture, not to mention Madeleine's usual assortment of jumble. The table at which I hastened to reseat myself was a creamy marble slab, designed for the space. It was as if Madeleine, transported to Hollywood and fame, had now decided to exercise her early love for avant-garde adventure by collecting.

'Forgive me. You're punctual and I overslept.' Madeleine's husky, early morning voice breaks through my inventory.

'I'm glad you could make the time for me.'

'Not much of it, I'm afraid. I'm off again day after tomorrow, and the schedule is crowded.'

We talk nervously, hiding behind the armour of formal correctness. Her beauty in the flesh is so much more arresting than what my memory has fashioned that I hardly dare glance at her. Briefly I tell her about North Africa. With equal brevity, she recounts her latest ventures. Then suddenly she laughs her low secret laugh and says, 'It suits you, Pierre, this nomadic life.'

Our eyes meet and the electricity is still there, rustling between us, as potent as ever, and I find myself asking what I promised myself I wouldn't ask.

'Are you with anyone, Madeleine? I mean—'

She cuts me off. 'That's not a question you're allowed to put to me, Pierre.'

'No, of course.'

She busies herself with the croissant and coffee

her housekeeper, whom I now know as Mme Baudoin, has put on the table, then laughs again, differently now.

'Though if you'd been keeping up with your American film gossip you'd know that I'd broken at least two hearts and had mine broken once in return. There's an awful lot of heart in the film industry.'

Her face has that mixture of vulnerability and boldness which thrusts me back to our childhood prehistory and I would like to touch her, just once, chastely, to feel her skin. But the sound of the doorbell intervenes and a moment later an elegantly suited woman with dark, commanding features comes into the room.

It is my first meeting with Madeleine's new agent, Marie-Ange Corot, and as the woman sits and calmly examines me, I have the feeling that her early arrival has been pre-arranged, to prevent anything going amiss between Madeleine and myself. Oddly, the realization of this, or perhaps it is simply Marie-Ange's presence, soothes me and by the time I have drained my second cup of coffee I am relaxed. We are all relaxed, as if nothing had ever gone disastrously wrong between Madeleine and me and we still shared a life.

Madeleine sees me to the door. 'It's all right,' I tell her just before I leave. 'I'm not loony any more.'

'Good.' Madeleine gives me a serene smile. 'I knew it was a passing aberration. Where do you go now?'

'Closer to home. Ottawa.'

'Write to me. And go and see Mémère.'

I nod.

She hugs me swiftly, too swiftly for me to hold onto her, and steps back. Her golden eyes have an animal seriousness.

'And Pierre. Find yourself another woman. One to keep, I mean.'

I take Madeleine's advice. In Ottawa I strike up a relationship with Denise Lalande, a fellow journalist. We move in together. We are companionable. We have everything in common. We should be perfectly paired. Yet one morning, after some six months together, I wake up and look at my partner's sleeping face and have the odd sensation that I am living an afterlife, that all my gestures are hollow, that all passion is spent. Has long been spent. I push away the thought and bury it in activity.

Not long after that Madeleine rings me from Montréal. She is passing through, would like to meet for dinner and catch up – if I can make the time. I make the time. And we catch up in more ways than one. Dinner stretches and stretches and we can't seem to leave each other. We spend the night together in Madeleine's hotel. The excitement of it engulfs me. There seems to be nothing so dangerously illicit as spending the night with one's wife.

The next day the marvel of it is still there, a newness which is also repetition, and we drive down to Ste-Anne together. We see both Mme Tremblay and my father. We spend the night together in Madeleine's room. Mme Tremblay treats us like newlyweds, serves us a regal breakfast.

And then Madeleine is off. I take her to the airport where she is to catch the plane for her next destination. She turns to wave at me from behind her dark glasses, a star again, distant, mysterious.

There were three more interludes of this kind, erratic, fleeting, separated by months of silence or sporadic postcards. During one of them, Madeleine told me it was best like this. She was fated to passion, not to the everyday. Maybe it was the life she led. It demanded extremities, great surges of adrenalin, which left little over for what others called life. It was a kind of occupational deformation – one she knew she had both been intended for and had chosen.

Madeleine was aware of my relationship with Denise. When it ended, petering out on our own ill-temper at its lassitude, she told me she was sorry. Maybe that was why she would do no more than lunch with me when our paths crossed in Paris where I was chasing a Canadian delegation. Maybe it had more to do with our past there and an unwillingness to be seen with me where she was primarily a public person.

After I moved back to Ste-Anne, there were two more of our unpredictable couplings. Once she stayed with me at the house, laughing at the strange secrecy of it, as if we were children again hiding from some vigilant parent's eye. And then, just when I thought her acquisition of an official address in Montréal signalled a new departure for us, all that side of things stopped. I still don't quite know why.

Madeleine never talked about her other men. At first I assumed that one of them was the reason and soon she would tell me. She didn't. I scoured the gossip columns and though her name came up often enough, there was no other name I could tie her to with any certainty. Finally I asked her.

She looked at me with a surprised expression, her eyes wide, as if the matter hadn't occurred to her. It made me realize how small a point I was on her horizon, how much she packed into the months between our meetings. What she said was that she was going through that kind of phase, that she wanted us to be friends – it was the friendship that mattered – so old now, her oldest one, so much more important than anything else. Didn't I agree? We didn't want to sour that just because she stopped in Montréal more often these days. She was brutally frank then. With a catch in her voice she told me that I mustn't assume the stoppings were intended for me. They were for her grandmother, who was getting old, who couldn't come to her as easily as she once had.

I took all that. Took it lightly, at least on the surface. I agreed that our friendship was the crucial thing. I meant it. I enjoyed being Madeleine's confidant and the mainstay she had named me – a solid, certain figure, far from the glare and whirl of the publicity machine. Nonetheless, a part of me curled into a corner – offended, yearning, angry.

Maybe that was the me who spurred the writing

of the letters. It was certainly after that conversation that I began them.

I swallow the remains of my glass of brandy, feel the heat in throat and stomach and force myself to look once more at the letters. Unnaturally for Madeleine, they are in meticulous order of date.

The first sequence is an anatomy of her roles. Each letter, sometimes two or three, focuses on a film. I write of her hard, sexual radiance as Anne, the quality of her sharp, watchful innocence as Julie in *Secret Woman*. I rhapsodize about her ability to portray both falseness and a sullen sense of threat in *Jacob's Daughter*, her searing, wounded passion in *The Pink Tower*. I lacerate her for the flimsy frivolity of her role in *La Parisienne*. I talk about her eyes, their seductive downward flutter, or the savage purity of her rounded gaze. I evoke particular gestures of her hands or hips or feet. I analyse the films with the formal rigour of a reader of *Cahiers du Cinéma*. I am by turns playful, amusing, critical, enraptured. Yet I am always careful to put in only what anyone could know who saw her on the screen or followed her from the outside.

Madeleine showed me some of these letters once, not long after I had started writing them. She brought them to dinner and told me she had a new and perceptive fan who watched her films with the attentiveness one normally gave to Shakespeare or Racine. She was intrigued, enticed. She marvelled at their insight. She read me a passage and then another.

I sat very still. I was waiting for her to say she knew it was me. To say she had guessed. To pierce my cloak of anonymity. When she didn't, disappointment made me leave her early. I think she suspected I was jealous of her new and discerning fan.

Gradually a different note seeps into the letters. They become more personal, as intimate as a kid glove slipping over a familiar hand. The woman behind the many filmed faces is explored, the mystery of her talent grappled with. The letters delve into the circumstances which might have shaped this talent. They probe the character of the sexuality which feeds her arresting screen presence. There are hypothetical scenarios in which the writer puts himself into Madeleine's body and fantasizes her relationship to her shifting selves.

Even to my eyes now, these letters exude a kind of visceral heat, a fascination which borders on the unhealthy. Yet they are also love letters. They murmur love without naming it: 'You have an unerring instinct for detecting men's desires and being what they want. You have a gift for awakening and fulfilling dreams.' They ask for tokens, make small demands. 'Keep me in your mind.' 'Hold me close to your heart.' 'When you sit down, put me right there, between your thighs where your hand lay in the final scene of *Jacob's Daughter*.'

When Madeleine next spoke of the letters to me, her tone was rather different. She was still intrigued, but the pleasure in the puzzle had vanished. Instead, she was troubled. She told me she was certain her anonymous fan was in fact an actor or a director she had once worked with – he knew her so well, sexually, emotionally. She was taking steps to find out.

'You're sure it's someone you worked with?' I remember saying, the challenge clear in my voice. She nodded without looking at me.

I should have told her then, but by now the writing of the letters had become something of an addiction. I looked forward to it as one does to a secret rite, without quite acknowledging to oneself that one is intent on engaging in it. I didn't know what mood or moment might spur me. The letters had taken on a life of their own.

Towards the bottom of the pile come two letters which coil my stomach into tight knots and induce a dizzying nausea.

Madeleine!

I saw you the other night. Saw you in the flesh, so much softer, smaller, more pliable than that luminous presence on the screen. You were coming out of your apartment. I had tracked you, seen the lights go out on the eighth floor and stay out until you appeared, swathed in some glossy animal trapping, on the steps of the building. The superintendent waved. A car pulled up, a black saloon, and swallowed you until you re-emerged in the shadows of the Hôtel de Ville. A man rushed up to embrace you. Familiarly. An old friend or a lover . . .

I cannot read on.

It was the second time I had followed Madeleine, tailed her this time all the way up to Montréal from her grandmother's house. I don't know why I did it nor what led me to put it into writing, but when Madeleine told me she was being followed, I assumed she was referring to this letter, referring to me.

We were having dinner together at Louis', not far from the theatre. It was during the rehearsal period for *Hedda Gabler*. Madeleine was tense, as taut as a tightrope that might give the second any pressure was applied. She talked about her difficulties with the role. She told me she was having trouble making Hedda in any way sympathetic. And then, without any visible change of voice, she told me she was being followed. It scared her.

I thought of my letter and made light of her fear. I knew I should tell her then, confess everything. But there was something that made me hold back. She wasn't really paying attention to me. And the moment was wrong for admitting to a gigantic hoax. So I didn't speak, but I knew that soon I would have to tell her.

The whole enterprise had, in any case, begun to pall. I had no intention of frightening Madeleine. I didn't want her to suffer. I only wanted to show my love in a way that was permissible, to show her, too, that I didn't need to hit or be violent, that I could love her just as much in this pure, disembodied form.

I put a date to it. I told myself that over

Christmas in the long evening of the countryside I would tell her. Tell her softly with perhaps just a touch of whimsy in my voice so if the laughter gathered I would not be unprepared for it. I imagined her staring at me and then bursting into giggles as she did after our childhood pranks. Alternately I imagined her falling into my arms and whispering, 'I should have guessed. Only you could have known so much of me.'

I allowed myself only two more letters. The first was intended to heighten the joke once it was revealed. It described Madeleine and me leaving her apartment and going down to a Crescent Street café for a snack – as seen by a third person. I enjoyed writing it. I enjoyed finding a film equivalent for each of her gestures – the swing of her hair over her back, the slight slope of her face in the lamplight as she looked down into a boutique window, the touch of forefinger to generous lips. Here was Julie or Anne or another of her screen heroines in the flesh. The spirit was that of the first letters. Or so I thought when I wrote it.

Now, as I scan the sentences, the exactitude of the description frightens me. I can see Madeleine on my arm. As we move down the icy stairs, she nestles just a little into my shoulder. She pauses to pat the silky head of an Irish setter. The eyes of its sombre-faced owner are on her, then on me. Other eyes too – a brightly scarfed girl in the street, a big burly man slumped beside a car.

I pause at this figure. There is something about him which in retrospect is familiar, but I can't quite place it. Hastily I put the letter aside. I don't want to read any more. I don't want to remember that it would have reached Madeleine just after the killings at the Université de Montréal, at a time when she was in no mood to appreciate jokes.

There is only one letter to go – an announcement really, to tell Madeleine that this is the last letter, to tell her how our one-sided correspondence has engrossed me, to tell her how she will chuckle should she ever meet her principal fan.

But that letter isn't here. I suddenly remember it tucked into the palm of Contini's hand that day we left the apartment together. The sight of it made me shiver. Makes me shiver still. I am glad Contini has not seen the rest of these letters.

What confronts me now does nothing to reduce my uneasiness. It is a letter in Madeleine's own looped hand. The characters skate across the page as gracefully as she did on the edge of the river. Through tears I claw out their frozen sense.

Pierre!
I want to creep into a dark hole and die. I want to become utterly invisible, a heap of ash caressed only by the wind. How could you? How could you have? You whom I loved and trusted. All this time . . .
I had begun to suspect it was you. Now I am certain. You have given yourself away. No-one but you sitting opposite me in the café could have seen the fleck of mascara 'smudging my cheek like a dark tear'. No-one

*but you could have made out my whispered
words from the movement of my lips.*

*Perhaps you see it as an act of love. A
strange love it is which wants only to fathom
and control, to stalk my imagination more
insidiously than my movements.*

*For over a year now, I have been obsessed
by the knowledge this anonymous stranger
has of me. I have felt trapped by an omni-
science I don't recognize – like some baleful
god created only to watch me and fix me in
his perverse gaze.*

*You have made me an object to myself. I
can no longer lift a finger or a lock or pour
myself a glass of water spontaneously. On
stage or in front of the cameras, each gesture
carries with it one of your phrases. It is worse
still in bed. An analysis of yours rears up to
confound and pin me to a slide, like some
insect under a microscope. I am no longer
capable of loving. But perhaps this is what
you always intended.*

*Anatomy is what one performs on the
dead. With incisive brutality, you have
performed it on me and now I want to die. I
am superfluous, even to myself.*
*If it is an act of vengeance you intended, it has
been utterly successful. You have betrayed me
far more radically than I ever betrayed you.*

*There is only one part of me you have been
unable to touch. You will never know about it
now. It is too late.*

There is no signature on the letter. Madeleine has followed my example.

I read and reread Madeleine's words. My hands tremble. In the window my own shadowy face confronts me, as distorted and malevolent as any portrait of Dorian Gray. I have killed Madeleine. These letters, my letters, have tied the rope round her neck, kicked away the chair beneath her feet, more surely than if my limbs had taken part. Like a slow, certain poison, these letters have led to her death.

Apart from me, there is no other murderer. Will Henderson may or may not be guilty of many crimes, but Madeleine's death is mine alone. The law may see it as suicide. Contini will take this letter as the confirming suicide note he first looked for. But the responsibility is all mine.

In taking her own life, Madeleine has performed the one act I never described, the single act my imagination never followed her into. A gratuitous, an unnecessary act. An escape. An act without meaning. Except for me. An act intended for me. My act. Yes.

My head feels fuzzy. My eyes are blotched with tears. I close them for a moment and images leap and dazzle before me as bright and noisy and untouchable as fireworks. I force myself to stare at them, but their speed and brilliance makes sight impossible. As if some synapses had gone askew and produced a brainstorm.

Without realizing I have moved, I find myself leaving my bedroom. The letters are in my hand.

The key clinks in my pocket. It is time. I need to see Madeleine alive.

At the end of the hall there is a locked door which opens onto a narrow staircase. The room at the top spans half the space of the attic. Three windows poke out of each side of the sloping walls to form small gabled alcoves. The inside partition is starkly white. Every other space is hung with posters and photographs. This is not my father's collection. It is my own. It is my museum to Madeleine.

There are posters advertising each of her plays and films – in French and English and German and Italian. There is even one in Hebrew for *La Parisienne* and one in Greek for *Secret Woman*, oddly renamed *Janus Face*. The blocked shapes of the antique alphabet carry with them a whiff of the *collège classique* and confer a sculptural serenity to Madeleine's bent head.

There are stills and theatre photographs and publicity shots crammed into alcoves, making inroads on the ceiling, filed into a corner cabinet. The photographs carry Madeleine's signature. None of them is dedicated to me. In this room, I have no name. I am everyman.

Banked along the floor of the outer wall are a series of aluminium cases. Each one contains a reel of film. Each one is clearly labelled with name and part number. At the far end of the wall, a bookcase is stacked with video tapes. Some bear the glossy covers of store-bought product, others the uniform packaging of off-air tapes.

Behind the blue velvet sofa stands a 16mm projector. Tucked into an alcove on a wheeled pedestal is a television set and video recorder. An alcove on the opposite side contains a chair and a small desk on which my old office computer and printer sit. Apart from these, the only other furniture in the room is a radio-cassette player and a tiny fridge of the kind used as liquor cabinets in desultory hotel rooms.

I pour myself a drink now and prowl the length and breadth of the room. The single lamp to the back of the sofa casts a dim circle of light. In its shadows, Madeleine looks out at me, ever vivid, ever radiant.

From outside there is a faint whistle of wind through trees, the sudden hoot of an owl. I peer out the window and see a smattering of stars. In the distance I can make out, more by sense than sight, the blur of the copse beneath which the remnants of the barn lie.

Before the blaze overpowers me and the motion of memory reels me back to an intact barn and the sight of Madeleine's helpless swinging body, I veer away and switch on the projector. The whir of the machinery is soothing. It casts a pale creamy circle onto the white of the far wall.

Quickly, I prod open one of the aluminium cases and position the film onto the projector. It doesn't matter what movie I've picked. Anything will do now. Anything that blots out the real.

The sound of a flute and violins floats across the room, strains of Debussy. I lean into the soft warmth of the sofa and see Madeleine as large as life on the far wall. She is running across the slope of a meadow. The grass is very green. The sun shimmers and dances across leaves and field. Madeleine's face is troubled. For some reason I no longer know why, nor what film I have stumbled into. I only know that Madeleine is very young and in some distress and her dress is long with the pale embroidered flowers of the turn of the last century.

She stoops to pick a daisy and gazes at it for a moment as if its centre could solve a mystery. There is a soft glow on the arch of her cheek. Her eyelashes cast a shadow and then the flower is in shreds, tossed aside, and she runs again, her dress lifted and swaying, her stockings brightly white against the green of the field.

Madeleine's voice comes to me. But it doesn't come from the projector, where the flute still pipes.

'I hate the country,' she says.

'Nonsense,' I say.

'It's true. I hate all that green. All those trees, all those insects, all that life that could happily do without me. That does happily without me. That doesn't care. That doesn't see. That's indifferent. It went on before. And it'll go on after. The same green. The same trees. I hate it.'

But Madeleine on the wall which is a screen has stopped beneath a vast beech. There is a swing hanging from one of its branches. She perches on it. Her legs begin to move with that slightly hectic randomness I remember from *Lulu*, as if their motion were unwilled. Were utterly their own and utterly sexual.

Her face is still troubled, but she is swinging now, back and forth, her legs arching and swooping and slicing the air, higher and higher. Her mouth relaxes, her hair sweeps the ground and suddenly on a curve of ground nearby a man's booted feet appear and then his legs and torso and velvety face, shaded by a wide-brimmed hat. He is watching Madeleine, whose eyes are closed now, her face a map of the rustling leaves above her.

Despite myself, the stirring starts, a tug and tickle at my crotch which I am powerless to control. As Madeleine opens her eyes and meets those of her onlooker, my hand is already in my pocket.

He pulls her off the swing and I am there with him pulling her onto the ground. The earth is soft with moss. Her face beneath my fingers is soft too and her hair has a fresh fragrance of wind. She lifts her lips to him and I cover them with mine and wonder which one of us she is kissing and if it is the same or different with each and I see his fingers rising up her stockinged leg and the sudden wildness in her face as we taste the cleavage between her breasts. Then for a breathless moment everything is a painful sweetness of flutes and violins and a summer afternoon. And cut – we are in the salon of a comfortable house and Madeleine is talking to an older woman.

I let the film play over and through me until the spool winds its way to the end and flaps repeatedly into the air. Reluctantly I switch on the light and gaze at the bare white wall which minutes ago was covered with such heated activity. I get up and turn off the projector.

The room is a cavern of silence as echoing as that of a church. But this is a church, I remind myself. My very own shrine to Madeleine. Built out of love and devotion. Erected in her honour. Madeleine – Magdalene, the whore who bathed her saviour's feet with her tears and dried them with her hair and was purified in turn. Madeleine, who gave her name to a hundred sanctuaries and to that area of Paris where the upper-class call-girls drive round in their white convertibles and pick up their clients. Holy Madeleine who gave her name to those delicate little shells of cakes which, dipped in tea, brought the past back for Proust's Marcel.

How often in these last years have I visited this shrine and sweated through memories? Engaged in my rites in this hothouse of fantasy. Written those letters which began so innocently and ended in doom. I should have pinned them to the wall, like those devotees who offer their prayers in writing to the saints.

How often? Twice a month? Less? More? Does it matter? As religiously as a devout sinner in search of a confessional, I have returned here to bathe in memories and dreams which offer no absolution. For my shrine is also a brothel. A brothel in reverse. Not one in which dream is made flesh. But one in which flesh is made dream. My estranged wife become pornography.

The thought, so coldly put, startles me. Madeleine's dead body hurtles towards me. I don't want to see it. I thrust it aside with activity, push the television screen into the centre of the room, pick out a video tape and hurriedly press the play button.

The throb of a heavy-metal song fills the room, frightening away the ghosts. I pour myself another finger of brandy and tell myself I have unconsciously chosen well. Madeleine dies in this film. I have watched her die at least a hundred times. And each time, I knew that her death was a play of illusion. Each time, with a flick, I could rewind her into life.

Adept as I am in the world of fantasy, perhaps I can maintain that illusion for the length of another night. And postpone that cold weight of guilt which will drown me as surely as ice closing over a winter pool.

As I watch I find myself erratically thinking once more of Madeleine's tirade against the country. What did it mean but that she hated the country because she couldn't be seen in it? The trees, the grass, didn't watch her, didn't return her life to her. Is that what it meant to be an actress? To be enamoured of the gaze which confirms one's life?

But my gaze has killed her. She has said as much in her last letter. I had seen too much and given testimony to my seeing in words, blind to the imprisoning effect it might have.

My mind balks at the paradox. Can there be an excess of seeing which topples over into blindness as there is an excess of love which ends up as hate?

Or perhaps Madeleine didn't altogether mean what she said. She often didn't. Words for her were speculations and fancies, teasings as well as truths.

The images on the screen race and blear in front

of my eyes. I am fuddled with alcohol, exhaustion and too many emotions. I zap on the rewind button and watch life hurtle backwards. Video is the technology of dreams.

What would I not give to have real time move under my mastery in the way that these images do? Backwards and forwards, fast or slow, repeated at will. What would I not give to have been able to stop time on a frame like this one in which Madeleine throws back her hair, her face dreamy, secret, alive in every fragment and feature? Alive for me.

But I have never had any control over Madeleine's real life. That has always been the crux of the problem. If nothing else, that is clear to me now.

It comes to me with a fierce jolt of anguish that the only mastery I have ever had is over her death.

14

The bell sounds through a great blur of distance.

'Pierre,' my mother's voice calls. '*Pierre, vas-y. Réponds.* Get the door. *C'est le facteur.*'

'OK, Maman.' Without opening my eyes to the murky light, I look for my slippers. They are not at the side of the bed where I left them. Nor does the soft chenille of my robe meet the scrabble of my fingers.

The bell rings again and with it comes my mother's softly admonishing voice. 'Pierre?'

If I don't hurry she will go to the door and I will kill her. She is supposed to rest. To rest as much as is possible. My father has made that very clear.

'*J'y vais, Maman.*'

I rub my eyes and scramble out of bed. The floor is cold. Colder than it should be. The carpet has vanished in the night.

I open my eyes properly and realize with a start that I have been dreaming round the sound of the doorbell, which rings again now with an emphatic insistence. The cold floor at my feet is that of the attic. Madeleine's face smiles at me from a hundred pictures. I have fallen asleep on the sofa. In front of me, the television screen flickers black and white.

I pull on my socks and shoes and zap the screen into darkness. I pass a hand through my hair and glance at my watch. It is almost eleven. My wakeful nights are eating up my days. But who on earth has taken it upon themselves to visit me without a telephone warning? Perhaps it is Jerome again, willing me away.

I race down the stairs and try to put a semblance of order into shirt and sweater as I do so. Everywhere in the house, last night's lights are still on. I switch them off as I go and only pause at the door to take a deep breath, before opening it.

Above a black ski-jacket Contini's smooth face startles me.

'You sure know how to take your time,' he says by way of greeting. 'It's colder than a witch's teat out here.'

'I wasn't expecting anyone,' I mumble.

'No.' He brushes past me, stamping his feet on the indoor mat. 'And from the look of things, I'd say you hadn't bothered to wake up yet. Let alone to turn off the lights or take off your clothes before getting into bed. Your behaviour could get a man seriously worried.'

'What?'

'Yes, another few minutes and you'd have had me climbing through a window.'

'What are you talking about?'

He glares at me and I suddenly catch his drift.

380

'You don't think I'd—'

'Kill yourself? Why not? But if you make me a cup of coffee, I'll forgive you for making me worry. Though I have to say, you already look half-dead.'

'I didn't know you cared.'

He grunts at my sarcasm and follows me into the kitchen.

'What are you doing working on a Sunday?'

'Only half working.'

'So this is a social visit?'

'I drove the wife and the kids up to Mont-Gabriel for a day's skiing. That was the social part. Then I came back here. Murder inquiries don't take the weekend off.'

I grind the coffee and try to collect myself in the rush of noise.

'So you're still convinced it's murder and Henderson's your man?'

'Henderson's dead.'

A gasp escapes me. 'I . . . I'm sorry.'

'Yup. Died on the way to the hospital. Why're you sorry? Your chief of police is pleased. Fancies the case is closed.'

'I never really thought—' I begin slowly and he pounces on me.

'Why? You got someone better for me now?'

I shrug and busy myself with cups and brewing.

'All that tossing and turning last night lead to something new?' he asks as soon as I face him. 'No! Don't tell me. You're guessing it was suicide again.'

'Yes. Maybe. I don't know. Let me drink some of this and then I can think straight.'

'How about offering me a muffin or something. Given that it's Sunday.'

I stare into the all but empty fridge and pull out a sliced loaf that has seen better days.

'You don't take care of yourself properly,' Contini grumbles. 'You should get a woman to look after you.'

'The one I had wasn't up to much in the way of muffins.'

He chortles as I put some bread into the toaster and asks, 'Did you get my little message?'

'I haven't checked the answering machine yet. I was asleep when you came, remember.'

'Hmmm.' He digs in his pocket for cigarettes, thrusts them at me and sips his coffee.

I light up. A wave of dizziness hurtles through me. I close my eyes for a moment and open them to find him staring at me.

'You feeling sick?'

'Just tired. Find out anything more yesterday?'

'We couldn't get a match on the fingerprints.'

'Which prints?'

'Henderson's and the shoddy ones we lifted from Madeleine's bedroom – amongst yours and Mme Tremblay's.'

'Oh.' I smile.

The smile is a mistake. Contini is right in there.

'So you're pleased that that scumbag wasn't fucking your wife? Well, someone sure as hell was. Balling her I mean. So don't get too happy too soon.'

I stub out my cigarette. 'And Madeleine's car?'

'Everyone wears gloves these days, don't they? But they're testing the fibres the crime scene girls and boys picked up.' Contini cracks his knuckles, then asks with sudden cherubic sweetness, 'You sure you didn't get my message?'

'I told you, I haven't . . .' Like an electric jolt, something kicks in at the back of my head. 'You mean, you . . .' I struggle with words which fill me with too much horror. At the same time I am loath to give anything away. I find myself saying, 'You know, I think there was someone prowling around here last night. The logs in the woodpile tumbled. There was noise.'

'Oh?' Contini is all visible attention.

'Yes. I'm not sure, of course. It could have been an animal. But I've been thinking, maybe it was one of those kids who were gathered in front of the Rosenberg house.'

'You think the citizens of Ste-Anne don't like to see you crossing the barricades?' Contini chuckles.

'Something like that. Or maybe it's my imagination.'

'Yes. I have the impression your imagination is quite good.' He gives me a knowing look which I don't like, then reaches for the coffee pot and pours himself a second cup. 'Why have you started thinking about suicide again? I thought you'd gone right off that.'

The ringing of the telephone saves me from a reply. For once I pick up the receiver with alacrity.

A woman's voice I don't recognize greets me with firm precision. 'M. Pierre Rousseau?'

'Yes.'

'I'm calling from the Hôpital St-Joseph, on behalf of a patient here, Maryla Orkanova.'

'Maryla Orkanova?' I repeat dumbly.

'Yes. I'm afraid there was an accident last night. Nothing grave. But Mme Orkanova has asked that you visit. And if you can pick up her son from 14 Rue René Lévesque and bring him here, she would be grateful. He's expecting your call.'

She reads out a number to me which I jot down, my fingers as clumsy as wooden planks.

'What's happened?' Contini asks even before I have put the phone down.

'A friend of mine has been in an accident.'

'I'm sorry,' he says with genuine sympathy.

'Yes. Me too. I have to pick up her son and go to the hospital.'

'I'll take you. You're in no shape to drive anywhere.'

'No, no. Really. I can manage.'

'You can't manage. Go upstairs and get yourself cleaned up. Or you'll frighten your friend.'

There is a twinkle in his eyes, but his manner is determined.

'You'll miss your lunch,' I say in an attempt at resistance.

'All in the call of duty. And we can pick up something.'

Outside the wind is as icy as the snow's new crust. Contini drives carefully down the hill, his footballer's shoulders hunched over the wheel, his eyes intent.

I am glad of his silence, less glad when he breaks it once we have joined the through road.

'So you didn't recognize my signature on the package?' he says abruptly.

'I didn't see any signature,' I hear myself saying.

He laughs. 'But you received it all right. A packet chock-a-block with letters. I thought you might have noticed my stamp.'

'You sent them?' My voice is as rough as my head feels.

Contini nods, but his profile betrays nothing.

'And you read them?'

He shrugs. 'I'm a cop. They were in Madeleine's car. All wrapped and addressed and ready to go. To be posted by someone. By herself, perhaps. Or whoever was driving the car. To be delivered by someone.'

'I see.'

'Or perhaps they had already been delivered and were simply sitting there. Forgotten. Overlooked.'

'What?'

'You're not following me?'

I shake my head. 'Turn left here.'

Contini veers too sharply, but doesn't seem to notice. 'What I'm saying is that maybe she'd already given you the letters. Some time on Sunday. And you'd argued over them. Perhaps a little too violently . . .'

I glance at him in astonishment. 'I don't know what you're talking about.'

'Don't you?'

'It's the house with the red door. Just over there.'

Contini pulls up with a skid of tyres. He puts a staying hand on my shoulder. 'Here's how I see it. After midnight mass, Madeleine was in high spirits. Very high. She decided to give you a ring. Someone did ring you in the small hours of Monday morning, didn't they?'

My stomach heaves.

'So you walked over to see her. You talked, maybe you even did more. Inside, outside, I don't know. You walked under the stars and the talking got out of hand. You had a row. She was accusing you of stalking her. Harassing her. A big row. You were good at rows. I read that in her journal.'

He waits for my confirmation, but my lips won't move. I am with him, there on that night, on the path which leads to the barn.

'Anyhow, the row got a little out of hand. Your hands were round her throat.'

He looks meaningfully at my gloved hands, which suddenly seem very large. I thrust them into my coat pockets.

'Then, whoops, too late. Probably you didn't really mean to do it. So you strung her up. To make it seem like suicide. It wouldn't necessarily look all that different in the autopsy report. And you knew her letter would serve as a suicide note.'

I stare out into greyness.

'OK. Go get the kid. We'll talk it over later. I've got all day.'

Contini's eyes bore into my back as I clamber up the slippery steps to the house. I struggle to arrange my face. The woman who opens the door to me obviously doesn't think I have arranged it well enough for she stares at me suspiciously as she wipes her hands on a striped apron.

'M. Rousseau?'

I nod.

'I'll get Stefan.'

Stefan must already have heard the ring. He is right behind her, pulling his jacket off the banister and shuffling into it. He is a slim, sandy-haired boy, whose solemn timidity makes him seem older than his nine years. Maryla's grey eyes dart a wary look at me from his bony face.

'You'll bring him back here?' his hostess says. It is more a command than a question.

'If that's what Maryla wants.'

Stefan precedes me to the car without speaking. His shoulders are hunched like an old man's. Every movement of his body displays an anxiety he can barely control. Suddenly in that shuttered posture I see myself – picked up from school by a friend of my parents and driven to the hospital to visit my dying mother. I taste my sense of unreality, the muddle in my mind, the struggle to control uncontrollable events and incomprehensible emotions, the small boy's front of bravery.

My arm is around Stefan's shoulder. 'The nurse says your mother's fine. Just a little shaken up,' I murmur. 'Would you like to sit in front? With Detective Contini?'

'Detective?' Fear flashes across his face and disappears into stolid composure. 'No.' He opens the back door and huddles into the seat.

Fifteen long minutes later, we are at the hospital. It is not the one where my mother died. That has long since been pulled down.

Maryla is sitting up in a windowside bed at the far end of the ward. The only colour in her face is that of her lipstick. The rest is as milky white as the pillows. One arm lies swathed in a cast. She waves to us with the other and beckons Stefan to her side. Contini and I hold back as he rushes towards her. I see him struggle in her embrace, but his stiff features relax a little.

'Dumb ice,' Contini exclaims. 'Poor kid. No father, I presume?'

'He died when Stefan was three.'

'And your relation to the mother?'

'A friend,' I say emphatically.

Contini doesn't press me. Instead he urges me towards Maryla, who is gesturing to us.

'I should have brought flowers,' I mumble as we approach her.

'You've had other things on your mind.'

I cast him a quick look, but there is no sardonic smile on his lips.

'I'm so sorry, Maryla.' I squeeze her good hand. 'What happened?'

'I was just telling Stefan. I skidded, lost control. Just a little way from where your road meets the old highway.'

Her eyes are lowered and I can't read her expression.

'Silly, isn't it?' Her laugh is brittle. 'Still, not much

damage. Just the arm. You can be the first to sign my cast, Stefan.'

Contini swiftly brings a pen out of his jacket pocket and hands it to the boy.

'No, wait, this will be better.' He replaces it with a felt-tip.

'Draw me one of your cartoons,' Maryla urges and, while the boy is busy, she gives me a shadowy look.

'Sorry. I haven't introduced you. This is Richard Contini. Detective Richard Contini. Maryla Orkanova.'

'Oh yes. I . . .' She seems at a loss and Contini interjects.

'That road out of Rousseau's is an obstacle course. Don't know why any of us visit him in winter. How'd your car fare?'

'Not too badly . . .' She seems to be about to say something more when Stefan announces, 'There!'

'Oh, that's a beautiful dog, Stefan. Thank you. Isn't it good?' She displays the cast. 'A sad Sam. With sad eyes. Sad for my broken arm.'

'When can you get home, Maryla?'

'Tomorrow. I'm fine really, but the doctor wants to keep me quiet for another night. Funny way to spend New Year's Eve. Still, Stefan will be all right at the Lavalles, won't you, dear?'

The boy nods.

'But you must be starving now. Maybe . . .'

'We'll take Stefan out for lunch on our way back.'

'Or I can buy him a burger down at the coffee shop. What do you say, Stefan?'

Contini is suddenly all activity and I realize from Maryla's grateful smile that she has been trying to engineer a moment with me alone all along.

She seizes it as soon as they have left the vicinity of the bed. The smile and forced jollity disappear. Her face is all anxiety, her voice tremulous. 'I may be mad, Pierre. But I'm sure it wasn't an accident. This car appeared out of nowhere, no lights or anything. It forced me off the road. Bumped me on the side. I only said all that about skidding for Stefan's sake.'

'Are you sure?'

She nods.

'Did you tell the police?'

'Last night. I was in a bit of a state though. I had to clamber out of the car through a drift. My door was wedged tight. And, well, eventually, I got to the main road and flagged someone down.' She shivers, her eyes huge with remembered fear. 'I don't think the police altogether believed me.'

'Poor Maryla. I'll speak to Gagnon about it. Can you describe the car?'

She shakes her head. 'No. He came from behind me. Maybe if I hadn't had the radio on, I would have heard in time.'

I squeeze her hand. 'Don't worry about it any more. I'll deal with everything.'

'Will you?' She is staring at me with that wide-eyed vulnerability which makes me so uncomfortable.

I nod and lower my gaze.

She laughs drily. 'You know, when I first noticed

the car coming up alongside me, I thought for a split second it was you. That you had come after me. That you had forgotten to turn on your lights in your haste. That you had changed your mind.'

'Maryla!' It is a gentle reprimand, but as I utter it, I am suddenly afraid. Who could have been coming down that dark lonely road so late at night? Who would want deliberately to hurt Maryla, who has had enough to deal with in her life?

As I chat Maryla into ease and wait for Contini and Stefan to reappear, I retrace the events of the preceding evening: Jerome's visit, the thud in the shed, my sense of an interloper. Giorgio's arrival. Before that, the demonstration, Will Henderson and the drugged youths. As the river flows – or freezes – the distances between us are not so very great. I stop myself from thinking of Madeleine. She is not part of the same story. Contini knows that too. But suddenly, our quiet stretch of countryside has become a treacherous place.

When Stefan and Contini reappear, I excuse myself for a moment and go and buy Maryla chocolates and flowers, a stack of magazines and a paperback from the hospital shop. The gifts bring tears to her eyes. She forces us to share the chocolates with her. Stefan gorges himself, as if he had a hole inside him which permanently needed filling. And then Catherine, a friend of Maryla's, arrives. She offers to take Stefan back if we need to go.

'We do, really,' Contini says.

'Of course.' Maryla gives him her good hand and a proud little nod of the head.

Stefan waves, more at Contini than at me, I notice. Maybe he is better at recognizing a father when he sees one than his mother.

'Nice lady,' Contini offers when we are already back in the car. 'With the emphasis on lady.'

'Mmmn.' I hesitate for a few minutes and then recount what Maryla has told me of her accident.

He listens carefully and instead of commenting, mutters, 'You haven't by any chance got a good bakery in town, have you? The food in that coffee shop would give a rat indigestion.'

'To the left of the church. Though I don't know if it's quite up to your standards.'

'Still, we'll stop. We're going to have a long afternoon together and I'd like to sweeten the pain.

'No, no, I'll choose,' he says when we pull up and I make to climb out of the car. 'You don't care enough. And it's my treat.'

I wait and as I wait I stare at the bulky grey-stone rump of Ste-Anne's. I have a sudden desire to run, to escape. A pure, unadulterated flash of desire. Like I had as a child when I was trapped inside those walls. Just to run. With no sense of destination. With nothing in my mind. A mind occupied only with the movement of limbs and the raggedness of breath. The desert gave me that. Burn-out.

But Contini is already back, carefully depositing a capacious white box in my hands.

'Good of you to have waited,' he says wryly as if he had read my thoughts.

He moves the car slowly away from the kerb,

glancing at the safety of the box in my hands.

'Isn't that your brother over there? Just coming out of the seminary. He's got one of his women in tow.'

He cackles and I look to the left and indeed see my brother.

'Want to stop and say hello?'

I shake my head. Jerome turns and spots me. His face crumbles visibly as he notes Contini's presence. With uncustomary speed he takes Monique Blais by the arm and charges away.

'Guess he doesn't want to see you either. Too bad. Who's the woman with him, by the way?'

I look at him in surprise. 'Madeleine's mother. I would have thought you'd grilled her.'

'Lavigne's terrain.' He chuckles. 'I talked to that son of hers. Now there's one I'd happily lock up. But no proof. His alibi for Christmas Eve checks out. So far, in any case.'

'You know he very much wanted Madeleine to hire him as a bodyguard?'

'You do get around,' he mutters. 'So what's your brother got against you? You been blabbing in confession or refusing to blab?'

'We're pretty good friends,' I murmur.

'And you're a pretty good liar. Have you told them about Mme Tremblay's suicide attempt?'

'No. I didn't think she'd like people here gossiping. And she's got enough on her plate at the moment.'

He nods, takes the next turn without my having to direct him.

'Do you have the keys to Mme Tremblay's house?'

'No. Why?'

'You're lying.'

I laugh for what feels like the first time in weeks. 'I'm glad you're not omniscient.'

He grunts. 'So maybe you're not lying. By the way, Mme Tremblay has been taken off by Gisèle Desnos. To stay at her place. She thought she could use an environment a little more cheerful than the hospital.'

'Thanks for telling me.'

Silence covers us. We drive in it for what feels too long. The sky is a sullen, heavy grey, the heat in the car overpowering. I have the impression Contini is looking forward to our tête-à-tête even less than I am.

'How much longer are you going to postpone the ordeal?' I find myself muttering.

'Only until I've bitten into a pastry.'

I make to open the box and he stops me. 'Not so fast. We're almost there.'

He turns off the highway and takes the narrow incline with exaggerated slowness, as if deliberately to tax my nerves.

'That's where Maryla Orkanova's car must have gone off the road.' He points abruptly and I see where the neatly banked snow has been pushed and toppled and tyre-tracks edge over the verge.

'Lucky about the snow, really. Broke her speed, cushioned the impact. Car might have turned over if it wasn't there.'

I shiver. 'Do you think . . . ?'

'Do I think that you suffered a second aberration and followed her down from your house and bludgeoned her over the edge with your car? The answer is no. I don't have you down as a frenzied serial killer.'

'I should thank my lucky stars.'

'Thank them.'

'Second aberration, you said?'

'You heard me.'

An imp of the perverse makes me open the box of pastries and take a bite out of an éclair. It is time.

'Good?' Contini asks.

'Not bad.' I have the odd impression I can hear him salivating. I chew with audible relish for a moment.

'I didn't see your little package until yesterday, you know. I'm sure of that. The only time I ever saw those letters before was when I wrote them. All except Madeleine's, that is. That I saw for the first time last night. That's what made me think of suicide again.'

'So you did write them,' Contini says softly, though I feel the words as emphatically as a clap of thunder.

'You didn't know?'

'I assumed. I had no way of knowing until you just told me. Madeleine could have been wrong.'

'Of course.'

We don't speak again until we are in the house. It feels gloomy. The morning's coffee is still on the table, the mugs rimmed with a grey-brown sludge.

Minou is whimpering oddly in her basket. Her ears are peeled back. She looks at me accusingly.

I turn on all the lights, pile the dishes into the sink.

'Ya. Let's cheer this place up a bit. It's almost the New Year, after all.' Contini reaches for a blue and white platter displayed on the pine dresser, gives it a wipe and arranges the pastries on it. 'I'll make the coffee and you light the fire. We can go next door. OK?'

'Sure.'

My luck to be given a policeman who's an Epicurean, I think as I open a tin for Minou and freshen the water in her dish. She doesn't come running. It occurs to me that her mentality is a little like Maryla's. I've been neglecting her and now I'll have to grovel. I bend to stroke her and she whimpers.

'That's one unhappy cat,' Contini says from behind me. 'You been beating her or something?'

I veer towards him and he holds up a staying hand. 'Just kidding. But she really doesn't look too good.'

'The avalanche in the woodshed frightened her last night.'

As if to contradict me, Minou stretches and slowly comes out of her basket. She is limping. Her back paw doesn't touch the ground as she covers the short distance to her bowls.

'She get hit by a log?' Contini asks.

I shake my head. 'She was fine last night.' I bend to examine her. She whimpers again, more emphatically this time. There is a great round gash

396

on her leg where the fur has been stripped away. 'She must have got caught in a rabbit trap,' I murmur. 'I'll have to take her to the vet.'

'Na. Don't bother.' Contini is right beside me scrutinizing the paw like a past expert. 'Get me a couple of sticks, Popsicle sticks if you've got them, or those things doctors are always sticking down your gullet. And a roll of bandage. I'll do as good a job.' He grins at my evident suspicion. 'I might not have been much use at Greek and Latin, but I've been through a sobering lot of pets in my day.'

By the time I've rummaged around and come back with the necessary, Minou is sprawled luxuriously in Contini's lap. She lies there unmoving until he has tied the splint.

I carry her, unprotesting, back to her basket.

'Cream,' Contini says. 'I gave her some pastry. Wish they were all that easy, eh? Now it's our turn.'

He busies himself with the making of coffee as if he had done it a hundred times before in my house. I leave him to it, go and lay and light a fresh fire. Minou's leg worries me. Who could be laying traps around here?

I don't have much time to consider it. Within minutes, Contini comes in with a tray and reminds me that I have far more serious things to think about.

'One pastry and then you're on.' He prods his fork through the centre of a *religieuse* and pops the top into his mouth. 'Not bad.' He wipes a trickle of cream from the corner of his mouth with a dainty gesture, then pours out coffee. 'Help yourself.'

'I've had one, thanks.'

'OK.' He finishes his pastry in two heaped mouthfuls. 'Let's take it from the top. You wrote all those drooling, anonymous letters to Madeleine Blais. Pretty strong stuff. She didn't take to them in a big way. Not after a while, in any case. Then you gave the game away somehow. She found out they were from you. You only learned she had found out yesterday. December 30th. Is that right?'

I nod.

'That's right then?'

'You got a tape-recorder going? You want me to say it out loud?'

'I've still got a brain,' he mutters and passes me a cigarette. When he lights it, the flame leaps too high and all but singes my hair.

'Heh! Should I have a lawyer here?'

'You're the lawyer. And this is just a chat. You'll feel better afterwards, I promise. Like a confessional. Now pay attention.' He leans comfortably back into his chair. His voice when it comes takes on a musing, intimate note.

'So the letters don't come into it just yet. But Madeleine rings you. Around one-fifteen a.m. on Christmas Day?'

'That's what you told me. I don't remember hearing a voice.'

He puffs at his cigarette. 'OK. But you knew it was her. Maybe she breathes a certain way. Like Marilyn Monroe.' He gives me a happy smile and then rushes on before I can protest. 'So you hotfoot it over to Mme Tremblay's. Madeleine is waiting.

Maybe she invites you in or maybe she suggests a stroll straight away. Which was it?'

I shrug. 'I don't remember.'

'Try.'

'OK. We went out.'

'You didn't fuck her first? In her bedroom? In that nice comfortably dishevelled bed. There are all those prints. Everywhere. On the bedposts.'

Maybe he has spiked my coffee. Maybe it's just me. But somehow confusion sets in and I can see it all. Like in a movie. A blue movie. Madeleine and me on that bed.

Contini is waiting. 'It doesn't matter,' he says. 'So you go out. She's got her big coat on and nothing underneath. Well, almost nothing. A slip of a night-gown. Soft silk, warmed by her flesh, but turning cold in the night air. The stars are shining. From somewhere an owl screeches. A perfect night with the love of your life. You slip your arm around her, beneath the coat. To warm her. You murmur sweet nothings. She's irresistible. Just like in the movies. And then suddenly, without warning, she turns on you.

'Women! They're always blowing hot, then cold.

'She says she knows it was you. Yes. She knows. All those letters. You've driven her to distraction. Persecuted her. Terrified her. Stalked her. She's been brought to the very edge. And all because of you. An obsession. A jealous obsession. Vengeful. You're trying to kill her.'

Contini's voice has grown hypnotically low and I am straining to hear, the images racing across my mind in time to his words. Like a dream or a night-mare. Already lived. More real than the real.

'No, no, you protest. You love her.

'Never, she insists. It's not love. You don't want her alive. You don't want her breathing freely. You're a pervert. Like that Marc Lépine. Like that assassin, who shot down all those women at the university. And she slaps you hard across the face.

'You slap her back. You hit her hard and she stumbles, slips, but her leg kicks you in the crotch. Once it's started, it's hard to stop and suddenly your hands are round her neck. You just want to stop her talking, to stop her railing against you, calling you names, and you squeeze, you squeeze hard and she goes all limp. She stops resisting.

'But you're not limp. You're hard. Too hard. And you take her hand and you wrap it round your cock and together you squeeze and there it is, your spunk all over her coat. You wipe it with your hand-kerchief and get up.

'Yet she doesn't get up when you do. She just lies there. And abruptly it comes to you. This time you've gone too far. Really too far. You didn't mean to. You love her. You really love her. But now it's too late.

'You don't actually know what you're doing. You're on automatic pilot. No-one will understand that it was an accident. Just a row that got out of hand. So you find the rope. It doesn't take long. You know exactly where everything is. And minutes later, you've strung her up. Too late you realize that her eyes have fluttered open. She wasn't dead. But now she is. She's hanging there. Madeleine. Poor Madeleine. Your great love.

'Is that how it was?' Contini whispers after a moment.

I can barely hear him. My head is buried in my hands. I think I am crying. The acrid fumes of my guilt clog my mind, paralyse limbs, stab at my eyes.

'Is that how it was?' His hand is on my shoulder.

I look up at his hazy face and see the features swim into solemnity. My head feels as if it is nodding. My voice creaks through my throat. 'Yes. That's how it was. More or less. I killed her.'

'You know you're confessing to murder.'

'Whatever.'

He stares at me from his protruding eyes.

'You got a toilet around here?'

15

Contini is gone a long time. Too long. Maybe the food really didn't agree with him.

I don't mind. My head feels light. My heart feels light. If I believed in an afterlife, I would run through the door now and scramble to the top of some tree or house and fling myself down. To join Madeleine.

But it doesn't matter. I don't have to hide any more. Don't have to construct reasons for myself. Don't have to get through each solitary day with a pretence of purpose. No more burden of guilt. So easy. Everything will be taken care of. A child again. With Contini as my mother. He feeds me pastries.

I stare at the flames.

Contini comes in so softly his voice startles me.

'Feeling better?'

I shrug, stretch out my arms in expectation of handcuffs.

They don't come. Instead Contini casts me a rueful look and settles into the sofa.

'Confessions are great, Rousseau. But what I need

402

is evidence. I've borrowed these.' He puts two blue sweaters down beside him and pats them reflectively.

'By the way. How'd you get Madeleine's body up to the loft?'

'What?'

'You heard me. How'd you string her up?'

My head is fuzzy. 'A ladder. There was a ladder.'

'A ladder. OK.' He reaches into his pocket and takes out a small black box, prods a button. 'It was on, by the way.'

We both stare at the tape-recorder.

'I'll tell you what. I'll trade you the tape for a sperm sample. Tuesday morning. Eleven o'clock should do it. At headquarters.'

I gaze at him in disbelief. 'You mean ... all that ...?'

'Could be true.' He ambles towards the liquor cabinet, takes out a bottle of whisky and pours us both a small shot. 'We could use this.' He lifts his glass to me.

'So, Tuesday at eleven?'

'I don't understand.'

'Don't you? Some men are very particular about their sperm. And for what purpose it's extracted.'

There is a dull thudding in my head. I try to shake off my confusion. 'What were you doing upstairs?'

'And the story works, doesn't it?'

'What were you doing upstairs?' I repeat more emphatically.

'Having a crap. Having a look round.' He grins. 'Some men are pretty particular about having their houses searched too. And warrants with guys like you . . . with the local police chief on their side, can take for ever.'

I feel for the attic keys in my pocket. 'What did you find?'

'These two.' He pokes the sweaters. 'And a whole lot of garbage. Christ, you've got a lot of garbage in this house. It would take me a year to sift through it.'

'Anything useful?'

He winks at me and plumps the tape-recorder into his pocket. 'Just get yourself to headquarters Tuesday, Rousseau. OK? That gives you two days' grace. A New Year's present from me. And bring Mme Tremblay along with you. Just so we can clear up loose ends, check on whether poor Henderson was or wasn't Madeleine's so-called hitchhiker. I want this case over and done with. Before anyone else gets hurt. The inquest is set for Monday week.'

He glances at the telephone where the tell-tale light is blinking again. 'And pick up your messages, will you? You've got to start behaving responsibly.' He presses the button and we both listen to the voice of Gisèle Desnos.

'Pierre. I've got Mme Tremblay staying with me. And we're having a little party tonight. Why don't you drive over? You can stay the night. About nine. See you then.'

'I think you should go,' Contini says. 'It will do you good. And you never know how long freedom will last.'

The next voice cuts him off. 'Pierre. It's Marie-Ange Corot. I'm flying into Mirabel on Wednesday at two-thirty. Air France. Meet me if you can. If you can't, I've got a room booked at the Ritz.'

Contini whistles beneath his breath. 'Classy woman. I talked to her on the phone. Good she's coming. And now I'd better get back to the wife. Or she'll murder me.'

I stiffen and he chuckles.

'You're not a bad man, you know, Rousseau,' he says as I walk him to the door. 'A little too obsessional maybe. But you were always like that. Even as a kid. All those patriots. All that remembering. Some of the boys in my class nicknamed you "*Je me souviens*" – after the motto on the licence plates. Did you know that?' He lets out a guffaw.

'No. I didn't.'

'Well, now you do.' He pauses for a moment as he pulls on his coat. 'Something else. Were you aware that Madeleine Blais had a child?'

'A child!' I can feel my mouth hanging open, but I can't quite close it.

'So you didn't know that either. Funny. I always thought men could detect that of their lovers. The change in their bodies, I mean. But maybe you never looked closely enough. Or maybe, afterwards, you didn't ... Oh, never mind. A better new year, eh!' He pats me on the shoulder. 'That's what we need.'

I grunt something that might be a return greeting and watch him as he unlocks his car.

The door is already wide open when he turns

back to me. 'Two more things I forgot to mention, Rousseau. We've located the last voice on Madeleine's answering machine. One Fernando Ruiz. Mean anything to you? No?' He glances at his watch. 'Lavigne should be talking to him right now. And this.' He shuffles through his trouser pocket and brings out a small gold plaque bearing the letter R. 'Belong to you? I noticed a bunch of keys in the hall that looked as if they could use it.'

I turn the plaque round and round. It burns a hole in my hand, but I can't let it go.

'Yes, I thought so. Funny that we found it in the snow just outside Madeleine's window . . .' He prises it from my fingers. 'Tuesday at eleven. Don't forget.'

I stand there gazing into the gathering darkness for a long time after he has vanished. Images of that fateful night scud across my mind with dizzying pace. Like the distorted fragments of a nightmare, they refuse clarity and sequence. Am I mad? I can no longer distinguish the lived from the fantasized.

But the imprint of the key-ring plaque squeezed in my hand brings me back, a small cold object in the midst of fugitive dreams. A small, cold, identifying object, like the pebble I wanted.

In some buried recess of my self, the phone rings. Yes, the phone rings, rupturing sleep. Despite my grogginess, despite the answering silence, I know it is Madeleine. The need to see her is overwhelming. I need to explain. To confess to those letters. Quietly, privately. Before Christmas traps us in a familial moment. Yes, now. I must. I leave the warmth of the blankets and like a sleepwalker set out across the familiar fields.

The lamp glows in her window above the landing. It casts shadows through the cold darkness. Madeleine is waiting for me. I will hurl a pebble at her window to catch her attention. Without waking Mme Tremblay. As in childhood.

But there are no pebbles. Only my key-ring with the tell-tale R.

And then I see the figures etched against the light. Madeleine and a man. Kissing. Her head is thrown back in the same way as when she is kissing me. One hand is firm on her buttocks. The other caresses her hair, her back. I stare.

This is why she phoned me. This is her revenge for the letters. Madeleine wants me to see. To bite into the bitter core of my suffering. I don't want to see and yet I cannot move. The cold creeps into my bones, but the fires of that old familiar jealousy have leapt and kindled and burn through me. Is it jealousy of a stranger or of a lost self that I feel? In fury, I lob my key plaque at the window. I want her to know that I am here. But Madeleine doesn't turn from her kiss. I want to throw the plaque again, but in the darkness I cannot find it.

Do I wait then? Wait for Madeleine to come down? Do I go home?

The images whirl and disintegrate and reshape themselves with kaleidoscopic frenzy. Only Contini's mesmeric voice provides a pattern. Is it a pattern I have lived? I need to find out.

* * *

Gisèle Desnos lives on Ridgewood, a winding road which slips up and over the mountain behind the gargantuan dome of the Oratoire St-Joseph where, in my childhood, the pilgrims still used to climb the thousand or so steps to the shrine of the beatified Frère André on their bloodied knees.

The area is a wealthy one and offers spectacular views of the city, but the picturesque is not what concerns me now.

For the entire length of the drive here, I have been snuffling through my memory like a boar in search of truffles, trying to remember, trying to recover the scene to which I so willingly confessed, lulled by Contini's voice and scenario. Lulled by my own wishes, too, perhaps. For I know I am guilty. I have done so much wrong. Yet I can't remember. Like a strip of film beyond which I cannot see, Contini's words usurp the space of my memory. Am I crazy? How and where will I find the truth? For my own sanity, I need to unearth the truth before the chains of what Contini calls evidence ensnare me irrevocably.

A young woman opens the door to me, takes my coat with the polite aplomb of hired help and waves me into a house which is all sheer angles and glass and split levels. I make my way up and down stairs towards the distant tinkle of glasses and laughter and soft music and find myself in a large beech-parqueted room perched on a sheer precipice. Gowned women and suited men cluster in small groups against a great gleaming pond of night.

'Pierre, I'm so glad.' Gisèle glides towards me and plants a scented kiss on either cheek. She is regal in an off-the-shoulder gown of vibrant blue. Her arm is firm through mine as she guides me through the crowd. I can feel the eyes on me, curious, apprehensive, the little uncomfortable pockets of air that open at our passage.

A crystal cup of champagne finds its way into my hand.

'Doesn't Mme Tremblay look wonderful in my dress? We had such fun trying things on. I think it cheered her a little.'

Gisèle points me towards a corner sofa where I almost fail to recognize Mme Tremblay, so different does she look from the woman I last saw lying on a hospital bed. A pearl clasp adorns her hair. There is a matching choker at her neck. The long dress is darkly severe, but gleams subtly where the light falls on it. Only her eyes still have that trace of vagueness. They fail quite to focus on the silver-haired man perched at her side. But they focus on me.

'Pierre.' She puts out her hand to me.

'No, please, don't get up.' The man beside her rises to give me his place. 'Do sit down, Rousseau,' he says, and I recognize him as a former diplomat in Trudeau's last government.

'Thanks.'

Mme Tremblay squeezes my hand as Gisèle walks away with her guest.

'Gisèle insisted that I come down, but now that you're here, I think she'll let me retire.'

She forces herself from the sofa and I catch her before the weight of gravity defies her. Slowly, I help her through the crowd and up the stairs. They take all her concentration. She doesn't speak again until she is propped against the pillows in her room.

'I'm sorry, Pierre. Sorry for all the trouble I caused. It just took me over.'

'No trouble. And I understand.'

'Yes.' Her pale eyes scrutinize me and she gives me a twist of a smile. 'I believe you do. That was why you came back to Ste-Anne, wasn't it, Pierre? So you could be certain of seeing Madeleine. Be as close to her as it was possible to be. Yes.'

I intrude on the vagueness which has taken over her eyes again. 'How do you feel now?'

'Better for Gisèle's company. She's told me so many interesting things about Madeleine.'

We exchange a look and in it I realize again the extent to which Mme Tremblay and I are kin. Like two fanatics engaged in a cult, we judge everything by a single measure. The only difference is that I would prefer my adherence to be secret, while she wears hers like a badge of honour.

'Better too, strangely, because of the barn burning. They're holding someone, aren't they?'

'So you know.'

'Gisèle told me. She thought it best that I find out from a friend.' She lets out a sound which is not quite a laugh. 'It proves my first intuition was right. Madeleine did not take her own life. The police definitely recognize that now, don't they?'

410

I don't want to think about what Contini does or does not recognize. 'Yes,' I say, too loudly.

'Tell me about the man they're holding.'

Her hand grips my arm and I cover it with mine.

'I'm afraid there was . . . an accident. He died.' I rush on before I lose my nerve. 'Detective Contini would like you to come to headquarters Tuesday and . . . and see if you can identify him as the man who was with Madeleine that night.'

For a long moment, she is silent. 'There's more, Pierre. There's something you're not telling me.'

I take a deep breath. 'Contini is not certain he was Madeleine's—'

She cuts me off. 'You'll have to help them, Pierre. I don't altogether trust that Contini to find the right man. Imagine thinking I had anything to do with Madeleine's death!'

I wish I could share Mme Tremblay's sense of outraged innocence. I change the subject. I tell her about Monique, her wish to stay at the house. For my brother's sake, I add that she seems a little lost, despairing. I tell Mme Tremblay that she will do her daughter good.

She doesn't answer for a moment. She fingers the choker at her neck. At last she says, 'Will I? I never quite managed to before. But I guess it's only right. She is Guy Tremblay's child. She is my daughter – even if we didn't always see eye to eye.' Her gaze is troubled. 'Go now, Pierre. Leave me. I need to sleep.'

I want to put to her one of the many questions that has been plaguing me. I want to ask her about

411

Madeleine's child. But I can't now. If she doesn't know, it might prove too much of a shock. Instead, I find the young woman who opened the door to me and ask her to bring Mme Tremblay a hot drink and make sure she can undress herself. Then I force myself towards the crowd.

In the far corner of the room, couples are dancing. They sway across the floor with easy languor. Their faces are bright, smiling. This is no place for me. But I need to speak to Gisèle. I spy her at last in front of a long buffet table. There is a striking black woman at her side in a sequinned thirties dress. In her hand she holds a large copper gong. The spectacled man I met in the restaurant with Gisèle raises a sparkling hammer. Gisèle is calling for quiet.

'It's time for the countdown,' she announces, her hand aloft. 'Ten ... nine ...' Voices join her. The gong sets up a clatter. Corks pop and everywhere there are kisses and cries of 'Happy New Year'.

I plant what I hope has the semblance of a smile on my face and mingle with the crowd. The music has grown loud, and I can return the embraces of friends and acquaintances without pausing for impossible conversation. I find Gisèle to the corner of the buffet. She is urging everyone to dig in.

'Shall we talk when you have a moment?'

She nods. 'Give me five. And join me in the study. Up a few stairs on the right.'

I wait in a room which is a smaller version of its neighbour. There are books and a wall lined with fine costume drawings, a wave of a coral sofa and a large glass-topped desk which looks out on the night.

Gisèle is with me promptly. She closes the door behind her. 'Happy New Year,' she says with a bitter-sweet smile.

'And to you. Thank you for taking such good care of Mme Tremblay.'

She shrugs and points me towards the sofa. 'I like her.' She paces for a moment. 'What's the latest on the man the police are holding?'

With a dismal sense of what I can't say, I catch her up on events.

'That means they're more or less back to point zero.' She gets up restlessly. '*Ecoute, Pierre.* I want Mme Tremblay to stay here for a few more days. It may not be safe for her in Ste-Anne. Who knows what might happen next?' She throws her hands up in the air. 'If she's stubborn and insists on going back, you'll have to convince the police she needs protection. If there's a murderer and an arsonist running round . . .'

Gisèle's words shake me. They bring home a sense of danger I have been peculiarly immune to. Why?

'You're right. Of course. I'll do that.'

She offers me a cigarette and lights up herself with a long shaky puff. 'Yes. You know I talked to Marthe just after I saw you. That's the woman who plays Thea Elvsted. She got close to Madeleine during the run of the play. Anyhow, she told me that Madeleine was certain she was being followed. Stalked.' She shivers.

413

'I think there were only letters,' I say.

She gives me a surprised look. 'No. Maybe. I don't know. I didn't hear anything about letters. These were telephone calls. Heavy breathing ones. They started during the rehearsal period, I think. Or just before. And Madeleine was certain there was sometimes someone at the stage door. Waiting. All bundled up. Leering. And in a car. She started taking taxis home instead of driving herself. This was all before the massacre at the university. Marthe believed her too. She didn't think she was imagining it. She spent a few nights at Madeleine's place and twice she heard the nuisance calls. Madeleine was very depressed about it. Scared too. She thought of going to the police or hiring a private detective, but she told herself she would be off soon enough. Then it would stop.'

I feel very cold. I want to bang my head against the wall to clear the noise in it.

'I told Detective Contini all this, but his partner had already had it from Marthe. You should meet her. She's next door.'

'Gisèle.' My voice sounds odd. 'What do you know about a Fernando Ruiz?'

'You mean the Portuguese? Madeleine's friend. I identified his voice on the answering machine for Contini. I'd spoken to him a couple of times when he was trying to get hold of Madeleine and his accent is pretty distinctive. But I've never met him.'

My heart is making more noise than Gisèle's New Year gong. Like sniper fire, the things I don't know

414

about Madeleine assault me continually and from unexpected directions. Why then, does the sense that I know her best nonetheless persist?

'Was he a close friend?'

Gisèle looks at me queerly. 'He was meant to be flying over for Christmas.'

'I see.' I don't see.

She stubs out her cigarette. 'Let's go back to the party. Come and meet Marthe.'

I nod and then stop her at the door. 'One more thing, Gisèle. Do you know anything . . . have you heard any rumours about a child of Madeleine's?'

'A child?' she echoes. 'No. Nothing.'

'Contini thinks there was one.'

She shrugs. 'A termination, maybe . . .'

'A termination? But when?' The words don't come out right and, with a determined gesture, Gisèle waves the subject and all speculation away. She wraps her arm through mine. 'You know what I've done? I've started the ball rolling. The Cinéma du Parc is going to run a big retrospective of Madeleine's films. I think the CBC will too. You'll be pleased about that, won't you? A fitting memorial . . .'

Marthe Ducharme has wavy copper hair, a smattering of freckles and a wide, sinuous mouth, which seems to speak without the necessity of words. What it says now, as Gisèle introduces us and we move towards a quieter corner of the room, is that she's sorry, but she doesn't trust me, though she'll speak to me because Gisèle insists.

415

'You and Madeleine grew very close during the run of *Hedda Gabler*,' I begin, my tone a little brusque, bullying, and oddly like Contini's. I clear my throat. 'You were wonderful as Thea Elvsted, by the way.'

She nods a formal thank you. 'What do you want to know?' she asks abruptly.

'I . . . I'm trying to help the police with their inquiries. You see, I knew Madeleine well and—'

'Did you?' She cuts me off. Her eyes are all defiance. 'Yet you didn't believe her, did you? Men!' She spits it out at me.

In the set of her face, I am suddenly aware that I am speaking to someone who has fallen under Madeleine's spell. Marthe idolizes her, is devastated by her death.

I don't let the thought that has suddenly leapt into my mind about a possible liaison between the two women deflect me. 'It was stupid of me,' I say. 'Very stupid. But tell me about the stalker. Maybe . . . maybe it will help.'

'I told the police everything there was to tell.'

'I did know Madeleine a little better than them. There might be some leads . . .'

Marthe can't refute the sense of that. 'Let's go next door,' she murmurs.

I fill her glass and we sit on the coral sofa. Marthe speaks quickly, as if she doesn't really want me to hear or as if she can't bear reiterating out loud her conversations with Madeleine. Some of what she tells me, Gisèle has already said. Other episodes stand out, forbidding in their augury. Again I curse

416

myself for being so blind to Madeleine's needs.

A few days into the rehearsal period, Madeleine told Marthe that she had had the oddest experience the night before. She didn't know quite why, but she had an uncanny sense that someone had been through her apartment in her absence. She had looked around, checked on jewellery and appliances and clothes, but nothing obvious seemed to be missing. She had talked to the superintendent about it, rung her cleaning lady. The first had seen nothing and the second confirmed that she wasn't due until the morning. Madeleine had roamed the apartment, unable to decipher what was wrong, some clothes out of place, perhaps, but she felt the difference – like an aroma of disturbance. She had joked to Marthe, 'With my clutter, it's not exactly easy to spot if anything has been taken.' But the laughter was jittery.

The following day she had come to the theatre visibly shaken. 'There was someone,' she told Marthe. 'It's not my imagination.'

On her dressing table she had found a small pair of tweezers, not her own. And the hairbrush which usually lay there was gone. Definitely gone. The night before she had presumed that she had simply misplaced it. It was as if the tweezers had been left as a token, a stand-in for the theft, as if the person wanted her to know he had been there. It spooked her. But she couldn't very well report a stolen hairbrush to the police, nor, as she amplified later in the week, a camisole which bore the label of a shop called Madeleine. An over-ardent fan, she determined. Perhaps the same one who sent her occasional anonymous letters. She changed her lock, added a new one.

The second episode Marthe recounts is even more ominous. On the day of the assassinations at the university, Madeleine was indeed there. She had gone to meet an Ibsen specialist. When she arrived, there was nothing amiss. After the meeting, the professor had walked her out of the building and a little way along one of the university roads. There they had confronted the tragedy, seen the commotion of ambulances and police and bodies brought out on stretchers from the engineering faculty.

In the midst of it all, Madeleine had dropped the bag she was holding. It contained a book the professor had given her – one of his own, a study of Ibsen.

When she got home late that night, the superintendent had handed her the lost bag. She had thanked him, though in the midst of the day's terror, she was barely aware of the loss. Marthe was with her at the time, had come back to the apartment to keep her company. When they got upstairs and opened the bag, they saw that the book it contained had been savaged. The picture of the professor on the back cover had had its eyes gouged out. His name had been obscured from the title pages with ink that looked not unlike blood, as had the dedication to Madeleine. Pages were scrawled over.

'Madeleine cried. Cried for hours,' Marthe tells me. 'It was dreadful. It was mostly over what had happened at the university, but the desecrated book somehow released her tears. The next day . . .' she pauses as if she is still trying to make sense of events, 'Madeleine was unnaturally calm. She told me that the book was an omen. The play, *Hedda*, would not go well. I wasn't to take any of the reviews to heart. There were times like that in life and we were being let off lightly. With that, she picked up the book, took my hand and marched me down the hall. She had an odd look on her face, a smile that wasn't really a smile. When we reached the incinerator door, she opened it and thrust the book down the chute. Then she clapped her hands. Like a little girl.'

The gesture is pure Madeleine. I can see it clearly. What I see less clearly is the questioning glance Marthe gives me.

'I'm still not sure why she did that. I was sure she should take the book to the police.'

'It was an offering to the gods,' I tell her. 'And a doubling of Hedda. You know, in character. Hedda, too, burns a crucial book which kills a man.'

The next morning Gisèle won't let us go. She takes me aside and tells me again that Mme Tremblay is not yet ready to face Ste-Anne. It is exactly a week since the death, a terrible anniversary she points out, as if I needed to be reminded, as if I hadn't spent the entire night trying to give flesh to leaping shadows. Another few days away from home and memories will do her good. She also tells me it won't do me any harm.

I try to still my restlessness and behave as one

ought to behave at the breakfast which welcomes in a new decade. Gisèle's periodic worried glances tell me I am not altogether succeeding.

Marthe's story has finally convinced me that Madeleine had a stalker other than myself. And if that is the case, even if what I have confessed to Contini is the truth, it is up to me somehow to find him. First, however, there are a few tasks to perform.

I manage to track down Gagnon and convince him of the need for security at Mme Tremblay's house from tomorrow on. He agrees readily. He feels he owes me favours. The hunt through the woods around the Rosenberg place has yielded results. Gagnon is very pleased. Trebly pleased because, as he underlines, his success is one in the eye for our pompous mayor. Yes, yes, he assures me. Of course he has told that disgruntled Contini. He makes it sound as if he has told him in order to make up for Henderson's death – not that he has spared a tear for the man he, at least, is still certain is Madeleine's murderer. We have reason to be proud of the Ste-Anne police force, he emphasizes.

After a bit of a chase, I track down Jerome. His voice tells me he is not altogether happy to hear from me. I convey an invitation from Mme Tremblay to Monique and to him. I also tell him about Maryla's accident and suggest he check in on her and Stefan. Then I try to grill him about what it is that he knows, about his sources too, but he refuses that conversation. Having done his best for me, he has now given me up to the mercy of a greater authority.

With Gisèle's permission, I ring Marie-Ange Corot in Paris and tell her answering machine that if it is at all possible I will be waiting for her at the airport.

Then I drive through the half-empty city. I park in front of Madeleine's apartment. I gaze up at her window for too long. Chastising myself for my musing, the lapse into a perennial reverie, I force myself into practicality. Like some deputy of Contini's, I confront the super at his polished teak desk and barrage him with questions about the day of the university assassinations. He looks up at me blankly.

'Hey. You got yourself the wrong man. I'm only filling in. Old Olivier will be back on Wednesday.'

'When did he leave?'

'Christmas Day I started.'

I curse my bad luck. From the pay telephone in the corner coffee shop, I ring all the friends Madeleine and I had in common. Two of them are at home. I pay them visits and repeat my questions. I find out nothing new, except that Madeleine had talked of going back to Paris as soon as the run of *Hedda Gabler* was finished.

I try the political editor of *Le Devoir* who contacted me not so many days ago. Journalists always hear things.

We meet for an early evening drink at a bar on St-Denis. By the end of our circuitous chat, a weighing of motive and circumstance, he has me convinced that Madeleine's killer could have come only from Ste-Anne.

This does nothing to ease my sleep. The mists still won't lift from my memory. Contini's hypnotic voice maps out terrain and strategy. Pierre Rousseau again emerges as a more than plausible murderer.

At eleven o'clock the next morning, Mme Tremblay and I are sitting in the lobby of the Sûreté du Québec building and I am far more nervous than I thought possible. Maybe it's because I still don't know what I am going to say to Contini. I need time.

The sight of a man in handcuffs, his head bowed, two policemen at his side, underscores the fact that I may not be allowed to leave this building. Freedom suddenly beckons to me in all its fleeting glory. I am about to make my apologies and head for the door, when I hear my name called.

'M. Rousseau, Mme Tremblay.' Ginette Lavigne, her hair too bright against the sobre grey of her suit, addresses us. Her voice seems to rebound through the expanse of the lobby.

'Here,' Mme Tremblay says, as if she were marking her presence at a school roll-call.

Ginette's smile is only for her. 'Detective Contini would like to see you first and then I'll take you down for the ID.'

The elevator door swishes shut behind us with an eerie finality. Yet it does manage to open at the ninth floor. We are ushered into a long rectangle of an office ranked with desks. The grimy light which comes through the tall windows does nothing to cheer the functional blandness of the half-empty room. Soiled paper coffee cups are everywhere. Telephones ring into the void. The occasional officer picks one up, sprawls in a chair and scribbles on a sheet of paper.

'You wait here, M. Rousseau.' Lavigne points me to one of the unoccupied desks.

I am about to protest, but she has already whisked Mme Tremblay through a door at the side. I doodle on a pad, pretend indifference. There is nothing I can do to prevent Contini warning Mme Tremblay about me. My drawing takes on the semblance of a row of prison bars.

When Mme Tremblay re-emerges she casts me a searching look, but she winds her arm through mine as Lavigne leads us back to the elevator. This time, when its doors open, there is a palpable chill in the air. We are in the basement. We are in the morgue.

Lavigne must notice Mme Tremblay's shudder, for she addresses her with an air of apology. 'It should only take a moment.'

The long windowless room is cold yet airless. It smells of chemicals and something I don't want to identify. Mme Tremblay leans heavily on my arm as a grey-faced, spectacled man exchanges a few murmured words with Lavigne, then pulls open a vault in the wall. Mme Tremblay looks away, but I am riveted, as if Will Henderson's prone body contained my own mortality.

The sack is pulled back to reveal a pale waxy face, pain etched in its mouth, its eyes closed in sleep. The long dark hair gleams, somehow too alive. In death, Will Henderson looks like a Renaissance Christ. Only his mourning mother's lap is missing to complete a *pietà*.

'No!' Mme Tremblay's wail is loud in the stillness of the room. 'Too young. So young.' She hides her face in her hands.

Ginette Lavigne and I hold her up on either side. Her eyes meet mine for the first time. The look is too stark. I turn away in confusion.

In the lobby, Lavigne deposits me, like some lesser package, with a woman in a white lab technician's coat and takes Mme Tremblay away to the canteen.

The woman gives me a cursory smile, one that barely creases her face, and waves me once more towards the elevator. 'Follow me, please.' Her voice is as thin as her face and whistles slightly.

'Where is Detective Contini?'

'Oh, we don't need him. It's a very simple, standard procedure.'

'I need to see him.'

'Really, I promise you. There's no need. And there's nothing to be nervous about.'

'I have to see him,' I repeat.

The elevator door opens and shuts again as I refuse to precede her into it. The woman's smile vanishes.

'Very well,' she says through gritted teeth. 'We'll go up to the ninth. But he may not have time to see you.'

'He'll make time.'

She casts me the kind of look one gives to troublesome time-wasters and reluctantly leads me to Contini's cubicle of an office.

Contini sits behind his desk, a telephone balanced between ear and shoulder.

'Ya, the security guard,' he mutters. 'Just check his alibi for Christmas Eve and get him there.' He throws me an impatient glance, then swivels his chair to turn his back on me.

I gaze at the picture on the wall. It shows a steeply wooded valley beneath iridescent blue skies. A sculptured stone village studs a distant mountain top. 'Umbria', the caption reads. On his desk there is a photograph of a darkly severe woman and two plump children.

Contini swivels back to me. 'What are you doing in here, Rousseau? I'm a busy man.' The brusqueness of his words is undercut by the smile which flickers across his lips. 'Nervous, eh? Don't worry, Mlle Johnson knows just what she's doing. She's a very experienced hand.'

The lab technician turns a stern headmistress's face on him. He waves her out through the door and shuts it behind her.

'So you're afraid I won't keep to my side of the bargain? You think I'm just a corrupt policeman whose word can't be trusted. Here.' He takes the recorder from his jacket pocket and flicks the tape into my hand.

'It's not that.' I put the tape between us on the table. 'I've changed my mind.'

'Changed your mind? What the . . . ? Look,

425

Rousseau, you're wasting my time. And I'm not feeling great today.'

'I'm not going to do it. No sperm-test. You can keep the tape.' I don't know why I am saying this except that I don't want Contini to know more than I do about myself. And I don't want to be held captive until I have worked it out.

'OK. No problem. Is that all?'

His response astonishes me. 'You mean I can go?'

'Go. For the time being.'

I don't move. 'I . . . I'd like to see Madeleine's journals.'

'Sure. When we're through with them. If Mme Tremblay allows it, that's no skin off my nose.'

'I want to see them now.'

'No can do. They're evidence.'

I sit there stubbornly and he bursts out laughing. 'There's nothing in the journals about a child, Rousseau.'

'What! So how do you know?'

'The post-mortem, of course. I wish you'd stop being such a romantic.'

A vision of Madeleine's poor mutilated body flashes across my mind. In the morgue. Like Will Henderson. I force away vertigo and heave myself to my feet.

'But you should do the test, Rousseau. For your own peace of mind. Be a good boy now and run along with Mlle Johnson.'

I shake my head.

'All right. Have it your way.' He plops the tape into his drawer. 'Go. I've got things to do.'

426

I skirt the lab technician and hurry towards the elevator. I have almost reached it when Contini calls me back.

'Heh, Rousseau. How close was this Oscar Boileau to Madeleine? Lavigne tells me he's done a painting of her. And he appears in the journals.'

'I don't know,' I mumble.

He gives me his inquisitorial stare, the one that fixes me in my tracks, then grins maliciously. 'Did your beloved police chief mention to you that they found Charlie? Charlie McNeil? Apparently he turned up in that lovely wood near your river. Convenient, eh? And now Gagnon can be a white-gloved hero and wrap things up in a nice clean package. Pats on the shoulder all round. Ste-Anne once again a drug-free zone. For the time being at least.'

'You mean . . . ?'

'Ya. A witness to name Will Henderson as the major bad guy.'

I study his face. 'Did Charlie say anything about Madeleine and Will?'

'Thought you'd never ask.' He puts his arm around me conspiratorially, loosens a tie which is already loose enough. 'Apparently both Charlie and Will went to midnight mass – a little early. Henderson met up with Madeleine in front of one of the confessionals and something – innocent Charlie doesn't quite know what, of course – changed hands. Then Madeleine went into the booth.'

'So that's how Jerome—' I stop myself.

'What about your brother?'

'Oh, nothing.'

Contini pats me too hard on the back. 'Stay close to home, Rousseau.'

16

The thick silence of separate solitudes reigns in the car as Mme Tremblay and I drive back to Ste-Anne in the half-light of a sombre afternoon.

But when we reach the road to her house she suddenly grips my arm. 'Turn off at the barn, Pierre. Never mind the ice.'

'OK. But there's nothing to see.'

'An absence,' she whispers. 'That's something.'

She is right. We both stand there in front of the car and I suspect we see the same thing. A process. A barn which is also a stable which contains a horse that Madeleine rides, and chickens and rabbits. A barn that is full of life. And then gradually the barn empties until there is nothing in it but the chipped and broken relics of past days and Madeleine's fractured lifeless body. And now, there is only absence, white curves and ridges and hollows tracing out a lack.

The last of the light vanishes as we stand there.

'Let's go,' Mme Tremblay says. 'Maybe it's better that the barn's gone. Fitting. Like a pyre.'

I drive right up to the porch of the house so that she doesn't have far to walk.

There are flowers strewn on the steps, poking through the wooden posts of the balcony, tied to the banister. Red carnations, amber chrysanthemums . . .

'The people of Ste-Anne have taken Madeleine into their hearts at last,' I murmur.

'Because . . .'

'Because of the fire.'

'Yes, I see. Not too soon,' Mme Tremblay says, with no visible bitterness.

The dogs have already set up their barking. A bearded figure opens the door even before I have helped her out of the car. It is only then that I notice that the lights are already on.

'Michel. It was good of you to come.' Mme Tremblay greets her handyman and smiles for the first time in days as the dogs rush round her. I hadn't realized she had rung him.

'Is the fire going?'

He nods.

'And you've managed the basics? Good. Thank you. Thank you very much. I'm expecting some visitors.'

'I know.'

'You'll stay for a cup of tea, Michel? Or a glass of whisky. For the New Year.'

Dubois shakes his bulky head.

'Had enough over the last days, did you? Never mind. It's only fitting for the New Year. Have the dogs been behaving?'

'Yes. Very good.'

The doorbell rings and I glance at my watch. Monique and Jerome are early.

'You answer it, Pierre.'

Mme Tremblay's face has grown taut. She arranges an invisible strand of hair back into its knot and hastily puts things into the fridge. 'Take them into the salon,' she calls after me.

But it is not my brother and Monique. A tousle-haired young man in a black motorcycle jacket and leather trousers confronts me. Noël Jourdan.

'Oh!' he says. 'I thought . . . What are you doing here?' The words come out in a challenging hiss, as if I were a spy from an enemy state and it were treason to be seen fraternizing with me.

'Visiting Mme Tremblay.'

'You . . .' He gives me a contorted look, half fear, half suspicion. 'So you've changed sides again.'

'And you?' I match his aggression. 'What are you doing here?'

He holds out a flat white box. 'Gran'mère asked me to bring this round. A *tourtière*. For Mme Tremblay. But if she's not here . . .'

'She's here. Maybe you had better come in.'

He shrugs, waves to someone behind him. I see a motorbike. A figure slides off the seat and removes a helmet.

'Martine!' The sight of her reassures me. 'Come on in. I'm sure Mme Tremblay will be pleased to see you.'

'Hello, M. Rousseau. Thank you.'

Martine has more social grace than her sullen

friend. As I usher them inside, I realize that they are both painfully shy and slightly bewildered. They don't know where to put their hands or their feet and they gaze up at the pictures of Madeleine with a mixture of awe and avid curiosity. Noël makes brash remarks to hide it and holds onto the *tourtière* as if I might steal it away.

I urge Mme Tremblay through from the kitchen and tell her I will see to supper. She should be resting and sipping whisky. Dubois skulks after her, like some protective genie. As they go into the living room, I hear Noël say with a laugh, 'Hey, Michel, found any more murdering Anglo arsonists lately?'

Minutes later, as I am warming a couple of store-bought onion pies in the oven alongside the *tourtière*, the doorbell rings again.

This time I am right in presuming it is Monique and my brother. He holds a small case in his hand. His other is at his collar which seems to be chafing. He refuses my gaze.

Monique is full of artificial excitement. She kisses me loudly on both cheeks and lets out a spew of words about the weather and the roads as she hands me her padded coat. Beneath it, she has on a tidy skirt over ample hips and a pink sweater which is just a little too tight. Something about her reminds me unhappily of my stepmother.

While I hang coats, Michel Dubois comes into the hall and tries to slip out the door with a muttered '*Bonsoir.*'

Jerome holds him back. 'I didn't see you at mass on Sunday, Michel.'

'Busy.' He grunts a second '*Bonsoir*' and is down the steps before my brother can say any more.

There is a hollowness in the living room when I usher Monique and Jerome through, a silence which Monique ruptures with a breathless, echoing 'Maman' as she rushes over to Mme Tremblay who sits as motionless as an effigy in the sofa.

'Welcome, Monique. Welcome, Jerome.' Mme Tremblay's voice comes fractionally too late and barely disguises the effort that has gone into her words.

'Thank you, Mme Tremblay.' Jerome shakes her hand solemnly. 'I haven't had the opportunity . . .'

She waves away his condolences.

Martine is standing up. 'We should go now.'

'These kind children have been delivering a *tourtière* for our supper. Why not stay and join us?' Mme Tremblay says with sudden inspiration.

'No, no. We're due elsewhere.' Noël is stealing unhappy sidelong glances at my brother. 'Aren't we, Martine?'

She nods. I notice that the scarf round her neck is still Madeleine's.

'We're off, then.' Noël shuffles from foot to foot.

'You'll come again. I would like that.' Suddenly Mme Tremblay rises. Rises slowly. 'You probably haven't met Monique yet. Monique Blais, Madeleine's mother.' She gives it the emphasis of a public proclamation.

'Oh.' Martine's exclamation fills the quiet in the room like a train's whistle.

'You'll thank your grandmother for me, Noël.

433

And you take care on that motorbike. From my peek through the window, it looks much bigger than the one my husband used to drive.'

Noël's chest swells to the amplitude of a champion's facing a cheering studio audience. 'Don't worry, Mme Tremblay.'

I see them to the door. Outside I notice a police car parked to the side of the drive. Noël sees it too, and tenses dramatically.

'Take it slow,' I tell him, but he isn't paying attention. He pulls his helmet on with a swagger, eases himself in front of Martine and revs with exaggerated force. I watch them whiz away and sink into a moment's self-pity.

In the living room, my brother is holding forth on the moral challenges faced by contemporary youth. I realize it is a staying ploy. He doesn't know what to do with the two women. He is as nervous as a virtuous thirteen-year-old in the company of rank temptation.

Mme Tremblay is staring at her lap as if it contained the answer to the riddle of the Sphinx. She refuses Monique's imploring glances. But suddenly she asks, in a pointed voice, 'Where is your son, Monique?'

'I haven't mislaid him, if that's what you're implying,' Monique fires back, and then, covering her rudeness, moans a little. 'Those Montréal cops were beastly to him. He preferred to stay away.'

'And your other children?'

'Louis is working in Galveston. He's got three

kids of his own now, you know. I'm a grandmother.' Monique glances at my brother and laughs girlishly. 'And you're a great-grandmother. How the years fly! But I don't see them very much. Louis had a terrible row with his father and then, well . . .' Her voice dies away, but she picks it up again, brightly. '*C'est la vie*, as you say around here. And Rachelle, well, she's living with a man in Pittsburgh. Awful man.' She flushes suddenly and races on. 'But Martin, he's the good one. He's a teacher. He inherited your brains. He lives in Omaha. I go and visit them in the summers for a week or so. His wife is . . . is very refined. Madeleine helped him out, you know. When he was at university.'

'That was kind of her.' There is a sudden leap of tears in Mme Tremblay's eyes.

'But when I wrote to her . . . oh, never mind.'

'What?'

Monique pushes the *tourtière* round her plate and then swallows a forkful.

'When I wrote to her about poor Arthur, my husband, being ill, she didn't even bother to answer.'

The self-pitying whine in her voice grates on my skin.

'No. I would imagine not.' Mme Tremblay is severe.

'Why would you imagine not?' Monique flutters her eyelashes and, like some rebellious adolescent, mimics her mother's dry tones exactly.

'Because she had no affection for him. And if you stop to think about it for more than two seconds, you'll know exactly why that was.'

'Why was it?' Monique's voice rises in stridency. 'Because you turned her against us. Little Princess Goldilocks, spoiled by you until she thought she was too good for us.'

As the two women confront each other, they seem to take on age-old postures. We have entered a time-warp. Like fossils which have lain untouched in some deep geological stratum and awaited this moment to spring back into life, they can only replay ancient familial wars.

'And I'll tell you why it was, you wilfully stupid woman. It was because as soon as your belly grew big, Arthur Blais started to beat her. Worse. I saw it with my own eyes.' Mme Tremblay's face is twisted into a scowl.

'Ridiculous! You even turned her against Marcel who wanted only to be useful to her. You treat your handyman better than us. He wouldn't even have let us in out of the cold, if it hadn't been for Père Jerome.'

'Michel Dubois has always been loyal and kind. Unlike that brute of a man you married.' Mme Tremblay scrapes her chair back from the table and rises slowly. 'I'm tired now. If you want to stay here, I won't throw you out. You can sleep in the guest room. But no more of this.'

'I just hope Madeleine has seen fit to rectify your joint sins in her will,' Monique mutters under her breath and then, as Mme Tremblay leaves the room, turns tearful eyes at Jerome. 'She hates me, you know. She's always hated me. I'm not clever enough for her. But family ties should be stronger than that.

You understand that, Jerome. You're like your father.'

'Maybe if you behaved just a little better,' I hear myself saying.

'Pierre!' Jerome chastises. 'You of all people.'

'She's an old woman. She's suffered a severe shock.'

'And me? What about me?' Monique strikes the pose of a bereaved mother.

'You—'

'Pierre!' Jerome cuts me off.

The stark severity of his face catapults my guilt to the surface. I want to shake him so that all the things he thinks he knows about me will at last tumble out into the open. Instead, with barely a nod, I push my chair back from the table and leave.

There are no stars tonight. My house rises out of the gloom like some ungainly prehistoric creature, its cavernous jaw opening at my approach. For a moment, I rue the human, bickering warmth of Mme Tremblay's, but by then the garage door has already slid shut behind me.

The cold wind blowing down the basement stairs alerts me. It whistles and gusts with unusual force as I make my way into the kitchen. Have I, in my abstraction, left a door or window open?

I switch on the lights and rush through the dining room where a table lamp lies toppled. But the front entrance is shut and locked. I hurry towards the salon.

Glass crackles and skids beneath my feet. Myriad

shards and splinters cover the floor, stipple the old floral sofa. I stumble over something hard and recognize the outline of a brick even before I see it.

The double-paned window gapes, a vast yawning mouth fed by hooligans flushed by recent exploits. I check the brick for a message. But this one contains none. It doesn't need it.

Did the boys come here, drunk with their New Year's Eve celebrations, to teach me a lesson, Noël Jourdan amongst them? The room is cold enough to have been open to the wind for some time. On the window ledge a small heap of crusty snow has gathered.

Quickly I fetch a pan and broom and cardboard box from the kitchen and clear away the principal mess. In the basement, I find two large pieces of ply, a hammer and nails.

It is as I am about to fix the boards that the thought creeps up on me, treacherous, more chilling than the wind. A brick has indeed shattered the window. But the cavity in front of me is larger than that, different too. The glass has been picked at and eased away, leaving a gap big enough for a man to crawl through.

My eyes scud across the room, searching for signs of theft. There doesn't seem to be anything missing. The stereo is in place, the artefacts still neat on their shelves.

I hammer the wood into position across the frame. The blows echo uncannily through the house, making it creak and judder. When I finish, the silence is heavy. Too heavy – as if a deep anticipatory breath had been taken and held. The certain sense that I am not alone suddenly overtakes me. The intruders are still here, crouching in some dim corner, waiting to pounce. Why have I assumed that the brick was launched on New Year's Eve? Why not today? Why not just moments before my return?

I stop all my activity and listen. Listen for the shift of floorboards, the whisper of feet on rugs. Nothing. I can hear nothing but the wind wailing round the cracks.

From the fireplace I take a poker and creep towards the stairs. Half-way up, I pause to listen again. I stand there for a good few minutes. Still nothing. I try to calm my fear. The kids wouldn't get up to anything really vile. A group protest, yes, an egging each other on against the outsiders. Even a drunken threat against the faithless authority I might be seen to represent. But nothing more than that. No. Certainly not.

Yet what if some vengeful character really does want to pay me back for taking sides against the crowd? Or what if someone knows that it is I who tipped off Gagnon about the drugs? Worse still, what if there is someone out there who, like Contini, suspects I am guilty of Madeleine's death and wants to take immediate revenge?

I switch on the upstairs lights and stealthily open doors. Fear prickles at the base of my spine. As I struggle to calm it I wonder at myself. Why is it that I am prepared to believe the worst of myself yet am so unwilling to suspect anyone I know of violent malice? Is my tolerance simply a defence against emotion or a deep knowledge of my greater guilt? I run through the faces in the crowd outside the Rosenberg house, discounting them one by one, pitting reason against dread.

When I open the door to my bedroom, dread wins. Everything here is helter-skelter. Clothes have been tumbled from drawers, lamps broken, books ripped, their spines arched and cracked like so many broken necks.

My eyes refuse the worst of it. At the tip of my dishevelled bed there is a bundle of streaked and burnished fur. Minou. Her head is at an odd angle, the pillow behind her red with the blood that has oozed from her mouth.

My stomach heaving, I cover her gently with the sheet. Foreboding clutches at my throat and with it a rising anger. I race from the room and down to the far end of the corridor.

The door is closed, intact. The keys still in my pocket. I almost walk away and then something makes me twist the knob. It gives. I have forgotten to lock the attic. I hold my breath. Poker at the ready, I walk stealthily up the stairs.

Through the glimmer of light from the door, I scan the alcoves, the only possible hiding places. Nothing moves. I take a step forward and then another. Something rustles and crunches beneath my feet.

'Get your hands up,' I hear myself shouting as if Contini had once again lent me his guise.

There is no answering stir.

I switch on the light and look round. A groan comes to my lips. The floor is heaped with film, loops and coils and strands of it, like the rapids of a stream rippling down blue velvet, breaking across smooth aluminium stones. Ripped posters and crumpled photographs indent the flow. Here and there Madeleine's mutilated face looks up at me with a plea.

The shrine has been desecrated. Its altar toppled. The shattered lens lies next to the projector on the floor.

I walk slowly round the graveyard of my dreams. For some reason, I can't bring myself to touch anything, to move or right.

It is only on my third trajectory that I notice that the video tapes and recorder are gone. Oddly, the television is untouched. It stands just where I left it.

My legs are unsteady as I move down the stairs. The poker scrapes the wall, reigniting my fear. Who would do such a thing? Why?

I cannot think straight. Not here in this burial site. Not now.

With sudden speed, I make for my bedroom. From the cupboard, I extract a clean white sheet. Carefully I wrap Minou in it and head down to the basement. There is a small metal moulded trunk here which still houses a childhood collection of tin soldiers. I pour these out and delicately place Minou in the box, then carry her out through the front door. Like Madeleine, she cannot yet be buried. It would take a flamethrower to break the ground tonight. Instead, I place her between two ornamental garden firs and cover the casket with snow.

The outdoor light illuminates the porch and as I approach it again I can see fragments of glass sparkling amidst the iced blue of the gathered snow. The pieces of pane are bigger here than on the inside and amidst them, despite the hardness of the snow, there is the indentation of a boot.

I gaze at it for a moment, then with a shiver race inside and double lock the door behind me. I leave all the lights on and head for the garage. I do not want to be here. Fear claws at me. An odour of death stifles my breathing.

It doesn't get better in the car. I am so intent on the rear-view mirror that I can barely focus on the curves in front of me. I think of Maryla and the car that bludgeoned hers off the road as she left my house just three nights ago. Was that accident really intended for me? A warning, perhaps?

With a surge of gas, I speed past the place. I recall my sense of being followed on my way home from the Rosenbergs', my assumption, probably mistaken, that it was Contini. And later that evening, the incident in the shed, a first attempt perhaps to perpetrate the abomination which I discovered tonight – a first attempt foiled by Jerome's presence with me in the house. Was Minou's crushed foot also a warning?

I check the road for shadows and, signalling in the opposite direction, turn right into the highway, then zip into the first gas station.

No-one comes after me. I fill up and take off

again, with too much speed. Yet I don't quite know where I am going. I can't contaminate any local household with my potentially dangerous presence. Somewhere, it comes to me with sudden stinging clarity, there is a madman poised to strike a second time. Yes. A second time.

I know I should contact Gagnon and report the break-in. But I am not ready. Not quite ready to have him trekking through my inner sanctum. Pride perhaps. Or shame.

Suddenly I notice a car behind me. It is cruising at the same speed. Its beams are low. I cannot make out the model or licence plate. As I speed up, it matches my pace. I slow down to let it overtake me, but it creeps along, maintaining its distance. With sudden decision I veer into the slip road which leads to the autoroute. I take it fast and the car disappears from view. But it is there again at the junction. I rev away, winding in and out of the hurtling traffic, and after some five miles I assume I have lost him.

My brain feels addled. All the faces I have seen this last week float and churn through my mind like figures in a nightmarish identity parade. Their features fade into each other, blur into other faces. Figures remembered, seen dimly on street or screen, propped against desks or walls or pillows, moving forward or back, gliding, screaming, chanting, lying ripped on the ground. Swinging. Madeleine.

With a shudder, I collect myself and check the rear-view mirror. The cars in front and behind are indistinguishable. So, too, on this starless night, is the section of the autoroute I have reached. I drive until a sign appears. With it comes a sudden grim suspicion.

The road is quieter than when I was last here. There are no night-time skiers on the slopes. Chair-lifts swing desultorily in the wind and cast strange robotic shadows onto the snow as my headlights graze them. The holiday amusement park is asleep.

I drive slowly, not altogether certain of my turn off. Last week I arrived from the opposite direction.

Where the mountain gives way to the lake, I hear a car behind me. Hear, but don't see. There are headlights nowhere, yet I can feel the vibration of another engine. I speed round a bend, but the noise is still there, coming closer and closer. Sweat moistens my brow. I am doing 110 and the road cannot take it. The banks of ploughed snow on my right look hard and steep. Then a house appears. I calculate where the drive might be and swerve towards it.

There is a terrible scraping noise as the car clips my right side and shears off my wing mirror. I am wedged on the bank. For a moment I think he may reverse back onto me in a funfair replay of bumper cars. But he doesn't slow. I have no time to read his plates. There is only the impression of redness. Nor do his lights go on. He accelerates into darkness.

In his wake my headlamps pick up something flying through the air, looping into the wind and landing not fifty feet from me.

I wait. I wipe my brow. And then, my lights still

on, I whisk out into the cold and retrieve what my tracker has dropped.

When I find it, the perspiration returns. The strip of film is some three feet long. I don't need to examine it to know whose image is embedded there.

For some fifteen minutes, I linger in the drive. It is better to wait here. I need to collect my wits, to make myself ready.

No lights flash across the Auberge Maribou sign tonight. In my tense state, I almost miss it and have to reverse back down the road. I leave my car at a little distance in the shadow of trees, then creep round to the parking lot. A single sedan is parked by the inn's side. I examine it closely for redness and dents. It has neither and the hood is cold. I search out the garage which is tucked behind the building. The doors are solidly locked.

A lone lamp illuminates the dining room. My fists clenched, I peer through the window. There is no-one visible. My shoulders squared, I ring the bell and wait for what feels like a long time.

'Pierre!' Giorgio Napolitano is clad in a burly tracksuit. His hair is wet and tousled as if he may just have emerged from the shower. 'Come in, come in. No problem with rooms tonight. Holidays are over.' He smiles at me with too much warmth. 'But I'm not so sure about the food. Paloma and Sylvie are in Montréal.'

'I'm not worried about food.' I try to peer behind his uncertain smile, glance at the snowshoes stored by the door.

'No.' He considers me. 'I can see that. But I'm glad you've come. We couldn't talk the other night.' He ushers me into the dining room, pulls a bottle of wine from the rack.

'How long have you been back here?' I keep my voice even.

'Back? Back from where?'

'Ste-Anne.'

The look he gives me is a study in incomprehension. 'Saturday. Just after I saw you. I'm sorry about bursting in on you like that.' He puts a glass of wine in front of me. Dark eyes meet mine. 'What's wrong, Pierre?'

'Where's your car?' I size him up as I ask. I am taller than him, but he seems sturdier.

'My car? What do you mean? Have you broken down? Paloma's taken mine to pick up Sylvie with. The old one's still here though.'

'In the parking lot?'

'No. That's our single guest. Mine's in the garage. Where do you need to go?'

My shoulders relax a little. 'Can I see it?'

'Sure. It's not much to look at. What's wrong, Pierre?' he asks again.

'Why did you come and see me on Saturday?'

He pulls out a chair and straddles it, waves me towards another. 'Sit down. Please. You look as if you're about to slug me.'

With a shrug, I perch on a chair opposite him.

'I came to see you, because I wanted to talk. Talk about Madeleine. About the fact that, as Detective Contini had made clear, she had been murdered.' He

446

shivers slightly. 'And . . . yes, there was something else.' He studies my face carefully, as if he were trying to make up his mind about something.

'What?' My fists are clenched again. I confront him boldly, note every shift in those mobile features. 'Did you prowl round my shed?'

'The shed? Why? No. No.' He gives the impression of being genuinely confused. 'It was something I ended up telling Contini. Perhaps I shouldn't have, but at the time, it seemed important.'

I slump back into the chair as if my spine had crumbled. I know what he is going to say.

He urges me to drink. My mouth is as dry as ashes. It transforms the wine to vinegar. But I drink it all the same while Giorgio with a diplomat's tact recounts how Madeleine, when he had last seen her, had mentioned a series of anonymous letters she had received, invasive letters that troubled her deeply, hateful letters she had at last angrily concluded could only have come from me.

'I told the detective that she suspected you. I wasn't sure I should have. So I came to see you.'

I massage my brow. A pain I can't get rid of has lodged itself there.

Giorgio gets up to stoke the fire into life. I barely hear his murmur. 'Were they from you?'

The 'Yes' hurts my throat.

'Tell me about it,' he says softly. 'Tell me why. If you want to.'

I tell him briefly, tersely, about the odd compulsion of the letters. There is a look of such

447

fraternal compassion on his face that I barely stop myself from recounting my doubts, my terror, concerning the fateful night of Madeleine's death. But I manage to skirt that. Instead I find myself telling him about the break-in, about Minou, about the chase – the events of the last few hours which brought me here to him.

Giorgio has a gift for listening, a peculiar intent concern which is also like a neutral space. Maybe he learned it as a priest. A good confessor. Or maybe, it was already him. I almost wish I could tell him everything, what I know and what I don't know. But I hold back. I finish by saying, 'I hope my coming here isn't irresponsible.'

'Auberge. That's what it means. A place of refuge. I'm glad you've come. Even if you suspected me.' He laughs and I look away in shame.

'No, no. Don't worry about it. We're all trapped in suspicion and fear. Murder is so much harder for us moderns to bear than suicide. It throws everything askew. The violation of it. The brute force. I have tried to reason it out for myself, but I have no answers.'

'No,' I echo him dismally.

'I console myself with the thought that at least Madeleine didn't act as her own judge and executioner. Didn't condemn the entirety of her life. Judge it null and void.' He throws me a glance full of whimsical irony. 'You see, I am good at self-consolation.'

'I see. I wish I could share it.'

He looks at me as if he could read my mad desire

to be somehow implicated in Madeleine's death.

'More selfishly – and this is my confession – the revelation that Madeleine's death was a murder stupidly eased a little of my hurt. I had told myself that we had become friends again, you see. Good friends. I thought she counted on me. And then, to have her pop herself off without consulting me, without coming to me – that was very difficult to bear. I knew that I had failed in friendship.'

I stare at him and find myself wondering again whether Madeleine ever went to bed with him. I don't ask. Somehow it doesn't seem to matter any more. That startles me. What surprises me more is that in an odd way I find myself hoping she did.

'And now?' I ask softly.

'Now? Now I think she's up there laughing at us. Revelling at the commotion she's caused. Flirting with the angels. Giving Gabriel a really hard time. Telling God he ought to do something about poverty and injustice.'

'You really believe that?'

'Maybe I do. Yes, maybe I do. The wine's not bad, is it?'

'But I'm afraid I have a hankering for coffee. It's been a long day.'

'And you want to make it longer?' He laughs and leads me into the kitchen which is all clean silver surfaces and arrays of giant pots.

'You know,' he says, as he fills a kettle, 'it seems to me – and probably this is my selfish side again – that murder is like an accident. Like an act of fate, or an act of God – if he doesn't mind my bringing his name into this again . . . We reproach ourselves, we do a litany of if onlys, we grieve. But we cannot be directly responsible. Only one person is directly responsible.'

I flinch.

He sees it, pushes the plunger down abruptly. 'You must ring the police, Pierre. Tell them about everything that's happened today. Do it now.'

'There are things I don't want them to know.'

'We all have things we don't want anyone to know.'

In the morning, which comes too soon – we have spent so much of the night talking and watching out for my tracker – he says to me, 'Would you like me to come with you? I could. Paloma and Sylvie won't be back until tomorrow.'

I shake my head.

'You'll go straight to the police?'

'I've left messages. For both Gagnon and Contini.'

'You'll keep in touch?'

'Yes. And thank you.'

He nods and follows me out to the car.

The day is perversely bright. The snow so dazzling we have to shield our eyes. Birds chirp and swoop at our passage.

'Someone, somewhere's done something right.' Giorgio's voice is rueful.

I turn to him. 'Contini told me Madeleine had had a child.'

'Oh?'

'So you had no inkling.'

He shakes his handsome head. 'When?'

'He didn't tell me. Maybe he doesn't know. And he could be wrong.'

We study each other again for a long moment and suddenly embrace.

Two potential fathers hugging against the gleaming snow.

Back on the autoroute, all the calm acquired in Giorgio's presence dissipates. My rear-view mirror preoccupies me with growing tenacity. I keep to the right-hand lane, hide between trucks. I decide not to confront my house for any fresh damage, nor to drop in on Mme Tremblay as I had planned. Instead I go straight to the office. I need the comfort of closely peopled streets and a sobering dose of normality to stop my fears from running away with me.

Arlette Gatineau, my secretary, is already at her desk. A thin, serious woman of my own age, she wishes me a happy New Year, then repositions her spectacles and reads from her message pad.

'A Detective Contini rang and says he'll ring back later. He's very busy today. Police Chief Gagnon phoned to say he's personally at your disposal and will come whenever it's convenient.'

She gives me a quizzical glance over the top of her glasses, but puts no questions into words.

I hired Arlette some eighteen months ago when she arrived in the vicinity of Ste-Anne. Her husband commutes to Montréal. I hired her because she is intelligent and doesn't gossip – though she takes in everything around her and when asked will give me a sharp little portrait of her impressions. We get on splendidly.

Now her quizzical glance lasts a second longer than usual and I know she needs confirmation about the unusual events which have upset the town. She is too new to it to know about my past relations with Madeleine.

I can't quite give the explanations she seeks. Instead I tell her that I'll be out much of today and probably a little erratic in my movements for the next few. She'll have to hold the fort. I also ask her to get hold of Maryla Orkanova for me and see if she needs any help. I am worried about Maryla and wonder if I should ask Gagnon to put her, too, on his security list.

'Mme Groulx is waiting for you,' Arlette informs me. 'I'm afraid she insisted and I couldn't put her off.'

We smile at each other. The ordinariness of that complicit smile gives me strength and I march calmly through to confront Mme Groulx.

'Pierre.' She looks at me in her most queenly manner. 'I'm not pleased with you. You didn't stand up for me in front of that horrid Montréal detective. What right he has to stick his nose into our business, I don't know.'

'What can I do for you on this bright morning, Mme Groulx?'

She narrows her eyes. 'So you know now?'

'Know what?'

452

'Who did it. It was that awful drugged youth, wasn't it?'

'Mme Groulx, this is not the police station, and I'm as ignorant as the rest of us. Now, please. Is there some business you want to transact?'

A smile plays over her thin lips. She shows me her gold tooth. 'Yes. A small change to my will. In favour of my great-grandson, Noël Jourdan.'

'You're sure of that? You know each change costs you.'

'I'm sure. He's a smart boy. A brave boy. He'll go far. I want you to put in five thousand for him. Subtract it from my donation to the seminary.'

I note the change in my black book. 'I'll send the amendment round for you to sign.'

'No. I'll drop in. Tomorrow morning?'

'That'll be fine.'

She doesn't get up. Instead, she clears her throat and shows me her tooth again. 'Did Mme Tremblay enjoy my *tourtière*?'

'Very much, I think. It was delicious.'

'And that Monique of hers?' She bends towards me. 'You know she isn't worth a tenth of Madeleine. A hundredth.' She lowers her voice. 'I have it that she only turned up here because of that arsonist. That murderer,' she emphasizes stubbornly. 'You know they both come from Maine. How much did Madeleine leave her in her will?'

'I'm afraid I don't know that, Mme Groulx. Madeleine Blais' will is not in my hands.'

'Hmmm.' She gives me a doubtful glance and then preens herself. 'I haven't told you. About that motorbike outside the church at midnight mass. I hadn't realized. That was Noël's. My great-grandson's. How about that! He offered Madeleine Blais a ride on it and apparently she gave him a big kiss.'

'What a pretty picture,' I say through stiff lips. The titbit of information makes the hair on my neck bristle. 'Did they take it? The ride, I mean?'

She looks confused for a moment. 'Well, I don't know. I'll ask.'

No sooner does Mme Groulx make her exit than my brother strides in. He stands uncomfortably on the other side of the desk. 'They haven't locked you up yet, so maybe I misinterpreted.'

'What?' I want to lunge at him.

'Rumours.' He is dismissive. 'I haven't much time. The boys start coming back today.' He shuffles from foot to foot, his expression troubled. His reason for coming seems to have deserted him.

'Tell me, Jerome,' I say softly.

He clears his throat. 'It's about Mme Tremblay and Monique. They're so at odds. Perhaps, I don't know . . . if only Mme Tremblay could be a little more charitable. Monique doesn't mean ill. It's just that life has blunted her. She's grown coarse.' He gives me a sudden pained, naked look. 'Hasn't she?'

He doesn't give me time to answer. 'Tell her. Explain to Mme Tremblay. It will be a good deed.'

He rushes away, cloaked in virtue once more.

I sit there a little stunned and wonder at the dreams he must have clung to all these years. Even longer than myself. We are a family of dreamers.

Arlette's buzz wakes me to the present.

'Two Messieurs Lefèvre for you and I have Madame Orkanova on the phone.'

It takes me a moment to remember the appointment I set up in the middle of last week's distress. I talk briefly to Maryla, who sounds well enough. Dr Bergeron has given her a few days off and Mme Préfontaine has come to sit with her and help out with the house. I keep the anxiety out of my voice and tell her it will be nice for her to enjoy a few days' rest at home. I stress the home.

Then for the next hour I am caught up in a bitter saga which is not my own – and which for perhaps that reason seems to hold out solutions.

By the time the two Messieurs Lefèvre have left, my watch shows after one. I ring Gagnon, who is out. So, too, is Contini.

With a heavy heart, I make my way to the parking lot and covertly check for any cars with dents and scrapes on their passenger side. There are two, but neither of them bears the imprint of my paint-work or Maryla's. Despite my reluctance, I force myself to head home. It is daytime, after all. Nothing happens in the daytime. And I need to change.

In the bright midday sun, the house looks innocent and as sedate as the town dignitary who constructed it in his image. For a moment, I pretend to myself that all the events of the last days, from Madeleine's terrible death to the vandalism of yesterday evening, are the product of some wild nightmare, brewed out of indigestion and a guilty conscience.

In a flurry of optimistic fancy I walk round to the front door and tell myself reality will show no tell-tale signs. But the salon window really is boarded up, and between the ornamental firs Minou's casket makes a forlorn hump in the snow.

Without her, the house feels emptier than ever. I dash up the stairs two at a time and, averting my eyes from the bed, grab a suit from the closet and pick a shirt and underwear from the heaped jumble on the floor.

I change quickly in the bathroom. The sight of the razor lying open in the middle of the sink gives me pause. I am about to pick it up when I notice the blood on its edge. With a dreadful certainty, I realize it is Minou's. My skin feels as if it is crawling with maggots.

The ringing of the telephone jars me into movement. I pick up the receiver. Silence meets my '*Allo*', and then, as I am about to hang up, a high falsetto voice screeches, '*Sale cochon*.'

'Who is this?'

'Up your arse.'

The line goes dead.

I am about to head for the door when the ringing starts again. I hesitate. Could I identify this voice if it kept talking? Steeling myself, I pick up the receiver.

'Rousseau. It's Gagnon. You've been trying to reach me?'

With a sigh of relief I tell him about the break-in and about the cat.

'*Mauditcriss*,' he mutters beneath his breath. 'We'll get right over.'

I glance at my watch. 'How long will you be, Gagnon? I have to meet someone at the airport.'

'Fifteen minutes, no more.'

'OK. I'll let you in, then leave you here to get on with things.'

'There might be some prints on the window ledge,' he says in his new confident manner. 'Don't touch anything.'

Too late, I think to myself as I hang up. Too bloody late. I kick a stray pair of underwear into the centre of the heap and in a fury of self-deprecation, walk to the end of the corridor and turn the key in the lock of the attic room.

PART THREE

17

The arrival lounge at Mirabel Airport is busy with returning holiday-makers. Taxi-drivers hold up signs with boldly printed names. People cluster around gates. Grandmothers and toddlers wave erratically at the doors as if in rehearsal for the great moment. A few suited businessmen stroll impatiently between the Avis and Hertz and Budget kiosks and back again.

My impatience matches the businessmen's. I scan the arrival monitors and pace the elongated corridor. Near the escalator, I am surprised to see Contini. He is lounging in an armchair.

'I didn't know you were coming,' I greet him.

'It seemed convenient.' He takes a big juicy bite from the apple in his hand and munches reflectively. 'Had to skip lunch, though.'

A little to one side of him, I notice Serge Monet, Contini's sometime partner, talking to a man I don't recognize.

'Oh yes. I don't believe you've met.' Contini gestures the two men over. 'Fernando Ruiz, meet Pierre Rousseau.'

Ruiz is smaller than me, dark and wiry with a hawk-nose and unblinking yet shifty eyes. He wears a leather jacket and cord trousers and his glossy black hair falls in a wave across his brow. I stare at him in nervous fascination.

'*Enchanté*, M. Rousseau,' he says in a heavily aspirated accent, and stretches a bony hand towards me.

'He had a haircut back in Lisbon. I'm pretty sure he's Mme Tremblay's pony-tailed guest. You certain you've never seen him before?' Contini's tone is insinuating and loud enough for the man to hear.

Perhaps Ruiz doesn't, or he doesn't understand, for he says, 'I was so deeply sorry to hear about Madeleine's tragic death. Anything I can do to help the investigation . . .' He is addressing me as if someone has told him who I am. Maybe Madeleine has mentioned me as a friend.

Contini shatters my illusions. 'I explained you were her ex.' He gives me one of his ostentatious winks and with an oafish gesture hurls his apple into a neighbouring bin.

I don't know why he is playing the clown. It is Monet who is being scrupulously polite today. His lean form is encased in a smart suit, his drooping moustache carefully combed. He comes over to shake my hand and points to the screen overhead. 'Mme Corot's plane has just landed. It shouldn't be long now.'

'She is a fine woman, Marie-Ange Corot. I am happy to see her here,' Ruiz intones.

'You know her?'

'Oh yes. We have met on occasion.' He looks down at his boots, which are pointed and shiny, like a stage cowboy's. 'Spoken mostly. We are in the same line of work.'

'Ya,' Contini interjects. 'Ruiz makes movies. A director. He tells me I have a really good cop's face. So I'm auditioning right now. Maybe he'll give me a part. Give us both parts. You can play the murderer and I can play myself.'

With a smirk, he winds his arm through mine and pulls me in front of the two men.

'Did you get my message?' I ask, all my irritation suddenly in my voice.

'We're always leaving messages for each other, you and me. It's getting to be quite a little love affair.' Again that wink.

'Have you been drinking?'

'No, just thinking. Too much thinking. And I'm pissed off at you for wasting my time yesterday. The formidable Mlle Johnson was not pleased to have her schedule disturbed.'

I let his enquiring glance pass.

'And I'm not exactly happy about Ruiz having his hair cut. You think the old lady will recognize him? Lisbon–Montréal is a long way to come for a non-identification.'

'You brought him over?'

'To be fair, he didn't fuss.' He gives me his slow assessing glance implying a comparison in which I show to no advantage. 'He'd been away in some remote Atlantic pleasure spot and hadn't heard of

Madeleine's death until the weekend. He was suitably distressed.'

'You trust him?'

'I don't trust anybody. But his story holds together. More or less.'

The loudspeaker forestalls my next question. Monet and Ruiz, I notice, have gone outside for a smoke. They hover by the doors. Monet wears his inscrutable, wooden face. Ruiz looks preoccupied, abstracted, but when he catches my glance, his face settles into a bleak half-smile. He waves a pack of cigarettes in my direction. I shake my head.

'What's his story?' I ask Contini.

'Ruiz came over before Christmas to see Madeleine. They've had a possible movie cooking for some time. She wanted to show him the place she'd grown up in, so they drove down to Ste-Anne together on Christmas Eve. He went back up to town in her car and then left it for her at the airport, since he was flying back to Lisbon on Christmas Day. Via Paris. Some people have all the luck!'

'But he had time to . . .'

'To do the deed? Just about. He was back in his hotel soon after three a.m. We've checked. But where's the motive? And why ring and leave a message for her if you know she's dead?'

'So you know the message came after her death?'

'Yes, of course we know. That's what he says. He says he wanted Madeleine to do this film they were planning, but when he got back to Lisbon, his producer put his foot down. So he phoned to tell her. He also faxed the bad news to Mme Corot. When he read about Madeleine's death – read about it as a suicide – he claims he was devastated.'

'It could still all be a ploy.'

'Don't you worry. We're checking him out.' Contini gives me a look of casual scrutiny. 'You sound as if you're retracting your confession.'

I scowl at him. 'Why didn't he stay the night with Madeleine, once he was here?'

'Maybe you'd better ask him that.' He takes off his hat and arranges the creases with artful precision. 'After all, you both know the lady in question somewhat more intimately than I do. Maybe she sent him packing. Maybe she wanted to have Christmas morning alone with Granny. Maybe he'd had enough of her. But as far as we know, he was the last person to see Madeleine. Apart from you, of course.'

I refuse the bait and stare at the arrival gates which are now releasing a fresh horde of passengers.

'And how was Madeleine supposed to pick up her car?'

He shrugs. 'I don't know. Maybe you were supposed to give her a lift. So what were you ringing me about?'

'My house was broken into. Brick through the window. And entered. While I was in Montréal. Out, in any case. It's a mess.'

He darts me a quick look and repositions his hat at a rakish angle. 'You sure you're not just telling me this to blind me to your guilt? Make me feel sorry for you?'

'Come and see for yourself.'

'Was anything taken?'

I hesitate. 'Whoever it was killed the cat.'

'Damn!'

A child has started to howl. People brush past us, their voices raised in agitation. A capped driver flashes a name board in my face and slinks off as I shake my head.

'Anything taken?' Contini repeats.

I swallow. 'My video recorder.'

'From the Madeleine Blais museum?'

'You . . . you went in?' My throat creaks, a casket prised open to reveal worms.

Contini is avoiding my eyes. 'Nice collection,' he murmurs, searching the faces in the crowd.

'Yes, from there. And some tapes.'

'Excuse me, inspector . . .' Fernando Ruiz is at our side.

'Detective.'

'Detective, yes. Mme Corot has come through. There, see. By the flower stand.'

Against the vibrant background, Marie-Ange Corot is a fashion designer's vision of mourning. There is a heavy dark fur slung over a tailored suit of un-relieved black and a sleek dark helmet of a hat. She looks like some great glossy raven and as for-bidding. She doesn't smile at our approach, merely acknowledges us with a stiffening of her etched features.

'Pierre.' She shakes my hand and drops it quickly, as if I had some contagious and unacknowledgeable disease. I have the sudden sense that Contini has

466

alerted her. The signs are all there in the suspicious glance she casts at me, the refusal to meet my eyes.

Though he manages to plant airy kisses on her cheeks, her greeting of Fernando Ruiz is hardly warmer. She stands there rigid as a mannequin. Only when I introduce Contini and Monet does the fluidity I remember return to her features.

'Mme Corot will come with me,' Contini announces to my surprise. 'You take Ruiz and Monet, Rousseau. And by the way, we're going to Mme Tremblay's.'

'What?'

'You heard me.'

'But Mme Corot—'

'Just do as I say.'

Like a past master of chivalry, Contini picks up Marie-Ange's case and ushers her towards the escalator.

Monet's arm is on my shoulder, as if he thinks I might dart after them. 'Where's your car?' he asks.

Fernando Ruiz sits beside me in the front. He doesn't really sit. Like some caged wolf, he twists and turns and edges and looks longingly out the window. He crosses and uncrosses his legs and arms. He smokes continuously. He covers my silence with eruptions of words which grow in confidentiality with each passing kilometre. Maybe he has forgotten Monet in the back seat or maybe this is all a show for his benefit. In my mirror, I can gauge the intensity of Monet's listening by the way he strokes his moustache. It comes to me that

Contini has set us up with his usual canniness.

'Marie-Ange thinks I am partly responsible for Madeleine's death. I can feel it. She thinks I shouldn't have left Madeleine.'

My voice isn't working properly. It changes registers against my will. 'What happened exactly on Christmas Eve? Why did you leave Madeleine?'

Ruiz closes his eyes and squeezes the bridge of his nose, as if he were in pain or didn't want to remember.

I edge into the right-hand lane and drive more slowly. I don't want to miss any of his words.

'We were good friends, you know, Madeleine and I. Close friends.'

I clutch the wheel, but he doesn't say anything more for a moment. The contradictory thought that he is both savouring his memories and rehearsing his story takes hold of me.

'Close friends?' I urge him on.

'Yes.'

He must sense my mistrust for his tone changes, becomes drier. 'We drove down to the country after dinner. She was full of childhood stories. About her grandmother in particular. She wanted me to meet her, to show me the sights, but when we arrived the poor woman was asleep. Then ... well, after Madeleine had changed, we went to midnight mass. In the church in town. We were a bit early.'

'Did you see her talking to a dark, rather beautiful young man?' I interrupt.

He shakes his head. 'Inspector Contini asked me about that. There were so many people around, wanting to talk to her too. I stood aside. I noticed she went into the confessional. That surprised me.'

He pauses and I can feel the look of enquiry on his face, but all I can think of is Jerome and his warnings. My instincts, about that at least, were right. Madeleine may not have made her confession to Jerome directly, but he got wind of it.

'How did Madeleine seem then?'

'Happy. Excited even. But after we got back to the house, afterwards . . .' Ruiz shakes his head, lights another cigarette. I know what he can't talk about. 'Well, her mood shifted. She decided it would be better if I didn't stay the night. Maybe because of her grandmother . . . I don't really know.'

With too much vividness, I see the state of Madeleine's room as Mme Tremblay and I found it on Christmas Day. My foot presses down on the accelerator and I lurch out to pass. The car on my left honks.

'Hey,' Monet grunts from the back seat. 'Watch it. What happened to your wing mirror?'

'I'll tell you later,' I mutter and resume my more sober pace.

Ruiz is silent for a few minutes, then says, 'In any case, Madeleine offered me her car to drive back to Montréal in. She said she could always get a lift to Mirabel. It was no distance at all from Ste-Anne.'

'Was there anything in the car?'

'What do you mean?'

'A large envelope.'

'I didn't notice anything. To tell you the truth, we had both had a fair amount to drink.'

'And that was it? Nothing else. She didn't say anything? You didn't go for a walk?'

He gives me a peculiar look, then sits up straighter in his seat. 'We did have a little walk. To . . . to clear my head. It's just come back to me. There was a noise from somewhere. A crackle. Something. You know what the countryside's like. Anyhow, I jumped. And Madeleine, well, she called out, "Pierre!" and laughed. Then she whispered something to me about her grandmother's neighbour being in love with her, liking to spy on her, and she gave me a very large kiss.'

Both men's eyes are on me.

'In case you've forgotten, Rousseau, it's the next exit,' Monet says from behind me.

Monique opens the door to us when we arrive at Mme Tremblay's. She is visibly cool to me, but rustles up a smile for Monet and Ruiz and manages an artful tear when the Portuguese realizes who she is and offers condolences.

'It is a great loss to us all,' she breathes, not without dignity. Mme Tremblay's tone is creeping into her, I suddenly realize.

The fire is lit in the living room. Contini and Marie-Ange are already installed on the sofa opposite Mme Tremblay, all of them balancing teacups.

'Ah, there you are!' Contini booms, but his eyes are on Mme Tremblay.

Her cup has set up a rattle in its saucer. She is staring at Ruiz, her neck craned, her mouth poised in an inaudible gasp.

'So you've met Fernando Ruiz before, Mme Tremblay?' Contini says with a gleam of self-satisfaction.

'I . . . Yes.' She turns her face away.

I rush to her side and put my arm round her shoulder.

'I'm afraid it wasn't an auspicious occasion,' Ruiz mumbles.

Her eyes dart back to his face as if she would claw it. She takes a deep breath. 'You knew Madeleine before . . . ?' She pauses and Ruiz finishes for her.

'For some time. We had hoped to work together.'

Contini has evidently sprung this meeting on Mme Tremblay with no preparation.

'Yes,' Marie-Ange breathes. She is playing with the silver brooch at her neck and the face she turns on Ruiz is all recrimination. But what she says to Mme Tremblay has a neutral ring. 'Fernando is in the process of casting a new film and—'

'I know.' Mme Tremblay cuts her off. 'And Madeleine wasn't good enough for him. That's what you told her, wasn't it? I heard the message.'

'More than good enough.' Ruiz shifts from foot to foot, but somehow stands up to her venom. 'It was my producer who wasn't certain . . . about the suitability of the part.'

'A little tea?' Monique flutters towards him with a cup.

'Not for you, Rousseau,' Contini mutters. 'We need to go back to your place for a little while.' He gestures Monet aside and they carry on a whispered

471

conversation. Monique's sudden burst of babble makes it impossible for me to hear and then Contini is at my side. 'You'll excuse us, ladies, gentlemen.'

He puts his arm through mine and before I can say anything he has propelled me through the door.

'What are you doing, Contini?'

'My job. Your place has been broken into, right?'

'Yes, but Gagnon's already been. There's no need for you—'

'There's every need,' he says.

A local police car is parked in my drive. The lights are on in my bedroom and throughout the ground floor. Contini looks so alert his nose seems to twitch as we walk round to the front door.

'Tell me again, from the top. What time did you get home? What did you notice? I didn't get it straight at the airport.'

As I speak, he looks from the garden to the porch to the boarded window and back again. 'You sure took your time over calling the police, Rousseau! Any reason?'

I shrug, but my trembling hands give away my agitation as I ring the bell and then unlock the door.

Plump, pink-cheeked Miron comes bounding down the stairs.

'Oh, it's you, M. Rousseau. Whoever it was sure made a mess of your bedroom. We're just finishing dusting for prints up there.'

Contini gives him a surly greeting. 'You know what you're doing?'

Miron blushes and nods.

'Well, get back to it then. And don't let me hear any gunshots.' He prods me towards the living room. 'Where did you find the cat?'

'On my bed.'

'Bed?'

'Head on the pillow, to be exact.'

'Ouch. Someone sure has it in for you.' He paces the room slowly, scrutinizes the boarded window, the floor and all the neighbouring surfaces, then suddenly whispers, 'Did you tell Gagnon about the Madeleine room?'

I feel I am flushing as brightly as Miron as I shake my head.

'Right, let's have a look at the cat first of all.' He precedes me towards the stairs and I stop him.

'Minou's outside. I . . . I put her in a box.'

'What the—! Don't you know yet not to touch anything, Rousseau?' He cracks his knuckles with slow deliberation. 'My patience is wearing as thin as a strip of puff pastry. All right. Forget the cat for now. Let's go up to the attic.'

I unlock the door. Half-way up the stairs, I hesitate. 'You look round on your own, Contini.'

'What's the matter? All getting too much for you?'

'Maybe it is,' I hear myself say.

He flashes me the look of a disappointed parent. 'All right. Wait for me downstairs. Don't relax too much though. We've still got a lot to do today.'

With a glance at his watch he hurries up the remaining stairs. I stand there for a moment, trapped between spaces I don't want to be in, an

473

alien in the only home I know. I hear him emit a low whistle, an ejaculation of '*Putana!*' and, despite the barrier of a thick wall, I can see in acute detail what confronts him. I hasten down the stairs and stand like a lost child in the cold formality of the dining room. I gaze out the window.

The sun is setting. Rosy fingers fondle the darkening blue of the sky and tinge the glistening snow a pale pink.

Madeleine was right. Nature doesn't care. It is too big for us.

I will away the cosy blanket of self-pity which beckons with such seductive warmth. I pour myself a stiff whisky, pretend to dilute it with a sprinkling of water and try to focus my recalcitrant mind on the night of Madeleine's death.

The phone rings and for a moment I have the uncanny feeling that I will hear that silence again, the silence I recognize as Madeleine. I take a hefty sip of whisky and force myself to lift the receiver.

'Pierre, it's Elise.'

'Elise!' My voice registers my surprise.

'Look, Oscar's out and . . . well, can you come round? I need to talk to you. Alone.' Her voice is low as if she didn't want anyone to overhear.

'Alone?' My skin prickles uncomfortably.

'Yes. It's important.'

There is an odd beating in my heart. I have a sinking sense that I know what she is going to tell me. Oscar and Madeleine . . .

'I can't get away right now,' I murmur. 'But a little later. I'll try and make it a little later.'

'OK.' She pauses. 'If Oscar's back, don't say I phoned you.'

She hangs up before I can question her.

I am so immersed in what Elise will tell me that when Contini appears I jump.

A smug little smile plays over his lips. He looks as if he has just secretly swallowed a prize delicacy.

'OK, Rousseau. I'm done.' He pats his pocket. 'It's back to Mme Tremblay's for the two of us. I've had a word with the boys upstairs.'

'You told them?'

He toys with me as if I were a hamster in a cage. 'No need to be indiscreet. Not just yet. I heard the phone, by the way. Anything interesting?'

'Just a friend.'

'Which friend?' His tone makes me realize that my freedom is utterly in his gift.

'Elise Boileau.'

'Oscar Boileau's wife.' He considers for a moment. 'So why are you looking as if the sky had just fallen in?'

'Am I?'

He grunts. 'What did she want?'

'To see me. I thought I'd pop over there now. When you're all through in here.'

'Oh no, Rousseau. You're mine tonight, as the crooners say.' His laugh has an edge of malice. 'Come on. Get your coat. We're off.'

Outside it has grown dark and the wind has come up, the chill wind that brings with it an arctic blast of bad weather. I pull my coat more tightly round me and wish I had a toque on my head, rather than this useless brimmed felt donned for Marie-Ange's benefit and an expedition to the Ritz.

'Hope you're ready for the excitements of the evening,' Contini says as he slips something into the glove compartment.

'To tell you the truth, I've had about all the excitement I can handle. What have you got in mind?'

'You'll see.' He chuckles mysteriously.

I don't like the sound of that chuckle.

18

The traffic on the twisting hill road that leads between my house and Mme Tremblay's is unusually dense. Tail-lights gleam red ahead of us, appear between trees like furtive animal eyes. Behind, headlights dazzle, ricochet searching beams through the pines.

When we arrive two marked police cars flank the drive. As if poised for an outdoor concert, a uniformed officer directs oncoming cars into parking spaces.

Contini glances at the car clock and flashes me a smug smile.

'You planning a party? Or a press conference?' I ask.

'Neither. Hope you'll enjoy it though. Meet you at the house in fifteen minutes.' He waves me away and disappears between parked cars.

I walk slowly. Despite the agitated barking of the dogs and the commotion of cars, there is an odd hush in the air. To the left, beneath the old gnarled oak, men huddle in a small, tight group. Gagnon's capped head is distinguishable amongst them. So too is the mountainous bulk of Georges Lavigueur. Next to him stand Noël Jourdan, Michel Dubois and, to my surprise, Oscar. I make my way towards them, but Gagnon shoos me away as if he didn't recognize me.

Closer to the house, I spy a torch glimmering among the ranked cars. A woman officer materializes behind it and next to her a figure I am certain is Maryla. They are talking in low voices as the woman plays her light over the cars. The one being examined at the moment is mine. The small pool of light beams across its scratched left-hand side and broken wing mirror.

Maryla sees me and takes a step in my direction, but the officer puts a staying hand on her shoulder, flashes the beam in my face and hurries me along towards the house.

Suspicion chills me more certainly than the wind. With it comes a sudden spurt of fear. I have a distinct feeling that I am being set up.

Out of the shadows of the porch, young Miron emerges like an eager puppy.

'Hello again, M. Rousseau. Managed to get here before you. Go right in. They're expecting you.'

'What's up, Miron?'

He averts his eyes, shuffles his feet. 'It's Contini. He's . . . Just go on in.' He rings the bell for me and Monique appears at the door. Her cheeks are flushed.

'Can't stand that Detective Monet,' she mutters as she takes my coat. 'He's been bullying me.

Treating me like a servant. Not that you'd care. And no-one explains anything. The way he talked to Marcel—'

'Is he here?'

She gestures vaguely towards the door. 'Out there somewhere.'

I edge towards the living room, but she bars my way, prods me in the chest. 'You didn't help, did you? Not a sou for her real mother in her will. As if I hadn't carried her in my belly for nine months.'

'I don't know anything about Madeleine's will, Monique. Not a thing.'

'I bet you don't. Her executor. With that high and mighty Marie-Ange Corot. Don't know anything!'

I stumble as I take in this information and try to order my jumbled thoughts. The sight of the unexpected group gathered round the hearth sends them racing.

Mme Groulx is here, wearing a black felt hat complete with feather, as if Madeleine's funeral had been scheduled for this evening and the coffin already set up for ghoulish viewing. Mme Préfontaine sits between her and Mme Rossignol, who from the glazed look on the assembled faces must be recounting one of her interminable stories. Mme Tremblay has her profile to me. It is as taut as a mask. Next to her, I recognize one of Mme Groulx's daughters and old Senegal.

In the far corner of the room, Serge Monet leans his gangling form against a table and peers through the window. Near him Marie-Ange is engaged in what seems to be desultory conversation with my brother, Jerome. On the far side of the room, a pretty blonde woman I don't recognize is leafing through a magazine.

I utter a generalized hello and all eyes turn to me for a moment, only to be as quickly averted. Only Mme Tremblay stands to greet me by name. Her mouth is tilted in stubborn defiance, her eyes bewildered. At a sign from Monet she sits down again. He beckons me towards him.

'Only a few more minutes, Rousseau.'

'Is anyone planning to tell me what's going on?'

'You'll find out soon enough.' His face is as impassive as a carved totem. He leans it towards the window again.

'Sit with us, Pierre.' Jerome gestures to me, a little stiffly. 'I was just saying to Mme Corot that Ste-Anne is usually a sleepy little place. There haven't been so many policemen around since . . . well, since the Duplessis days.'

Marie-Ange stares at me strangely, then rotates her chair by 180 degrees.

It occurs to me that only Fernando Ruiz is missing. What has Contini done with him?

'OK, everyone.' Monet suddenly unfurls his lean form from the window seat, switches off the overhead light and pulls the chain on the standard lamp in the corner. 'Quiet now.'

All eyes are turned towards the empty doorway. A figure steps through it and pauses. In the dim light, it takes me a moment to recognize Fernando Ruiz. The collar of his leather jacket is turned up. His profile as he turns towards the lamp is all cheekbones and jagged plains. He crosses his arms and claps them against his shoulders, as if a blast of cold air had whipped through the room. With a sidling movement, he walks slowly towards the corner of the room where the blonde woman turns to greet him.

She has pulled on a coat while I wasn't looking. It is golden and plush. Its leopard spots leap and dance and blur my vision. Madeleine's coat. I rub my eyes.

The woman lifts her face to Ruiz and coils her arm round his waist. He draws her close and, smiling, plants a kiss on her lips.

There is a startled exclamation from Mme Groulx, a note of discord from one of her neighbours. I can't make out its content in the generalized shushing.

As Ruiz and the blonde woman disappear through the door, the room seems to release a collective breath. A moment later the central light comes on and, with it, Contini enters the room, closely followed by Monique, who carries a tray of wine glasses.

My brother scrapes his chair backwards across the floor and throws me an embarrassed glance.

'Our detective has a remarkable way of holding an identity parade. Doesn't play by the rules, does he? Trouble is, from the distance of an altar ... Even that woman could be Madeleine.' He shakes his head. 'What did you think?'

'What was I meant to think?'

He bends towards me, his mask of composure

slipping, his face suddenly strained, and whispers, 'Pierre, tell me truthfully, on the night, did you—?' He stops himself as Monet approaches.

'We need you, Rousseau. Follow me.'

Maybe he thinks my brother has tipped me off about something, for he claps a hand on my shoulder and propels me towards the kitchen, where I can hear the dogs yelping and straining against the door.

When I open it, they yap and leap and lick at me with enthusiastic familiarity. At least they, unlike my neighbours, seem to know that I am the same person I was yesterday and the week before.

'Keep them quiet, Rousseau,' Monet mutters as I bend to greet them. 'Settle them into the corner or something.'

As I do so, a pair of cord-clad legs appears beside me. They bend and Fernando Ruiz's face is level with mine. He pats the dogs and gives me a smirk. 'What did you think of my performance?'

'Authentic,' I murmur.

'OK, you dog-lovers in the corner,' Contini's voice hails us from the other end of the room. 'Pay attention. That was act one. Now we're about to stage act two. You too, Rousseau. You first, in fact.'

'What?'

'You heard me. Ruiz, you come along and coach him. You're the pro.'

'What are you concocting, Contini?'

'Just follow orders, Rousseau.' He prods me towards the stairs as if I were a stranger and we hadn't by now shared too many dinners.

'OK,' he says when we reach the landing. 'Now this is how it goes. Ruiz will give you a dry run with the curtains shut tight. And then you're on. *Con brio*.'

I stare at him in incomprehension.

'There's no time for explanations. The guys out there will freeze. Show him, Ruiz.'

We have reached Madeleine's bedroom and after a quick check of the curtains Contini switches on the bedside lamp, gestures Ruiz and the blonde woman who has now joined us through, and comes to stand with me at the entrance. His arm holds me back, as sturdy as a metal gate.

The woman pulls off her coat and then quickly, with only a sideways glance of embarrassment at Contini, her trousers and sweater. Underneath, she is wearing a pale blue slip of a garment. Ruiz eyes her approvingly and moves towards her, only to be stopped abruptly by Contini's 'No. Take your jacket off. I want you in shirtsleeves. You too, Rousseau.'

Ruiz removes his jacket and sweater.

'OK, action.'

'You want my job, eh, inspector?' He grins at Contini.

'Detective. Go.'

Ruiz shakes himself, head, arms, hips, legs, and then smiles seductively at the woman, who is standing within the frame of the curtained window. He moves towards her, lifts her chin, looks into her eyes and holds her gaze for a beat. Then he winds his arm round her, places his hand firmly on her bottom and draws her closely to him in an embrace. With his other hand he ruffles her hair and cups her head. He kisses her. It is a long slow kiss.

'That'll do. Or "cut", as they say.' Contini is enjoying himself. 'OK, Ginette?'

With a start, I recognize Ginette Lavigne. The flowing blond wig over her hennaed spikes, her concoction of make-up and clothes have completely fooled me.

Now she looks a little dazed.

'You think you can do that, Rousseau? Make it last a bit longer. And I want you to end up on the bed. You're taking Madeleine Blais to bed.' He smirks. 'For our audience, of course.'

Briskly, he switches off the light and motions Ruiz from the room.

'But I can't possibly—'

'But nothing. Get on with it. And turn off the hall light for me.'

Reluctantly, I do as he asks and hear the sound of the curtains being pulled open. Then Contini is beside me in the darkness, prodding me, telling me to turn on the bedside lamp as I go in.

I am standing in Madeleine's room, framed by the window. Outside everything is black and still. Peeking out from the far corner of the artfully rumpled bed is a frowsy old teddy bear, one of its eyes askew. A pair of stockings hangs from the bed frame. On top of the dresser stand an assortment of perfume bottles, a comb and a brush. Next to them is an open enamel jewellery box. It looks as if someone has recently gone through it.

From the box's edge, a leather thong droops. I

follow it upward and see the spangled silver of a sun, the signs of the zodiac clustered round its centre. My childhood medallion. Dizziness assaults me.

'Jacket,' Contini hisses invisibly from the doorway.

The woman who is and isn't Ginette Lavigne stands in front of me in her silk slip. I can see the arch of her nipples, the outline of her breasts through the thin material as she moves to ease my jacket off my shoulders. She throws it on the bed. I raise her chin so that our eyes meet. Her eyes are not the colour of Madeleine's. They are two angry points of light. She doesn't like me.

With an impatient gesture, she takes my hand and curls it round her.

'Kiss her, for Christ's sake!' Contini orders.

She raises her lips to mine and I kiss her and as I kiss her I hear Madeleine's voice ringing in my ears. Telling me all those years ago, too many years ago, 'It's not sex, Pierre. It's cinema. When you're asked to repeat a gesture for the fifth take, arousal is not what you feel.'

I battle against the voice. Perversely I try to make this encounter real. I kiss this blonde Ginette, who resists and isn't allowed to resist, kiss her hard. I stroke her back, I pull her down on the bed, oblivious to her muted struggle. And all the time Madeleine is there, laughing, until Contini hisses a 'Cut', and Ginette switches off the lights.

'Enjoyed that, did you?' Contini cackles as he leads me away from darkness.

I am too confused to answer.

'Off with you, now.' He hands me my jacket. 'Monet will tell you what to do. I want you to watch closely.'

Before I can get my bearings, Monet has pushed me out the front door of the house, where a uniformed officer stands waiting. 'We've saved you a good seat,' he says enigmatically. 'Just follow Jean, here, and don't move once you're in position. We regroup when the siren goes.'

A light snow has started to fall. The wind whips the feathery moistness across my face and whistles faintly through the trees. Jean doesn't speak. He treads as noiselessly as a cat through the darkness. I concentrate on his back, concentrate so hard that as we go round the house and trail through the wood, I lose my orientation.

He leaves me amidst clustered firs and raises his finger to his lips as a parting salute. His shadowy outline disappears in seconds. Then all I can make out are gradations of gloom.

I lean against prickly branches and wait. The cold seeps through my joints. What am I waiting for? What is this elaborate game Contini is staging? Why has he not alerted me to it? I have a certain sense that the show is for my benefit. Yet he has also made me a player. What more does he want from me, since he already has my confession?

Madeleine's laugh rings in my ear and as I listen to it a light comes on in the house. It illuminates Madeleine's room. A figure moves into the light.

The policewoman, her wig bright, dishevelled, her face uplifted. She could be Madeleine at this distance. Why not? A man steps into the frame. I cannot make out his face. All I can see is the blackness of his hair and a suggestion of pale features. His arm comes towards her and she moves into its circle. I watch. I have the sudden impression that I am in a movie theatre and around me, wrapped in the secret dimness, a hundred faces are raised towards the same screen.

The figures clasp, play out the pantomime of sex, and despite myself, despite the fact that I know the scenario, I am drawn in, grow warm with the heat of their mingled bodies, am bound by the spell of the darkness and the illuminated frame.

Suddenly the script shifts. The man raises his hand. It comes down on the woman's face with a searing slap. I want to move nearer. I ache for the camera to give me a close-up and show me her pain. But my feet are fixed in the ground.

The woman's hand moves swiftly to return the man's slap and then he is shaking her. Rage is unleashed. His fingers move to her throat. She eludes him, runs towards the window, flings it open. She screams. The scream echoes through vastness.

Near me, there is a flutter and swoop of bird's wings, a sound like the scraping of a gate against stone. Phosphorescent eyes leap through the night.

My mind is racing. It provides a dialogue. A narrative. But the narrative isn't my own. I hear Contini's voice again, low, mesmerizing, giving me the script I need to hear.

The man is dragging the woman back from the window. There is a rope in his hand. Thick cord, loosely looped at its end. She looks at him. Her mouth is open. His hand grasps her shoulder. Moves to her neck. Squeezes. Her head slumps. Her whole body slumps. He holds her up.

I hear a rush of breath. My own. No, no. Not my own. There is a presence near me. A stir. A movement. Another release of breath, almost a moan as the rope makes its way round the woman's neck.

Sleepwalker's mists lift from my mind. Suddenly for the first time since Madeleine's death, everything moves into crystalline focus.

This is not my script. No, definitely not my script, but Contini's. Yes, in my half-sleep, I did come out that night after the telephone call. I did see Madeleine framed with a man in the window – and, after the initial spurt of jealous anger, the key plaque hurled at the pane, I walked on. This was not something I wanted or needed to see. This was something to forget, to repress. I didn't want the coils of a fresh jealousy strangling me. I had seen nothing. I went home, the memory wiped, a blank tape in place. I had done nothing but lie in bed that night and dream, dream as I so often do, of a shadowy, elusive Madeleine.

No, however little I may be able to bear that ultimate separation from her which death marks, I am not Madeleine's killer.

As the scene above me is acted out, I find myself

anatomizing my derangement with surgical precision.

No, I could not bear the shock of Madeleine's death. In the event, death by suicide provided an almost tolerable notion. Somehow or other I could be implicated in a suicide, enmeshed in the emotions which had led to it. They had something to do with me.

Possessed by love, by a jealous possessiveness, by a desire to recapture what I had lost, I could only come to terms with the possibility that Madeleine had been murdered if I could be named as her murderer. No-one else must touch Madeleine in that ultimate rite of passage. She had put her virginity into my care. She had called me her earth. I had to continue to be so. Only I could be responsible for her death.

Contini's blue movie provided me with a script to which I could confess.

A sperm sample would have obliterated both bond and confession.

Whatever my lover's delirium, I do know the difference between the stuff of dreams – the Madeleine of fantasy over whom in the image-lined chamber of my attic I had a zapper's power – and the embodied woman who danced away from my every attempt at control. At last, I know.

The man's back now all but fills the illuminated window frame. I have decided it is Ruiz. The acting is so good. Too good, perhaps. As he turns, his face has the cast of a tragic mask. Anguish and terror are there. There in his posture, as he brings his hands to cover his eyes, in his tensed shoulders, in the barely controlled movements with which he leaves the frame.

Where he stood, the woman's legs hang – thin, frail, swinging slightly.

Behind me, beside me, there is that sound again, a choked rasping.

How has Contini managed these particular effects?

From somewhere a creature lets out a thin, high screech. I think of poor Minou and in her wake of the desecration of my attic room, of the brutal pounding of Maryla's car and my own. I think of the blazing barn. I know now with a physical certainty that someone far more dangerous than myself has stalked Madeleine's landscape.

Yet Contini, I am now equally certain, suspects primarily me.

The light in the window is extinguished. In its place, as if to echo my new racing clarity, the moon appears amidst hurtling clouds. It casts furtive shadows on the snow. Amidst them I see the outline of a man. His head has the solid mass of a helmet, but fuzzier round the edges and peaked at the top, like some prairie buffalo.

I wait for the promised siren call and as I wait, the shadow shifts its position. There is something in that hovering outline which makes my skin prickle, a tugging at the edges of sensation – a shape, an impression of bulk, a particular stance. A line from one of my last anonymous letters to Madeleine comes back to me, a description of a man watching her as she came down the steps of her apartment.

Suddenly the shadow moves. On the snow there is an agitated blur of feet and arms and wavering boughs, like an exotic dance.

The impact takes me by surprise. All I see as shoulder and head butt me to the ground is a thick bullish huddle of a coat.

My shout echoes through silence, but the boots have already gone.

As I extricate myself from branches and find my breath, the light in the window comes on again. I do not stay to watch Contini's stagecraft. Anger fuels me. It is clean and strong. It creates its own purpose. I race across the thin fresh layer of snow which carries tracks even the greenest of scouts could follow.

The man knows the woods well. He has dropped down into the dip at the nearest opportunity, forsaken fields and a straight line, skirted the sharpest incline and moved into the density of forest. Where is he heading? I can hear the creak of branches. But if I can hear, so can he. I fall back a little and wait.

The ground is uneven here, packed and hard, then, abruptly, it swallows my leg and I have to clutch at a trunk to regain my footing. The only light now comes from the snow itself. A silvery sheen indicates ice. I slither down it on my bottom.

When I can stand again, there are no more tracks. There is no sound either. Even the night creatures are silent. I hold my breath and listen. And then I hear it, the slight rustle of a footfall. I can't distinguish its direction.

A wave of panic flows through me. Who is pursuing whom? Is my assailant behind me or in front? I take a step and then another when a sudden eruption of noise, a lurching and crack of branches, makes me freeze into position. A deer bounds across my path, swifter than an arrow. In the cover of its steps, I walk swiftly downhill.

And then it is there in front of me: the river, a sheer stretch of ice. Across its expanse, on the southern shore, lights flicker. With sudden decision, I slip down the bank and examine the ground. Nothing.

I turn left, treading carefully. Within a few metres, the prints emerge – sliding indentations on the fresh, powdery surface. I hasten my pace.

At first, when I hear the sound, I mistake it for the whirr of a saw poised to cut through wood. But the bulge of an old boathouse which emerges on my side clears my mind. I heave myself up the bank, slip along the side of the building. I have almost reached its front when a car emerges. Its headlights dark, it lumbers stealthily up the track.

I know that car. I have seen that car. Where have I seen it? I listen to its rumble until it disappears into the night.

Half-way up the track, in the shelter of the tall arching maples which all but obliterate its existence, it comes to me with a thud as jarring as the one to my body. I want to sit down and nurse the impact, but my feet are already running, bolting over the surface of the snow at a pace which is also the pace of fear.

19

The narrow track opens onto a country road which is not much wider. To the right it twists round a bend. To the left, it rises and dips into nothingness. Behind me the narrow lane to the boathouse is all but invisible in its density of snow-clad vegetation.

I cannot make out where I am. My head is swirling with too much knowledge, my heart beating too fast.

I turn to the right and follow the road round the curve hoping that a car may turn up, any car but that one. The wind is icier here. It blows down the gully of the road as if the passage had been constructed for that very purpose. Flurries come with it, a glut of racing whiteness in the air, dissolving the solidity of shape and contour.

My country has too much wilderness. I am neither trapper nor *voyageur* used to covering it on foot. Familiarity comes only with an engine roaring in front of me, a speed which tames distance and domesticates it.

I walk. Numbness has taken over my extremities.

Feet and fingers and nose have moved beyond coldness. Like a robot powered only by some distant radar source, I place one foot in front of the other.

Round the turn of the second bend, lights appear. Their gleam steadies the landscape. Suddenly, as if the grail were within my reach, I am running, running fast.

When the house takes on form and size, I feel a laugh rising in my throat. I blunder towards the door and press the bell. A shadow appears in front of the eyehole. A cautious voice asks, 'Who is it?'

'Pierre.'

Elise unlatches the door. There is bewilderment in her face.

'Pierre! How'd you get here? I was listening for your car, though I'd all but given up waiting.' She takes in my state and urges me towards the fire. 'Did you have an accident?' She pours a glass of brandy and forces it into my hand.

I shake my head. 'But I need to borrow your car, Elise. And a telephone directory.'

She gives me a queer look, then opens a cupboard and pulls a directory down from a top shelf.

I leaf through the pages quickly. Yes, the address is here. I jot it down.

'I wanted to talk to you because Oscar's upset. Very upset,' she says as I write. 'You're angry with him. Because of the portrait of Madeleine Blais.'

'I can't talk now, Elise.'

'It's not what you think.' Now that she's started, she can't seem to stop herself. 'Though I thought it too. He didn't sleep with her. OK? I know that. I'm

494

his wife. But she asked him to keep it secret. So it felt like that. Funny woman. I guess he wanted to, though. Guess you all want to.'

I squeeze her shoulder. There are tears in her eyes. The speech hasn't been easy for her.

'I have to go, Elise. But do something for me. Do it now.' I write down Mme Tremblay's number and pass her the slip of paper. 'I want you to ring here and speak to Detective Contini or Serge Monet. Tell them to get to this address quickly. Insist. As a last resort, try Gagnon. Ring him at home if necessary.' I hold out my hand. 'Car keys.'

She gives them to me. 'You're going to do something crazy, Pierre. I can feel it.'

'Less crazy than some of the other things I've been doing this last week. Thanks for telling me about Oscar.' I give her a quick kiss and go out into the night.

The blizzard is restless, tossing the snow as erratically as confetti blown by some great whirling fan. Its force prevents speed. My thoughts charge ahead of the car. They are noisier than the heater.

I quiet them and concentrate on the route. It occurs to me, as I pass the darkened hulk of the Rosenberg house, that I had never realized how much shorter the distance from Mme Tremblay's to Oscar's was cross-country than along the road. That would explain Will Henderson's appearance on the morning of the blaze. Will may have been guilty of a great many things, but I suspect not that.

Another kilometre passes. On my left an old gas

station emerges from whiteness. Its two rounded pumps stand like sentinels to the past, reminders of a time when this road led to the busy army camp. Now both station and camp are deserted.

I creep along, my eyes peeled for a sign of the house which should be somewhere along here. But nothing materializes to left or right and abruptly the road comes to an end.

Two high metal-meshed gates topped by barbed wire block my route. On either side, the perimeter fence stretches into oblivion. From it a battered sign creaks, its letters so defaced that only a U and an S are distinguishable.

Could anyone have been granted permission to inhabit the derelict barracks?

Baffled, I leave the car engine running and try the gates. The heavy padlock is firm, if rusty. I peer through the fence. It comes to me that somewhere I have heard a rumour about strays bedding down in the camp. But strays don't have telephone numbers, I remind myself.

Cursing the lost time, I turn the car round and retrace my route, crawling now, my imagination willing shapes out of the storm of whiteness.

The outline of the garage takes hazy shape in my headlights. From this direction, I can make out a cluster of barnlike buildings behind it. I have almost passed them when within the blur of white I detect a change of tone, a flicker of yellow, a rapid movement of light.

I reverse into the garage and realize as I do so that someone has cleared the snow here not too long ago or my entrance would not be so easy. Quickly, I kill lights and engine and head round the side of the building.

It is dark here, too dark. My eyes have grown accustomed to the glow of headlights, my body soft in the warmth of the car. I steel myself, test the anger which will give me cunning and strength. For a fleeting second, Madeleine's pale face, as it looked there, hanging in the barn, flashes before me. I tread quickly, the snow muffling all sound.

At the far edge of the garage building I bump into something that blocks my path. Not a fence, no, too soft. I try to edge round it, but it is still there, a resilient barrier. I scrape away snow and the blackness of piled tyres emerges. I hoist myself over them and leap down to the other side.

I am behind the garage. To my right is an assemblage of massed shapes among which I can no longer detect the yellow flicker of light I was so certain I saw.

Staring begins to give the shapes a kind of meaning. I am in some kind of yard, a dump perhaps, with three, maybe four structures, their roofs sloping irregularly. From my vantage point, they tumble into each other like a portion of some erratic cityscape after a bomb has fallen.

I edge along, find myself face to face with a tractor, its attached snowplough lifted like a giant's mittened hand. I weave my way round it, between tyres, a stack of timbers, tin barrels, a redundant refrigerator, concrete blocks, unidentifiable rubble. Another turn and I find myself in front of two large wooden doors. They creak slightly in the wind. I prod one and it swings towards me on rusty hinges. Through the gap I make out the shape of a truck and a car. That car. My pulse beats faster.

I turn a corner and see the light. It comes from a window in the furthest of a series of sheds and shacks. Flickering shadows play into the night. Television.

I tread carefully, hugging the sides of walls, until for a few metres I dare the narrow ploughed path. In front of me is the window, cut high, slightly above eye-level. I look down at the ground. The heaped snow makes a mound against the wall. I test it for solidity and clamber to its top. It sinks beneath my weight. But I can see. Yes. Now I can see. I shudder.

A pot-bellied stove stands at the far end of a shabby room. Next to it are two straight-backed wooden chairs. A doll sits on one chair – a large doll, with a porcelain smile and crimped golden hair and thick glistening lashes lowered over cornflower-blue eyes. She wears a long blue chequered dress and a white pinny.

I know that doll. She used to be Madeleine's. She disappeared during that second summer of our friendship. 'Mémère threw her away,' Madeleine told me in a voice which was half-way between laughter and tears. 'I forgot her in the barn and Mémère threw her away. She thinks I'm too big for her. She's right. I'm not going to say a word about it.'

Draped over the second chair is a woman's frock,

a spattering of daisies on pink ground. Edging out from beneath it is a creamy camisole. On the floor stand a pair of high-heeled sandals. Are these, too, all Madeleine's? I don't know. I don't want to know. Nor do I want to see the images moving across the screen. But my eyes are drawn to them in confirmation of what I already suspect.

Madeleine is there, her face slightly lowered in that expression which is at once seductive and pure, transgressive in its very purity. There is a man's hand on her shoulder. The camera follows its movement to pause at the cleavage between her breasts. Madeleine's skin glistens. Her lips move.

I do not need to watch this. I know it too well. I could speak her words for her, breathe her poignant sigh. It is my tape. The recorder sits on the floor next to the television set.

My eyes veer towards what I have been avoiding.

The man sits in a dilapidated armchair just below me to one side of the window. His mouth is crimson against the darkness of his beard, his lips slightly parted. His tongue moistens them, as if they were parched. One hand grips the arm of the chair. The fingers are thick and splayed.

His other hand holds a black stocking. Partly wrapped in the stocking is his penis. He caresses it with a growing urgency and then his whole body shakes, as if some predator had him by the neck.

I look away, my stomach turning in a spasm of pity and disgust. '*Mon semblable, mon frère,*' I find myself thinking and then a terrible clatter ruptures the stillness of the night and I am lying in the snow on my back, my platform dispersed into an assortment of lead pipes and ducts and cylinders.

I pick myself up quickly and run round to the far side of the building. The advantage of surprise has been lost and suddenly the fear that I have kept at bay grips me more fiercely than a man-eater's claw.

'*Qui est là?*' a voice booms.

I hear the creak and bang of a door, the clink of pipes, a curse. Then nothing. Silence and darkness. I tread softly through deeper snow and cling to the side of the house. Why didn't I pick up one of those pipes?

Before me stretch desolate fields on which every print will be clearly visible. To my right is the maze of shacks and sheds. I dip round to the right. My hand grazes a curve and I make out an upright barrel. One heave and I am on top of it, a second and I am lying flat on the slight incline of a sheet-aluminium roof, icier than the snow which covers it. I slither towards its lower edge and peer round.

A flashlight points a beam at my tracks. He is picking them out, one by one, slowly. His right hand is raised. In it he holds a stretch of piping. In the shadows, he looks as big as a grizzly and more terrible.

I ease myself into a crouch. When he has moved just past me, I leap. I scream a scream I didn't know I possessed. The scream of a banshee. It rebounds through the snow-muffled night as I topple him to the ground. Then everything is in a fast forward which is also a dizzying slow motion illuminated by the feeble light of the fallen torch.

I am astride him, but the pipe is still in his hand and he won't release it, no matter how much I tug. I am tumbling, thrown back like a squealing puppy by a mammoth. He stands above me, the whites of his eyes huge.

'You!' he grunts. 'You!' His lips twist into a venomous leer and the pipe is coming towards me.

My legs arch into a kick and hit solid muscle. The pipe flies through the air. I hear a groan. I am on my feet. But he is coming towards me again, a looming vastness. I take a few steps backward. My heels hit something rubbery. In the flush of instinct my hand reaches behind me. I heave the tyre at him.

He reels. I lunge, my head a butt. His arms close round me like a vice, squeezing, squeezing, toppling us both to the ground.

He is on top of me now, pummelling, thrashing, his knee at my groin. There is a kind of dazed ecstasy on his face. I claw at it, try to worm out from under him. His weight is so great, each breath requires an effort of diminishing return. There is something sticky and hot in my mouth.

An immense longing to sleep comes over me, as sweet as the brush of angel's wings. And then I am being carried. My legs flail uselessly, skim the ground. My head and back are thrust against the wall of the house. Again and again. It judders. I am falling. The snow above me is falling, cascading from the roof. We crumple to the ground together.

My hand touches something solid. The message takes a long time to reach my brain. The length of piping. I finger it, get a firm grip just as he comes

501

down on me. I can hit him now, land a killing blow on the head of Madeleine's murderer.

Our eyes meet and hold. His are crazed, black and shiny like stones washed by the tide.

Yes. Now.

I try to find the centre of my fury, try to unleash the blow. But I can't. I have this aching sense of affinity, a painful compassion. I scream at my hesitating hand and already it is too late. He has seen the pipe. He wrests it from me. Lifts it.

I am going to die here, my blood a fugitive smear in the falling snow.

I close my eyes and wait for death. My life races before me and away in a kaleidoscope of images. My mother's voice calls, 'Pierre, hurry.' A placard-bearing crowd gathers round a steeple and cheers. The hot yellow sands of the desert trickle through my fingers. A golden Madeleine materializes from them like an oasis. She stretches her arms out towards me. There is a lingering smile on her face. It shapes itself into the sound of my name.

But the voice isn't Madeleine's. It is raucous, raging. It booms out orders like a cannon. It pulls me to my feet.

With an effort I open my eyes. Contini is at my side, his arm round me. Everywhere there is the beam of flashlights.

'Lunatic,' he grumbles. 'Trying to play the hero. Can you walk? Miron, you, get over here.'

Two men take hold of my elbows.

Contini plays the light over my face. 'He'll live. But get him checked out by a medic. I'll catch up with you later, Rousseau.'

He walks away before I can shape a word.

In the distance, I make out three shadowy figures. The burliest one is in the centre. Like a tethered animal, he drags his feet reluctantly through the snow. His keepers push and prod.

As we pass them, he snarls and spits in my direction.

'Good thing we got here in time,' Miron stammers.

My yes falters and doesn't quite make it to my lips.

Streaks of pale lemon sun criss-cross the bed. The house is quiet. The only pounding is in my head. It detracts from the stiffness of my body and the ache round my ribs as I shift position. But last night old Dr Bertrand declared me fit, if somewhat battered, before popping a pill into my mouth to enforce dreamless sleep.

I push away grogginess, then get up before the succession of nightmarish images which hover over me can leap and pounce. My mouth feels as if a winter of grit had settled in it. I empty the glass of water by the bedside to wash it away, find a robe folded over the back of a chair and make my way down the hall to the bathroom.

When I come back, Oscar is standing there, a pile of clothes folded in his arms.

'Heard you moving. You OK?' He inspects me obliquely, veils a frown. 'Thought you might like these.'

He puts the clothes on the bed and gestures at the rumpled heap in the corner. 'Breakfast when you're dressed. Elise has taken the kids off to school. Then she's going to the supermarket.' He hastens to add this, as if one or other of us might not be fit company.

A glance in the small mirror tells me why. My face is mottled and lumpy, a battleground of bruises and cuts, as if I had blundered into the ring with the world's champion heavyweight.

I pull on Oscar's jeans and turtleneck and look out the window. The sky is an icy, pitiless blue. Trees and ground and studio roofs are covered in a pristine coat so lustrous it hurts the eyes. If I stand here long enough, maybe the brilliance will pierce through the shroud of depression which encases me.

Oscar's voice wills me down the stairs. I pad along slowly, my legs not quite my own.

He grins as I come into the kitchen. 'I could use you in the studio. Change my palette to Francis Bacon's.'

'Thanks.'

'By the way, Elise told me she spoke to you . . .' He hesitates, puts a mug of steaming coffee in front of me, scoops eggs onto a plate. 'About Madeleine. I . . . She had asked me not to talk about it.' His glance is at once embarrassed and stubborn.

'It's OK.'

'Ya?'

I nod. We all have our secrets about Madeleine.

'Tell me about last night.'

I sip my coffee and try to construct a narrative that makes sense, but Oscar is impatient.

'Michel Dubois, eh! Whoever would have thought he had that in him. Not that I know the man well, but he was always so helpful. He never struck me as . . . as . . .' His voice evaporates into silence.

We look at each other. On this bright morning at this comfortable family table, we are both unequal to the notion that there has been a murderer in our midst.

Finally I shrug. 'Yes. Dubois. Mme Tremblay's trusted Dubois. Or at least it would seem so. Certainly, he didn't take kindly to me last night.' I finger the rawness of my face. 'The police will tell us more.'

As if on cue, the doorbell rings and Contini strides in, only to slump into the first available chair. He looks haggard.

'Long night,' he mutters. 'Any more of that coffee going?'

'So you've found your man, detective. It really is Michel Dubois.'

Contini nods. 'He confessed to everything, poor bugger. Great floods of tears.'

'And you believe him?' My voice holds a challenge.

His features dimple into wryness. 'The evidence won't be far behind. There's enough of it already. Ya. I believe him.'

'To everything?' Oscar asks.

'Yes, everything. Murder, arson, breaking and entry – even pushing Mme Orkanova's car off the road. Yours too. You forgot to tell me about that,

505

Rousseau.' His expression as he empties his cup of coffee is querulous.

'But why?'

'Rousseau will have to explain that to you later, M. Boileau.'

'How are you feeling by the way?' Contini asks me as we get into his car.

'Like I'd rather not have a body.'

He flashes me a grin. 'Know the feeling. Guess I owe you a thank you for leading us to Dubois. How did you guess he was our man?'

'I didn't. Not until he lunged at me last night. Outside. During your little show.'

He chuckles. 'So it worked. I had a hunch it would flush our man out.'

'You suspected him already?' I am aghast. 'But you led me to believe—'

'That I had you in my sights.' He laughs. 'I've had several of you in my sights. You, Dubois, Boileau . . . Yes, him too. Any man who knew Madeleine Blais and was big enough to carry her dead weight, heave her up to that height. Not easy. I told you before, Rousseau. I'm democratic in my suspicions. As democratic as Madeleine Blais was with her favours.'

The pounding in my head takes on a new intensity. 'You mean Madeleine and Michel Dubois . . .'

'No, no. Not quite like that. I was thinking of Fernando Ruiz. But tell me your side first.'

I tell him about the attack, the trek through the woods, the car in the boathouse which confirmed

Dubois' identity. He drives slowly, listens intently to my every word as I run through the events of the evening.

'One of my men followed you, but he lost you in the woods. Those were the orders. Follow anyone who tries to leave the scene. But you're dumb, Rousseau. You should have come to me and told me. Dubois had it in for you. I don't like to think what would have happened if we hadn't turned up in time.'

'I'm here. More or less in one piece.' I finger my face. 'But you did think it was me?'

'For a minute. Well, maybe a minute and a half. When I got the breakdown of phone calls from the Tremblay number. The one to you at around one-twenty on Monday morning gave me pause, I have to admit. On top of that there was the key-ring. And then . . . but you don't know this: Dubois pointed the finger at you.'

'At me?'

He nods. 'When Ginette Lavigne first interviewed him, he told us he'd been out late on the night of Madeleine's death, after midnight mass, and thought he'd just make sure everything was OK at the Tremblay place. He saw the light on in Madeleine's room and the man with her, he said, looked like you. That's what gave me the idea for the mime. From a distance – maybe it's just the distance of jealousy – all you guys have not a little in common.'

'Michel Dubois was jealous of me?' My voice rises to a pitch of disbelief and Contini throws me one of his cynically knowing looks.

'What's so strange about that? I'm no fancy psychologist but it's clear to me that Dubois loved Madeleine in his own deranged way. You had her and he didn't. So he hated you. As for the rest, he was also around when the barn was ablaze. In fact it was he who handed Henderson over to Gagnon. The two of them were together, though Dubois isn't mixed up in the drug stuff.'

'Wait a minute. You're telling me Will Henderson saw Dubois set light to the barn?'

'What Henderson saw was the blaze. He could hardly miss that. And he saw Dubois. Though he couldn't remember or didn't know his name. As for the rest, he was as vague as he was about everything except his daily fix. It doesn't matter. Dubois admitted everything. It makes perfect sense. Unlike your two-bit confession. Giving me the run-around like that. Adding nothing to my story. Telling me you carried Madeleine Blais up to the loft on a ladder, when the only ladder in the barn had half its rungs missing. I should charge you with wasting valuable police time.'

'And I should charge you with extorting confessions.'

He snorts and suddenly veers the car towards a scruffy roadside diner. 'What do you say to another cup of coffee? I'm not quite ready to face the old lady yet. I don't think she's going to like this.'

'Is that where we're going?'

'That's where we're going.'

The diner is one I've never stopped at, though it

reminds me of the site that led to my first affair. A couple of truck-drivers sit on scuffed mock-leather stools at a less than sparkling counter. A plump woman with ample breasts and steaming face stands behind it. There is a smell of frying onions and thrice-percolated coffee.

Contini beats his chest like a stage King Kong and breathes deeply. 'Good stuff. Fancy a burger? Got to keep the energy levels up.'

'Coffee will do me.'

We slide into padded windowside benches. They squeal and squeak at our weight.

'But you wanted me to do the sperm-test?' I mutter as soon as the coffee has arrived.

'Sure. In the daze of it all, you could have forgotten the platform.'

'What platform?'

'The one on the pulley system that went up to the loft in the barn. Lavigne spotted it on her second visit. It was all neatly tucked away to the right of the beam, but Lavigne saw it. Dubois installed it himself. So he knew just how it worked. He used it on the night, then put it back in place, almost out of sight if you didn't know where to look. Neat job.'

'So tell me what Dubois said.'

'What do you want to know?' Contini's lips fold into coyness. 'Oh, the big night. Sure. But, here.' He passes me a cigarette. 'You're going to need this – though it's pretty much as I imagined it for you. I just wasn't altogether sure of my man.'

'Get on with it, Contini.'

'You don't look as pretty as usual, with your

509

puffy face. I feel I'm revealing secrets to a stranger.'

'Thanks.'

'Drink your coffee.'

I swallow a few bitter mouthfuls.

'OK. This is the précis version – without the tears. Dubois blubbered like a baby. Couldn't wait to tell us, really. Though words aren't altogether his métier. You would have made it sound more elegant.'

'Get on with it.'

'Right. So he sees Madeleine Blais at midnight mass with a man. He follows them back. He's her stalker by the way. He's been tailing her for ages. Whenever the opportunity arose. He followed her to Boileau's for her portrait sitting. Even went into her apartment. It was easy enough to borrow Mme Tremblay's set of keys. And he was there on the day of the polytechnic assassinations. That excited him. It may even have planted a seed. And, of course, he was around when Madeleine came here to visit. Quite an intimate in his own way.'

He sets his face in challenge, waiting for me to contradict him.

I don't. My fingers are digging into my palms. My head is still pounding.

'So, on the night, he spies. He sees the light go off downstairs and on again in Madeleine's room. There's a bit of kissing, maybe a bit of nudity. Anyhow, I imagine he's excited. And angry. His rationale seems to go something like this – if the beautiful, unattainable Madeleine can do it with some stranger, right here on home ground, then why not with me?

510

'After Madeleine waves off Fernando Ruiz in her car, Dubois is still lurking. She must hear something, for she calls out. She calls out your name. Pierre. Ruiz told us that too, so this must be the second time.'

'What?'

'That's what Dubois claims. She had already phoned you. So she probably thought you'd hot-footed it over. And so, she calls out "Pierre". That's another reason Dubois has it in for you. It seems he's loathed you for years. Envied you. I imagine he's even mentioned you obliquely in his confessions to your brother.'

There is a speculative gleam in the eyes Contini turns on me as he takes a bite out of his burger and I look away.

'I don't know anything about this,' I mumble.

He shrugs. 'The man has imagination. By his lights, it seems you were the one who took Madeleine away from him. Before you appeared on the scene, she was all his.'

'Madeleine never mentioned him. Not in all the years.'

'No. Well, the man's obviously got his *idée fixe*. Imagines all the signs of requited love, whether they're there or not. There are people like that. Not all that rare, apparently. They send letters. They stalk. They do worse. Sometimes they've never even met the objects of their obsession. I read a book about it once. Ya, I do sometimes read. A syndrome named after some Frenchman.'

'Clérambault.'

'That's it. So you know.'

He pauses, munches. 'Anyhow, back to the night. When Madeleine called your name, that really got him worked up. He had it in his head anyway that since she was sleeping with everyone now, she could also sleep with him. But Madeleine refused. She laughed at him when he propositioned her. That laugh – I can almost imagine it. Astonished, contemptuous, provocative. It sent him over the edge. Things got rough. She struggled. My scenario wasn't wrong. You remember?'

'I remember.' I don't like to remember.

'He got his fingers round her throat and she went limp, unconscious. That was the bruising our lot found. It wasn't quite consistent with the marks left by the rope. In any case, Dubois thought he'd strangled her, so he strung her up to make it look like suicide – though what he said was that he didn't like to see her lying there, looking pathetic on the ground. Maybe it just made the grounds a little too messy for him. After all, he was in charge of them. At the last, she apparently opened her eyes and landed him a kick. That excited him again. He finished himself off with a hand job. Remember the spatter of sperm on her coat?'

I stare at the creamy white splodge the milk has left in my coffee and I feel I am going to be sick. I grab one of Contini's cigarettes and rush outside to take a deep puff of air and nicotine. I lean against the wall and close my eyes to the glaring light, but darkness brings a rush of images so hideous I open them again quickly. The world swims before me, everything doubled up on itself, askew, as if the landscape had spawned a maze of distorting mirrors.

When he comes out, Contini pats me lightly on the shoulder. We don't speak again until he has pulled back onto the road. And then I find myself asking, 'So Dubois was pleased when you all thought it was suicide.'

'No, not pleased, troubled. Deep down, these guys always want to be found out. They feel guilty at having gotten away with it. But not quite guilty enough to confess right away. He saw Mme Tremblay on television insisting that Madeleine had been murdered. That spurred him to set fire to the barn – both to burn the site of the crime he couldn't face and to give us a signal. Maybe to get rid of any possible evidence, too. Meanwhile, you were everywhere. Mme Tremblay kept going to you for this and that. It became clear to him that she depended on you more than on him. That she, too, preferred you. And he worships her.

'He decided to make you pay. You and yours. All those years of simmering resentment reached their boiling point. And he had nothing to lose. He came to your house the night Maryla Orkanova was there. The noise you heard in the shed – that was Dubois. So was the accident, hers and yours, the cat's paw, and finally, the poor beast herself. And your attic collection, that really sent him into a frenzy. He'd watched you up there before, seen the flicker of the big screen casting shadows into the night. I'm glad you didn't happen to be there when he finally broke in. Though he'd checked on that. He wasn't quite prepared for face-to-face confrontation.'

He pauses. 'You OK?'

I notice that my hand is shaking. 'Just about.'

'Sometimes it only hits you later.'

We drive in silence for a few minutes.

'So that's that,' he says. 'I'm sure the prints on the film I found in your place will match his. He's wearing a sweater which I can swear is the same as the one we found a strand of in Madeleine's fingernail. His car has got all the necessary bits of matching paintwork. And we've got a full confession. We're home.'

'*Crime passionel*,' I murmur.

He laughs a deep throaty laugh. 'Except in Mafia-land, they're usually passionate. Love or money, with a little dash of perversion.'

We bump into Mme Tremblay's drive. I have a sudden image of Michel Dubois standing on the porch steps and staring at me from his dark, unmoving eyes. A sense of his unbearable jealousy overtakes me. Not so very different from my own. Except that for him Madeleine was both tantalizing and wholly unattainable, the desired object he could never begin to possess. Whereas I couldn't face losing what I had once had. Two spurned lovers at opposite ends of a continuum. Both enveloped in fantasy.

I turn to Contini. 'I don't know that I can face Mme Tremblay.'

'She stood up for you yesterday. When Serge

Monet was busily planting the seeds of suspicion about you to all and sundry, she was the only one who was emphatic in your defence.'

'But . . .'

'You're going to have to, Rousseau. You're just going to have to. You're a hero, remember.'

20

After the crowded commotion of yesterday evening, the house has a quiet fragility about it, as if its foundations have grown uncertain. Nothing is altogether in its proper place. Chairs are scattered. The pictures of Madeleine haven't returned to the piano. Christmas tree baubles sit abandoned on a shelf, their glow diminished by the light streaming through the windows. Even the dogs are subdued.

Impeccably groomed from the dark sleekness of her hair to the tips of her well-polished shoes, Marie-Ange Corot ushers us into seats. She has the manner of a woman used to being mistress of a grand house. Her politeness gives away nothing and asks for nothing. It shrouds us in formality.

'Mme Tremblay should be down in a moment. I imagine it is her you want? Monique has gone into Ste-Anne for groceries.'

'Yes, it is Mme Tremblay we need to speak to.' Cowed into correctness, Contini smoothes the crease in his trousers and sits at the edge of his chair. He has acknowledged a force greater than himself.

Marie-Ange still hasn't met my eyes, nor blinked at my appearance. I wonder again exactly what Contini or indeed Madeleine told her about me. The silence in the room lengthens.

Contini breaks it at last. 'Ah, a family album.' He leans towards the coffee table and scrutinizes a page of pictures. 'May I?'

'I thought it would do Mme Tremblay good to take me through it,' Marie-Ange murmurs, melting a little. 'I have also suggested that after the funeral, she come back to Paris with me. She can oversee the disposition of Madeleine's house. Perhaps it will help her. I just hope she's strong enough.'

'You should invite M. Rousseau, too,' Contini says unexpectedly.

Marie-Ange's gaze flickers in my direction, but she doesn't say anything.

Footsteps deflect this uncomfortable line of conversation. Mme Tremblay comes into the room. The merciless brightness of the morning light makes me aware that in these last days time has swept over her with hurricane savagery. She has grown smaller – all fragile bones with a loose covering of parched skin. Her hair is askew, her eyes sunken.

The brightness can't be kind to me either, for she stares at me in dismay.

'You didn't do this to him, detective! I won't believe it of you.'

'No, no. Not me. Sit down, Mme Tremblay. Get her a cup of tea, Rousseau.'

'No. I've had tea. Thank you. What happened to

you, Pierre? What have you come to tell me, detective?'

Contini and I look at each other. He takes a deep breath. 'Michel Dubois attacked Pierre, I'm afraid.'

'Michel! It's your doing, detective. I told you all these suspicions you were spreading, all these amateur theatricals would lead to no good. Poor Pierre. I'm sorry. Michel's not the cleverest of men.'

Contini coughs. 'Michel Dubois didn't only attack Pierre. He murdered your granddaughter, Mme Tremblay.'

She stares at him, all colour drained from her face. 'Did I hear you correctly, detective? This isn't just another of your games?'

'I'm afraid not.'

'Pierre, you tell me.'

'It seems to be true.' My voice sounds hollow so I reinforce it: 'He's confessed.'

Mme Tremblay slumps back into her chair.

'Get that tea, Rousseau. Plenty of sugar,' Contini mutters.

Marie-Ange follows me into the kitchen. She hesitates for a moment as I fill the kettle, then she throws her arms around me.

'Pierre, thank God. That Contini put such ideas into my head. I was told not to talk to you.' Her eyes are moist. 'And there's so much we need to talk about. Later. Quietly. Just the two of us.'

I don't know why it hits me now, but suddenly, like a small boy who has held back his tears for too long, I have a desire to go into a dark room and

518

weep. To weep my grief to the stroke of an invisible woman's fingers in my hair.

Mme Tremblay's back has the rigidity of a poker as I place the tray on the table. It is as if her hold on life were all in the straightness of her back. Her eyes don't move. They are focused on some elsewhere we can't see.

Contini grimaces at me and takes hold of the teapot with such force that I have the impression it will crumble in his fingers.

'I've explained briefly,' he mumbles.

I take a cup of sugary tea to her. 'Drink this, Mme Tremblay. It'll do you good.'

Her eyes flutter towards me. 'It's all my fault, Pierre. I should have sent him away. Years and years ago. I had no idea . . .' Cup and saucer shake in her hand. She sets them down, spilling the liquid.

'Everyone always feels guilty in these cases, Mme Tremblay,' Contini interjects reasonably. 'A great series of if onlys—'

'You don't understand.' She cuts him off. 'I was the one who took Michel in, who offered him a place when he was in trouble. He'd been expelled from school. A big lad. Too big for his years. Fifteen, I think he was. Terrible family. Anyhow, I offered him a job, when no-one would have him. Let him stay here until he found his own place. He was useful, good with his hands, good with the animals. He taught Madeleine to ride. She was just a child, friendly with him, friendly with everyone. And he was gentle with her.'

Her voice fades off. She is talking to herself, sifting through memories, trying to make sense of things.

'Once, I think it was just after Madeleine and I had come back from Europe, '64 or '65 that must have been – Michel had taken good care of the place in our absence – I caught him looking at her in a particular way. The look was repeated. I took him aside and talked to him. I told him Madeleine would be going away to school soon and then probably away from Ste-Anne for ever. She wasn't for him. I was stern with him. Stern with her, too. She had learned to be flirtatious in France. She was always so jaunty with Michel. As if she was still a child.'

She sighs. The sound is so loud that it startles her from her reverie. She takes a gulp of tea. When she speaks again, her voice has changed. It is sharper, streaked with anger and self-recrimination.

'And that was it. Or so I thought. Madeleine went off to school in Montréal. There wasn't really enough work here to keep Michel fully occupied. He got other jobs, though I kept him on part time.'

She gives me a sudden sharp look and I have a terrible feeling that she has found me out, that she has seen the hideous parallels between Michel and myself. But she hurries on.

'When I told him that Madeleine and you were getting married, he wasn't happy. He threw a spade with such force against a tree that the metal broke away from the wood. I was furious, I scolded him.' She lets out a single sob, covers her mouth with her hand, so that we strain to hear her. 'Yet a part of me felt sorry for him and I kept him on. I didn't see the growing resentment. I didn't understand that he was harbouring a secret passion ... that in some mad way he felt entitled to her.'

She shivers and stands up abruptly. 'I want to see him, detective. See him now.'

The force of her determination is such that it transforms her back into the stubbornly resolute woman I have always held in awe.

Contini falters. 'It's not customary, Mme Tremblay.'

'Murder isn't customary either, detective.'

In front of the police station there is more traffic, both on wheels and human, than I have ever seen. Mme Tremblay is stopped at every step and only Contini's footballer's shoulders manage to create a space for her through the fray.

'Your mayor insisted on a press conference here, at one o'clock,' he mutters. 'Wouldn't listen to me.'

Inside there is a warren of activity, but a hush spreads around us as Mme Tremblay's presence is noted.

'You two better wait out here.' Contini motions to Marie-Ange and myself. 'He's a strong bugger and as we know he's not over fond of you.'

Gagnon emerges from his office and, after a brief word with Contini, the two of them lead Mme Tremblay down the corridor towards the cells.

Marie-Ange slips her hand through mine as we wait. We don't wait long. After some five minutes, Mme Tremblay reappears followed by the two men.

She doesn't look at either of us. Her cheeks are flushed with two brightly pink spots as she makes for the front door.

I hold Contini back. 'What happened?'

He shrugs and gives me a lopsided grin. 'They eyeballed each other and she landed him two surprisingly hard smacks. Sounded a bit like a guillotine. I think he might have preferred that.' He glances at her receding back with open admiration.

'So . . . Miron will drop you home now, unless you want to stay for the press conference?'

I shake my head.

'No. The old lady doesn't want to either. That's it, then. I'm back to Montréal this afternoon. I'll try and make it to the funeral, but if I don't, offer my apologies. I'll see you at the trial. Or if you feel like it, come and have lunch with me.'

He puts his arm round my shoulder, squeezes hard enough to make me wince, and winks. 'And Rousseau, I'm glad it wasn't you. The old school, even with all its changes, wouldn't have been pleased. *Je me souviens*, eh?'

I find myself smiling. It makes my battered face ache.

Marie-Ange and I stroll along the stretch of river near Le Lion d'Or. The walk is her idea. She says the light is too beautiful to miss, but I suspect she is building herself up to an announcement about Madeleine's will. She can't know that Monique has already let slip.

I don't mind. The cold air acts like an anaesthetic

on my face and my stiff limbs need stretching.

Mme Tremblay refused to join us for lunch. Instead, with an air of defiance, she handed me a glittering parcel. 'It's your Christmas present from Madeleine. Open it, open it now.' Under the two women's watchful eyes, I steadied my trembling hands and tore open the paper. Inside, there was a hand-painted box, bright with candy colours. When I unfastened the lid a stage popped up, on it a beautifully crafted Colombine blowing a kiss at a Pierrot, his face a melancholy mask. Very Madeleine. For a moment, I felt she had forgiven me.

I gaze at the icy river, the snow-encrusted trees, the distant huddled houses on the opposite shore. It all feels so civilized in Marie-Ange's presence, like a landscape waiting for the hand of a talented painter. I can even see the frame. Last night's forbidding trek seems to belong to another life. A dream life, perhaps. Maybe Michel Dubois' pummelling gave me the punishment I needed to wake to an existence without Madeleine.

Yet with Marie-Ange at my side, Madeleine's death takes on the aura of an absence. Its finality is kept oddly at bay. As if there were still that residue of hope, whose embers I have fanned for so long.

I cut off the cloying fingers of wish which have proved so disastrous and ask her whether Madeleine and she had spoken much of late.

She nods. 'I was just thinking of that.' She brushes at her face and I notice there are tears in her eyes. 'We spoke almost daily. She was upset. Upset at everything. That's why at first, when I heard, I thought it was suicide. Reaching a certain age as an actress isn't easy. There are hurdles to cross. Then, too, the play was going badly and there was that dreadful event at the university. She was scared. I've never known Madeleine to be frightened of anything. She had an intuition – an accurate one as it turns out.'

'Her intuitions were always good. We should have listened to her. I should have listened to her.'

Marie-Ange is silent for a moment. She wraps her fur more closely round her to hide a shiver.

'Shall we go in?'

She nods and drapes her arm through mine for the climb.

'She was angry at you, too, that last week. The week before Christmas. Had you had a row?'

'Not exactly,' I prevaricate, and then find myself stammering and telling her. 'I'd been writing her letters. Anonymously. Stupidly. They were meant to be fan letters, love letters, I guess, but they somehow got out of hand. Madeleine guessed they were mine. They didn't feel like love letters to her. Nor a joke. Or maybe she just didn't want anything like that from me. I curse myself for it. There was never a chance to explain.'

It is a long, halting speech and I wait for her response, but again she doesn't say anything. I am not about to be blessed with second-hand forgiveness.

At last she murmurs, 'It was foolish of you.'

'The trouble was I could never come to terms

with the fact that she had stopped loving me.'

She flashes me a queer look. 'Madeleine made a will a few years back. You and I were named as joint executors.'

'At least she trusted me.' An idea leaps into my mind, spurred by something in Marie-Ange's tone. 'Or . . . Did she decide to change it that last week?'

'She toyed with the idea. She was very angry with you. Then she cooled down and said no. About some things you were responsible. She wanted to talk to you about it.'

'I see,' I say, but in fact I don't see. 'Why didn't she talk to me before? When she first made the will?'

We have reached the restaurant and Marie-Ange slips off her gloves and makes a sweeping gesture with her ringed hand. 'Madeleine talk about death if she could avoid it? Don't be silly. The will was altogether my idea.'

Only Marie-Ange's aplomb and haughty Parisian voice see us past the disapproval of the maître d' as he looks at my less than clean jeans and bruised face.

'A window table,' she commands. 'And bring us the wine list immediately. We need a drink, don't we, Pierre?'

She gives me an imperceptible wink as the man rushes away with a '*Tout de suite, madame*'.

We drink. Marie-Ange works her way through salad and steak, while I sip soup and try to make my swollen face behave appropriately over morsels of soft fish pie. We talk about Madeleine, randomly at first, exchanging slivers of memory. Gradually it comes to me that the randomness is not simply that. Marie-Ange's questions are probing. They suggest that although in fact we are virtually strangers she knows a good deal about me. It comes to me that in some obscure way I am being tested.

By the time coffee cōmes, I seem to have arrived at a subliminal decision.

'Look, Marie-Ange, it might be more appropriate if I withdrew as the second of Madeleine's executors and you named another. I imagine most of the estate will be handled in France and it would be simpler if—'

She cuts me off, her face severe. 'It was Madeleine's wish.'

'Though not on your advice,' I say softly.

She gives me a hard, assessing look, the look of a woman who is used to making quick judgements and fighting her corner.

'Not against my advice either.' She fingers the gold chains round her neck. A wry smile moves up from her lips to her eyes. 'You haven't asked me what's in the will yet.'

I shrug. 'I imagine Madeleine's been reasonably fair. Mme Tremblay . . .'

Her expression stops me.

'Oh, I see. You mean there's a Madeleine flourish. Some theatre school or prize for young Québec actors for us to administer?'

'You're right. There is a flourish.' Marie-Ange pats her lips with her napkin and reaches for her bag, then changes her mind and puts it aside. 'A very real flourish. I wish she'd told you herself. She half intended to.' She pauses. 'Madeleine had a child, Pierre.'

The words, uttered with Marie-Ange's authority, hit me with the force of an inescapable tidal wave. For a moment, I am submerged, struggling. When I surface, I hear myself saying, 'So Contini was right . . . I thought . . . It doesn't matter. Where is the child?'

'She lives in France. Just outside Aix.'

'A girl, then.' My words sound inane. 'She lives with her father?'

'Madeleine had her adopted.' She scans my face searching for a reaction and I try to adjust my features into a semblance of sense.

'Adopted. I see.'

'I don't think you do. When Madeleine found out she was pregnant – it's some years back now – she considered abortion and then realized she couldn't go through with it. She just skipped her appointment, put it off and off again. But nor did she really want a baby. A kind of visceral fear came over her when we talked about it – maybe because of her own troubled infancy. In any case, she was in a state of considerable confusion. What she was certain of was that the kind of life she led wasn't right for a child. Her movie career was in full swing . . .'

I listen. I don't dare speak. I am there with Madeleine trapped in her agitation, as tangible as if it were my own.

'In the latter stages of her pregnancy, I suggested

to her that she might consider adoption. She was more or less holed up in the house in Neuilly then. We were very close, saw each other almost daily and I told her about a cousin of mine who couldn't conceive and was desperate to adopt a child. To make a long story short, they met and liked each other. Liked each other very much. They came to an understanding. If, once the child was born, Madeleine still wanted to give it up, then my cousin and her husband, who is a lawyer, and could arrange the papers with minimal fuss, would adopt.

'Madeleine made up her mind within days of the birth. She wasn't easy with the child. She treated her like some precious bowl that it was too hazardous to touch.'

She hesitates, then presses on. 'It was, I am convinced, the right thing to do. Caroline and Jean-Jacques have been good parents. And they were happy to make all kinds of accommodations. Madeleine became a kind of informal godparent – eventually, that is. At first she didn't want anything to do with Louise, Lulu, as she called her.

'But then, when the girl was about four, she started to take an interest in her, was fascinated by her. She's a pretty child, vivacious. Madeleine would visit when time allowed – birthdays, holidays, spend a few days sometimes. And you know Madeleine, she always came with lavish presents.

'It all went swimmingly until a few years ago, when Madeleine suddenly felt hemmed in by the arrangement. She wanted to come clean. I told her that would be destructive. Destructive and unfair to everyone concerned. Lulu, of course, knows she's adopted. But suddenly acquiring a second mother, let alone a mother who is the famous Madeleine Blais, wouldn't be a simple matter for any child to come to terms with. I insisted that only when Louise was eighteen, and only then if she wanted to know who her parents were, could anything be revealed. I quoted the law at Madeleine.

'Madeleine saw sense, of course. Though she wasn't altogether happy about it. And now . . .' Her voice drifts off.

Around us the restaurant has grown empty. We sit in a pool of dying light and gaze out the window.

'Poor Madeleine,' I murmur. 'She never told me. I never suspected . . .'

'No. She said to me she was considering telling you soon. She wanted, well I think she wanted to be able to talk about the fact of Lulu to someone here.'

The last line of Madeleine's letter unfurls before me like an emblazoned medieval banner rich in mysterious insignia and defiance. 'There is only one part of me you have been unable to touch. You will never know about it now. It is too late.'

It comes to me again with a terrible force how my very love for the glittering, seductive Madeleine – that Madeleine of the screen who had become my familiar – had blinded me to the living woman's real needs. I had prided myself on knowing her. Yet what had I known but the fantasy she engendered? And all the time the drama of her real life had passed me by.

I scrabble for some reassurance and tell myself

that it hadn't always been thus, not in the beginning, not when we lived together.

'You don't look well, Pierre.' Marie-Ange breaks into my thoughts. 'I think we should go. Take me to your place. I'd like to see it.'

My body doesn't seem capable of movement. I stare at Marie-Ange and utter the question which has rumbled insidiously in my mind since the start of this conversation. 'Do you know who Lulu's father is, Marie-Ange? Did Madeleine know?'

Marie-Ange fumbles in her purse and only meets my eyes for a moment before rising.

'Madeleine was an extraordinary woman, Pierre. I don't need to tell you that. And her life made it easy for her not to have to confuse love and fidelity. She was no puritan. And she had strong feelings about independence.'

I follow her out of the door and try to decipher her words. I have an odd feeling that Marie-Ange loves Madeleine as much as I do, if differently, and is working to protect her memory. A little like Mme Tremblay when she sent me in search of journals which might provoke scandal.

In the car I say to her, 'So you've told me all this because Madeleine's will, I take it, is largely in favour of her daughter.'

'When she turns eighteen.'

'I see. How old is she now?'

'About ten.'

Despite myself, my mind races with calculations which lead me nowhere.

Marie-Ange is silent until we arrive at the house.

In the greying dusk, it looks bleak. I hurry her past the casket where Minou lies, past the boarded-up window. Tomorrow I will have everything fixed, create a new order out of the devastation.

'Perhaps we should have left this until tomorrow.' Marie-Ange sniffs my mood.

'No. I'm glad you're here. I wasn't looking forward to coming back alone.'

She looks around with her perceptive gaze as I turn on lights. 'Funny that after all these years you never found another woman to live with.'

I shrug. I place Madeleine's present on a corner table and stare at the two figurines and think they are perhaps a fitting goodbye. I try to find words with which to explain to Marie-Ange, but they don't come.

'Though after the whirlwind of Madeleine, it can't have been easy.'

'Thank you,' I hear myself mumble, as if she had paid me a compliment.

'I hadn't imagined it like this.' She waves her arm in a graceful arc.

'No?'

'I had imagined something more modern, open plan, lots of white spaces.' She stops herself, puts her hand over her mouth. 'I'm being rude.'

'Not at all. I never quite expected this of myself either. It's my father's house. He was a bit of a collector. And I've grown into it. Or slumped into it would be more accurate.'

She laughs. 'You're very hard on yourself, Pierre. Madeleine never told me that.'

531

'What did she tell you?'

'Oh . . . lots of things. But show me round. I'm curious. Show me everything.'

I show her. I take her through my father's collections, give her anecdotes, titbits of history, like a guided tour through a museum which has become myself. I even show her the police-sifted dereliction which is my bedroom. Her presence, her comments, approving or wry, with an occasional glint of humorous malice, are oddly liberating – as if this fresh eye on my accumulated life gives me a necessary perspective.

It is when we reach the last room that I decide.

'I'm afraid the attic's a bit of a mess. Vandalized by Michel Dubois. But I'd like you to see.'

I hesitate on the last step then fling open the door. For a moment vertigo overtakes me. The kilometres of film still undulate on the floor, topped by their flotsam of torn pictures and posters. Madeleine's eyes gaze out at me. Her lips curl and pout.

'I see,' Marie-Ange whispers. 'Yes, I do see.' She throws me a keen look and stoops to pick up a reel. Then, in a calm, matter-of-fact voice, she says, 'We'd better get to work, hadn't we? Put this on the projector and let's see how far we get. It should still wind.'

While I right the heavy machine, she opens windows. Cold air blasts through the room. The projector whirrs.

'It's only film, Pierre. Film and paper. All replicable.' She holds a strip up to the light with an experienced eye. 'I'll get you duplicates.'

532

I shake my head. 'Probably better that I pay for my seat at the cinema.'

She gives me a hint of a smile, then unfurls the strips to feed them onto the loop, throws torn film aside, finds an empty spool and we begin again.

We work. Gradually the room takes on a semblance of order, the walls bare, the pictures and posters neatly stacked on the table, the reels back in their cases, unmanageable strips heaped in a sack.

'You owe me a drink,' Marie-Ange says. 'And this. I'd like this. I've never seen it before.' She holds up a picture of Madeleine which has survived Dubois' rage. It is an early photo. It dates from our days together in Montréal and shows Madeleine leaning against a mountain-top balustrade, the skyscrapers of the city hazy beneath her. She is wearing jeans and a sweater. Her hair is piled on top of her head and her smile is pure carefree gamine.

'I took that.'

'I guessed. I'll give you something in return.' There is an air of mystery on her face.

'You've given me enough. You've helped me clear this place.'

I want to tell her that it has done me good, that she has both helped to rupture a kind of perverse magic and to expel Dubois' shadow. I feel chastened. As if the cloistered stables of my mind had been swept clean. But I don't know how to say all that.

Maybe she guesses a little of it for, as we make our way downstairs, she asks, 'Did Madeleine ever come up here?'

I shake my head.

'Too bad. Your loyalty might have pleased her.' She laughs, suddenly rueful. 'Or maybe she would have ripped it all up herself. You could never tell with Madeleine.'

'No. You could never tell.'

She squeezes my hand in a gesture of complicity.

The fire in the hearth blazes. We have pulled one of the sofas up to it and pushed the other, which might still contain a litter of splinters, up against the boarded window. With a practised eye, Marie-Ange has rearranged a side table and a lamp, so that the room still has a semblance of harmony.

She is sitting at the opposite end of the sofa, her feet curled under her. Her feet, I have noticed, are surprisingly small. Despite her posture, despite all the work, she still looks immaculate. Maybe it is the smooth sheen of her hair. Maybe it is simply the Paris mould which I have forgotten.

She holds her whisky glass up to the light, gazes at it, then gazes at me. I am a little afraid of her, yet I trust her. We are easy in our silence here in front of the flames.

Then, abruptly, she gets up, only to come back a moment later with her handbag. 'Right. I've decided.'

'What have you decided?'

She doesn't answer. Instead she takes an envelope out of her bag and hands it to me.

I stare at it and with a shudder I hope she doesn't see pull it open. 'I don't know if I'm ready for any more letters.'

My tone manages lightness, but there is none in her face.

The envelope contains two photographs. They show a girl with liquid brown eyes and dark hair held back by an Alice band. She has high cheekbones, an impish smile which reveals gaps where teeth might be and a delighted dimple. She wears jeans and a yellow shirt and has a school bag hoicked over her shoulder. Behind her are the luminous colours of the south.

'Louise?' I ask.

Marie-Ange nods.

'Sweet. But . . . not at all like Madeleine. May I keep them?'

'If you like.'

I place the pictures on the mantel. When I turn around there is a puzzled expression on Marie-Ange's face.

'Can't you see it?'

'See what?'

'The resemblance.'

'No.' I look at the pictures again. 'She really isn't like her. Maybe it's the dark hair and eyes.'

'Not like Madeleine. Like you. Why else would I bother?'

'Me?'

Marie-Ange nods. Her voice is soft. 'She's your child, Pierre. Louise was born while you were in North Africa.'

My head swirls with greater frenzy than last night's blizzard. I think of Madeleine. I think of the nature of that explosive parting and her misery and mine. I think of my two-year near total silence. I think of the course of our subsequent relations and suddenly the face in the pictures settles into mine. My face as a child. Captured in photographs. My mother's face.

Marie-Ange touches my hand.

When I find my voice, it creaks. 'Why didn't she tell me at the time? Or didn't she know until later?'

'Madeleine was altogether certain. We talked about it during the pregnancy. She was equally certain you couldn't live together.' Marie-Ange avoids my eyes.

'No. I see.' I gaze into the flames which bear the corrosive colours of guilt. 'She was probably right.'

Silence falls over us. It is not so friendly this time. It carries the burden of my sins.

'We all live muddled lives, Pierre,' Marie-Ange says at last. 'Madeleine's ended in tragedy. But there was brightness along the way. A good deal of it. And in her own inimitable manner, she loved you. She was loyal. She named you as Louise's father on the birth certificate.'

She pauses. My breath is too loud. It whistles through the fingers which cover my face.

'So you see, I had to tell you. Prepare you. Just in case Louise, when she reaches the age of eighteen, wants to know. Though I wasn't sure I would be able to do it. Or you were the right man to receive the information.'

I look up at her. 'And you decided I was?'

She laughs. It is a warm, wry sound. 'You'll

do. You can even meet Louise some time if you like.'

Like a beacon to a shipwrecked man, her words beckon me to a future which is not repetition.

It is not a place I have imagined for what feels like a very long time.

21

The funeral of Madeleine Blais took place on Tuesday the ninth of January, 1990. The small cemetery on the outskirts of Ste-Anne couldn't contain the explosion of mourners. They thronged the snowy paths, spilled round the gates, flocked into the surrounding field.

All of the townspeople were there. So were Madeleine's friends and colleagues and a retinue of reporters and photographers. By the time everyone had trailed past the open grave, the flowers had reached the level of the ground. They decked the surrounding snow like exotic specimens.

Madeleine would have been happy. The very size of the crowd gave the ceremony a festive flavour. The sky turned out in its best blue and the sun made diamonds of the snow. The spray of dark glasses provided an additional touch of glamour.

She would have laughed too, giggled at the spectacle of Mayor Desforges, puffed up like a penguin, delivering a sonorous eulogy to follow on from my brother's more sombre rites. She would have smiled at the notion of a Centre des Arts, Madeleine Blais, soon to open its doors on the outskirts of Ste-Anne. Maybe she would have been chuffed as well.

A small group of us stood to one side of the grave until the sun set pink and the throng dispersed. There was Marie-Ange, Gisèle Desnos, Giorgio Napolitano, Fernando Ruiz, Detective Contini and myself. Madeleine was no longer with us, but she had thrown us together. For the moment at least, it felt as if we would maintain the bond.

When Mme Tremblay had finished with the shaking of too many hands, we lifted her up and like a triumphant figurehead carried her to the waiting cars. She protested, but smiled, waving on Jerome and a subdued Monique.

Later that night after too many drinks and spatterings of tears and stories and reminiscences, we sat in a hushed cinema and waited for the first of the films in the commemorative retrospective of Madeleine Blais' work. Contini was on my left, Marie-Ange on my right.

No sooner had the first few scenes of *Winter Spell* unfolded than he tapped my knee and murmured, 'Pretty powerful stuff. What a woman, eh? I can see it all now.'

His voice was reassuring, though I didn't know quite what it was he saw. I was waiting. Waiting nervously for that terrible and secret blue movie effect. Marie-Ange wound her hand through mine as if she too were waiting.

It didn't come.

Instead, I had a dazzling and fresh sense of Madeleine's remarkable talent. And with it a rush of freedom, as if I had burst out of the solitary circle of the self – that fuzzy, fantasizing self which blurred public and private passion into one muddy ball.

It came to me with a poignant clarity in the magical darkness of that hushed theatre that Madeleine was large enough to belong to everyone. Had to belong singly to everyone.

In the world of common images, love is always at once unique and uniquely shared.

THE END

ABOUT THE AUTHOR

Lisa Appignanesi was Deputy Director of London's Institute of Contemporary Arts before she became a full-time writer. Her non-fiction includes *Freud's Women* (with John Forrester) and, more recently, *Losing the Dead*. Her five previous novels have all been bestsellers. She lives in North London.